MW01674244

Otto's French Conversation Grammar

SALZWASSER
VERLAG

Emile Otto

Otto's French Conversation Grammar

Reprint of the original, first published in 1864.

1st Edition 2022 | ISBN: 978-3-75259-260-3

Verlag (Publisher): Salzwasser Verlag GmbH, Zeilweg 44, 60439 Frankfurt, Deutschland
Vertretungsberechtigt (Authorized to represent): E. Roepke, Zeilweg 44, 60439 Frankfurt, Deutschland
Druck (Print): Books on Demand GmbH, In de Tarpen 42, 22848 Norderstedt, Deutschland

OTTO'S

FRENCH

CONVERSATION GRAMMAR.

REVISED BY

FERDINAND BÔCHER,

BOSTON

1864.

PREFACE.

The first edition of Dr. EMILE OTTO'S "FRENCH CONVERSATION GRAMMAR" appeared at Heidelberg in 1859. A second edition was issued in 1863, upon which this first American edition is based. The present editor has not hesitated in making such changes as he deemed proper in the body of the work, abandoning, among other things, the names of the Latin cases, genitive, dative, etc., which, although they may be of help to the German student, can only confuse the American learner. The names of the tenses have also been changed, and, it is hoped, simplified. A few lessons have been added to Part I., and the chapter upon the Past Participle has been re-written. The preliminary lesson upon Pronunciation is also entirely new, and an English and French Vocabulary of the words that occur in the Themes has been added.

BOSTON, August, 1864.

CONTENTS.

PRONUNCIATION.

PART I.

PART II.

FRENCH GRAMMAR.

PRONUNCIATION.

THE ALPHABET.

1. The written French alphabet is the same as the English. W and K are found only in words borrowed from other languages.

The names of the letters are given below in the French spelling as they are of little or no value to the beginner. In the new names the *e* in *be, ke, de, gue,* etc., is only sounded enough to allow the utterance of the consonant that precedes it, as in glo*be*, ca*ke*, ma*de*, fati*gue*; j is sounded as *s* in *pleasure*. The vowels have their normal French sounds. — *W* when spoken of is called *double V*.

		OLD NAMES.	NEW NAMES.
A	a	a	a
B	b	bé	be
C	c	cé	ke (se)
D	d	dé	de
E	e	é	e
F	f	effe	fe
G	g	gé	gue(je)
H	h	ache	he
I	i	i	i
J	j	ji	je
K	k	ka	ke
L	l	elle	le
M	m	emme	me

		OLD NAMES.	NEW NAMES.
N	n	enne	ne
O	o	o	o
P	p	pé	pe
Q	q	ku	ke
R	r	erre	re
S	s	esse	se (ze)
T	t	té	te
U	u	u	u
V	v	vé	ve
X	x	ics	kse
Y	y	i grec	i
Z	z	zède	ze

DIVISION OF SYLLABLES.

2. Words are generally divided as in English; but whenever it is possible *a syllable must begin with a consonant.* Hence, verbal and other terminations beginning with a vowel must be joined to the consonant that precedes; thus *ai-mer*, but *ai-me-rai; chan-ter, chan-te-rai, chan-te-rons.*

As to *x* equal to *gs, cs,* its compound nature prevents its separation from the vowel that precedes: hence the following division *ex-em-ple.*

In writing, silent *h* apparently begins a syllable, as in *in-hé-rent;* but in the spoken syllables, silent *h* has no value whatever; and a consonant between a vowel and a silent *h* is separated from that vowel in the spoken though not in the written language; hence the following divisions.

Written.	*Pronounced.*
in-hu-main	i-nhu-main
in-ha-bi-le	i-nha-bile
in-hé-rent	i-nhé-rent
bon-heur	bo-nheur

If these words were pronounced according to the written divisions, they would begin with a nasal sound; but they do not. (See Nasal vowels, 37.)

SYLLABIC ACCENT, OR STRESS.

As compared with English, French is generally said to have no syllabic accent. Such a stress of voice as is heard in the words *ac'cent* and *accent'* does not occur in French; but the following rule explains the uniformity of the English accent on the last syllable in words newly introduced from the French, such as *barouche, surtout, machine, fatigue,* etc.

3. In French each syllable of a word must be pronounced smoothly, the voice resting upon the last, unless it ends in *e* mute, in which case the syllable before the last is slightly accented. Ex. *constitution, indubitable.*

ACCENTS, — ORTHOGRAPHIC MARKS.

4. Three orthographic marks, the *acute* (ʹ), the *grave* (ˋ), and the *circumflex* (ˆ), have received the name of accents.

These marks never affect a syllable; they can only modify the sound of a vowel over which they are placed. Sometimes they have a mere orthographic value. They must never be neglected in writing.

5. The ACUTE (ʹ) is used only over the vowel *e* (*é*), which then has the sound of *a* in *date*. Ex. *été*, *donné*.

6. The GRAVE (ˋ) or open accent is used principally over *e* (*è*), which then has the sound of *e* in *ebb* or of *e* in *there*. Ex. *fève*, *père*. Over *a* and *u* it is only used to distinguish words otherwise similarly spelled, and does not affect the pronunciation. Ex. la, *the;* là, *there;* a, *has;* à, *to;* ou, *or;* où, *where*.

7. The CIRCUMFLEX (ˆ) is used over all the vowels, which are then long. Ex. *âge*, *côte*, *sûr*.

The circumflex denotes that a contraction has taken place; thus *âge* and *sûr* were formerly spelled *aage* and *seur*. Often an *s* has been dropped in modern French which still remains in the English word taken from the old French. Ex. île, *isle;* hâte, *haste;* forêt, *forest;* tempête, *tempest*.

8. The CEDILLA is placed under the *c* (*ç*) when it has the sound of *s* before *a*, *o*, *u*. Ex. *façade*, *garçon*, *reçu*.

9. The DIÆRESIS (¨ *Tréma*) is used over *e*, *i*, and *u;* in which case these letters do not coalesce with the preceding vowel, but begin a new syllable. Ex. *haïr*, *Noël*, *aiguë*, are pronounced *ha-ir*, *No-el*, *ai-gu-e*, (the last e is silent.)

SIMPLE VOWELS.

A.

10. A long has the sound of *a* in *far*. Ex. âme, *soul;* pâte, *paste;* cas, *case*.

11. Short *a* differs from long *a* principally in quantity. It has

the sound of *a* in the Interjection *ha!* pronounced quick. Ex. la, *the;* patte, *paw.*

A is silent in Saône, taon, août, aoriste, Curaçao.

E.

12. E unaccented, when it ends a syllable in the middle of a word, and in the monosyllables *ce, de, je, le, me, ne, que, se* and *te*, has the indistinct sound of *e* in *Battery.* Ex. lever, *to raise;* regard, *look.*

13. E unaccented final is mute. Ex. table, *table.*

14. E with an acute accent (é) has the sound of *a* in *date.* Ex. été, *summer;* donné, *given.*

E unaccented takes the sound of *é* (*a* in *date*) before final *d, r, z*, mute, also at the beginning of a word before a double consonant. Ex. pied, *foot;* donner, *to give;* assez, *enough;* effet, *effect;* et, *and*, is always pronounced *é*.

15. E with the grave (è) or with the circumflex accent (ê) is more or less open, varying between *e* in *ebb*, and *e* in *where.* Ex. rêve, *dream;* père, *father;* forêt, *forest;* après, *after.*

E unaccented takes the sound of *è* (*e* in *ebb*) when preceding *c, f, l, r, s, t*, or *x* in the same syllable and in the middle of a word before any double consonant. Before *r*, the sound is more open than before the other letters. Ex. fer, *iron;* dessert, *dessert;* terre, *earth;* tendresse, *tenderness;* sonnette, *bell;* chef, *chief;* mes, *my;* est, *is;* esprit, *spirit.* In the last words the *e* is pronounced by many persons very nearly like *é* especially in rapid conversation. Even *ê* often loses its broad, long sound.

16. E takes the sound of French *a* in *femme, solennel, indemniser*, and in all adverbial terminations in *emment.*

17. E is silent between *g* and *a* or *o*. Ex. pigeon, *pigeon;* mangeons, (*we*) *eat;* mangeant, *eating.* In these words the *e* merely serves to prevent *g* from having the hard sound of *g* in *go.*

For further observations on *e* mute, see page 26.

I.

18. I has only one sound, that of *i* in *machine;*—long in vie, *life;* rire, *to laugh;*—short in fini, *finished;* ici, *here.*

O.

19. O, when long, has the sound of *o* in *rose*. Ex. côté, *side;* dose, *dose.*

20. O short has a sound between the *o* in *rob* and the *u* in *rub*. Ex. Rome, robe, mode.

21. O before final *re* or *r* and a final consonant has the sound of *o* in *lord*. Ex. aurore, *dawn;* alors, *then;* bord, *border*.

O is silent in Laon, paon, and faon.

U.

22. French *u* has no equivalent in English. To acquire the sound, place the lips as if about to whistle, leaving the aperture very small; keeping the lips in this position try to utter *e* as in *me*. Ex. murmure, *murmur*.

U may be long as in mûr, *ripe;* or short as in vertu, *virtue*.

23. U is silent after *q* and between *g* and *e* or *i*. Ex. guide, *guide;* question, *question;* quatre, *four;* fatigue, *fatigue*.

EXCEPTIONS. — U is sounded when the vowel after it is marked with the diæresis, as aiguë, *acute;* also in arguer, *to argue;* aiguille, *needle;* aiguiser, *to sharpen;* etc. Qu is sounded as in English in a few words directly derived from the Latin. These words are alike or nearly alike in French and English. Ex. équateur, équation, quadrupède, etc. In équitation, ubiquité, and a few other words, *u* retains the proper French sound.

Y.

24. Y, initial, or between two consonants, has the sound of French *i*. Ex. style, *style;* y, *there*.

25. Y between two vowels is eqnivalent to *ii*, the first *i* forming a diphthong with the preceding, the second with the following vowel. Thus, essayer, *to try;* royal, *royal;* appuyer, *to lean;* are pronounced as if written essai-ier, roi-ial, appui-ier. (See *ai* and *oi*.)

In pays, *country;* paysage, *landscape;* paysan, *peasant; ay* is equivalent to *ai-i*.

2

COMPOUND VOWELS.

AI and EI (ay).

26. Ai and ei are equivalent sometimes to è, sometimes to é. Ai final is always like é; in other cases it takes the sound of è, — whenever *e* unaccented would have that sound. (See under E.) Ex. reine, *queen;* j'aimai, *I loved;* j'avais, *I had;* lait, *milk.*

Ay, followed by a vowel, is equivalent to *ai-i*. Ex. rayer.

Ai in the present participle of the verb *faire* and in the corresponding syllables of all the forms derived from it, has the indistinct sound of *e* in *battery*. Ex. faisant, je faisais, tu faisais, il faisait, je défaisais, bienfaisant, etc. These forms were all written formerly as they are pronounced: *fesant, je défesais,* etc.; compare the future of the same verb, which is *je ferai* and not *fairai.*

AU.

27. Au and eau sound like *o* in *note*. Ex. haut, *high;* beau, *handsome.*

EU ŒU, (œ.)

28. Eu (œu) has no exact equivalent in English; it is somewhat like the *u* in *fur*. It is longer in jeûne, *fast*, peur, *fear*, cœur, *heart*, than in jeune, *young*, feu, *fire*, and œuf, *egg*.

Œ has the sound of *eu* before liquid *l*, — as in œil, *eye.*

Eu, whenever it occurs in the conjugation of the verb avoir, *to have*, has the sound of simple French *u*, so that J'eus, tu eus, il eut, etc., must be pronounced as if written *j'us, tu us, il ut*, etc.

OU.

29. Ou has the sound of *oo* in *poor*. It is long in roue, *wheel;* boule, *ball;* short in mou, *soft;* cou, *neck.*

DIPHTHONGS.

30. The vowels *i, u, ou, o,* preceding a vowel sound, may coalesce with it and produce a diphthong.

These vowel sounds (*i, u, ou, o,*) are the only ones that can be initial in a true diphthong; *i. e.* one in which *two* vowels are heard but coalesce into *one* syllable.

31. In French diphthongs the first vowel (*i*, *u*, *ou*, *o*) is uttered quick and short and the voice rests upon the second vowel element. The dipthongal combinations are: *i-a*, *i-e* (*i-ai*), — *i-o* (*i-au*), *i-eu*, *i-ou*, — *o-a*, *o-e*, *o-i* (wa), — *ou-a*, *ou-ai*, *ou-e*, *ou-i*, — *u-a*, *u-e*, *u-i*. The *e* in these combinations is not the *e* mute.

By paying attention to the above remark the diphthongs present no difficulty, as each vowel retains its proper sound, the first being very short; *oi* is the only exception.

OI. (oy.)

32. Oi is nearly like *wa* in *water;* more accurately *oi* is equivalent to French *a* preceded by a *w* sound. The *a* (ah) is more prolonged in voir, *to see;* poire, *pear;* than in roi, *king;* moi, *me.*

Oy, followed by a vowel, is equivalent to *oi-i*. Ex. royal.

NASAL VOWELS.

33. M and N, following a vowel in the same syllable, lose their power as consonants, and form with that vowel a nasal sound which is in every respect a vowel.

34. The nasals form four groups, viz.: —

A.	E, AI.	O.	EU.
an, am.	*ain, aim.*	*on, om.*	*eun.*
en, em.	*in, im.* (*ym.*)		*un, um.*

To acquire these sounds the organs of speech should be kept in *the same position* as they are in uttering the simple vowel that is to be nasalized; the back part of the tongue being raised enough to close the passage between the mouth and the nose. The same is done in English in such words as *anger, ink, want;* but in English the nasal sound is not detached from the next consonant, while in French it is. No *m* or *n* consonant sound must be heard. To avoid this, the tip of the tongue must be kept motionless and the lips disposed to articulate a vowel. French *a*, thus uttered, will give *an;* — *è* (ai), (not *i* in *machine*) gives *in* (ain); — *o* gives *on;* — *eu* (not French *u*) gives *un* (eun).

The nasal sounds may coalesce with a previous *i*, *u*, *ou*, or *o*, and form a *nasal diphthong*, to which all that has been said of the other diphthongs is applicable.

35. The following list presents the nasal combinations.

N. B. The English equivalents of the French nasal vowels are all necessarily imperfect, as *no consonant m* or *n* must be heard in the French sound they are meant to explain.

an		dans, lance, manger, vanter.
am	*an* in	camp, ambre, ample, lampe.
en	w*an*t	en, enfant, mentir, dent.
em		temps, empire, membre, trembler.
ian	is equivalent to	viande.
ien	*i-an*	patient. (See special rule for *ien*.)
in		pin, crin, vin, rincer.
im		impie, importe, imposer, imbu.
ym	*an* in	thym, nymphe, symphonie.
ain	*an*ger	sain, bain, saint, crainte.
aim		faim, essaim, daim.
ein		sein, peindre, feindre, ceinture.
ien	is equivalent to *i-in*,	rien. (See special rule for *ien*.)
oin	" " " *w-in*,	foin, coin, point, moins.
on	*on* in	non, conte, chanson, ronde.
om	s*ong*	nom, comte, plomb, compris.
ion	is equivalent to *i-on*,	action, passion, question.
un	no equivalent	un, brun, tribun, chacun.
um	in English, French	parfum, humble.
eun	*eu* nasal.	à jeun.

The nasal diphthongs *ian*, *ion*, are the simple sounds *an*, *on*, preceded by a short French *i*; *oin* is *in* preceded by a *w* sound. All other combinations may be decomposed in the same manner, as *ou-in*, *ou-en*, etc.

36. Ien final, and in verbs in *enir*, is equivalent to *i-in* or *yin*, (*yan* in *yankee*). Ex. *chien*, *bien*, *viendrai*, *tiendront*; in other cases, when followed by a consonant (not *n*), it is equivalent to *i-an* (*yan*) nasal. Ex. *science*, *audience*, *patient*, and all words in *ient*.

REMARK. In compound words, as *bientôt*, *chiendent*, *ien* retains the sound of the primitive words *bien*, *chien*.

37. M and N are *not nasal* when double or when between two vowels or a vowel and a silent *h*. Ex. année, innocent, homme, une, inouï, inutile, inhumain.

EXCEPTIONS. The nasal sound is heard in *ennui* and its derivatives; in *emmener* and all words beginning in *emm*; in *enivrer* and *enorgueillir*.

38. *Ent* in the third person plural of verbs is silent. Ex. ils aiment, *they love;* ils unirent, etc. In other cases *ent* final is equivalent to nasal *an*. Ex. content, *contented;* président, *president;* — while in the verbs, ils content, *they relate*, ils président, *they preside*, *ent* is silent.

39. *En* and *em* in a few foreign names have the sound of *in*. Ex. Mentor, Benjamin, Memphis. *Em* final, and sometimes *am* and *im* in foreign proper names, are not nasal. Ex. Jérusalem, Abraham, Selim. *Um* in words that still preserve their Latin form is not nasal, *u* having the sound of *o*. Ex. album, triumvir. In many other foreign words *m* and *n* final are not nasal. Ex. *Eden*, *Hymen*, *amen*, etc.

CONSONANTS.

GENERAL RULES.

40. Final consonants are silent except *c*, *f*, *l*, *r*. Ex. *était*, *après*, *croix*, pronounced as if written *étai*, *aprè*, *croi*.

REMARK. When several consonants occur at the end of a word with no vowel after them, they are all silent, except *c*, *f*, *l*, *r*. Ex. *est*, *faits*, *ils*, *dards*, pronounced as if written *è*, *fai*, *il*, *dar*.

EXCEPTIONS. In foreign proper names the final consonant is generally sounded. Ex. *Brutus*, *Job*.

41. A double consonant is pronounced as one letter. Ex. *abbé*, *frapper*, pronounced as if written *a-bé*, *fra-per*.

42. B, c, d, f, l, m, n, p, (ph,) q, v, and z are pronounced as in English.

Exceptions to the above general rules will be given under the various letters.

43. In English, consonants in the middle or at the beginning of words are often silent, as *p* and *l* in *psalm*; *g* in *phlegm*; *l* in *calm*. In French, consonants in a like position retain their proper sound. Thus in *psaume*, *flegme*, *calme*, the *p*, the *g*, and the *l* are fully sounded.

SPECIAL RULES.

B final is pronounced in *radoub*, *rumb*.

C has the sound of *g* in *second* and its derivatives.

44. Ç is pronounced as *c* in *façade*. Ex. *garçon*, *leçon*.

45. Ch has the sound of *ch* in *machine*. Ex. *chaise*, *chercher*.

Ch in many words derived from the Greek and in several proper names has the sound of *k*. Ex. *chaos*, *chœur*, *Michel-Ange*. But *ch* has the sound of *sh* in *Achille*, *patriarche*, *archevêque*. It is silent in *almanach*.

Cc before *e*, *i*, *and y* is equivalent to *k-s*. Ex. *accès*, *accident*.

C final is silent after *n*. Ex. *banc*. It is silent in *accroc*, *broc*, *clerc*, *estomac*, *lacs*, *tabac*.

D final is heard in *sud*.

Dd. Two *d's* are heard when *ad* precedes a syllable beginning with a *d*. Ex. *addition*.

F final is silent in *clef*, *chef-d'œuvre*, *bœufs*, *œufs*; though sounded in *chef*, *bœuf*, *œuf*. *F* is silent in *neuf*, nine, only when the next word begins with a consonant, before a vowel it has the sound of *v*. Ex. *neuf hommes*.

G before *a*, *o*, *u*, sounds like *g* in *game*. Ex. *garçon*.

46. G before *e*, *i*, and *y*, sounds like *s* in *pleasure*. Ex. *genre*, *gibet*, *général*.

47. Gn has a liquid sound something like *ni* in *union*. Ex. *agneau*, *magnifique*. This sound is produced with the body, not with the tip of the tongue against the roof of the mouth.

G is hard before *n* at the beginning of a word. Ex. *gnomon*; also in *stagnant*, *inexpugnable*, and in several words in *eg* and *ig* that seldom occur.

Gg. Two *g's* are heard in *suggérer*: the first hard, the last like *s* in *pleasure*.

G final is sounded in *joug*.

48. H is said to be mute or aspirate. When mute it is entirely disregarded in pronunciation, and the vowel that comes after it is pronounced with the preceding consonant, or causes the preceding vowel to be elided as if no letter intervened. Ex. *l'homme, deux habits.*

49. When *h* is *aspirated* no real aspiration is heard as in English; but the vowel that comes after it is pronounced strongly. H aspirate prevents linking and elision. Ex. *le héros, deux héros.*

50. There are about 300 words beginning with *h* aspirate. These comprise many marine terms, foreign words, and the words in the following list, and their derivatives.

REMARK. The derivatives of *héros—heroine, héroique, héroism,*—are not aspirated. But *hableur, haine, hausser,* etc., follow the anology of their primitives *habler, hair, haut,* which alone are given in the list.

habler	hameau	hargneux	hennir
hache	hanche	haricot	Henri
hagard	hangar	haridelle	héraut
haie	hanneton	harnais	hérisson
haillons	hanter	harpe	hérisser
haïr	harangue	harpie	héron
haire	haras	hasard	héros
hâle	harasser	hâte	herse
halle	harceler	haut	heurter
hallebarde	hardes	hâve	hibou
hallier	hardi	hâvre	hideux
halte	hareng	havresac	hiérarchie
homard	houblon	houx	humer
honte	houille	huche	huppe
horde	houlette	huée	hure
hors	houppe	huguenot	hurler
hotte	housse	huit	hussard

51. J is pronounced like *s* in *pleasure*; it is never silent nor double. Ex. *déjà, joujou.*

L when not liquid sounds as in English. Ex. *livre.*

52. *Ill* not initial, and *il* final, have a liquid sound somewhat like *ll* in *William, brilliant.* This sound, still prevalent in the southern

and central parts of France, has been softened down to nearly a *y* in the north and especially in Paris, so that there, *ill* in *tailleur* is scarcely more audible than *i* in *païen*. Ex. *fille*, *famille*, *gentille*.

53. The vowel that precedes liquid *ill* or *il*, retains its proper sound and does not coalesce with the *i*; *ue* and *æ* are then equivalent to *eu*. Ex. *muraille*, *patrouille*, *orgueil*, *œil*.

54. *Ill* is not liquid, that is, *l* retains its proper sound, in words that begin with *il*. Ex. *illustre*, *illisible*; also in *mille*, *ville*, *tranquille*, *pupille*, *Achille*, *osciller*, *vaciller*, etc.

Il is not liquid in *mil*, *fil*, *civil*, *profil*.

L final is silent in *baril*, *chenil*, *coutil*, *fournil*, *fusil*, *gril*, *gentil*, *sourcil*, *persil*, *outil*. It is also silent in *soûl*, *pouls*, *fils*, and in the terminations *auld*, *ault*, *ould*, *oult*.

M and N, when not nasal, are pronounced as in English. Ex. *manier*.

M is silent in *damner*, *automne*, and their derivatives.

P is silent in *baptême*, *sept*, *compte*, *dompter*, *exempter*, *sculpter*.

Q is always followed by *u* except in *coq* and *cinq*, when it sounds like k. (For *qu* see *u*, 23.)

55. R is rolled, but with less force at the end than at the beginning of a syllable. Ex. *grand*, *sœur*; *rr* and *rh* are generally pronounced with more force than *r* alone. Ex. *arriver*, *rhume*.

In the future and conditional of the verbs acquérir, *to acquire*, courir, *to run*, mourir, *to die*, the two *r's* must be distinctly heard to distinguish them from other forms that have but one *r*. Thus *nous courrons*, *vous acquerrez*, *ils mourraient*, must not be pronounced like *nous courons*, *vous acquérez*, *ilts mouraient*.

R final is generally pronounced, but final *er* is equivalent to *é*. Ex. *parler*, *aimer*. In monosyllables in *er* the *r* is sounded. Ex. *fer*, *cher*, *mer*. It is also sounded in *amer*, *enfer*, *hier*, *hiver*, and in a few words of foreign origin, as *magister*, etc. R is silent in *monsieur*.

56. S is generally sounded as in English; but in words ending *isme*, *asme*, etc., it has *not* the sound of *z*. Ex. *prisme*, *miasme*.

57. S between two vowels has the sound of *z*. Ex. *rose*, *base*, *vase*.

S has also the sound of *z* in words compounded with the Latin proposition *trans*, followed by a vowel. Ex. *transitif, transition*. It has the same sound before *b, d, v*, and after *l*. Ex. *presybtère, svelte, balsamique*.

As *s* initial has the hissing sound as in English, — when a word beginning with an *s* takes a prefix, the *s*, though between two vowels, retains its hissing sound. Ex. *vraisemblable* (compounded of *vrai* and *semblable*), *monosyllabe*.

Sch is generally pronounced like *sh*. Ex. *schisme*. It has the sound of *sk* in a few words.

S final is sounded in words that have been taken from Greek and Latin without any change of orthography. Ex. *atlas, blocus, gratis*, etc. *S* is also sounded in *cens, en-sus, maïs, mœurs, vis, Rheims, fils, sens* (in some of its meanings), *lis* (not in *fleur-de-lis*), *tous* (when used without a noun).

T is generally sounded as in English.

58. In words corresponding in form to those in which *t* has in English an *sh* sound, it has in French the sound of *ss*. This occurs in *tial, tiel, tier, tion*, not initial or preceded by *x* or *s*. Ex. *partial, essentiel, initier, nation*. But *bestial, bastion, mixtion*, have the pure *t* sound.

59. T has also the souud of *s* in words in *tie*, that have in English *cy*, or *tia*, in which *t* sounds like *sh*. Ex. *prophétie, démocratie, minutie, initier*, — also in *balbutier*. In other words in *tie* and *tier*, *t* retains the proper sound. Ex. *moitié, métier*.

Th is never pronounced as in English, but always like *t* alone, as *pathétique*.

T final is heard in *brut, chut, correct, dot, direct, déficit, fat, exact, net, suspect, strict*. In *sept* and *huit*, *t* is silent only when they precede a noun commencing with a consonant. Ex. *huit garçons*. In *Christ*, *s* and *t* are both pronounced; but in *Jésus-Christ* they are both silent. In *vingt*, *t* is pronounced only in the series between 20 and 30. Ex. *vingt-cinq*.

X has the sound of *gs* in words beginning with *x* or *ex* before a vowel or an *h* mute. Ex. *Xavier, exil, exhumer*.

In a few proper names *x* has the sound of *ss*. Ex. *Bruxelles, Auxerre*; it has also this sound in *soixante*, — and in *six* and *dix* when standing alone. In *dix-huit* and *dix-neuf*, *x* sounds like *z*.

X in other cases has the sound of *ks*. Ex. *luxe, Aix-la-Chapelle*.

Z is pronounced in *gaz*. When final in proper names it has the sound of s. Ex. *Metz, Suez*, etc.

LINKING OF FINAL CONSONANTS.

60. The final consonant of a word, closely connected in sense with the next word beginning with a vowel or silent *h* must generally be carried over. In that case *s* and *x* are sounded like *z*; *d* like *t*, and *g* (seldom linked) like *k*. Ex. *un grand homme, vous avez, ils ont, aux armes.*

No general rule can be given embracing *all* the cases in which a final consonant must be thus linked. In poetry and in impressive reading, the linking must be made in many cases where it would sound unnatural and affected in daily conversation. It may be stated in general terms that the more closely connected the words are in sense, the more imperative it is to link them together in pronunciation. Certain words, such as *et, riz, clef, plomb, loup,* etc., can never be linked. Words ending in a nasal sound are seldom linked, except short words that recur frequently, such as *on, en, un, mon, ton, son, bien, bon,* etc. When a nasal *n* is linked, either the nasal sound is heard and an additional *n* pronounced before the next vowel, or the nasal is dropped altogether, thus *un homme, on a,* as if written *un nhomme, on na;* or *u-nhomme, o-na.* In rapid speech the nasal sound almost always disappears; many omit it altogether. In some combinations, such as *bon homme, bien heureux,* it is never heard.

OBSERVATIONS ON *E* MUTE.

We have seen that *e* unaccented when final is mute, and that in the words *ce, de, je, le, me, ne, que, se* and *te,* and when it terminates a syllable not final, it has the indistinct sound of *e* in *battery.* In rapid utterance, however, even this feeble sound is not heard *whenever the articulation connected with it can be distinctly uttered without it.*

Hence the following rule:—

61. E unaccented ending a syllable is silent whenever the consonant before it can be pronounced either with a vowel that precedes or one that comes after it in the next syllable or word.

Practice and oral teaching only can make this law of euphony perfectly clear. In the following examples the *e's* printed in *italics* are not pronounced.

Voilà l*e* chemin d*e* fer.	There is the railway.
Je l*e* sais.	I know it.
Je n*e* te l*e* donn*e* pas.	I do not give it to thee.
Beaucoup d*e* monde.	Many persons.
Je n*e* me l*e* propos*e* pas.	I do not propose it to myself.
Etr*e* attentif.	To be attentive.
Nobl*e* ardeur.	Noble ardor.

In the last two examples the *r* and *l* that precede the *e* are virtually carried over to the next word as if no *e* intervened, and *tr* and *bl* were final.

Note. Care must be taken not to pronounce *tre, dre, ble, ple, cre,* etc., as they are in English, that is as *ter, der, bel, pel,* etc., in *order, temple, noble.* In French the *l* and *r* must not be separated by any intervening sound from the consonant that precedes. Ex. ordr*e*, aimabl*e*, quatr*e*, nacr*e*, peupl*e*.

I. PREMIÈRE LEÇON.

THE ARTICLE.

1. In the French language there are only *two genders*, viz., the *masculine* and the *feminine*. This distinction applies also to inanimate objects, which are either masculine or feminine.

2. The *definite* article has a peculiar form for each gender: *le* before a masculine, *la* before a feminine substantive; *les* is the plural of both genders. Ex.:—

Masc. *Le roi*, the king.
le père, the father.

Fem. *La reine*, the queen.
la mère, the mother.

3. *Le* and *la* in the singular lose their vowels and take the apostrophe (*l'*) before a noun beginning either with a vowel or *h* mute. Ex.:—

Masc. *L'ami*, the friend.
l'homme, the man.

Fem. *L'amie*, the (female) friend.
l'histoire, (the) history.

4. The *indefinite* article, answering to the English *a* or *an*, is *un* for the masculine; *une* for the feminine. Ex.:

Masc. *Un roi*, a king.
un père, a father.
un ami, a friend.

Fem. *Une reine*, a queen.
une mère, a mother.
une amie, a (female) friend.

VOCABULARY.

Le livre, the book.
le pain, the bread.
le cheval, the horse.
le chien, the dog.
l'oncle, the uncle.
l'enfant, the child.
l'or, the gold.
un jardin, a garden.
un chapeau, a hat, bonnet.
la rose, the rose.
la fleur, the flower.
la plume, the pen, feather.
la tante, the aunt.
une poire, a pear.
une pomme, an apple.
et, and.

S. *J'ai*, I have.	*Ai-je*, have I?
tu as, thou hast.	*as-tu*, hast thou?
il a, he has.	*a-t-il*, has he?
elle a, she has.	*a-t-elle*, has she?
Pl. *nous avons*, we have.	*avons-nous*, have we?
vous avez, you have.	*avez-vous*, have you?
ils ont, they have.	*ont-ils*, have they?
elles ont, they (fem) have.	*ont-elles*, have they?

REMARK 1. *J'ai* is for *je ai*. The *e* of *je*, I, is elided when the verb begins with a vowel or silent *h*.

2. Observe the hyphen by which the verb and pronoun are always joined in interrogations.

3. The *t* in *a-t-il*, *a-t-elle*, is merely euphonic. It is inserted to prevent the hiatus between two vowel sounds, when the third person singular of a verb ends in a vowel, and is followed by *il*, *elle*, *on*.

4. The use of the 2d person singular is much more frequent in French than in English. It generally denotes familiarity and intimacy. In addressing inferiors, it denotes authority; in poetry, its use is the same as in English.

5. When, in a question not beginning with an interrogative pronoun or an adverb, the subject is expressed by a *substantive*, it must begin the sentence, and the pronoun still be put after the verb. Ex.:—*L'enfant a-t-il?* has the child? *La mère a-t-elle?* has the mother?

READING EXERCISE 1.

J'ai le livre. Tu as un livre. J'ai la rose. As-tu la rose? Il a le cheval. Elle a le pain. Le pèrea un cheval. La mère a un jardin. L'enfant a une poire. Nous avons un chien. Avez-vous un chapeau? Ils ont un oncle et une tante. Elles ont une tante. L'enfant a-t-il une plume? La mère a-t-elle la fleur? Le roi a-t-il un cheval? Il a le cheval. Les amis (*plu.*) ont les livres. Les enfants ont les plumes.

THEME 1.

1. I have the horse. 2. I have a friend. 3. Thou hast the book. 4. He has a dog. 5. She has the bonnet. 6. The father has a garden. 7. The mother has the rose. 8. The king has the gold.

9. The uncle has a friend. 10. We have the bread. 11. You have a pear. 12. They (*masc.*) have an apple. 13. They (*fem.*) have a flower. 14. Has the friend a horse? 15. The friend has a horse and a dog.

CONVERSATION.

Ai-je la rose?	Vous avez la rose.
As-tu le pain?	J'ai le pain.
A-t-elle la fleur?	Elle a la fleur.
L'enfant a-t-il le livre?	Il a le livre.
Avez-vous un cheval?	Nous avons un cheval et un chien.
L'enfant a-t-il une poire?	L'enfant a une poire et une pomme.

II. DEUXIÈME LEÇON.

FORMATION OF THE PLURAL.

1. General Rule. The plural is formed in French as in English, by the addition of an *s* to the singular. Ex.: —

Le roi,	Plur. *les rois.*	*la pomme,*	Plur. *les pommes.*
le livre,	*les livres.*	*l'enfant,*	*les enfants.*
l'homme,	*les hommes.*	*l'ami,*	*les amis.*

EXCEPTIONS.

2. Nouns ending in *s*, *x*, *z*, in the singular, remain unchanged.

Le fils, the son.	Plur. *les fils*, the sons.
la noix, the walnut,	*les noix*, the walnuts.
le nez, the nose.	*les nez*, the noses.

3. Words ending in *au*, *eu*, form their plural by adding *x* instead of *s*, as: —

Le chapeau, the hat *or* bonnet.	Plur. *les chapeaux*.
le feu, the fire.	*les feux*.
le lieu, the place.	*les lieux*.

REMARK. Seven nouns in *ou* take *x* in the plural, viz.:

Le chou, the cabbage.
le bijou, the jewel.
le caillou, the pebble.
le hibou, the owl.
le pou, the louse.
le genou, the knee.
le joujou, the plaything.

Plural: *les choux, les bijoux, les cailloux*, etc.

The others ending in *ou* follow the general rule and take *s* in the plural, as: *le clou*, the nail; plur. *les clous; le trou*, the hole; plur. *les. trous*, etc.

4. Nouns ending in *al, ail*, change these terminations into *aux*, to form the plural, as:

Le cheval, the horse.	Plur. *Les chevaux*.
l'animal, the animal.	*les animaux*.
le travail, the work.	*les travaux*.

REMARK. This rule, however, has a few exceptions, which follow the general rule, simply taking *s* in the plural, as: *le bal*, the ball; *le carnaval*, the carnival; *le portail*, the doorway; *le gouvernail*, the helm; *l'éventail*, the fan, etc. Plur. *les bals, les carnavals*, etc.

5. The following words form their plural irregularly. (The first three have also a regular plural. See Part II, L. II.)

Le ciel, heaven.	Plur. *Les cieux*, heavens.
l'œil, the eye.	*les yeux*, the eyes.
l'aïeul, the great-grandfather.	*les aïeux*, the ancestors.
le bétail, the cattle.	*les bestiaux*, the cattle.

VOCABULARY.

Le canif, the penknife.
le frère, the brother.
la sœur, the sister.
la porte, the door, gate.
la maison, the house.
le château, the castle.
le palais, the palace.
un tableau, a picture.
le chat, the cat.
le général, the general.
la noix, the walnut.
le jeu, the play, game.
la souris, the mouse.
le nom, the name.
le chameau, the camel.
le couteau, the knife.
mon, ma, my.
vu, seen. *ou*, or.
deux, two. *trois*, three.
quatre, four. *cinq*, five.
le bras, the arm.

Voici, here is, this is, here are, these are.
Voilà, there is, that is, there are, those are.

Voici is compounded of the imperative of *voir*, to see, and *ici*, here. It means therefore literally, *see here*. *Voilà* means *see there*. They both govern the objective case. Ex. *me voici*, here am I; literally, *Behold me here*.

S. *J'avais*, I had.	*Avais-je*, had I?
tu avais, thou hadst.	*avais-tu*, hadst thou?
il avait, he had.	*avait-il*, had he?
elle avait, she had.	*avait-elle*, had she?
Pl. *nous avions*, we had.	*avions-nous*, had we?
vous aviez, you had.	*aviez-vous*, had you?
ils avaient, they had.	*avaient-ils*, had they?
elles avaient, they had.	*avaient-elles*, had they?

READING EXERCISE 2.

Nous avons un canif. Vous aviez deux canifs. Mon frère a les couteaux. La maison a deux portes. Avais-je les noix? Aviez-vous les joujoux? Oui, nous avions les joujoux. Le roi avait trois châteaux. La reine a les bijoux. Voici quatre souris. Les enfants avaient trois pommes. Mon oncle avait deux chevaux. Ma tante a cinq tableaux. Les chameaux ont une bosse (*hump*). Ma mère a deux sœurs et trois frères.

THEME 2.

1. I have three brothers. 2. (The)* man has two arms. 3. I had four horses. 4. Hadst thou the flowers? 5. I had the roses. 6. There are the apples, the pears, and the walnuts. 7. There are also the games and the pictures. 8. Have you seen the houses, the castles, and the gardens? 9. My uncle has four pictures. 10. I have seen five horses and two camels. 11. The children have three mice. 12. Have you seen the games of the (*des*) children?

* In the Themes, words placed in parentheses (—) must be expressed in French, though redundant in English. English words printed in *italics* must be omitted in French.

13. Has my aunt three dogs or three cats? 14. She has three dogs and two cats. 15. The eye is blue (*est bleu*). 16. I have two eyes. 17. My brother has two knives, and I have two penknives.

CONVERSATION.

Avez-vous un canif?	J'ai deux canifs.
Avais-je les couteaux?	Vous aviez les couteaux.
As-tu vu les chameaux?	J'ai vu les chameaux et les chevaux.
Avez-vous aussi vu les châteaux?	J'ai vu les châteaux et les palais.
Avez-vous les bijoux?	Ma tante a les bijoux.
Les enfants ont ils les habits (*coats*) ou les chapeaux?	Les enfants ont les habits et les chapeaux.
Avaient-ils vu les feux?	Ils avaient vu les feux.
Avez-vous les tableaux?	Je n'ai pas (*not*) les tableaux.
Mon père a-t-il un chat?	Il a un chat et un chien.
Combien de (*how many*) frères avez-vous?	J'ai trois frères.
Combien de sœurs avez-vous?	J'ai deux sœurs.
Avez-vous vu les amis?	Nous n'avons pas vu les amis.

III. TROISIÈME LEÇON.

CASE—*A*—*DE*.

1. French nouns have no variation of termination to indicate case; the nominative and objective are, as in English, alike in form, and the possessive is expressed by the preposition *de* (*of*) and its object.

2. The possessor must, in French, follow the object possessed,

and be preceded by the article. *e. g.* The king's throne, must be transposed as if it were, the throne of the king; *Le trône du roi.*

3. The preposition *de* (of, from,) appears either unchanged or contracted with the article. A contraction takes place whenever *de* occurs before the article *le* or *les;* in the first case, it takes the form *du* (singular), in the second *des* (plural). Ex.

S. *du roi* (instead of *de le roi,*) of the king, *or* the king's.
du père (instead of *de le père,*) of the father, *or* the father's.

Pl. *des rois* (instead of *de les rois,*) of the kings, *or* the kings'.
des mères (instead of *de les mères,*) of the mothers.

4. Before *la* and *l'*, *de* remains unaltered, as:—

de la mère, of the mother, *or* the mother's.
de l'ami, of the friend, the friend's.
de l'homme, of (the) man, the man's.

5. Before the indefinite article *un*, *une*, an apostrophe is put instead of the *e* of *de*, as:—

d'un roi, of a king.	*d'une reine,* of a queen.
d'un ami, of a friend.	*d'une amie,* of a female friend.

6. Before *le*, the preposition à (to) is contracted with this article to *au;* and before *les* into *aux;* as:—

au (à le) *roi,* to the king.	*aux* (à les) *rois,* to the kings.
au " *frère,* to the brother.	*aux* " *frères,* to the brothers.

7. The definite article must be used in French before all nouns used in a general sense or denoting a whole species of objects, though in English the article is not employed; as:—

Man, *l'homme.*	nature, *la nature.*
life, *la vie.*	summer, *l' été.*
fortune, *la fortune.*	dinner, *le dîner.*

Hence, of man, of life, of fortune, etc., are to be translated in French *de l'homme, de la vie, de la fortune, etc.;* to man, to life, to nature, etc., *à l'homme, à la vie, à la nature.*

8. In French the article is to be repeated before each substantive of a sentence, as:—

The salt, pepper and vinegar,—*le sel, le poivre et le vinaigre.*
The men, women and children,—*les hommes, les femmes et les enfants.*

VOCABULARY.

Dieu, God.
le créateur, the creator.
le monde, the world.
l'ennemi, the enemy.
le sommeil, sleep.
l'image, f. the image.
la mort, death.
la feuille, the leaf.
à qui, to whom, whose?
l'oiseau, the bird.
votre, your.
l'arbre, the tree.
la fenêtre, the window.
le cousin, the cousin.
la cousine, the cousin, f.
la fille, the daughter.
la ville, the town.
je donne, I give.
le voisin, the neighbor.
est, is. (belongs) *sont*, *are*.
oui, yes. *non*, no.
Monsieur, Sir.
Madame, Madam.
Mademoiselle. Miss.

READING EXERCISE 3.

Le père de l'enfant. La mère des enfants. La porte de la maison. Les portes des maisons. Les fenêtres du palais. Le chat est un animal. Les chats sont les ennemis des souris. Le sommeil est l'image de la mort. Le château est au roi et à la reine. Je donne la plume à l'enfant. Je donne le jeu aux enfants. Le jardin est aux frères et aux sœurs. Les images des rois. Les feuilles des arbres. Les fenêtres de la maison.

THEME 3.

1. The father of the son. 2. The mother of the daughter. 3. The mother of the children. 4. The door of the house. 5. The gates of the town. 6. The houses of the towns. 7. The windows of the houses. 8. God is the creator of the world. 9. The dog is the enemy of the cat. 10. I give the book to the brother. 11. I give the coats to the brothers and sisters. 12. The dog is the friend of man. 13. The feathers of the birds. 14. My cousin's bonnet. 15. My cousins' bonnets (the bonnets of my cousins). 16. Sleep is the brother of death. 17. Of the trees of the garden. 18. The

eyes of the horses are large (*grands*). 19. The friend's name. 20. The windows of the castle. 21. The neighbor's house and garden. 22. I give the roses to the sister of the general. 23. Give (*donnez*) the pen to the father.

CONVERSATION.

Ai-je le livre du cousin?	Tu as le livre du cousin.
As-tu l'image de la tante?	Oui M —* j'ai l'image de la tante.
A-t-il vu le jardin du roi?	Non M — il a vu le château du roi.
Les enfants ont-ils les jeux?	Oui M — les enfants ont les jeux.
Qui (*who*) a les ciseaux (*scissors*) de ma sœur?	Voici les ciseaux de votre sœur.
A qui sont les noix?	Elles sont à l'enfant.
A qui sont les poires?	Elles sont aux enfants du voisin.
A qui est ce (*this*) jardin?	Il est au roi et à la reine.
Avez-vous vu le chien de l'oncle?	Voilà le chien de l'oncle.
A qui sont ces (*these*) roses?	Elles sont à ma cousine.

IV. QUATRIÈME LEÇON.

PREPOSITIONS.

1. The following list includes the French prepositions of most frequent occurrence.

à, to, at, in.	*dans*, in, into.	*par*, through, by
après, after.	*de*, of, from.	*parmi*, among.

* This *M* —, which will always be inserted after *Oui* and *Non* should be read *Monsieur*, *Madame*, or *Mademoiselle*, as the case may require.

avant, before, (time).	*devant*, before, (place).	*pendant*, during.
avec, with.	*derrière*, behind.	*pour*, for.
chez, at, with, at the house of.	*en*, in.	*sans*, without.
	entre, between.	*sous*, under.
contre, against.	*envers*, *vers*, towards.	*sur*, on, upon.

As to the contraction of *à* and *le* into *au*, of *à* and *les* into *aux*, of *de* with *le* into *du*, of *de* with *les* into *des*, see page 34.

2. After prepositions no article is used whenever the noun is taken in a wide and indeterminate sense, and forms with the preposition a sort of adverbial phrase, as : *avec plaisir*, with pleasure ; *sans crainte*, without fear.

3. *Chez* means *at the house of*. It governs the noun or pronoun as any other preposition. Ex. *chez moi*, at my house, (at the house of me); *chez vous*, at your house ; *chez mon oncle*, at my uncle's, (at the house of my uncle).

For remarks on the employment of some prepositions, see P. II., L. 16.

VOCABULARY.

La cour, the court, yard.	*la chambre*, the room.
l'école, f. the school.	*l'église*, f. the church.
le maître, the master, teacher.	*la nuit*, the night.
l'eau, f. the water.	*le jour*, the day.
la main, the hand.	*la cuisine*, the kitchen.
la pluie, the rain.	*la poche*, the pocket.
le toit, the roof.	*demeure*, lives. *notre*, our.
où, where.	*qui*, who, whom ?

S. *Je suis*, I am.	*Suis-je*, am I ?
tu es, thou art.	*es-tu*, art thou ?
il est, he is.	*est-il*, is he ?
elle est, she is.	*est-elle*, is she ?
Pl. *nous sommes*, we are.	*sommes-nous*, are we ?
vous êtes, you are.	*êtes-vous*, are you ?
ils sont, they are.	*sont-ils*, are they ?
elles sont, they are.	*sont-elles*, are they ?

READING EXERCISE 4.

Je suis dans la cour. L'oiseau est sur le toit. Es-tu au jardin (dans le jardin)? Louis est chez mon père. Les chevaux sont devant la porte. Après la pluie. Pendant la nuit. Avant le jour. L'enfant est sous l'arbre. Parmi les enfants. Nous sommes derrière les arbres. Ils sont entre la porte et la fenêtre. Ce livre est pour mon frère. Ma tante est à l'église. Sans argent (*money*.) Avec les chevaux de mon oncle. Contre l'ennemi. Notre ami demeure à Paris dans la maison de sa tante.

THEME 4.

1. In the yard. 2. During the night. 3. I am before the house. 4. Louis is in the garden. 5. Are you in the yard? 6. Before night. 7. I speak (*je parle*) of the house, — of the coat, — of the flowers, — of my father, — of my mother. 8. The two knives are in my pocket. 9. Where are the cats? 10. They are in the kitchen. 11. The birds are on the roof. 12. The three children of my cousin (*m.*) are in (the) town. 13. Against the rain. 14. With my father. 15. Without a master. 16. Louis is in his (*sa*) room. 17. The book is for my sister. 18. Between the two windows. 19. Under the roof of the house. 20. Are they before the door of the church? 21. No; they are behind the church. 22. The children are at (the) school.

CONVERSATION.

Où est Louis?	Il est dans la cour.
Où est mon fils?	Il est au jardin.
Où sont les enfants?	Ils jouent (*play*) devant la maison.
Votre cousine est-elle á l'école?	Non M—, elle est à l'église.
Êtes-vous dans le jardin?	Non M—, nous sommes dans la cour.
Ton père est-il au jardin?	Non M—, il est dans sa chambre.
Sont-ils à la fenêtre?	Oui M—, ils sont à la fenêtre.
Avez-vous vu les canards (*ducks*) dans la cour?	Nous avons vu les canards et les oies (*geese*).

V. CINQUIÈME LEÇON.

THE PARTITIVE ARTICLE.

1. The partitive article answers to the English *some* or *any*, expressed in French by *du* before a noun masculine beginning with a consonant, by *de la* before a noun feminine beginning with a consonant, and by *de l'* before a noun of either gender beginning with a vowel or an *h* mute. Ex: —

Du pain, some *or* any bread.	*de la bière*, some beer.
du vin, (some *or* any) wine.	*de la viande*, some meat.
de l'argent, some money (Silver).	*de l'huile*, some oil.

In the plural the partitive article is *des* for both genders. Ex.

Des livres, (some) books.	*des fleurs*, flowers.
des enfants, children.	*des roses*, roses.

Some is not always used in English, whereas *du, de la, de l', des*, must always be expressed in French.

2. In questions the English use *any* instead of *some*; in French it must be rendered by the same article, as: —

Have you any bread? *avez-vous du pain?*
Is there any water? *y a-t-il de l'eau?*

3. The partitive article must be used whenever in English *some* or *any* is expressed or understood before a substantive; it must be repeated before every substantive in a sentence. Ex.: —

Have you bread and cheese? *Avez-vous du pain et du fromage?*
Bring me some mustard, oil and vinegar.
Apportez-moi de la moutarde, de l'huile et du vinaigre.

4. However, when the substantive is preceded by an adjective, the simple preposition *de* or *d'* takes the place of the partitive article, in the singular as well as in the plural, as: —

S. *de bon vin*, some *or* any good wine.
de bonne viande, some *or* any good meat.
de mauvais café, some *or* any bad coffee.
d' excellente farine, some *or* any excellent flour.

Pl. *de bons livres*, some *or* any good books.
de belles fleurs, some *or* any beautiful flowers.
d'excellents vaisseaux, some *or* any excellent vessels.

VOCABULARY.

La farine, the flour.	*le fruit*, the fruit.
le fer, (the) iron.	*le sucre*, the sugar.
l'argent, m. silver.	*le café*, the coffee.
le papier, the paper.	*la prune*, the plum.
l'encre, f. the ink.	*le beurre*, the butter.
le fromage, the cheese.	*le crayon*, the pencil.
le garçon,* the boy.	*le soulier*, the shoe.
le plomb, the lead.	*le bas*, the stocking.
le sel, the salt.	*acheté*, bought.
le canard, the duck.	*que*, what. *mais*, but.
l'œuf, m. the egg.	*là*, there. *six*, six.
il y a, there is, there are.	*c'est*, this is, that is.

8	*J'aurai*, I shall have	*Aurai-je*, shall I have?
	tu auras, thou wilt have.	*auras-tu*, wilt thou have?
	il aura, he will have.	*aura-t-il*, will he have?
	elle aura, she will have	*aura-t-elle*, will she have?
Pl.	*nous aurons*, we shall have.	*aurons-nous*, shall we have?
	vous aurez, you will have.	*aurez-vous*, will you have?
	ils auront, they will have.	*auront-ils*, will they have?
	elles auront, they will have.	*auront-elles*, will they have?

READING EXERCISE 5.

J'avais de la farine et du sel. Aviez-vous aussi du sel? Le roi a de l'or et de l'argent. Il a aussi des bijoux. Tu auras du fromage. Louis a acheté du papier et de l'encre. Nous aurons des livres, des plumes et des crayons. Avaient-elles des fleurs et des fruits? Je donne à ton cousin des noix et des pommes. Dans la cour il y a des canards. Mon cousin avait des chevaux et des chiens. Ma cousine aura des chats, mais ma tante aura des oiseaux. Dans les jardins il y a des arbres, des fruits et des fleurs.

* *Garçon* means *waiter* and *bachelor* as well as *boy*. *Petit*, small, is therefore generally prefixed in speaking of a young boy.

THEME 5.

1. We had some butter and (some) cheese. 2. You had butter and eggs. 3. Here is (L. II.) bread. 4. There is some bread. 5. My father bought lead and iron. 6. The child has flowers. 7. My cousin (*f.*) will have some flour and bread. 8. There are eggs and fruits. 9. The man has sugar and coffee. 10. The queen has gold and silver. 11. I gave (*to*) the boys books, pencils and pens. 12. They will also have some paper and ink. 13. Louis has horses and dogs. 14. My sister will have shoes and stockings. 15. I give (*to*) the boy stockings, clothes, (*habits*) and hats. 16. Have you (any) friends (m). 17. They (f.) will have friends (f.). 18. At my uncle's (L. IV. 3.) house there are books and pictures. 19. Will you have (*voulez-vous*) some money? 20. No; give me (*moi*) some bread. 21. Read (*lisez*) good books. 22. This is bad coffee. 23. We have seen beautiful roses.

CONVERSATION.

Avons-nous de la farine?	Nous avons de la farine.
Avons-nous aussi du sel?	Nous avons aussi du sel.
Aurons-nous du beurre et du pain?	Non M—, mais vous aurez des fruits.
Qu'avez-vous là (*there*)?	Nous avons de la viande et du pain.
A-t-elle des crayons?	Non M—, mais elle a des plumes.
Les enfants ont-ils des poires?	Non M—, ils ont des pommes.
Qu'as-tu sous le bras (*arm*)?	J'ai des livres.
Pour qui sont ces livres?	Ils sont pour mon maître.
Ta sœur a-t-elle du sucre?	Elle a du sucre et du café.
Ton cousin a-t-il du papier?	Mon cousin a du papier, des plumes et de l'encre.
Qui a du fromage?	Le garçon a du fromage.
Y a-t-il des fruits?	Oui M—, il y a des fruits.
Qu'y a-t-il chez mon oncle?	Il y a des livres et des images.

VI. SIXIÈME LEÇON.

FURTHER USE OF *DE*.

De is used without the article.

1. After nouns expressing *measure*, *weight*, *number*, as:

Une bouteille de vin, a bottle of wine. *Une livre de sucre*, a pound of sugar.
Un morceau de pain, a piece of bread. *Une paire de bas*, a pair of stockings.

2. After adverbs of quantity.

Assez, enough.
beaucoup, much, many, a great many, a great deal.
combien, how much, how many.
guère, but little, but few.
peu, little, few.
plus, more.
moins, less.
ne—rien, nothing.
quelque chose, something.
trop, too, too much, too many.
trop peu, too little, too few.
tant, so much, so many.
autant, as much, as many.

Ex.: — *Assez de vin*, wine enough, (*assez* before the noun).
Combien d'argent, how much money?
Tant de fleurs, so many flowers. *Trop de fautes*, too many mistakes.

Remark. But after *bien*, much, many, and *la plupart*, most, the article must be used. Ex.: —

Bien des hommes, many men. *La plupart du temps*, most of the time.

3. After *pas*, *point*, *jamais*, *de* alone must be used instead of the partitive *du*, *de la*, *des*. Ex.: —

Je n'ai pas de sucre, I have no sugar. *N'avez-vous point d'encre*, have you no ink?

4. *De* is used as a connective of a word denoting a material.

Une bague d'or, a gold ring. *Une cuiller d'argent*, a silver spoon.
Une bourse de soie, a silk purse. *Une table de bois*, a wooden table.
Un chapeau de velours, a velvet bonnet.

VOCABULARY.

Une feuille, a sheet.
un verre, a glass.
le thé, tea.
une boîte, a box.
la montre, the watch.
le drap, the cloth.
reçu, received.
l'aune, f. the ell, yard.
une douzaine, a dozen.
la botte, the boot.
la personne, the person.
le bois, the wood.
que, than.
bu, drunk.

READING EXERCISE 6.

Voici une bouteille de vin. Nous avons trois livres de sucre. Nous aurons aussi deux livres de café. La reine avait beaucoup de bijoux. Aviez-vous assez d'argent? Mon oncle aura une douzaine de bas. Avez-vous reçu la boîte de crayons? Vous aurez une feuille de papier. Aviez-vous assez de pain? Les enfants avaient moins de poires que de noix. Je donne assez d'argent à mon fils. Il a bu trop de vin. Nous aurons une chaine d'argent. Vous aurez une montre d'or. Ma mère a un chapeau de velours. La plupart des hommes sont heureux.

THEME 6.

1. I have a dozen (*of*) pens. 2. Thou wilt have a sheet of paper. 3. She has cheese and butter enough. 4. We had a glass of wine. 5. I shall have also a piece of meat and two glasses of wine. 6. He had a bottle of oil. 7. We had two pounds of sugar, six pounds of coffee, and five pounds of tea. 8. You will have a great many pencils and books. 9. I have bought a dozen stockings and two pairs of shoes. 10. In this (*cette*) box there are six yards of cloth. 11. I had a silver watch and a gold ring. 12. This is a wooden table. 13. How many persons have you seen (*vues*)? 14. We have seen few persons. 15. My cousin had a wooden box. 16. Have you drunk a bottle of wine? 17. Give me a sheet of paper. 18. My brother will have something. 19. My sister has bought two gold rings and three silver spoons. 20. The child has as many pears as (*que de*) apples.

CONVERSATION.

Qu'avez-vous là ?	Nous avons un verre d'eau.
Qu'avez-vous acheté ?	J'ai acheté deux livres de sucre.
Avez-vous aussi du café ?	Oui M—, j'ai du café.
Avez-vous de l'argent, mon fils ?	Oui mon père, j'ai de l'argent.
Combien d'argent avez-vous ?	J'ai six francs.
Est-ce assez pour vous ?	C'est assez pour moi (*me*).
Où avez-vous vu le maître de musique ?	J'ai vu mon maître de musique au jardin.
Avait-il des fleurs ?	Oui M—, il avait des fruits et des fleurs.
Combien de chevaux avez-vous ?	Nous avons trois chevaux.
Avez-vous une paire de bottes ?	J'ai une paire de bottes et deux paires de souliers.

VII. SEPTIÈME LEÇON.

PROPER NOUNS.

A distinction must be made between names of *persons* and *towns*, and names of *countries*, *provinces*, *mountains*, *rivers*, *lakes*.

1. The former, as in English, take no article, such are :—

CHRISTIAN NAMES.

Guillaume, William.	*François*, Francis.
Henri, Henry.	*Elise*, Eliza.
George, George.	*Hélène*, Helen, Ellen.
Jean, John.	*Jeanne*, Jane.

NAMES OF TOWNS.

Vienne, Vienna.	*Lyon*, Lyons.
Genève, Geneva.	*Bruxelles*, Brussels.

2. We must except from the above rule the names of several Italian authors before which the article is used: *le Tasse*, Tasso (*du Tasse*, etc) ; *l'Arioste*, Ariosto ; *le Dante*, Dante ; — titles of books or plays, as : *le Télémaque de Fénelon*, *l'Athalie de Racine*, etc. ; some names of towns, as : *le Havre*, Havre ; *le Caire*, Cairo ; *la Nouvelle Orléans*, New Orleans.

3. Before proper names of countries, provinces, rivers and mountains, the definite article is used in French, as : —

La France, France.	*la Prusse*, Prussia.
la Belgique, Belgium.	*l'Europe*, Europe.
l'Angleterre, England.	*l'Afrique*, Africa.
l'Italie, Italy.	*l'Asie*, Asia.
la Suisse, Switzerland.	*l'Amérique*, America.
l'Allemagne, Germany.	*la Seine*, the Seine.
l'Espange, Spain.	*le Rhin*, the Rhine.
la Suède, Sweden.	*les Alpes*, the Alps, etc.

EXCEPTIONS.

4. The names of *countries* and *provinces* take no article when they are preceded by the preposition *en*, which corresponds to both *to* and *in*. Ex.: —

Je vais en Italie, I am going to Italy.
Il demeure en Allemagne, he lives in Germany.

5. *To* and *at* or *in*, before names of cities, towns, and villages, are rendered by *à*. Ex.: —

Nous allons à Londres,	——	*à Paris*,	——	*à Bade, etc.*
We go to London	——	to Paris,	——	to Baden, etc.
Mon oncle demeure à Berlin	——	*à Lyon, etc.*		
My uncle lives at (in) Berlin,	——	at (in) Lyons, etc.		

(Further explanations will be given in the second part.)

Most names of towns are spelled in French as in English, with a few exceptions ; those that end in *e* mute are feminine, the rest are masculine.

VOCABULARY.

Le cahier, the copy-book.	*la ville*, the city, town.
la carte, the map.	*le cours*, the course.
la fable, the fable.	*le marchand*, the dealer, tradesman.

le manteau, the cloak.	*le négociant*, the merchant.
le gant, the glove.	*la capitale*, the capital.
le pays, the country.	*donnez*, give. *votre*, your.
où, where. *lu*, read.	*était*, was. *étiez-vous*, were you?

READING EXERCISE 7.

J'ai le cahier de Frédéric. Voici les fables de La Fontaine. J'ai vu le château du roi de Belgique. Donnez la boîte *à* Sophie. Donnez la plume *à* Henri. Où est Monsieur H? C'est le chapeau de mademoiselle Elise. C'est le canif de George. Nous sommes *à* Paris. Étiez-vous à Vienne? Mon cousin est en Amérique. Le cours du Rhin est long. Voici une carte d'Allemagne. Louis Phillippe, roi de France, est mort (*died*) en Angleterre. Voici les chevaux de Charles. Avez-vous lu les œuvres (*the works*) de Corneille? Donnez ces gants à Henri.

THEME 7.

1. William is my friend. 2. I am William's friend (the friend of William). 3. Here is John's brother. 4. Where is my sister Ellen? 5. She is with Caroline. 6. Where are Eliza's gloves? 7. Speak (*parlez*) to Henry and Francis. 8. I have received the book from Paris. 9 Brussels is the capital of Belgium. 10. Florence is a city in Italy. 11. I am going to Switzerland. 12. The merchants of New York. 13. My uncle lives in Germany. 14. Are you going (*allez-vous*) to Berlin or to Vienna? 15. I am going to Frankfort and to Vienna. 16. Paris is the capital of France. 17. Is your aunt in America? 18. Yes; she is in New Orleans. 19. My brother has travelled (*voyagé*) in Russia, in Sweden, and in Germany. 20. This is John's hat. 21. I have seen Geneva, Lyons, and Rome. 22. Give me Mary's copy-book and George's pencil. 23. I have seen the apple-vender (dealer in (*de*) apples).

CONVERSATION.

Oú étiez-vous?	J'étais à Paris.
Et ton frère où était-il?	Il était aussi à Paris.

Où sont les gants d'Hélène?	Ils sont sur la table.
Quelle est la capitale de la Belgique?	C'est Bruxelles.
Quelle est la capitale de la Prusse?	C'est Berlin.
Qui est là?	Les enfants de madame B.
A qui donnez-vous ces livres?	Je les (*them*) donne à Marie.
A qui est ce chapeau?	Ce chapeau est à Guillaume.
Où trouve-t-on (*is found*) beaucoup d'or?	En Californie.
Où trouve-t-on de bon fer?	En Suède (*Sweden*) et en Angleterre.
Quels pays avez-vous vus?	J'ai vu la Suisse et l'Italie.
Avez-vous lu les poëmes de Béranger?	Non M—, mais j'ai lu les poëmes de Victor Hugo.
Combien de crayons Caroline a-t-elle achetés?	Caroline a acheté quatre crayons et Jeannette a acheté six plumes.
Où sont les enfants de Madame L?	Ils sont au jardin.
Donnez moi (*me*) mes. gants s'il vous plaît (*if you please*).	Les voici, M—, (*Here they are*).
Avez-vous lu cette (*this*) fable?	Oui M—, j'ai lu toutes (*all*) les fables de La Fontaine.

VIII. HUITIÈME LEÇON.

CONJUGATION OF *AVOIR*, TO HAVE, — AFFIRMATIVELY.

INDICATIVE MOOD.

PRESENT.		COMPOUND OF THE PRESENT.	
J'ai,	*I have*	J'ai eu,	*I have had*
Tu as,	*thou hast*	Tu as eu,	*thou hast had*
Il a (elle a, on a),	*he has*	Il a eu,	*he has had*
Nous avons,	*we have*	Nous avons eu,	*we have had*
Vous avez,	*you have*	Vous avez eu,	*you have had*
Ils ont,	*they have*	Ils ont eu,	*they have had*

IMPERFECT.		COMPOUND OF THE IMPERFECT.	
J'avais,	*I had, was having, or used to have*	J'avais eu,	*I had had*
Tu avais,	*thou hadst*	Tu avais eu,	*thou hadst had*
Il avait,	*he had*	Il avait eu,	*he had had*
Nous avions,	*we had*	Nous avions eu,	*we had had*
Vous aviez,	*you had*	Vous aviez eu,	*you had had*
Ils avaient,	*they had*	Ils avaient eu,	*they had had*

PRETERITE.		COMPOUND OF THE PRETERITE.	
J'eus,	*I had*	J'eus eu,	*I had had*
Tu eus,	*thou hadst, etc.*	Tu eus eu,	*thou hadst had*
Il eut,	*he had*	Il eut eu,	*he had had*
Nous eûmes,	*we had*	Nous eûmes eu,	*we had had*
Vous eûtes,	*you had*	Vous eûtes eu,	*you had had*
Ils eurent,	*they had*	Ils eurent eu,	*they had had*

FUTURE.		COMPOUND OF THE FUTURE.	
J'aurai,	*I shall or will have*	J'aurai eu,	*I shall* or *will have had*
Tu auras,	*thou wilt have*	Tu auras eu,	*thou wilt have had*
Il aura,	*he will have*	Il aura eu,	*he will have had*
Nous aurons,	*we shall have*	Nous aurons eu,	*we shall have had*
Vous aurez,	*you will have*	Vous aurez eu,	*you will have had*
Ils auront,	*they will have*	Ils auront eu,	*they will have had*

CONTITIONAL MOOD.

PRESENT.		COMPOUND OF THE PRESENT.	
J'aurais,	*I should have*	J'aurais eu,	*I should have had*
Tu aurais,	*thou wouldst have*	Tu aurais eu,	*thou wouldst have had*
Il aurait,	*he would have*	Il aurait eu,	*he would have had*
Nous aurions,	*we should have*	Nous aurions eu,	*we should have had*
Vous auriez,	*you would have*	Vous auriez eu,	*you would have had*
Ils auraient,	*they would have*	Ils auraient eu,	*they would have had*

IMPERATIVE MOOD.

Aie,	*have (thou).*
Ayons,	*let us have.*
Ayez,	*have (ye or you).*

SUBJUNCTIVE MOOD.

PRESENT.			COMPOUND OF THE PRESENT.		
Que j'aie,	*that I may*	*have*	Que j'aie eu,	*that I may*	*have had*
Que tu aies,	*that thou mayest*		Que tu aies eu,	*that thou mayest*	
Qu'il ait,	*that he may*		Qu'il ait eu,	*that he may*	
Que nous ayons,	*that we may*		Que nous ayons eu,	*that we may*	
Que vous ayez,	*that you may*		Que vous ayez eu,	*that you may*	
Qu'ils aient,	*that they may*		Qu'ils aient eu,	*that they may*	

IMPERFECT.			COMPOUND OF THE IMPERFECT.		
Que j'eusse,	*that I might*	*have*	Que j'eusse eu,	*that I might*	*have had*
Que tu eusses,	*that thou mightest*		Que tu eusses eu,	*that thou mightest*	
Qu'il eût,	*that he might*		Qu'il eût eu,	*that he might*	
Que nous eussions,	*that we might*		Que nous eussions eu,	*that we might*	
Que vous eussiez,	*that you might*		Que vous eussiez eu,	*that you might*	
Qu'ils eussent,	*that they might*		Qu'ils eussent eu,	*that they might*	

INFINITIVE MOOD.

PRESENT.		COMPOUND OF THE PRESENT.	
Avoir,	*to have*	Avoir eu,	*to have had*

PARTICIPLE.

PRESENT.		COMPOUND.	
Ayant,	*having*	Ayant eu,	*having had*

PAST OR PASSIVE.

Eu, *had*

It would be a good plan to conjugate the whole verb *avoir* together with a noun, as; *J'ai une pomme, j'avais une pomme, etc.*—After that, with the pronoun *l'* (*le*), it, and *les*, them, as: *je l'ai*, I have it; *tu l'as, il l'a, etc.; je les aurai, tu les auras, etc.*

VOCABULARY.

Le temps, time.
le courage, the courage.
le plaisir, the pleasure.
la voiture, the carriage.
la bourse, the purse.
hier, yesterday.
demain, to-morrow.
l'encrier, the inkstand.
la règle, the ruler.
perdu, lost.
aujourd'hui, to-day.
et, and. *si*, if.

THEME 8.

Pres. 1. I have a book. 2. He has a hat. 3. We have a house and (a) garden. 4. They (*masc.*) have a horse. 5. They (*fem.*) have flowers and fruit. — Imperf. 6. I had a friend. 7. Thou hadst a friend. 8. Louisa had two cats. 9. You had money enough. 10. The children had bread. — Pret. 11. He had the courage. 12. You had the pleasure. 13. The son of the king had a carriage. — Fut. and Cond. 14. I shall have apples. 15. He would have seen the castle. 16. We shall have some coffee to-day. 17. We would have some sugar. 18. You will have two horses. 19. They would have an inkstand and a ruler. — Compound Tenses. 20. We have had much trouble (*peine*). 21. You have had a great (*grand*) pleasure. 22. She has had a great many nuts. 23. They had had two copy books. 24. I shall have paper and pens. 25. You will have had my horse. 26. Charles's sisters will have many flowers. 27. I should have had a great deal of (*beaucoup de*) trouble. 28. Thou wouldst have had more pleasure. 29. You would have had a good friend. 30. The boy would have had a penknife.

ADDITIONAL THEME UPON AVOIR.

1. My (*ma*) aunt has apples, I have many plums and you have flowers enough (L. VI. 2). 2. The merchant's cousin will have a ball to-morrow. 3. Yesterday I had money, but I have lost my purse to-day. 4. To-morrow I shall have the pleasure of seeing (*de voir*) my cousin, (f) my aunt and my sister; I should have had the pleasure of seeing them (*des les voir*) yesterday if I had been in (*en* without article) town. 5. We shall have time enough to-morrow. 6. We had too much time yesterday. 7. Have the cour-

age to do it (*de le faire*) ; you have time enough. 8. Let us have the carriage and we shall have much pleasure. 9. We should have had the carriage yesterday if we had wished (*voulu*). 10. Though (*quoique*) you may have had time, you have not had the courage. 11. Though we have (pres. Subj.) two horses, we have not (*n'avons pas*) the courage to ride them (*de les monter*). 12. We have money to-day, and to-morrow we shall have bread, meat, and wine. 13. It is you, who (*qui*) will have the most (*le plus de*) pleasure. 14. I do not think (*je ne crois pas*) that he would have had the courage. 15. During the night he had lost his (*sa*) purse. 16. If he had had an inkstand he would have had ink. 17. They will have silver spoons on the table. 18. They would have jewels if (*s'*) they had money.

IX. NEUVIÈME LEÇON.

IDIOMATIC USE OF AVOIR.

1. *Avoir* is used idiomatically with the nouns *chaud*, warmth; *froid*, cold; *faim*, hunger; *soif*, thirst; *raison*, reason; *tort*, wrong; *peur*, fear; *honte*, shame; *envie*, desire; *sommeil*, sleep; *besoin*, need; as:—

J'ai chaud.	I am warm.
J'avais froid.	I was cold.
Il aura faim.	He will be hungry.
Elle aurait soif.	She would be thirsty.
Nous avons raison.	We are right.
Vous avez tort.	You are wrong.
Nous avons eu peur.	We were (have been) afraid.
Ils ont honte.	They are ashamed.
Elles avaient envie.	They were desirous.
Avez-vous sommeil?	Are you sleepy?
Nous avons besoin.	We need. We want.

2. *Avoir quelque chose*, literally, to have something, is also used idiomatically in the sense of *to be the matter with;* thus: —

Qu' avez-vous?	What is the matter with you?
J'ai quelque chose.	Something is the matter with me.
Vous avez quelque chose.	" " " " " you.
Il a " "	" " " " " him.
Elle a " "	" " " " " her.
Nous avions " "	" was the matter with us.
Vous aviez " "	" " " " " you.
Ils auront " "	" will be the matter with them.

REMARK. The opposite of *avoir quelque chose* is *n'avoir rien (ne* before the verb and *rien* after it. See L. XI. 2). As: —

Je n'ai rien.	Nothing is the matter with me.
Vous n'avez rien.	" " " " " you.
Il n'a rien.	" " " " " him.
Elle n'a rien.	" " " " " her.
Nous n'avions rien	" was the " " us.
Vous n'aviez rien.	" " " " " you.
Ils n'auront rien.	" will be the matter with them.

3. *Avoir l'air* means to have the appearance, to look; — *avoir l'intention de*, to have the intention, to intend; — *avoir soin de*, to take care of; — *avoir mal à*, to have a sore, an ache, or a pain in. As: —

Il avait l'air content.	He looked glad.
Vous avez l'air heureux.	You look happy.
Ils ont l'air malheureux.	They look unhappy.
A-t-elle l'intention d'aller en France?	Does she intend to go to France?
Non, Monsieur; elle a l'intention d'aller en Italie.	No, sir; she intends to go to Italy.
Ayez soin de mon chapeau.	Take care of my hat.
J'aurai soin de votre chapeau et de votre canne.	I shall take care of your hat and cane.
J'ai mal à la tête.	I have a headache.
Avez-vous mal aux dents?	Have you the toothache?
J'avais mal au bras.	I had a sore arm.
Il avait mal au genou.	He had a sore knee.

VOCABULARY.

Le chien, the dog.
la tête, the head.
le bras, the arm.
la gorge, the throat.
la dent, the tooth.
le manteau, the cloak.
content, glad, pleased.
malade, sick, ill.
aller, to go.
votre, your.
mon, my.
le parapluie, the umbrella.

READING EXERCISE 9.

A-t-il peur? Oui Madame; il a peur. Avez-vous honte de parler (to speak) français? Non, Mademoiselle; mais j'ai peur de parler français. Aviez-vous froid hier? Oui, Monsieur, j'avais froid hier mais j'ai chaud aujourd 'hui. Avez-vous eu peur du chien? Non, nous avons eu peur du cheval. Votre ami, a-t-il quelque chose? Oui, il a quelque chose. Qu' a-t-il? Il a mal à la tête. Qu' avez-vous? J'ai sommeil. Votre ami a-t-il besoin de moi? Aurez-vous soin de mon cheval? Oui, Monsieur; j'aurai soin de votre cheval. Qui a besoin de l'encrier? Votre cousine a-t-elle mal au bras? Elle a mal au bras. Le negociant a l'air content. Mon frère a l'intention d'aller à Paris et à Londres. Votre frère, qu' a-t-il? Il a honte.

THEME 9.

1. Where do you intend to go to-morrow? 2. I intend to go *and* see (*voir*) the merchant. 3. I was wrong and you were right. 4. Was he sleepy? 5. He was sleepy. 6. Were you glad? 7. I was glad. 8. What is the matter with your father? 9. Nothing is the matter with him. 10. What was the matter with that (*ce*) boy? 11. He was ashamed. 12. Was he afraid of the horse? 13. No, sir; he was afraid of the dog. 14. Do I look sick? 15. Yes, sir; you look sick. 16. Have you a headache? 17. No, sir; I have a sore throat. 18. Has that young lady the toothache? 19. She has the toothache. 20. Take care of my watch. 21. We shall take care of your watch, your cloak, and your umbrella.

X. DIXIÈME LEÇON.

CONJUGATION OF ÊTRE, *TO BE*—AFFIRMATIVELY.

INDICATIVE MOOD.

PRESENT.		COMPOUND OF THE PRESENT.	
Je suis,	*I am*	J'ai été,	*I have been*
Tu es,	*thou art*	Tu as été,	*thou hast been*
Il est (elle est, on est),	*he is*	Il a été,	*he has been*
Nous sommes,	*we are*	Nous avons été,	*we have been*
Vous êtes,	*ye* or *you are*	Vous avez été,	*you have been*
Ils sont,	*they are*	Ils ont été,	*they have been*

IMPERFECT.		COMPOUND OF THE IMPERFECT.	
J'étais,	*I was* or *used to be*	J'avais été,	*I had been*
Tu étais,	*thou wast*	Tu avais été,	*thou hadst been*
Il était,	*he was*	Il avait été,	*he had been*
Nous étions,	*we were*	Nous avions été,	*we had been*
Vous étiez,	*you were*	Vous aviez été,	*you had been*
Ils étaient,	*they were*	Ils avaient été,	*they had been*

PRETERITE.		COMPOUND OF THE PRETERITE.	
Je fus,	*I was*	J'eus été,	*I had been*
Tu fus,	*thou wast*	Tu eus été,	*thou hadst been*
Il fut,	*he was*	Il eut été,	*he had been*
Nous fûmes,	*we were*	Nous eûmes été,	*we had been*
Vous fûtes,	*you were*	Vous eûtes été,	*you had been*
Ils furent,	*they were*	Ils eurent été,	*they had been*

FUTURE.		COMPOUND OF THE FUTURE.		
Je serai,	*I shall be, will be*	J'aurai été,	*I shall*	*have been*
Tu seras,	*thou wilt be*	Tu auras été,	*thou wilt*	
Il sera,	*he will be*	Il aura été,	*he will*	
Nous serons,	*we shall be*	Nous aurons été,	*we shall*	
Vous serez,	*you will be*	Vous aurez été,	*you will*	
Ils seront,	*they will be*	Ils auront été,	*they will*	

CONDITIONAL MOOD.

PRESENT.		COMPOUND OF THE PRESENT.		
Je serais,	*I should be*	J'aurais été,	*I should*	*have been*
Tu serais,	*thou wouldst be*	Tu aurais été,	*thou wouldst*	
Ill serait,	*he would be*	Il aurait été,	*he would*	
Nous serions,	*we should be*	Nous aurions été,	*we should*	
Vous seriez,	*you would be*	Vous auriez été,	*you would*	
Ils seraient,	*they would be*	Ils auraient été,	*they would*	

IMPERATIVE MOOD.

Sois,	*be (thou).*
Soyons,	*let us be.*
Soyez,	*be (ye or you).*

SUBJUNCTIVE MOOD.

PRESENT.		COMPOUND OF THE PRESENT.		
Que je sois,	*that I may be*	**Que j'aie été,**	*that I may*	*have been*
Que tu sois,	*that thou mayest be*	**Que tu aies été,**	*that thou mayest*	*have been*
Qu'il soit,	*that he may be*	**Qu'il ait été,**	*that he may*	*have been*
Que nous soyons,	*that we may be*	**Que nous ayons été,**	*that we may*	*have been*
Que vous soyez,	*that you may be*	**Que vous ayez été,**	*that you may*	*have been*
Qu'ils soient,	*that they may be*	**Qu'ils aient été,**	*that they may*	*have been*

IMPERFECT.		COMPOUND OF THE IMPERFECT.		
Que je fusse,	*that I might be*	**Que j'eusse été,**	*that I might*	*have been*
Que tu fusses,	*that thou mightest be*	**Que tu eusses été,**	*that thou mightest*	*have been*
Qu'il fût	*that he might be*	**Qu'il eût été,**	*that he might*	*have been*
Que nous fussions,	*that we might be*	**Que nous eussions été,**	*that we might*	*have been*
Que vous fussiez,	*that you might be*	**Que vous eussiez été,**	*that you might*	*have been*
Qu'ils fussent,	*that they might be*	**Qu'ils eussent éte,**	*that they might*	*have been*

INFINITIVE MOOD.

PRESENT.		COMPOUND OF THE PRESENT.	
Être,	*to be*	**Avoir été,**	*to have been*

PARTICIPLE.

PRESENT.		COMPOUND.	
Étant,	*being*	**Ayant été,**	*having been*

PAST OR PASSIVE.

Été, (invariable) *been*

VOCABULARY.

Riche, rich.
appliqué, diligent.
malheureux, unhappy.
content, pleased, contented.
faible, weak.
paresseux, lazy, idle.
heureux, happy.
jeune, young.
sage, good.
encore, still, again.

THEME 10.

I am ill. Thou art young. Charles is my friend. We are happy. You are also happy. The child will be good. Louisa was ill. William and Julius have also been ill. This boy has been idle. This girl was very good. He will be contented. You would also be contented. She has been at Paris. Her (*son*) brother has been in London. We have been in France. Your mother may (*peut*) have been (Comp. Inf.) ill. Yes, indeed (*en effet*) she has been ill long. Who was (has been) with (*chez*) your father? A merchant has been with my father. He had been before (*auparavant*) with my uncle.

ADDITIONAL THEME ON ÊTRE CONJUGATED AFFIRMATIVELY.

1. Having been sick, he is still weak. 2. The spoons were on the table. 3. We were still sick. 4. The young boy was at the helm. 5. I am among my (*mes*) friends. 6. I shall be with my friends to-morrow. 7. I was at your (*votre*) father's *house* yesterday (L. IV. 3). 8. She is in the room. 9. My neighbor's name is William. 10. I should be happy if you were pleased. 11. If you are unhappy, how can you (*pourrez-vous*) be (inf.) contented? 12. I shall be pleased to see you (*de vous voir*) to-morrow. 13. The merchant has been here (*ici*) to-day. 14. He had been at his friend's yesterday. 15. Be at my house (*chez-moi*) to-morrow. 16. Let us be happy. 17. Though he is (Pres. Subj.) rich, he is more (*plus*) unhappy than you.

XI. ONZIÈME LEÇON.

NEGATIONS.—THE NEGATIVE AND INTERROGATIVE FORMS OF THE AUXILIARIES.

1. The negation *not* is rendered by the two words *ne . . . pas*. *Ne* is placed before the verb and becomes *n'* before a vowel or silent *h*; *pas* is placed immediately after the verb. In compound tenses *pas* is placed between the auxiliary and the participle. In the infinitive *ne* and *pas* generally both precede the verb. Ex.

Je *ne* suis *pas*.	I am not.
Je *n'*ai *pas* eu.	I have not had.
Ne pas être, *less frequently*, n'être pas.	Not to be.

2. The words *jamais*, ever, *personne*, person, and *rien*, anything, used with a verb preceded by *ne* mean respectively *never*, *nobody*, *nothing*. When the verb is understood, as in answers, the *ne* is omitted, and they have none the less a negative meaning. When used with a verb not preceded by *ne* they are always affirmative. Ex.

Avez-vous jamais rien vu de pareil?	Have you ever seen anything similar?
Je n'ai rien.	I have nothing.
Il n'a jamais tort.	He is never wrong.
Personne n'a sommeil.	Nobody is sleepy.
C'est une personne qui a sommeil.	It is a person that is sleepy.
Qui a sommeil? Personne.	Who is sleepy? Nobody.
Qu' avez-vous? Rien.	What is the matter with you? Nothing.

3. The words *aucun*, *nul*, no; *nullement*, nowise, not at all; *ni . . . ni*, neither . . . nor; *guère*, but little, but few; and *que* in the sense of but or only; also require the verb to be preceded by *ne*. *Ne* (the verb) *plus* means, no more, not any more left. Ex.

Je n'ai plus de pain.	I have no more bread.
Il n'a ni pain ni vin.	He has neither bread nor wine.
Elle n'a guère de patience.	She has but little patience.
Nul n'est parfait.	No one is perfect.

REMARK. After *ni . . . ni* nouns used in a partitive sense take neither preposition nor article; as, *ni pain ni vin.*

For further rules on the negative see P. I. L. 33, and P. II. L. 15.

4. In interrogations the pronoun which is the subject of the verb is placed after it, and both are joined by a hyphen, as: *aurez-vous? avez-vous eu?* When the verb ends with a vowel, *-t-* is placed between the verb and *il, elle,* or *on,* as: *aura-t-il? a-t-on?* See also L. I. Rem. 5.

5. AVOIR AND ÊTRE CONJUGATED NEGATIVELY.

INDICATIVE MOOD.

PRESENT TENSE.

Je n'ai pas,	*I have not*	Je ne suis pas,	*I am not*
Tu n'as pas,	*thou hast not*	Tu n'es pas,	*thou art not*
Il n'a pas,	*he has not*	Il n'est pas,	*he is not*
Nous n'avons pas,	*we have not*	Nous ne sommes pas,	*we are not*
Vous n'avez pas,	*you have not*	Vous n'êtes pas,	*you are not*
Ils n'ont pas,	*they have not*	Ils ne sont pas,	*they are not*

COMPOUND OF THE PRESENT.

Je n'ai pas eu,	*I have not had,* etc.	Je n'ai pas été,	*I have not been,* etc.

IMPERFECT.

Je n'avais pas,	*I had not* or *did not have,* etc.	Je n'étais pas,	*I was not,* etc.

COMPOUND OF THE IMPERFECT.

Je n'avais pas eu,	*I had not had,* etc.	Je n'avais pas été,	*I had not been,* etc.

And thus with all compound tenses.

PRETERITE.

Je n'eus pas,	*I had not,* etc.	Je ne fus pas,	*I was not,* etc.

FUTURE.

Je n'aurai pas, etc.	Je ne serai pas, etc.

CONDITIONAL MOOD.

Je n'aurais pas, etc.	Je ne serais pas, etc.

SUBJUNCTIVE MOOD.

PRESENT.

Que je n'aie pas, etc.	Que je ne sois pas, etc.

IMPERFECT.

Que je n'eusse pas, etc.	Que je ne fusse pas, etc.

IMPERATIVE MOOD.

N'aie pas, etc.	Ne sois pas, etc.

INFINITIVE MOOD.

Ne pas avoir. (N'avoir pas.)	Ne pas être. (N'être pas.)

PARTICIPLES.

N'ayant pas. N'ayant pas eu.	N'étant pas. N'ayant pas été.

INTERROGATIVE CONJUGATION.

INDICATIVE MOOD.

PRESENT TENSE.

Ai-je,	*have I?*	Suis-je,	*am I?*
As-tu,	*hast thou?*	Es-tu,	*art thou?*
A-t-il,	*has he?* etc.	Est-il,	*is he?* etc.

COMPOUND OF THE PRESENT.

Ai-je eu,	*have I had?* etc.	Ai-je été,	*have I been?* etc.

IMPERFECT.

Avais-je, etc.	Etais-je, etc.

PRETERITE.

Eus-je, etc.	Fus-je, etc.

FUTURE.

Aurai-je, etc.	Serai-je, etc.

CONDITIONAL MOOD.

Aurais-je, etc.	Serais-je, etc.

NEGATIVE AND INTERROGATIVE CONJUGATION.

PRESENT.

N'ai-je pas,	*have I not?*	Ne suis-je pas,	*am I not?*
N'as-tu pas,	*hast thou not?*	N'es-tu pas,	*art thou not?*
N'a-t-il pas,	*has he not?* etc.	N'est-il pas,	*is he not?* etc.

IMPERFECT.

N'avais-je pas, etc. | N'étais-je pas, etc.

PRETERITE.

N'eus-je pas, etc. | Ne fus-je pas, etc.

FUTURE.

N'aurai-je pas, etc. | Ne serai-je pas, etc.

CONDITIONAL.

N'aurais-je pas, etc. | Ne serais-je pas, etc.

VOCABULARY.

La nouvelle, the news.
la lettre, the letter.
le chagrin, the grief.
les parents, the parents.
le tailleur, the tailor.
le bottier, the boot-maker.
la cerise, the cherry.
très, very.
pauvre, poor.
mécontent, discontented.
mangé, eaten.
autrefois, formerly.
longtemps, long, a long time.
vos, plural of *votre*, your.

THEME 11.

1. I have a friend. 2. Hast thou also a friend? 3. We have friends. 4. Have you also friends? 5. I am happy. 6. I am not happy. 7. Are you happy? 8. Are you not happy? 9. No, we are not happy; we are poor.[1] 10. Formerly we were very happy. 11. You are not rich.[1] 12. Thou hast been poor. 13. She has been rich. 14. Have you had any cherries? 15. You have been idle. 16. Hast thou been ill? No, I have not been ill long. 17. They have not received the letter. 18. Were you (have you been) at (*chez*) the tailor's? 19. I have not been at the tailor's. 20. I have been at the boot-maker's; but (*mais*)

[1] These adjectives take *s* in the plural (*pauvres — riches*).

he was not at home (*à la maison*). 21. How many horses had you? 22. I had two horses. 23. Charles would not have been ill, if he had not eaten too much (*trop*). 24. Be contented. 25. Take care of your books.

CONVERSATION.

Quand (*when*) avez-vous été au spectacle (*théâtre*)?	Nous avons été hier au spectacle.
Charles, seras-tu content?	Oui, M—, je serai content.
Avez-vous un ami?	Nous avons beaucoup d'amis.
Avez-vous reçu une lettre?	J'ai reçu une lettre de Paris.
Où était ton ami Louis?	Il était à Berlin.
Vos parents sont-ils riches?	Non, M—, ils sont pauvres.
Où avez-vous été hier?	Nous avons été à l'église.
Où serez-vous demain?	Nous serons à l'école.
Ta sœur a-t-elle été malade?	Oui, elle a été longtemps malade.
Avez-vous des affaires (*business*)?	Oui, M—, nous avons beaucoup d'affaires.
N'êtes-vous pas contents?	Non, M—, nous sommes mécontents.
Pourquoi (*why*) êtes-vous mécontents?	Nous avons eu une triste (*sad*) nouvelle.
Pourquoi avez-vous du chagrin?	Notre mère est trés-malade.
Serais-tu content, si tu avais beaucoup de livres?	Oui, M—, je serais bien content.

XII. DOUZIÈME LEÇON.

DEMONSTRATIVE AND INTERROGATIVE ADJECTIVES.

Adjectives in French agree in gender and number with the nouns they limit; — form the plural according to the rules given for nouns (L. II.); — form the feminine by adding *e* mute to the masculine. If the masculine ends in *e*, the feminine is the same. Irregular formations will be given in the vocabularies until the full rules are given, L. XVII.

1. The Demonstrative Adjectives are: —

Ce, fem. *cette*, this, that; plur. *ces*, these, those.
Ce—ci, fem. *cette—ci*, this (here); plur. *ces—ci*.
Ce—là, fem. *cette—là*, that; plur. *ces—là*, those.

2. As *ce* means either *this* or *that*, whenever in English the words *this*, *that*, *these*, *those* are emphatic, either *ci* (abbreviated form of *ici*, here) or *là* (there) are appended to the noun. Ex.: —

Ce chapeau, this hat.
cette ville, this town.
Ce garçon-ci, this boy (here).
cette femme-ci, this woman (here).
ces arbres-ci, these trees.
ces hommes, these men.
ce même livre, this same book.
ce garçon-là, that boy.
cette femme-là, that woman.
ces arbres-là, those trees.

3. Before a masculine noun which begins with a vowel or *h* mute, *cet* is used instead *ce*. Ex.: —

Cet arbre, this tree (instead of *ce arbre*.)
Cet habit, this *or* that coat (instead of *ce habit*).

4. The Interrogative Adjective is, in the singular, *quel*, fem. *quelle*; plur. *quels*, *quelles*, which *or* what? Ex.: —

Quel livre, which book? plur. *quels livres*, which *or* what books?
Quelle fleur, which *or* what flower?

It answers also to the exclamative *what a —!* Ex.: —

Quel beau tableau! what a beautiful picture!

VOCABULARY.

La plante, the plant.
le champ, the field.
la couleur, the color.
la fille, the girl.
le bœuf, the ox.
la vache, the cow.
l'heure, f. the hour.
la robe, the dress.
l'œuf, m. the egg.
haut, f. *haute*, high.
beau, f. *belle*, beautiful.
grand, f. *grande*, large, great.
bon, f. *bonne*, good.
trop, too. *mais*, but.
connaissez-vous, do you know?

READING EXERCISE 12.

Ce verre. Cette pomme-ci. Cet homme. Ces bas. Ces bottes-là. Cette boîte est haute. Ces enfants sont pauvres. Le frère de ce garçon. Deux livres de ce café. Je donne ces poires à cette fille-ci. La même couleur. Nous avons acheté les mêmes plumes. J'ai vu ces chiens-là. Quels chiens avez-vous vus? Quel beau cheval! Quelle belle maison! Le fils de cet homme-là est très grand. Quelle heure est-il? Il est trois heures (*o'clock*). Il est une heure.

THEME 12.

1. This king is rich. 2. This queen is also rich. 3. This man is poor. 4. These men are poor. 5. That child is not good (*sage*). 6. That woman is not contented. 7. This tree is very high. 8. Those trees are not very high. 9. Whose (*à qui*) is this pencil? 10. Whose are these pens? 11. The color of that dress is beautiful (*belle*). 12. The field of that man is large. 13. These oxen are larger (*plus grands*) than those cows. 14. I give the bread to this boy. 15. I give these flowers to those girls. 16. The parents of those children are very good. 17. Which boy? 18. Which apples? 19. What a beautiful picture! 20. The pleasure of those girls was not very great. 21. What o'clock is it (*transl.* which hour is it?) 22. It is four o'clock (*transl.* four hours). 23. We have read (*lu*) the same books.

CONVERSATION.

A qui (*whose*) est ce canif?	Il est à ma sœur.
A qui sont ces gants?	Ils sont à Mademoiselle Julie.
Où est la fille de cette femme?	Elle est au jardin.
Connaissez-vous cette fleur?	C'est une rose.
Connaissez-vous le père de ce garçon-lá?	Non M—, mais je connais (*I know*) sa mère.
Quel papier voulez-vous?	Donnez-moi ce papier-là.
Ces plumes-ci sont-elles bonnes?	Oui, M—, elles sont très-bonnes
Cette église est-elle haute?	Oui, elle est très-haute.
A qui donnez-vous ces fleurs?	Je les donne à cette fille-ci.
A qui donnez-vous ces crayons?	Je les donne à ce garçon-là.
Trouve-t-on de l'or dans ce pays?	Oui, M—, ce pays-ci est riche en or.
Voulez-vous (*do you wish*, literally, *wish you*) ces bas-ci ou ces gants-là?	Donnez-moi ces gants-là.
Trouvez-vous ces couleurs belles?	Oui, ces couleurs sont très-belles.
Quelle heure est-il?	Il est quatre heures.

XIII. TREIZIÈME LEÇON.

POSSESSIVE ADJECTIVES.

I. The Possessive Adjectives are: —

mon,	fem.	*ma*,	plur.	*mes*,	my.
ton,	"	*ta*,	"	*tes*,	thy.
son,	"	*sa*,	"	*ses*,	his, her, its.
notre	"	*notre*,	"	*nos*,	our.
votre,	"	*votre*,	"	*vos*,	your.
leur,	"	*leur*,	"	*leurs*,	their.

Ex.: — Mon père, ta mère, ses frères, notre ami, vos livres, leurs parents.

2. The possessive adjectives are repeated in French before each substantive, and agree with it in gender and number: —

Mon frère et ma sœur, my brother and sister.

3. *Mon, ton, son,* are used instead of *ma, ta, sa,* before feminine words beginning with a vowel or *h* mute, in order to avoid the hiatus which would result from the meeting of the two vowels. Ex.: —

Mon amie, my (female) friend; *son âme,* his soul.

4. *Son, sa, ses,* each mean his, her, and its; they agree in gender with the following noun, as: —

Le père aime son fils, the father loves his son.
La mère aime son fils et sa fille, the mother loves her son and her daughter.

5. In French, *votre* is, from politeness, often preceded by the words: *Monsieur, Madame, Mademoiselle;* plur. *Messieurs, Mesdames, Mesdemoiselles,* which are not expressed in English, as, —

Monsieur votre père, your father.
Mademoiselle votre sœur, your sister.
Messieurs vos frères, your brothers.

6. In expressions such as "a friend of yours," the possessive adjective must be used in French, preceded by *de,* as, *un de vos amis, une de mes tantes,* an aunt of mine.

7. A possessive adjective must always precede a noun denoting a degree of relationship when a relative or friend is addressed, though none is used in English. Ex. *Bonjour ma sœur,* good morning, sister; *adieu, mon cousin,* good-by, cousin. The words *papa, maman,* and a few terms of endearment are excepted, as, *bonjour papa, bonsoir maman.*

VOCABULARY.

La demoiselle, the young lady.
la tante, the aunt.
la canne, the cane.
la casquette, the cap.
le grand-père, the grandfather.
vieux, old.
la grand'mère, the grandmother.
la poche, the pocket.
arrivé, e, arrived.
parti, e, departed, gone.
perdu, lost.
trouvé, found.

READING EXERCISE 13.

Mon père est bon. Ma mère est bonne. Ton frère est grand. Ta sœur n'est pas grande. Notre oncle a été riche. Votre tante est pauvre. Leurs parents seront contents. Mes cousins et mes cousines sont arrivés. Les pères aiment (love) leurs enfants. Notre grand'mère a perdu sa bourse. J'ai trouvé la bourse de votre grand'mère. Mon amie est arrivée. Madame votre mère est-elle ici (*here*)? Non, elle n'est pas ici; elle est à Londres. Mesdemoiselles vos sœurs sont parties.

THEME 13.

1. My dog is old. 2. Thy book is good. 3. My book and (my) pen. 4. My books and pens. 5. Your garden is beautiful. 6. Your flowers are beautiful (*belles*). 7. My sister has lost her watch. 8. Our sisters have found their letters. 9. These children have lost their father. 10. These parents have lost their children. 11. Here is (*voici*) thy stick. 12. Your cousins (*f.*) have been in our garden. 13. My soul is immortal (*immortelle*). 14. We have received this letter from our aunt. 15. Our uncle's horse (the horse of our uncle) is old. 16. Where is your father? 17. Where is your sister? 18. I have found the purse of your mother.

CONVERSATION.

Où est mon frère?	Il est allé (*gone*) au jardin.
Où est ton livre?	Le voilà sur la table.
Qui a perdu sa casquette?	Charles a perdu sa casquette.
Qui a trouvé nos crayons?	Henri les (*them*) a trouvés.
Que cherchez-vous (*are you looking for*)?	Je cherche mes plumes.
A qui est cette canne?	Elle est à Monsieur votre oncle.
A qui sont ces gants?	Ils sont à Mademoiselle votre sœur.
Voulez-vous mes crayons?	Non, merci (*thank you*).
Connaissez-vous mon amie?	Oui, je la connais (*know her*).

Où était Monsieur votre père?	Il était à Berlin.
Où as-tu trouvé ta bourse?	Elle était dans ma poche.
Qui est arrivé aujourd'hui?	La fille de mon oncle.
Avez-vous été dans votre champ?	Non, Monsieur, nous avons été dans notre jardin.
De qui avez-vous reçu cette belle canne?	C'est un cadeau (*present*) de ma grand'mère.

XIV. QUATORZIÈME LEÇON.

CARDINAL NUMBERS.

1. The Cardinal Numbers are: —

Un, une, one.
deux, two.
trois, three.
quatre, four.
cinq, five.
six, six.
sept, seven.
huit, eight.
neuf, nine.
dix, ten.
onze, eleven.
douze, twelve.
treize, thirteen.
quatorze, fourteen.
quinze, fifteen.
seize, sixteen.
dix-sept, seventeen.
dix-huit, eighteen.
dix-neuf, nineteen.
vingt, twenty.
vingt et un, twenty-one.
vingt-deux, twenty-two.
vingt-trois, twenty-three.
vingt-quatre, twenty-four.
vingt-cinq, twenty-five, etc.
trente, thirty.
quarante, forty.
cinquante, fifty.
soixante, sixty.
soixante-dix, seventy.
soixante-onze, seventy-one.
soixante-douze, seventy-two.
soixante-treize, seventy-three.
soixante-quatorze, seventy-four.
soixante-quinze, seventy-five.
soixante-seize, seventy-six.
soixante-dix-sept, seventy-seven.
soixante-dix-huit, seventy-eight.
soixante-dix-neuf, seventy-nine.
quatre-vingt, eighty.
quatre-vingt-un, eighty-one.
quatre-vingt-deux, eighty-two.

quatre-vingt-dix, ninety.
quatre-vingt-onze, ninety-one.
qnatre-vingt-douze, ninety-two.
quatre-vingt-treize, ninety-three, etc.
cent, a hundred.
cent un, a hundred and one.
cent deux, a hundred and two, etc.
deux cents, two hundred.
trois cents, three hundred, etc.
quinze cents, fifteen hundred.
mille, mil, a thousand.
un million, a million.

Ex.: *Cinq enfants*, five children.
Trente-six chevaux, thirty-six horses.
Trois cent quatre-vingt-quinze aunes, 395 yards.
L'an mil huit cent soixante-cinq, the year 1865.

Et, and, must be expressed before *un* after *vingt*, *trente*, *quarante*, *cinquante*, *soixante*, as : *vingt et un*, etc. *Et* is also often used in *soixante et onze*.

2. The cardinal numerals do not admit of change in their terminations except *un*, which takes an *e* in the feminine, and *cent* and *quatre-vingt*. *Cent* takes an *s* when several hundreds, not followed by another number, are mentioned, as : —

Trois cents francs, 300 francs.
Sept cents personnes, 700 persons. — But:
Sept cent vingt personnes, 720 persons.

3. *Quatre-vingts* loses its *s* when followed by another numeral. Ex.: —

Quatre-vingts écoliers, 80 pupils. — But:
Quatre-vingt-deux aunes, 82 yards.

4. *Cent* and *mille* are not accompanied by the indefinite article as in English. Ex.: —

A hundred or a thousand pounds, *cent ou mille livres*.

5. When one thousand is used for dates it is rendered in French by *mil*, with one *l* only, thus : —

L'an or *en mil huit cent cinquante-huit*, in the year 1858.

6. The expression, "I am 20, 30, 40, etc., years old," cannot be rendered literally, but must be expressed thus : *J'ai vingt ans*, — *trente ans*, etc. How old are you? is translated thus: *Quel âge avez-vous?* Ex.: —

Quel âge a votre frère, how old is your brother?
Il a dix-huit ans, he is eighteen years old.

7. Collective numbers are:

Une huitaine, a series of eight.
Une dizaine, a series of ten, half a score.
Une douzaine, a dozen.
Une vingtaine, a score.
Une centaine, a hundred.
Un millier, a thousand.
Un million, a million.

VOCABULARY.

La fille, the daughter.
le veau, the calf.
le cochon, the pig, swine.
la brebis, the sheep.
le lièvre, the hare.
le chevreuil, the deer, the roe.
né, f. *née*, born.
la rue, the street.
l'habitant, m. the inhabitant.
l'âge, m. the age.
la semaine, the week.
encore, still. *fois*, times.
compte, contains.
environ, about.
chasse, hunting.
le jour, the day.
la nuit, the night.
le mois, the month.
le fièvre, the fever.
l'an, m. and *l'année*, f. the year.
l'heure, the hour.
la minute, the minute.
le pied, the foot.
vivait, lived. *mourut*, died.
combien, how much, how many.
font, make. *ou*, or.
vendue, sold.
en, in. *en*, of them.

READING EXERCISE 14.

J'ai trois fils. Vous avez quatre filles. Mon oncle a eu dix enfants. Il a perdu cinq fils et deux filles. Nous avons vu 35 bœufs, 42 vaches, 88 veaux, et 76 cochons. Notre voisin a eu 495 brebis. Combien de lièvres avez-vous tués (killed)? Nous avons tué 23 lièvres et 14 chevreuils. Sept et huit font quinze. 24 et 36 font 60. — 4 fois 8 font 32. — 7 fois 9 font 63. — 21 fois 32 font 672. Je suis né en 1814, et mon frère en 1818. Ma mère est née en 1829. La ville de Londres compte 10,000 rues, 600 églises, 249,500 maisons et plus de (*more than*) deux millions d'habitants. Lycurgue vivait en 880 avant Jésus-Christ. Quel âge avez-vous? J'ai quinze ans.

THEME 6.

1. I have had three horses and five dogs. 2. My cousin has 34 sheep. 3. My neighbor (*m.*) had 36 oxen. 4. A week has 7

days. 5. 30 days make a month. 6. 12 months or 52 weeks make a year. 7. A year has 365 days. 8. I was (*je suis*) born in the year (*en*) 1828. 9. I am 35 years old. 10. My sister was born (f.) in the year 1841; she is 17 years old. 11. How much is (*font*) three times nine? 12. 3 times 9 make 27. 13. 6 times 8 are 48. 14. 35 and 42 are 77. 15. How much is 125 and 264? 16. My mother has had the fever during 6 weeks. 17. A (the) day has 24 hours, an (the) hour 60 minutes. 18. Give (to) Charles 32 florins and (to) Louis 33 florins. 19. Here are 200 pounds of sugar.

CONVERSATION.

Combien de fils votre oncle a-t-il?	Il a encore trois fils.
Combien d'enfants a-t-il eus?	Il a eu sept enfants.
Où sont vos deux cousines?	Elles sont à l'église.
Quelle est la hauteur (*the height*) de cette église?	Elle a 327 pieds de hauteur.
Combien font 5 et 7?	5 et 7 font 12.
Combien font 15 et 25?	15 et 25 font 40.
Combien font 20, 35 et 45?	20 et 35 et 45 font cent.
Combien font 6 fois 8?	6 fois 8 font 48.
Combien font 12 fois 24?	12 fois 24 font 288.
Quel âge avez-vous?	J'ai quatorze ans.
Quel âge a votre sœur?	Elle a 18 ans.
Combien de florins avez-vous reçus de votre père?	J'ai reçu 50 florins.
Combien de jours a une année?	Une année a 365 jours et six heures.
Combien de semaines font un mois?	Quatre semaines et deux ou trois jours font un mois.
Combien de mois font une année?	Douze mois font une année.
Avez-vous été à la chasse hier?	Oui, Monsieur, toute la journée (*all day*).

Avez-vous tué beaucoup de lièvres?	**Nous avons tué 35 lièvres.**
Charles a-t-il assez d'argent?	**Oh, oui, il a 22 francs.**

XV. QUINZIÈME LEÇON.

ORDINAL NUMBERS.

1. Except *le premier* and *le second*, the ordinal numbers are formed from the cardinal by changing *e* mute into *ième;* and by adding this syllable to those which end in another letter. But *cinq* takes *u* before *ième* (*cinquième*), and *neuf* changes the *f* into *v* (*neuvième*). They are as follows:—

Le premier, *la première*, } the first.
le second, *la seconde*, *le, la deuxième*, } the second.
le troisième, the third.
le quatrième, the fourth.
le cinquième, the fifth.
le sixième, the sixth.
le septième, the seventh.
le huitième, the eighth.
le neuvième, the ninth.
le dixième, the tenth.
le onzième, the eleventh.
le douzième, the twelfth.
le treizième, the thirteenth.
le quatorzième, the fourteenth.
le quinzième, the fifteenth.
le seizième, the 16th.
le dix-septième, the 17th.
le dix-huitième, the 18th.
le dix-neuvième, the 19th.
le vingtième, the 20th.
le vingt et unième, the 21st.
le vingt-deuxième, the 22d, etc.
le trentième, the 30th.
le quarantième, the 40th.
le cinquantième, the 50th.
le soixantième, the 60th.
le soixante-dixième, the 70th.
le soixante-onzième, the 71st.
le soixante-douzième, the 72d, etc.
le quatre-vingtième, the 80th.
le quatre-vingt-unième, the 81st.
le quatre-vingt-dixième, the 90th.
le centième, the 100th.
le cent et unième, the 101st.
le cent deuxième, the 102d, etc.
le cent vingtième, the 120th.
le deux centième, the 200th.
le six cent soixante-quinzième, the 675th.
le millième, the 1000th.
le dernier, the last.

2. *Unième* is used only after *vingt*, *trente*, *quarante*, *etc.*, as: *Charles est le vingt et unième de sa classe.*

3. Days of the month (except *le premier* and *le dernier*) are expressed by cardinal numbers, as:—

The first of April, *le premier Avril.*—But:
The 2d, 3d, 4th, etc., of May, *le deux, trois, quatre, etc., mai* (or *de mai*).
The eleventh of March, *le onze* (without apostrophe) *mars.*
The twentieth of June, *le vingt juin.*

The question, "What day of the month is it to-day?" is translated: *Quel quantième avons-nous aujourd'hui?* or, *Quel jour du mois avons-nous?*

The English "on the sixth," etc., is rendered in French, without preposition, *le six* —— Ex.: On the sixth of May, *le six mai.*

4. Proper names of princes, etc., take in French the cardinal numbers without the article, except the first and sometimes the second, as:—

Henri premier, Henry the first.
Henri second or *deux*, Henry the second.
Henri quatre, Henri the fourth.
Louis quatorze, Louis the fourteenth.

Note. The German Emperor, *Charles V.*, bears in French the name of *Charles-Quint*, and the Pope *Sixtus V.* that of *Sixte-Quint.*

5. Numeral adverbs are formed from ordinal numbers by adding *-ment* or *-ement* to the final:—

Premièrement, firstly. *Deuxièmement*, secondly. *Troisièmement*, thirdly, etc.

6. Fractional numbers are expressed by ordinal numbers, as in English, but only from five upwards, as:—

Un cinquième, a fifth. *Un sixième*, a sixth.
Un huitième, an eighth. *Un dixième*, a tenth.

The others are as follows:—

Half (adj.), *demi.* f. *demie.* The half, *la moitié* (noun).
A third, *un tiers.* A quarter *or* fourth, *un quart.*
One pound and a half, *une livre et demie.*

7. The hours of the day or night are expressed thus: —

Two o'clock, *deux heures.*
A quarter past two, *deux heures et (un) quart.*
Half past two, *deux heures et demie.*
A quarter to three, *trois heures moins un quart.*
At twelve o'clock (at noon), *à midi.*
At twelve o'clock (midnight), *à minuit.*

8. Proportional numbers which express a quantity multiplied, are: —

Simple, simple.
double, double, twofold.
triple, triple, threefold.
quadruple, fourfold.
centuple, centuple, a hundred-fold.

VOCABULARY.

Janvier, January.
Fevrier, February.
Mars, March.
Avril, April.
Mai, May.
Juin, June.
Juillet, July.
Août, August.
Septembre, September.
Octobre, October.
Novembre, November.
Décembre, December.
en janvier, in January.
nous vivons, we live.
nombre, number.
Dimanche, Sunday.
Lundi, Monday.
Mardi, Tuesday (and on Tuesday).
Mercredi, Wednesday.
Jeudi, Thursday.
Vendredi, Friday.
Samedi, Saturday.
le siècle, the century.
l'incendie, m. a fire, conflagration.
la partie, the part, portion.
la place, the place.
la classe, the class.
à présent, at present.
numero, number (denoting order, as number of a house, of a rule, of a page).

9. RULE FOR *il* AND *ce* AS EXPLETIVE SUBJECTS OF *être*. Use *il* if the verb is followed: 1. by an *adjective* limiting something which comes after it in the sentence; 2. by *temps* or by the hour of the day. In all other cases use *ce*. Ex. *Faites cela, c'est facile*, do that, it is easy. But, *Il est facile de faire cela*, it is easy to do that. *Il est temps de le faire*, it is time to do it. *Il est six heures*, it is six o'clock. *C'est vous, ce n'est pas moi*, it is you, it is not I.

READING EXERCISE 15.

Je suis dans ma soixante-douzième année. Charles est le premier de sa classe. Louis est le neuvième, Henri le dix-huitième et Jules le dernier. Le pape (*pope*) Grégoire VII était l'ennemi de Henri IV. Nous vivons dans le dix-neuvième siècle. Romulus fut le premier, Numa Pompilius le second roi de Rome. Pierre premier fut surnommé (*was surnamed*) le grand. Avril est le quatrième, Juin le sixième et Décembre le dernier mois de l'année. La semaine est la cinquante-deuxième partie de l'année. Ma sœur Élisabeth est née le vingt-huit juillet, mil huit cent trente-cinq. J'ai reçu trois livres et demie de café et cinq livres et un quart de sucre. Charles XII était roi de Suède. Le 27 (de) septembre 1829, un incendie détruisit (*destroyed*) à Constantinople 11,000 maisons; 700 personnes périrent (*perished*) dans les flammes.

THEME 15.

1. A month is the twelfth part of a year. 2. What day of the month is it to-day? 3. It is the 24th [of] June. 4. I am the third, my cousin John the seventh. 5. January is the first, February the second, March the third month of the year. 6. Napoleon died at St. Helena (*Sainte-Hélène*) the 5th of May, 1821. 7. My grandmother is at present in her 78th year. 8. What o'clock (*quelle heure*) is it now? It is four o'clock, or half past four. 9. Louis the Sixteenth, king of (*de*) France, was beheaded (*fut décapité*) at Paris the 21st of January, 1793. 10. Frederick the Second was king of Prussia. 11. Peter the Great of Russia died at St. Petersburgh (*St. Pétersbourg*) the 8th of February, 1725, in the 53d year of his age. 12. We have received 6½ pounds of coffee, 1½ pounds of sugar, and 2½ pounds of tea.

CONVERSATION.

Quand êtes-vous arrivé?	Je suis arrivé le premier juin.
Quand avez-vous vu votre mère?	Hier à cinq heures.
Mademoiselle Sophie est-elle la première ou la deuxième?	Je crois (*I think*) qu'elle est la deuxième.

Quel âge a-t-elle ?	Elle a quinze ans.
Dans quelle année est-elle née ?	Elle est née en 1851.
Dans quel mois ?	Au mois d'Octobre.
Quel jour ?	Le onze.
De quel roi parlez-vous ?	Nous parlons de Louis XVI.
Quand mourut-il ?	En 1793.
Quelle heure est-il ?	Il est sept heures et (un) quart ou sept heures et demie.
A quelle heure êtes-vous parti ?	Je suis parti à huit heures moins un quart.
Quel quantième avons-nous aujourd'hui ?	Nous avons le vingt-cinq. C'est le vingt-cinq.
Combien d'aunes voulez-vous ?	Donnez-moi seize aunes et demie.
Quand mourut Charlemagne ?	Il mourut en 814, le 28 Janvier.
Quel âge a votre grand-père ?	Il est à présent dans sa quatre-vingtième année.

XVI. SEIZIEME LEÇON.

INDEFINITE ADJECTIVES.

1. The Indefinite adjectives precede the noun to which they belong, and agree with it in number and gender. They are sometimes used pronominally without a noun. They are as follows: —

Chaque, m. and f. } every, all.
tout, f. *toute*, }
aucun, e, } not one, no.
nul, nulle, }
maint, e, many a.
quelque, some, any.
quelques, pl. some.
certain, e, a certain.
plusieurs, pl. m. and f. several.
divers, f. *-es*, } *pl.* different.
différents, f. *-tes*, }

Ex. *Chaque maison*, every house.
toute ville, every town.
aucun pays, no country.
nulle règle, no rule.
maint homme, many a man.
quelque argent, some money.
quelques pommes, some apples.
plusieurs écoliers, several pupils.
certains mots, certain words.
différentes entreprises, different enterprises.

2. *Tout* has the double meaning of *every* and *all* or *whole;* in the latter case it is accompanied by an article or a possessive adjective. *Toute ville* (without article) signifies *every town; toute la ville* means *all the town* or *the whole town.* The plural of *tout* is masc. *tous*, fem. *toutes.* Ex.: *Tous les hommes*, all men; *toutes les lettres*, all the letters; *Tous ses enfants*, all his children.

3. *Aucun* and *nul* can only be used of individual things, and answer to the English *not one.* They require the particle *ne* to be prefixed to the verb. (In most cases the English *no* is translated *point de* or *pas de.*) Ex.:—

Je n'ai aucune faute, I have not one mistake.
Je n'ai pas de (or *point de*) *faute*, I have no mistake.

4. *Quelconque*, whatever, takes its place after the noun. Ex. *Un livre quelconque*, a (any) book whatever.

VOCABULARY.

L'épine, f. the thorn.
la chose, the thing.
le temps, time, weather.
la nouvelle, the news.
le nom, the name.
le paysan, the peasant.
prêtez, lend.
la faute, the fault, mistake.
l'erreur, f. the error.
la version, the translation.
mortel, -le, mortal.
la femme, the woman.
le motif, the motive.
l'ennemi, m. the enemy.
rare, rare.
froid, e, cold.
le même, the same.
depuis, since.
aime, loves.
quelque chose, something.

READING EXERCISE 16.

Nulle rose n'est sans épines. Notre maître de musique donne chaque jour six leçons. Plusieurs personnes sont arrivées de Vienne. Dieu est le père de tous les hommes. Chaque âge a ses plaisirs et ses chagrins. Tous les hommes sont mortels. Tout ce pays est pauvre. Toute chose a son temps. Je n'ai aucune nouvelle de mon frère. Je connais quelques familles riches dans cette ville. Nous avons reçu aujourd'hui diverses lettres. Plusieurs hommes ont le même nom. Maint paysan est très pauvre. On a parlé (*spoken*) de différentes entreprises. Prêtez-moi quelques livres.

THEME 16.

1. Every child likes playing (*le jeu*). 2. Each town has a church. 3. You have several faults in your translation. 4. Every man is liable (*sujet*) to error. 5. My brother has found some pencils, whose (*à qui*) are they? 6. The whole night was cold (*froide*). 7. All the houses of this town are very high (*hautes*). 8. I do not know the names of all animals. 9. John has lost several pens. 10. The king had different motives. 11. This father has lost all his children. 12. No rule without exception (*exception*). 13. Certain books are not good for young people (*la jeunesse*). 14. I have not one enemy. 15. Every mother loves her children. 16. All the children love (*aiment*) their parents. 17. It is rare to (*d'*) have several good friends.

CONVERSATION.

Ai-je des fautes dans ma version?	Oui, mon ami, vous avez plusieurs fautes.
Quelles sont les fautes?	Les voici.
Qui a dit cela (*said so*)?	Tous les enfants l'ont dit.
Où trouve-t-on cette plante?	On la (*it*) trouve dans tous les pays de l'Europe.
A qui sont ces maisons?	Toutes ces maisons sont à mon oncle.
Quels motifs avez-vous eus?	Nous avons eu divers motifs.
As-tu beaucoup de fautes?	Non, M—, je n'ai aucune faute.
Qui est mortel?	Tous les hommes sont mortels.
A-t-elle trouvé quelque chose?	Oui, elle a trouvé une bourse.
Où avez-vous été la semaine dernière?	J'ai été dans plusieurs endroits (*places*).
A quoi (*to what*) les hommes sont-ils sujets?	Ils sont sujets à l'erreur.

XVII. DIX-SEPTIÈME LEÇON.

ADJECTIVES.—FORMATION OF THE FEMININE AND OF THE PLURAL.

1. General rule. The feminine of adjectives is formed by adding an *e* to the masculine termination, if this does not end in *e* mute. Ex.: *Petit*, small, little, fem. *petite; joli*, pretty, fem. *jolie; appliqué*, diligent, *appliquée*.

2. Particular rules. Adjectives which end in *e* mute are alike in the masculine and feminine gender: *facile*, easy, fem. *facile; sage*, wise, fem. *sage*.

3. Adjectives ending in *el*, *eil*, and *n*,—further, monosyllables ending in *s* and *t*, double their final consonant before *e* mute of the feminine, as: *Cruel*, cruel, fem. *cruelle; pareil*, like, such, fem. *pareille; bon*, good, fem. *bonne; gros*, big, fem. *grosse; bas*, low, fem. *basse; sot*, stupid, fem. *sotte*.

4. Adjectives which end in *f* become feminine by changing *f* into *ve*, as: *vif* quick, lively, f. *vive; neuf*, new, f. *neuve; actif*, active, f. *active; bref*, short, f. *brève*.

5. Adjectives ending in *x*, change this *x* into *se*, as: *Heureux*, happy, lucky, f. *heureuse; jaloux*, jealous, f. *jalouse*.

6. Adjectives which end in *er* and *et*, take in the feminine the grave accent, as: *Léger*, light, f. *légère; complet*, complete, f. *complète*. Those in *gu* have *guë* in the fem. to preserve the sound of *u* (see p. 17, Excep.), as: *aigu*, acute, f. *aiguë*.

7. Of the adjectives ending in *c*, three change this *c* into *che*, viz: *Blanc*, white, f. *blanche; franc*, frank, f. *franche; sec*, dry, f. *sèche*.

The others ending in *c* take *-que*, as: *Turc*, Turkish, f. *turque; public*, public, f. *publique; Grec*, Greek, has in the fem. *grecque*.

8. The following adjectives do not quite agree with the foregoing rules: —

Long, long, f. *longue*.
frais, fresh, f. *fraîche*.
épais, thick, f. *épaisse*.
doux, sweet, soft, f. *douce*.
faux, false, f. *fausse*.
exprès, express, f. *expresse*.
muet, dumb, mute, f. *muette*.
sujet, subject, f. *sujette*.
malin, wicked, f. *maligne*.
bénin, benign, f. *bénigne*.

9. The following are more irregular in the formation of their feminine, as: —

Beau (bel), beautiful, f. *belle*.
nouveau (nouvel), new, f. *nouvelle*.
mou (mol), soft, f. *molle*.
fou (fol), mad, foolish, f. *folle*.
vieux (vieil), old, f. *vieille*.

Note. The forms in parentheses, *bel*, *nouvel*, etc., are used before masculine nouns beginning with a vowel or *h* mute, as: *un bel arbre*, a fine tree; *un nouvel ordre*, a new order; *un fol espoir*, a mad, wild hope.

10. The rules given for the plural of substantives apply also to adjectives. Ex.: —

Grand, f. *grande*; plur. *grands*, f. *grandes*.
appliqué, f. *appliquée*; plur. *appliqués*, f. *appliquées*.
gras, f. *grasse*, fat; plur. *gras*, f. *grasses*.
royal, f. *royale*, royal; plur. *royaux*, f. *royales*.
beau, f. *belle*, beautiful; plur. *beaux*, f. *belles*.
vieux, f. *vieille*, old; plur. *vieux*, f. *vieilles*.

Fou, *mou*, and *bleu* make in the plural *fous*, *mous*, and *bleus*.

11. The adjective must agree in gender and number with the substantive which it qualifies, as: —

La grande maison, the large house.
La maison est grande, the house is large.
La jolie rose, the pretty rose.
Ces roses sont très-jolies, these roses are very pretty.

The adjective is more frequently used substantively in French than in English. Ex. *Le paresseux*, the lazy (one).

VOCABULARY.

La médecine, the medicine.
l'ivoire, m. ivory.
la violette, the violet.
la montagne, the mountain.
la liberté, liberty.
la robe, the dress, gown.
l'herbe, f. the grass.
vrai, e, true.
la voix, the voice.
utile, useful.
agréable, agreeable.
amer, amère, bitter.
mûr, e, ripe.
aimable, amiable.
immortel, -le, immortal.
cher, chère, dear.
obéissant, e, obedient.
précieux, -se, precious.
corps, m. body.

READING EXERCISE 17.

Cet arbre est très-gros. Voici deux gros arbres. La médecine n'était pas bonne; elle était très-amère. Nos enfants sont heureux. Vos filles ne sont pas heureuses; elles sont très-malheureuses. Vous seriez aimable, si (*if*) vous étiez appliquée. Voici une très-jolie maison, elle est encore neuve. Cette église est vieille. Vos chevaux sont vieux. Les châteaux royaux sont très-beaux. Les dents longues et blanches de l'éléphant fournissent (*furnish*) l'ivoire. La fille de notre voisin est muette. Ils ne sont pas obéissants. J'avais une oie qui (*which*) était grosse et grasse.

THEME 17.

1. The rose is pretty; the violets are also pretty. 2. My room is small; your house is large. 3. This news is not true. 4. My father is good; my mother is also good. 5. These geese are big and fat. 6. What beautiful houses! 7. Henry's books are useful and agreeable. 8. Your windows are very small and low. 9. My body is mortal, but my soul is immortal. 10. Our town is very old. 11. Her sister is not handsome. 12. This house is well situated (*bien située*). 13. This apple is not ripe, but these pears are too (*trop*) ripe. 14. Is this butter fresh? 15. The grass is very thick. 16. Ivory is white; my teeth are not so (*si*) white. 17. Her voice is very sweet. 18. I have received a long letter from my father. 19. What a foolish (§ 9, *Note*) hope! 20. That medicine was very

bitter. 21. Louisa's dress is beautiful, but her bonnet is not very beautiful. 22. My shoes are very old. 23. The leaf is dry. 24. My mother is happy; my sisters are also happy. 25. Your letter was too short. 26. That girl is very foolish and idle.

CONVERSATION.

L'âme de l'homme est-elle mortelle?	Non, elle est immortelle.
Qui est malade chez vous?	C'est ma tante qui est malade.
Prend-elle (*does she take*) de la médecine?	Oui, M—, elle prend une médecine tres-amère.
Qui est arrivé?	Mon oncle Richard.
A-t-il apporté quelque chose?	Il a apporté un bel oiseau, un perroquet (*parrot*).
Êtes-vous heureux?	Oh! non, nous sommes malheureux!
Comment trouvez-vous (*how do you like*) cette rose?	Je la trouve très-belle.
Votre robe est-elle vieille ou neuve?	Elle n'est pas vieille; elle est toute neuve.
Notre version est-elle longue?	Non, elle n'est pas bien longue.
Comment trouvez-vous ces deux écoliers?	Ils sont très-paresseux.
Sont-ils obéissants?	Non, M—, ils ne sont pas obéissants.
Avez-vous perdu quelque chose?	Oui, Monsieur, j'ai perdu ma vieille casquette (*cap*).

XVIII. DIX-HUITIÈME LEÇON.

THE PLACE OF ADJECTIVES.

1. GENERAL RULE. ADJECTIVES GENERALLY FOLLOW THEIR NOUNS.

2. PARTICULAR RULES. The following generally *precede* the substantive:

Beau, fine.	*méchant*, wicked.
bon, good.	*meilleur*, better.
grand, great, large.	*moindre*, less, least.
gros, big.	*petit*, little.
jeune, young.	*saint* holy.
mauvais, bad.	*vieux*, old. *vrai*, true.

Ex.: — *Un beau pays*, a fine country.
Une grande ville, a large town *or* city.
Un jeune lion, a young lion.
Un mauvais lit, a bad bed.
Un meilleur avis, a better advice.
Un vieux soldat, an old soldier, etc.

Note. *Grand* is placed after its noun, when it signifies tall: *un homme grand*, a tall man.

N. B. It is to be observed, that substantives preceded by an adjective, when used in the partitive sense, take only *de* before them, instead of *du*, *de*, *la*, or *des*. (See L. v., 4.) Ex.: *De bon vin*, (some) good wine; *de belles fleurs*, beautiful flowers.

Note. Exceptions to this rule are: *du bon sens*, good sense; *des jeunes gens*, young men; *des petits pois*, green peas; and other expressions in which the noun and adjective form really but one compound word.

3. Monosyllabic adjectives, except those denoting some physical property (color, taste, form, etc.), *precede* the noun. Ex.: *Un long discours*, *un fol amour*.

4. Adjectives qualifying a noun followed by a limiting phrase or clause, *precede* the noun. Ex.: *L'immortel auteur du Paradis perdu*.

5. Many adjectives, when taken in their literal sense, follow, when taken figuratively, precede the substantive, as: —

FIGURATIVELY.	LITERALLY.
Un tendre amitié, a tender friendship.	*De la viande tendre*, tender meat.
mon pauvre enfant, my poor child.	*un enfant pauvre*, a poor (indigent) child.
un profond silence, a deep silence.	*un fossé profond*, a deep ditch.

6. Many adjectives take their place sometimes before, sometimes after the noun, without changing their signification, simply for the sake of euphony or stress. This is mostly to be seen when the adjective is preceded by the *definite* article or by *ce*, *cette*. We say, for instance: *une vérité affreuse*, a frightful truth, but, l'*affreuse* or *cette affreuse vérité*:

L'inflexible dureté des riches.
The inflexible hardness of the rich.

Cette affligeante nouvelle se répandit dans la ville.
This afflicting news spread (soon) in the town.

7. Some adjectives have a different meaning, according as they stand before or after their noun: —

Mon cher ami, my dear friend (denoting affection).	*Un livre cher*, a dear book (denoting the price).
un brave homme, a worthy man.	*un homme brave*, a brave (courageous) man.
un honnête homme, an honest man.	*un homme honnête*, a civil or polite man.
la dernière année, the last year (of a certain space of time).[1]	*l'année dernière*, last year (the past year).

VOCABULARY.

Le soldat, the soldier.	*américain, e*, American.
les gens, people.	*simple*, simple.
attentif, -ve, attentive.	*modeste*, modest.
vert, e, green.	*vertueux, -se*, virtuous.
bleu, e, blue.	*laborieux, -se*, laborious

[1] For instance: He spent the last year of his life at Paris, *il passa la dernière année de sa vie à Paris.*

aveugle, blind.
la musique, the music.
noir, e, black.
romain, e, Roman.
l'armée, f. the army.
le malheur, misfortune.
le vaisseau, the vessel.
naturel, -le, natural.
le sentiment, the sentiment.
la fumée, the smoke.
incroyable, incredible.
l'application, f. the application.
déjà, already.

NOTE. Adjectives denoting nationality are not written with a capital. Ex.: *La langue française.*

READING EXERCISE 18.

J'ai des raisins doux. Ce sont des jeunes gens attentifs. La couleur verte est la couleur de la nature. Notre voisin a un habit bleu et une casquette rouge. Voici une jeune fille aveugle. Voulez-vous cette petite boîte? Elle a reçu une lettre amusante de sa vieille (*old*) cousine. Avez-vous de bonne encre? J'aime la musique italienne. Voici deux aunes de drap vert et quatre aunes de drap noir. Les soldats romains étaient très-braves. Un été sec est très-nuisible aux plantes. Mon maître de musique est un brave homme. Voici de grands vaisseaux américains. Les colibris (*humming birds*) sont de beaux petits oiseaux. J'aime les jeunes filles douces, simples et modestes.

THEME 18.

1. France is a fine country. 2. We have a large house. 3. Henry has a bad pen. 4. My aunt is a virtuous woman. 5. She is also very active and laborious. 6. Frank is an attentive boy. 7. Miss B. is an amiable young lady. 8. Is Mr. A. a polite man? 9. Yes, he is very polite. 10. The wasp (*la guêpe*) is a hurtful insect. 11. Our neighbor has three small horses. 12. This is a natural sentiment. 13. The young man studies (*étudie*) with (an) incredible application. 14. I have bought a round table. 15. Give me some red paper and four black pencils. 16. Yesterday we had an easy translation, but our exercise for to-morrow is difficult. 17. I like the blue sky, (the) high trees and (the) green fields. 18. Have you ripe pears? 19. No, sir, the pears are not yet (*pas encore*)

ripe, but we have ripe cherries. 20. Italian music is very agreeable. 21. The French soldiers under Napoleon [the] first were very brave. 22. Here are beautiful flowers and beautiful fruit (*pl.*). 23. The English have large vessels. 24. The rose and [the] lily are beautiful flowers.

CONVERSATION.

Avez-vous des noix mûres ?	Elles ne sont pas encore mûres.
Quand seront-elles mûres ?	Dans huit jours.
Aimez-vous la musique allemande ?	J'aime mieux (*better*) la musique italienne.
Ce marchand a-t-il de bon beurre ?	Son beurre n'est pas frais, mais sa crême (*cream*) est fraîche.
Comment trouvez-vous ces jeunes lions ?	Ils sont très-beaux.
Votre thème est-il difficile ?	Non, Monsieur, il est facile.
Combien coûte cet habit ?	Il coute cent francs. C'est un habit cher.
Où est mon cher ami Lucien ?	Il est allé au concert.
A qui est ce livre amusant ?	Il est à mon oncle.
Qui a perdu une casquette rouge ?	C'est Jules qui l'a perdue.
Avez-vous de bon pain et du fromage ?	Voici un gros morceau de pain et du fromage.

XIX. DIX-NEUVIÈME LEÇON.

DEGREES OF COMPARISON.

1. The comparative is formed by placing the adverb *plus*, more, before an adjective. The superlative by placing the article before the comparative, as:

Haut, e, high; comp. *plus haut,* higher; sup. *le plus haut,* the highest; fem. *haute,* comp. *plus haute,* sup. *la plus haute.*

Mauvais, e, bad; comp. *plus mauvais, e,* worse; sup. *le plus mauvais,* f. *la plus mauvaise,* the worst.

Rem. When a possessive adjective is placed before the superlative, the article *le, la, les,* is dropped, as: *Mon plus jeune frère,* my youngest brother.

2. There is in French also a lower and lowest degree which is effected by the words *moins*, less, for the comparative degree, and *le moins*, f. *la moins*, the lest, for the superlative, as:

Cruel, -le, cruel; comp. *moins cruel,* f. *moins cruelle,* less cruel *or* not so cruel; sup. *le moins cruel,* f. *la moins cruelle,* the least cruel.

3. The following adjectives have an irregular comparison:

Bon, f. *bonne,* good; comp. *meilleur, e,* better; sup. *le meilleur,* f. *la meilleure,* the best.

(*Mauvais, e,* in the sense of wicked), comp. *pire,* worse; sup. *le pire,* f. *la pire,* the worst.

(*Petit, e,*); comp. *moindre,* less; sup. *le moindre,* f. *la moindre,* the least.

Petit and *mauvais* are also regular.

4. *As* before an adjective is rendered *aussi*; *as* after it, and *than* are both translated *que*. Ex.: — *Il est aussi heureux que moi,* he is as happy as I am. *Charles est plus fort que son frère,* Charles is stronger than his brother.

5. *In* after a superlative and before the name of a place is rendered by *de* and not by *dans*. Ex.: *Les plus belles églises* DE *Paris,* the finest churches *in* Paris.

VOCABULARY.

La Hollande, Holland.	*fort*, *e*, strong.
l'abeille, f. the bee.	*chaud*, warm.
le métal, the metal.	*encore*, still.
l'éléphant, the elephant.	*toujours*, always.
fidèle, faithful.	*l'autre*, the other.
peuplé, *e*, peopled, populous.	*le matin*, the morning.
le pays, the country.	*le soir*, the evening.
pesant, *e*, heavy.	*court*, short.

READING EXERCISE 19.

L'Europe est plus petite que l'Asie. L'Allemagne est plus fertile que la Hollande. L'abeille est l'insecte le plus utile. L'or est le métal le plus pesant. Ta robe est moins belle que la robe de ta sœur. Monsieur S est un homme très-fort. Son frère aîné (*elder*) est encore plus fort ; c'est l'homme le plus fort que (*that*) je connaisse. L'éléphant est le plus grand de tous les animaux terrestres. Les livres d'Émilie sont plus amusants que les nôtres (*ours*). Les chats sont moins fidèles que les chiens. Ces pommes-ci sont meilleures que vos poires. Les nôtres sont les meilleures. Votre tante est plus laborieuse que sa fille. Londres et Paris sont les villes les plus grandes et les plus peuplées de l'Europe.

THEME 19.

1. The morning was warm ; the evening was warmer. 2. This church is higher than the other. 3. Mary is the happiest girl in the world. 4. She is prettier than Louisa ; she is the prettiest of the sisters. 5. This house is not so (*si*) old as (*que*) the other. 6. This mountain is very high, higher than all the other mountains of this country. 7. The 22d [of] June is the longest, and the 22d of December the shortest day of the year. 8. The rose is the finest of all (the) flowers. 9. This wine is worse than water. 10. Have you any (*de*) better wine? 11. Yes, the red wine is better. 12. My wine is the best. 13. John is my best friend.

CONVERSATION.

Mademoiselle Marie, êtes-vous heureuse?	Oh! oui, je suis très-heureuse, plus heureuse que ma sœur.
Votre voisin est-il malheureux?	Il est moins malheureux que son frère qui est en Amérique.
Quel est le métal le plus utile?	C'est le fer?
Quels métaux sont les plus pesants?	L'or, le platine et le plomb sont les plus pesants.
Quelle est la plus attentive de toutes vos écolières?	C'est Madeleine, la fille de Monsieur B.
Quel est le plus fort des animaux terrestres.	C'est l'éléphant; c'est le plus grand et le plus fort de tous les animaux terrestres.
Quel est le mois le plus froid de l'année?	C'est le mois de Janvier.
Votre robe est-elle aussi belle que la robe de Julie?	Non, elle est moins belle.
Le tigre est-il cruel?	Oui, c'est le plus cruel de tous les animaux.
Où trouve-t-on le meilleur fer?	Le meilleur fer se trouve (*is found*) en Suède.

XX. VINGTIÈME LEÇON.

REGULAR VERBS.—FIRST CONJUGATION.—*DONNER.*

1. There are in French three regular conjugations, viz.: in *er*, *ir*, and *re*. Verbs in *-oir* belong to the irregular ones, as their root undergoes manifold changes.* The Infinitive mood is to be considered as the radical part or

*Only *six* other verbs are conjugated like *recevoir*, which is often given as the model of one conjugation. They will all be found L. XL.

ground-form on which the conjugation depends. What precedes the termination *er, ir,* or *re,* is the root, which, with regular verbs, always remains unaltered. To this are added the different terminations, by which persons, tenses, and moods are distinguished, and which are common to all the verbs of that same conjugation.

FORMATION OF THE TENSES OF REGULAR VERBS.

2. There are *primitive* tenses and *derived* tenses. The primitive tenses are: the *infinitive,* the *participle present,* the *past participle,* the *present indicative,* the *preterite.*

3. From the *present infinitive* are formed: the *future,* by adding *ai,* and the *conditional,* by adding *ais,* as: Inf. *donner:* Fut. *je donnerai,* and Cond. *je donnerais; finir:* Fut. *je finirai,* Cond. *je finirais.* In the third conjugation the final *e* is dropped: *vendre:* Fut. *je vendrai,* Cond. *je vendrais.*

4. From the *participle present* are formed: the *present* of the *subjunctive,* by changing *ant* into *e,* as: *donnant: que je donne; finissant: que je finisse; vendant: que je vende;* and the Imperfect Indicative by changing *ant* into *ais,* as: *finissant: je finissais, etc.*

5. With the *participle past* are formed all the *compound tenses,* by means of the auxiliaries *avoir* or *être,* as: Part. past: *donné, fini, vendu —: j'ai donné, j'avais fini, j'aurai vendu, etc.*

6. From the *present of the Indicative,* viz.: from its 1st person singular and the 1st and 2d persons plural, the *Imperative* is formed, by suppressing the pronouns *je, nous, vous,* as: *donne* (give), *donnons, donnez; finis* (finish), *finissons, finissez, etc.*

7. From the *preterite* is formed the *Subjunctive imperfect,* by changing the final *ai* into *asse* for the verbs of the first conjugation, and *is* into *isse* for the second and third conjugations. Ex.: *je donnai: que je donnasse; je finis: que je finisse; je vendis: que je vendisse.*

CONJUGATION OF *DONNER,* — TO GIVE.

INDICATIVE.

PRESENT TENSE.

Je donne, *I give,*	nous donnons, *we give.*
tu donnes, *thou givest.*	vous donnez, *you give.*
il donne, *he gives,*	ils donnent, } they give.
elle donne, *she gives.*	elles donnent, }

IMPERFECT.

Je donnais, *I gave* or *was giving*.	nous donnions, *we gave*.
tu donnais, *thou gavest*.	vous donniez, *you gave*.
il donnait, *he gave*.	ils donnaient, *they gave*.

PRETERITE.

Je donnai, *I gave* or *did give*.	nous donnâmes, *we gave*.
tu donnas, *thou gavest*.	vous donnâtes, *you gave*.
il donna, *he gave*.	ils donnèrent, *they gave*.

FUTURE.

Je donnerai, *I shall give*.	nous donnerons, *we shall give*.
tu donneras, *thou wilt give*.	vous donnerez, *you will give*.
il donnera, *he will give*.	ils donneront, *they will give*.

CONDITIONAL.

Je donnerais, *I should give*.	nous donnerions, *we should give*.
tu donnerais, *etc*.	vous donneriez, *etc*.
il donnerait, *etc*.	ils donneraient, *etc*.

IMPERATIVE.

Donne, *give*.	donnons, *let us give*.
(donnes-en),* *give* (*of it*).	donnez, *give*.

INFINITIVE.

Donner, *to give*.	(de *or* à donner), *to give*.

SUBJUNCTIVE.

PRESENT.

Que je donne, *that I* (*may*) *give*.	que nous donnions, *that we* (*may*) [*give*.
que tu donnes, *etc*.	que vous donniez, *etc*.
qu'il donne, *etc*.	qu'ils donnent, *etc*.

* The Imperative mood of the first conjugation takes an *s*, in the singular, when followed by *en* (of it, of them, some), or *y* (to *or* of it, to them). Ex.: *offres-en*, offer some, *penses-y*, think of it.

IMPERFECT.

Que je donnasse,	*that I (might) give.*	que nous donnassions.
que tu donnasses,	*etc.*	que vous donnassiez.
qu'il donnât,	*etc.*	qu'ils donnassent.

PARTICIPLES.

PRESENT.	PAST.
Donnant, *giving.*	Donné, f. donnée, *given.*
(en donnant), *by* or *in giving, etc.*	

COMPOUND TENSES.

In active verbs these are formed with the Part. past and the auxiliary *avoir,* to have.

INFINITIVE.

Avoir donné, *to have given.*

INDICATIVE.

COMPOUND OF THE PRESENT.

J'ai donné, *I have given.*
tu as donné, *thou hast given.*
il a donné, *he has given.*
nous avons donné, *we have given, etc.*

COMPOUND OF THE IMPERFECT.

J'avais donné, *I had given, etc.*

COMPOUND OF THE PRETERITE.

J'eus donné, *I had given, etc.*

COMPOUND OF THE FUTURE.

J'aurai donné, *I shall have given, etc.*

CONDITIONAL.

J'aurais donné, } *I should have given.*
J'eusse donné, }

SUBJUNCTIVE.

COMPOUND OF THE PRESENT.

Que j'aie donné, *that I (may) have given, etc.*
Que tu aies donné, *that thou (mayest) have given, etc.*

COMPOUND OF THE IMPERFECT.

Que j'eusse donné, *that I (might) have given, etc.*

PARTICIPLE.

Ayant donné, e, *having given.*

REMARK 1. There is but one way to render the expressions: *I give, I do give, I am giving;* viz.: je donne: — *I was giving;* je donnais, etc.

2. In the interrogative and negative form the auxiliary *do* is not expressed. (See also the 11th Lesson, 4.) Ex.:

PRESENT.

INTERROGATIVELY.

Est-ce que je donne, *do I give?*	donnons-nous, *do we give?*
donnes-tu, *dost thou give?*	donnez-vous, *do you give?*
donne-t-il, *does he give?*	donnent-ils, } *do they give?*
donne-t-elle, *does she give?*	donnent-elles, }

NEGATIVELY.

Je ne donne pas, *I do not give.*
tu ne donnes pas, *thou dost not give.*
il ne donne pas, *he does not give, etc.*

NEGATIVE-INTERROGATIVE.

Est-ce que je ne donne pas, *do I not give?*
ne donnes-tu pas, *dost thou not give?*
ne donne-t-il pas, *does he not give?*

3. The forms *donné-je* (acute on the *e*), *donnais-je, donnai-je,* are little used, except in poetry and in studied prose; they are replaced by *Est-ce que* (is it that) prefixed to the common form, as: *est-ce que je donne,* do I give; *est-ce que je donnais,* did I give (was I giving), etc. The future and conditional *donnerai-je, donnerais-je* are more common, though *est-ce que* may be used in all cases to form an interrogation, especially in common conversation, as: *est-ce que je donnerai,* shall I give; *est-ce qu'il donne,* does he give; *est-ce que vous donnez, est-ce que tu ne donnes pas,* etc.

COMPOUND OF THE PRESENT,

Ai-je donné? as-tu donné? a-t-il donné? etc.
Je n'ai pas donné, tu n'as pas donné, etc.
N'ai-je pas donné? n'as-tu pas donné? etc.

Conjugate in the same manner: *parler*, to speak; *porter*, to carry, to take; *admirer*, to admire; *aimer*, to love, etc.

VOCABULARY.

Le prochain, the neighbor.
apporter, to bring.
tomber, to fall.
l'escalier, m. the stairs.
la santé, health.
le cœur, the heart.
le canif, the penknife.
les gens, the people.
la chasse, the chase.
le chasseur, the hunter.
la poste, the post-office.
magnifique, magnificent.
manger, to eat.
chercher, to look for.
trouver, to find.
penser, to think.
jouer, to play. *pleurer*, to cry.
arriver, to arrive.
prier, to pray.
l'autre, the other.
pas encore, not yet.

READING EXERCISE 20.

Aimez Dieu et votre prochain. Les parents aiment leurs enfants. Portez cette lettre à la poste. Tu porteras cette robe à ta sœur. J'apporterai ces livres à mon maître. Apportez-lui (*him*) aussi cette boîte. L'enfant tomba de l'escalier. J'ai pensé á mon ami. Pensez à votre cousin. Jouons. Nous cherchions longtemps votre chien. Vous ne le (*him*) trouverez pas. Les jeunes gens parlaient souvent de leurs amis. Les chasseurs parlèrent de la chasse. Tu ne mangeras pas cette poire-ci; elle n'est pas mûre. Qui a mangé l'autre? N'admirez-vous pas cette magnifique couleur?

THEME 20.

1. I love my father. 2. Thou lovest thy mother. 3. He loves his sister. 4. We love our parents. 5. Do you like flowers? 6. I give an apple to my brother. 7. We were speaking of your aunt. 8. I admired the beautiful palace of the king. 9. We played yesterday. 10. The child cried. 11. The children cried. 12. The

boy will look for his copy-book. 13. The boys will look for their copy-books. 14. I have found my knife. 15. Have you found your gloves? 16. We have not found our gloves. 17. Play, my child. 18. Eat these apples. 19. Do not eat these pears; they are not ripe. 20. She would fall. 21. We should admire your garden. 22. They would have eaten some bread and butter. 23. I think that our friends will arrive to-day. 24. They will arrive to-morrow. 25. Will you take this letter to the post-office? 26. Pray [to] God every morning and every evening. 27. Why do you cry? 28. Why have you not brought your money? 29. I have not brought my purse.

CONVERSATION.

Avez-vous cherché votre montre d'or?	Je la (*it*) cherche encore.
Qu'avez-vous apporté?	J'ai apporté les gants de Mademoiselle Mathilde.
Voulez-vous (*will you*) manger du pain?	J'ai déjà mangé un gros morceau de pain.
Votre mère parle-t-elle français?	Oui, elle parle français et anglais.
Quel commandement Jésus-Christ a-t-il donné?	Il a dit: Aimez Dieu et votre prochain.
Qui est notre prochain?	Tous les hommes.
Qui portera cette lettre à la poste, Antoine ou Théodore?	Ce sera Théodore.
Qu'apporte le chasseur?	Il apporte deux lièvres.
Avez-vous aussi été à la chasse?	Oui, Monsieur, nous avons été à la chasse hier.
A quoi pensez-vous?	Je pense à mon thème français.
A quel jeu jouerons-nous demain?	Nous jouerons à la balle (*ball*).
Que cherchez-vous?	Je cherche mes gants.
Qu'admirez-vous là?	Nous admirons ce magnifique vaisseau anglais.

READING LESSON.

LE CHAMEAU ET LE CHAT.

Le chat au chameau. Soyez le bien-venu, mon frère.

Le chameau. Comment, moi (*I*) ton frère!

Le chat. Oui, certes. Voyez un peu (*see a little*): ne puis-je pas (*cannot I*) faire une aussi jolie bosse que vous?

Le chameau. Cela peut (*can*) être; mais peut-elle aussi porter autant que la mienne (*mine*)?

Le chat. La sotte demande! donnez-moi seulement (*only*) votre petit paquet, je le porterai, comme si ce n'était rien.

Le chameau. Mais penses-y bien: n'est-il pas trop gros pour toi (*you*)?

Le chat. Ah! quel conte! donnez-moi, vous dis-je, donnez.

Le chameau. C'est bien; approche un peu, le voilà.

Le chat. Ah! quelle charge! je suis écrasé!

Le chameau. Tu as ce que (*what*) tu mérites!

Celui qui veut entreprendre de grandes choses, doit (*must*) auparavant éprouver ses forces.

Le chameau, the camel.
le chat, the cat.
le bien-venu, e, welcome.
comment, how.
certes, to be sure.
faire, to make.
une bosse, a hump.
la demande, the question.
le paquet, the pack.
comme si, as if.
y, of it (to it).
le conte, the tale.
approcher, approach.
la charge, the weight.
écrasé, crushed.
mériter, to deserve.
entreprendre, to undertake.
auparavant, before.
éprouver, to try.
la force, the strength.

XXI. VINGT ET UNIÈME LEÇON.

REMARKS ON THE ORTHOGRAPHY OF SOME VERBS OF THE FIRST CONJUGATION.

Some regular verbs in *-er* are, for the sake of euphony, liable to the following modifications:

1. Some verbs ending in *-ter*, as: *jeter*, to throw; *rejeter*, to throw back; and those polysyllabic verbs ending in *eler*, as: *appeler*, to call; *renouveler*, to renew, etc.; double the *t* or *l*, when they are followed by an *e* mute.

This is the case in some persons of the Present, Future, and Imperative, viz.:—

PRESENT.	IMPERATIVE.	FUTURE.
Je je*tt*e — nous jetons.	Je*tt*e.	Je je*tt*erai.
tu je*tt*es — vous jetez.	*pl.* jetons.	tu je*tt*eras.
il je*tt*e — ils je*tt*ent.	jetez.	etc.
J'appe*ll*e — nous appelons.	Appe*ll*e.	J'appe*ll*erai.
tu appe*ll*es — vous appelez.	*pl.* appelons.	tu appe*ll*eras.
il appe*ll*e — ils appe*ll*ent.	appelez.	etc.

Except the verb *acheter*, to buy, and a few others that seldom occur, which never double the *t*, but take the grave accent è:

Pres. J'achète, tu achètes, il achète, nous achetons, vous achetez, ils achètent.

Fut. J'achèterai. *Imper.* achète, *pl.* achetez.

2. Dissyllabic verbs ending in *-eler*, as: *geler*, to freeze, and all others that have an *e* mute in the last syllable but one, such as: *semer*, to sow; *mener*, to lead; *lever* to lift up, take the grave accent, è, when the final consonant of the root is followed by an *e* mute:

Infinitive: *Mener*, to lead, to conduct.

Pres. Je mène, tu mènes, il mène, nous menons, vous menez, ils mènent.
Imperf. Je menais, tu menais.
Fut. Je mènerai, tu mèneras. *Imp.* mène, menons, menez.

The same change takes place with those verbs which have *é* in the last syllable but one. They, however, retain the *é* in the Future and Conditional.

Infinitive: *Espérer*, to hope.

Pres. J'espère, tu espères, il espère, nous espérons, vous espérez, ils espèrent. *Imperf.* J'espérais.

Imper. Espère, espérons, espérez. *Fut.* J'espérerai.

Verbs in *éger* retain the é, as: *je protége.*

3. In verbs ending in *-ger*, as: *juger*, to judge; *partager*, to share, divide, the *e* is retained in those tenses where *g* is followed by the vowels *a* or *o*, in order to give the *g* the same soft sound as in all other tenses and persons. Ex.:

Infinitive: *Manger*, to eat.

Pres. Je mange; *pl.* nous mangeons. *P. pr.* Mangeant.

Impf. Je mangeais, tu mangeais, il mangeait, nous mangions, vous mangiez, ils mangeaient.

Pret. Je mangeai, tu mangeas, il mangea, nous mangeâmes, vous mangeâtes, ils mangèrent. *Imp.* Mangeons.

4. In verbs ending in *-cer*, as: *commencer*, to begin, a cedilla must be placed under the *c*, when this letter is followed by *a* or *o*. Ex.:—

Infinitive: *Placer*, to place.

Pres. Je place, tu places, etc.; *pl.* nous plaçons, etc.

Impf. Je plaçais, tu plaçais, il plaçait, nous placions, vous placiez, ils plaçaient. *Imper.* Plaçons, etc.

Pret. Je plaçai, tu plaças, il plaça, nous plaçâmes, etc.

5. Verbs ending in *-ayer, -oyer, -uyer* change the *y* into *i*, whenever the letter *y* would be immediately followed by an *e* mute. Such are:—

Payer, to pay.	*employer*, to employ.
effrayer, to frighten.	*essuyer*, to wipe.

Pres. Je paie, tu paies, il paie, *pl.* nous payons, vous payez, ils paient. *Part. pr.* Payant.

J'emploie, tu emploies, il emploie, *pl.* nous employons, vous employez, ils emploient. *P. pr.* Employant.

J'essuie, tu essuies, etc.; *pl.* ils essuient.

Impf. Je payais, etc.; *pl.* nous payions, vous payiez, etc.

J'employais, etc.; *pl.* nouns employions, etc.

J'essuyais, etc.; *pl.* nous essuyions, etc.

Fut. Je paierai, etc.; j'emploierai, etc.; j'essuierai, etc.

Imper. Paie — payez. Emploie — employez. Essuie — essuyez.

6. Verbs which in the Infinitive end in *-ier*, as: *prier*, to pray; *crier*, to cry, are in some cases spelled with a double *ii*. This takes place in the 1st

and 2d persons plural of the Imperfect of the Indicative, and of the Present of the Subjunctive: —

Infinitive: *Oublier*, to forget.

Ind. Imperf. pl. nous oubl*ii*ons, vous oubl*ii*ez, ils oubliaient.
Subj. Pres. pl. que nous pr*ii*ons, que vous pr*ii*ez, etc.

VOCABULARY.

La vertu, virtue.
la beauté, beauty.
préférer, to prefer.
l'amitié, f. friendship.
le vent, the wind.
la pluie, the rain.
la terre, the earth.
élever, to bring up, to educate.
sécher, to dry.
bien, well.
la force, strength.
le bruit, the noise.
la servante, the servant.
la chambre, the room.
le chemin, the way, road.
nettoyer, to clean.
la pierre, the stone
la cuisinière, the cook.
posséder, to possess.
le jardinier, the gardener.

READING EXERCISE 21.

Le sage préfère la vertu à la beauté. L'amitié se paie (*is paid*) par l'amitié. Les parents élèvent leurs enfants. Il gèlera cette nuit. Il a gelé. Elle achète un livre. Les vents sèchent la terre trempée (*wet*) par la pluie. Nous achetons des fruits. Vous achèteriez cette maison, si elle n'était pas si chère. Appelez Jean. Nous partageons avec nos amis tout ce que (*all that*) nous avons. Ce jeune homme emploie bien son temps. Nous emploierons toutes nos forces. Cela m'effraie. Ce bruit m'a effrayé. La servante nettoie les chambres. Les maîtres aiment les écoliers qui emploient bien leur temps.

THEME 21.

1. The boy throws a stone. 2. You always throw (throw always) stones. 3. Call thy brother. 4. Call the servant. 5. I shall call John. 6. The cook buys eggs. 7. I buy a horse. 8. My father will also buy a horse. 9. Where dost thou take[1] this horse? 10. I hope to see you (*vous voir*) to-morrow. 11. What

[1] Mener is applied to what moves of itself, *porter*, to what is carried by lifting from the ground.

do you hope? 12. We hope nothing. 13. What are you eating there (*là*)? 14. The child ate an apple. 15. You ate walnuts. 16. I placed the books on the table. 17. I pay everything (*tout*). 18. Thou payest nothing. 19. Let us well employ our time. 20. My sons pay [for] what (*ce que*) they buy. 21. My uncle possesses a large garden. 22. The gardener cleans the ways. 23. Wipe your tears (*larmes*). 24. The dog frightens the children. 25. We wiped the table. 26. I prefer coffee to tea (*thé*).

CONVERSATION.

Qui a appelé?	Ton père a appelé.
Avez-vous nettoyé les chemins?	Pas encore; je les nettoierai ce soir.
Qui me protégera (*protect*)?	Dieu te protégera.
Nettoies-tu la chambre?	Je nettoie toute la maison.
Trouvez-vous cela cher?	J'appelle cela très-cher.
Que mangeais-tu?	Je mangeais des noix.
Où mène-t-on ce cheval?	On le mène chez le maréchal-ferrant (*farrier*).
Crois-tu (*do you think*) qu'il gèle cette nuit?	Il a déjà gelé.
Achèterez-vous du thé ou du café?	Je n'aime pas le thé, j'achèterai du café.
Où achetez-vous cette farine?	Chez le meunier (*miller*).
Qui a jeté cette pierre?	Je crois que c'est Richard.
Que fit (*did — do*) un jour un père?	Il partagea ses biens entre ses trois fils.

XXII. VINGT-DEUXIÈME LEÇON.

SECOND CONJUGATION: *FINIR*.

INDICATIVE.

PRESENT TENSE.

Je finis, *I finish.*	nous finissons, *we finish.*
tu finis, *thou finishest.*	vous finissez, *you finish.*
il finit, *he finishes.*	ils finissent, *they finish.*
elle finit, *she finishes.*	elles finissent, *they finish.*

IMPERFECT.

Je finissais, *I finished* (*was finishing*).	nous finissions, *we finished.*
tu finissais, *etc.*	vous finissiez, *etc.*
il finissait, *etc.*	ils finissaient, *etc.*

PRETERITE.

Je finis, *I finished* (did finish).	nous finîmes, *we finished.*
tu finis, *etc.*	vous finîtes, *etc.*
il finit, *etc.*	ils finirent, *etc.*

FUTURE.

Je finirai, *I shall finish.*	nous finirons, *we shall finish.*
tu finiras, *etc.*	vous finirez, *etc.*
il finira, *etc.*	ils finiront, *etc.*

CONDITIONAL.

Je finirais, *I should finish.*	nous finirions, *we should finish.*
tu finirais, *etc.*	vous finiriez, *etc.*
il finirait, *etc.*	ils finiraient, *etc.*

INFINITIVE.

Finir, *to finish.* de *or* à finir, *to finish.*

IMPERATIVE.

Finis, *finish.*	finissons, *let us finish.*
	finissez, *finish.*

SUBJUNCTIVE.

PRESENT.

Que je finisse, *that I (may) finish.*	que nous finissions, *that we finish.*
que tu finisses, *etc.*	que vous finissiez, *etc.*
qu'il finisse, *etc.*	qu'ils finissent, *etc.*

IMPERFECT.

Que je finisse, *that I (might) finish.*	que, n. finissions, *that we (might) finish.*
que tu finisses, *etc.*	que vous finissiez, *etc.*
qu'il finît, *etc.*	qu'ils finissent, *etc.*

PARTICIPLES.

PRESENT.	PAST.
Finissant, *finishing.*	Fini, f. finie, *finished.*
en finissant, *by finishing.*	

COMPOUND TENSES.

INFINITIVE.

Avoir fini, to have finished.

INDICATIVE.

COMPOUND OF THE PRESENT.

J'ai fini, *I have finished.*
tu as fini, *thou hast finished.*
il a fini, *he has finished.*
nous avons fini, *we have finished, etc.*

COMPOUND OF THE IMPERFECT.

J'avais fini, *I had finished, etc.*

COMPOUND OF THE PRETERITE.

J'eus fini, *I had finished, etc.*

COMPOUND OF THE FUTURE.

J'aurai fini, *I shall have finished, etc.*

CONDITIONAL.

J'aurais fini, } *I should have finished, etc.*
J'eusse fini, }

SUBJUNCTIVE.

COMPOUND OF THE PRESENT.

Que j'aie fini, *that I (may) have finished, etc.*

COMPOUND OF THE IMPERFECT.

Que j'eusse fini, *that I (might) have finished, etc.*

PARTICIPLE.

Ayant fini, *having finished, etc.*

Conjugate in the same manner: *bâtir*, to build; *choisir*, to choose; *remplir*, to fill, etc.

REM. 1. The verb *haïr*, to hate, loses in the Present and Imperative singular its diæresis. Otherwise it is quite regular and retains the two dots.

Pres. Je *hais*, tu *hais*, il *hait*, nous haïssons, vous haïssez, etc.
Imper. Hais; *pl.* haïssons, haïssez. *Pret.* Je haïs, *I hated.*

REM. 2. The verb *fleurir*, to flourish, has a second form for the Imperfect tense: *Je florissais*; and also a second for the Part. present: *florissant, e,*— both of which are only used in a figurative sense, as: *une ville florissante, etc.*

VOCABULARY.

Nourrir, to feed, nourish.
obéir, to obey.
remplir, to fill, fulfil.
bâtir, to build.
embellir, to embellish.
punir, to punish.
le vice, vice.
le devoir, the duty.
la flatterie, flattery.
le menteur, the liar.
saisir, to seize.
rendre, to render, return.
la tâche, the task.
la pomme de terre, the potato.
l'occasion, f. the opportunity.
salir, to soil.
la palais, the palace.
choisir, to choose.
la couleur, the color.

READING EXERCISE 22.

Le pain nourrit les hommes. Les bons enfants obéissent à leurs parents et à leurs maîtres. Remplis ce verre. Remplissez ces verres. Qui a rempli les bouteilles? Romulus et Rémus bâtirent la ville de Rome, l'an 753 avant Jésus-Christ. Les fleurs embellissent les jardins et les prairies. On punira les enfants qui n'obéissent pas à leur maître. J'espère que vous aurez puni ce méchant garçon. Le maître a puni le petit menteur. Notre voisin bâtit une grande maison. Nos voisins bâtissent de grandes maisons. Je bâtirais aussi, si j'avais plus d'argent. Je hais le vice, j'aimerai toujours la vertu. Haïssez le vice, il vous rend malheureux. J'ai toujours haï le vice. Nous haïssions la flatterie. Ne salissez pas vos habits. Les sciences nourrissent la jeunesse et réjouissent la vieillesse.

THEME 22.

1. I finish my exercise. 2. The pupils finish their translations. 3. We seize the opportunity. 4. We seized the opportunity. 5. Why have have you not seized the good opportunity? 6. The children soil their clothes. 7. Bread and potatoes nourish a great many men. 8. Do not punish Henry; he has been ill. 9. Fill the glasses. 10. We should fill the bottles, if we had wine enough. 11. The king builds a new palace. 12. Will you build a house? 13. I should build a large house, if I were rich. 14. Here are two colors: choose. 15. Which (*laquelle*) will you choose? 16. I shall choose the blue. 17. If I had to (*à*) choose, I should choose the green color. 18. Obey your (*à vos*) parents and (your) masters. 19. I hate nobody. 20. Hate nobody. 21. We hate vice. 22. We have always hated vice.

CONVERSATION.

Voici deux couteaux: un grand et un petit. Lequel (*which*) choisirez-vous?	Je choisirai le petit qui est le plus joli.
Cet homme remplit-il ses devoirs?	Pas toujours.
Avez-vous rempli toutes les bouteilles?	Non, Monsieur, je n'avais pas assez de vin pour les remplir.
Qui bâtit cette belle maison?	C'est mon voisin qui la bâtit.

Ne bâtirez-vous pas aussi?	Oui, je bâtirai aussi l'année prochaine (*next*).
Pourquoi ne bâtissez-vous pas à présent (*now*)?	Je bâtirais encore cette année, si j'avais assez d'argent.
Qui a sali ce livre?	C'est Martin.
Comment as-tu fait (*done*) cela?	La plume est tombée dessus (*upon it*).
Avez-vous fini votre thème?	Nous finirons notre thème ce soir.
Qui a bâti la ville de Rome?	Romulus et Rémus.
Qui a puni mon fils?	Le maître de musique.
Ne trouvez-vous pas que j'ai embelli mon jardin?	Certainement, ce jet d'eau (*fountain*) embellit beaucoup votre jardin.
Haïssez-vous le vice?	Oui, je hais tous les vices.
Pourquoi haïssez-vous votre voisin?	Je ne le (*him*) hais pas; je hais seulement ses flatteries.

READING LESSON.

LE MOINEAU ET SES PETITS.

Un moineau avait placé son nid dans le trou d'un mur. Il élevait tranquillement sa famille. Il aurait été bien heureux, si ses petits eussent voulu l'écouter: mais à chaque instant ils venaient sur le bord du nid. Le pauvre oiseau tremblait dans le crainte de les voir tomber. Il leur disait de rester dans le fond du nid, mais ils ne le voulaient point (*would not do so.*)

Un jour qu'il était *sorti*, ils profitèrent de son absence et s'avancèrent tant qu'ils tombèrent à terre. Ils n'avaient pas encore de plumes aux ailes; ainsi ils ne purent (*could not*) se sauver. Un gros chat, qui passait par-là, les vit (*saw them*); il n'avait pas dîné, il les *saisit*, et les *mangea* sur-le-champ. C'est ainsi qu'ils furent *punis* de (*for*) leur désobéissance.

Le moineau, the sparrow.
les petits, the young ones.
le nid, the nest.
le trou, the hole.
le mur, the wall.
tranquillement, quietly.
écouter, to listen, obey.
l'instant, m. the moment.
ils venaient, they came.
la crainte, the fear.
rester, to remain.
le fond, the bottom.
tant, so much.
l'aile, f. the wing.
sauver, to save ; *se* —, to fly away.
passer, to pass by.
par-là, there.
dîner, to dine.
sur-le-champ, at once, immediately.
la désobéissance, disobedience.

XXIII. VINGT-TROISIÈME LEÇON.

THIRD CONJUGATION: *VENDRE*.

INDICATIVE.

PRESENT TENSE.

Je vends, *I sell.*	nous vendons, *we sell.*
tu vends, *thou sellest.*	vous vendez, *you sell.*
il vend, *he sells.*	ils vendent, } *they sell.*
elle (on) vend, *she (one) sells.*	elles vendent, } *they sell.*

IMPERFECT.

Je vendais, *I sold (was selling).*	nous vendions, *we sold.*
tu vendais, *thou soldst.*	vous vendiez, *you sold.*
il vendait, *he sold.*	ils vendaient, *they sold.*

PRETERITE.

Je vendis, *I sold (did sell).*	nous vendîmes, *we sold.*
tu vendis, *etc.*	vous vendîtes, *etc.*
il vendit, *etc.*	ils vendirent, *etc.*

FUTURE.

Je vendrai, *I shall sell.*	nous vendrons, *we shall sell.*
tu vendras, *etc.*	vous vendrez, *etc.*
il vendra, *etc.*	ils vendront, *etc.*

CONDITIONAL.

Je vendrais, *I should sell.*	nous vendrions, *we should sell.*
tu vendrais, *etc.*	vous vendriez, *etc.*
il vendrait, *etc.*	ils vendraient, *etc.*

IMPERATIVE.

Vends, *sell.*	vendons, *let us sell.*
	vendez, *sell.*

SUBJUNCTIVE.

PRESENT.

Que je vende, *that I (may) sell.*	que n. vendions, *that we (may) sell.*
que tu vendes, *etc.*	que vous vendiez, *etc.*
qu'il vende, *etc.*	qu'ils vendent, *etc.*

IMPERFECT.

Que je vendisse, *that I might sell.*	que nous vendissions.
que tu vendisses, *etc.*	que vous vendissiez.
qu'il vendît, *etc.*	qu'ils vendissent.

PARTICIPLES.

PRESENT.	PAST.
Vendant, *selling.*	Vendu, f. vendue, *sold.*
en vendant, *by selling.*	

COMPOUND TENSES.

INFINITIVE.

Avoir vendu, *to have sold.*

INDICATIVE.

COMPOUND OF THE PRESENT.

J'ai vendu, *I have sold.*
tu as vendu, *thou hast sold.*
il a vendu, *he has sold.*
nous avons vendu, *we have sold, etc.*

COMPOUND OF THE IMPERFECT.

J'avais vendu, *I had sold, etc.*

COMPOUND OF THE PRETERITE.

J'eus vendu, *I had sold, etc.*

COMPOUND OF THE FUTURE.

J'aurai vendu, *I shall have sold, etc.*

CONDITIONAL.

J'aurais vendu, } *I should have sold, etc.*
J'eusse vendu, }

PARTICIPLE.

Ayant vendu, *having sold.*

SUBJUNCTIVE.

COMPOUND OF THE PRESENT.

Que j'aie vendu, *that I (may) have sold, etc.*

COMPOUND OF THE IMPERFECT.

Que j'eusse vendu, *that I (might) have sold, etc.*

Conjugate after this model: *perdre*, to lose; *attendre*, to wait, to expect; *répondre*, to answer, etc.

Rem. 1. The verb *battre*, to beat, is regularly conjugated; except that in the singular of the *Present Indicative* and in the *Imperative* it loses one *t*.

Pres. Je *bats*, tu *bats*, il *bat*, nous battons, vous battez, etc. *Imp. bats*, *Part.* battu.

Rem. 2. The verb *rompre*, to break, is conjugated in the *Pres. Indicative* as follows:

Je romps, tu romps, il rompt, nous rompons, etc. (All the rest is regular.)

Rem. 3. The verb *rire*, to laugh, is of the 3d conjugation: *Pres. Je ris, tu ris, il rit, nous rions, etc.* But the *Part. past* is *ri*, and the *Pret. Je ris, tu ris, il rit, nous rîmes, vous rîtes, ils rirent. Fut. Je rirai, etc.*

Rem. 4. *Conclure*, to conclude, is regular, as: *Pres. Je conclus, tu conclus, il conclut, nous concluons, etc. Fut. Je conclurai.* Except that in the *Preterite*, it has *je conclus* (not *je concluis*).

VOCABULARY.

La bague, the ring.
répandre, to spread, to shed.
le bruit, the report, the noise.
la mort, death.
défendre, to forbid, to defend.
entendre, to hear.
fumer, to smoke.
répondre, to answer.
le sang, the blood.
l'œil, the eye.
gauche, left.
droit, e, right.
les armes, the arms.
la sagesse, wisdom.
la Grèce, Greece.
l'honneur, m. the honor.
perdre, to lose.
attendre, to wait for, expect.
un peu, a little.
le tonnerre, the thunder.
le travail, the work.
désirer, to wish.

READING EXERCISE 23.

J'ai vendu mon cheval. Nous avons vendu nos chevaux. Je perdis hier ma bourse. Vous perdîtes votre bague. La vieille femme vendait des cerises. Nous vendions du fromage et du beurre. On a répandu le bruit de la mort du roi. Il est défendu de fumer ici. Qui défend cela? Entendez-vous le bruit? Qui a battu mon chien? Il bat son cheval. Répondez-moi (*me*), mon fils. Réponds à ton maître. Je répondis que j'étais malade. Ce tyran cruel a répandu beaucoup de sang innocent. Jules a déjà perdu son œil gauche, il perdra aussi son œil droit. Tu perds ton argent. Nous perdons tout notre temps. Le bataillon prit les armes et défendit la ville. Socrate répandit beaucoup de sagesse à Athènes et dans toute la Grèce. Pourquoi riez-vous? Je ne ris pas. Je n'ai pas ri.

THEME 23.

1. I sell my dogs. 2. My friend sells his horses. 3. We sell our houses. 4. I defend my honor. 5. Do you defend your friends? 6. Thou losest thy time. 7. You lose your time. 8. I lost my money. 9. My brother has lost his cane. 10. He will lose everything. 11. The pupils will lose their places. 12. We expect a letter from our grandfather. 13. Do you also expect a letter? 14. No, sir, I expect nothing. 15. James (*Jacques*) and William expect (a) good news. 16. We have waited an hour.

17. Wait a little. 18. Why don't you wait? 19. Do you hear the music? 20. I hear nothing. 21. I did not hear the thunder. 22. Have you answered (to) her letter? 23. I have not yet answered. 24. I shall answer to-morrow. 25. Answer me (*moi*). 26. When (*quand*) I heard the thunder, I came down from the mountain. 27. The poor children have lost their father. 28. They will lose also their mother; she is very ill. 29. Do not break my stick.

CONVERSATION.

Qui a perdu cette bourse?	Je crois (*I think*) que Jules a perdu une bourse.
A-t-il aussi perdu de l'argent?	Je crois qu'il a perdu deux francs.
Pourquoi perdez-vous votre temps à jouer?	Nous n'avons rien à faire (*to do*), nous avons fini notre tâche.
A quoi (*at what*) jouez-vous?	Nous battons le cerceau (*hoop*).
Qui défend les brebis (*sheep*)?	Le chien du berger (*shepherd*).
As-tu fini ton travail?	Oui, M—, mon travail est fini.
Ton frère a-t-il fini sa version?	Je ne crois pas; il la (*it*) finira demain.
Avez-vous entendu le bruit du vent (*wind*)?	Le vent est terrible.
Qui a défendu de manger de ces pommes?	Notre mère l'a défendu ce matin.
Comment êtes-vous descendu?	Je suis descendu par l'escalier (*stairs*).
Pourquoi salissez-vous vos mains?	Nous nettoyons la cage de nos oiseaux.
Pourquoi ne punit-on pas ce méchant enfant.	Il sera puni après la leçon.
Qui (*whom*) attendez-vous?	J'attends Monsieur le professeur.
Attendiez-vous quelqu'un (*some one*)?	J'attendais mon cousin de Paris.

READING LESSON.

LE ROI DE PERSE.

Un roi de Perse certain jour
Chassait avec toute sa cour;
Il eut soif, mais dans cette plaine
On ne trouvait point de fontaine,
Près de là seulement était un grand jardin
Rempli de beaux cédrats, d'oranges, de raisins:
"A Dieu ne plaise que j'en mange!"
Dit le roi; "ce jardin courrait trop de danger:
Si je me permettais d'y cueillir une orange,
Mes visirs aussitôt mangeraient le verger."

Certain jour, one day.
chasser, to go a hunting.
la soif, thirst.
seulement, only.
la plaine, the plain.
la fontaine, fountain, spring.
près de là, in the neighborhood.
le cédrat, the lemon.
à Dieu ne plaise, God forbid.
courrait, would run.
permettre, to permit.
cueillir, to gather. *y*, there.
aussitôt, immediately.
le verger, the orchard.

XXIV. VINGT-QUATRIÈME LEÇON.

DISJUNCTIVE PERSONAL PRONOUNS.*

With personal pronouns it must be observed whether they are intimately connected with or governed by a verb, as: *I speak, we go, I give you, etc.*; if this be the case, they are *conjunctive (pronoms conjoints)*; or if they are employed by *themselves* or *with a preposition*; in this case they are termed *disjunctive (pronoms disjoints)*. We begin with the latter.

1. The disjunctive personal pronouns are: *moi* (I or me), *toi* (thou or thee), *nous* (we or us), *vous*, (you), *lui* (he or him), *elle* (she or her), *eux* (they or them, masculine), *elles* (they or them,

* See P. II, L. IX.

feminine), and *soi* (self, one's self). These pronouns, it will be perceived, do not change their form to indicate *case*, the nominative and objective being the same.

Ex.: *Qui a dit cela?* *Moi, lui, elle, nous, etc.*
Who has said this? I, he, she, we, etc.

C'est pour moi, pour toi, pour elle, etc.
That is for me, for thee, for her, etc.

Je parle de toi, de vous, d'elles, d'eux, etc.
I speak of thee, of you, of them, of them, etc.

Nous pensons à lui, à vous, à eux, etc.
We think of him, of you, of them, etc.

2. All these *disjunctive* pronouns may take the word *-même*, pl. *-mêmes*, whenever in English the word *self* is joined to a pronoun. Ex.:—

S. *moi-même*, (I) myself.	Pl. *nous-mêmes*, ourselves.
toi-même, thyself.	*vous-mêmes*, yourselves.
lui-même, himself.	*eux-mêmes*, } themselves.
elle-même, herself.	*elles-mêmes*, } themselves.

soi-même, one's self.

3. When a stress is laid upon personal pronouns, they are often preceded by *c'est, c'était, etc.*, as in English:—

S. *c'est moi*, it is I.	Pl. *c'est nous*, it is we.
c'est toi, it is thou.	*c'est vous*, it is you.
c'est lui, it is he.	*ce sont eux*, } it is they.
c'est elle, it is she.	*ce sont elles*, } it is they.

The verb *être* following *ce* is put in the plural only when the pronoun or noun which follows that verb is in the *third person plural: c'étaient mes amis ce sont eux*, but, *c'est nous.*

4. *Soi* is only used of mankind in a general sense, and of inanimate objects in the singular. Ex.:—

Doit-on toujours penser à soi, ought one always to think of one's self?

VOCABULARY.

Inconstant, inconstant.	*la pelote*, the ball.
ressembler, to resemble.	*venez*, come.
envoyer, to send.	*casser*, to break.
demeurer, to live.	*sorti*, gone out.
la corbeille, the basket.	*âgé*, old.
l'aimant, m. the loadstone.	*ni — ni*, neither, nor.
attirer, to attract.	

READING EXERCISE 24.

Qui dit (*says*) cela ? Moi, — lui, — elle, — eux-mêmes, — elles-mêmes. Penses-tu à moi ? Je pense à toi. Je pense à vous, — à elles, — à eux. Je n'ai pas pensé à toi, mon pauvre enfant. L'homme inconstant ne ressemble jamais à lui-même. Nous nous souvenons (*we remember*) de vous, — de lui, — d'elles, — d'eux. Envoyez-moi de l'argent. Sans moi, elle serait tombée. Je suis plus grand que toi, — que lui, — qu'elle. Qui a été ici, lui ou elle ? Venez avec moi, — avec nous. Joue avec lui. Jouez avec elles. On parle de nous. Tu parles de lui et d'elle. Nous parlons souvent (*often*) de vous. Je défends mon honneur moi-même. L'aimant attire le fer à soi. Nous nous moquons (*we mock at*) d'eux. Ah ! vous vous moquez de nous !

THEME 24.

1. My brother and I (we) have heard the noise. 2. Who will have the ball, thou or he ? 3. Who has broken the stick ? 4. Not I ! 5. You and he, (you) were not attentive. 6. She and Emily have gone out. 7. Who has gone out with them ? 8. Come with me. 9. Come to our house (*chez nous*). 10. Who speaks of me ? 11. I speak of you. 12. You speak of her and of her sister. 13. For whom is the medicine ? 14. It (*elle*) is for yourself. 15. Does she live with you ? 16. She lives with us. 17. He is older than I. 18. I think of (*à*) you. 19. You do not think of me. 20. You always* think of yourself. 21. One must not (*il ne faut pas*) always think of one's self. 22. Have you brought the book yourself ? 23. Yes, I myself. 24. Does she play with us ? 25. She plays with them (*m.*) 26. Is it himself ? 27. Yes, it is himself. 28. It is I ; it is not he.

CONVERSATION.

Qui a dit cela ?	Moi. — Lui. — Elle.
Qui vient là ?	C'est nous.
Pensez-vous à vos amis ?	Je pense souvent à eux.

* In French, the adverb usually follows the verb.

Est-elle tombée ?	Heureusement non ! mais sans moi elle serait tombée.
Pour qui sont ces bottes ?	Elles sont pour moi.
A qui pensez-vous ?	Je pense à vous et à votre mère.
De qui parle-t-on ?	On parle d'eux, — d'elles.
Qui a apporté cette corbeille ?	Ma sœur elle-même.
Qui a fait cela ?	Ni lui, ni elle, ni nous, ni eux.
Est-elle arrivée seule ?	Non, elle est arrivée avec moi.
Qui a écrit (*written*) cette lettre ?	Mon père lui-même.
Que fait l'aimant ?	Il attire le fer à soi.
Qui a battu cet enfant ?	Ce n'est pas moi, c'est Léopold.
Qui est venu avec toi ?	Mon amie Jules.
Où demeure-t-il ?	Il demeure chez son oncle.
Est-ce vous qui avez perdu cet argent ?	Non, ce n'est pas moi, c'est ma cousine Emilie.

READING LESSON.

LE ROSIER. (*The rose-bush.*)

"Qui veut (*will*) me donner un petit arbre pour mon jardin ?" disait Frédéric à ses frères et à sa sœur.

Leur père leur (*them*) avait donné à chacun un petit coin de terre à planter.

"Ce n'est pas moi !" dit Auguste. — "Ni moi !" s'écria Louis. — "Ce sera moi !" dit la bonne Charlotte ; "de quelle espèce le (*it*) veux-tu ?"

"Je voudrais (*I should like*) avoir un rosier," répondit Frédéric ; "le mien est tout jauni."

"C'est bon," répliqua Charlotte. Puis elle prit (*then she took*) une pelle et alla (*went*) le retirer de terre.

"Que vois-je (*what do I see*) ?" dit Frédéric, "tu *n*'en as toi-même *que* (*only*) deux, et encore (*besides*) il y en a un si petit ! Du moins ne me donne pas le plus grand."

"Non, non!" s'écria sa sœur, "il pourrait encore (*could again*) se sécher; je puis jouir du plaisir de le voir fleurir dans ton jardin."

(*To be continued.*)

Chacun, e, each.
un petit coin de terre, a corner of land.
ni moi, nor I either.
s'écrier, to call out, to cry.
l'espèce, f. the sort, kind.
le mien, mine. *tout*, quite.
jauni, e, yellow, withered.
répliquer, to reply.
puis, then.
la pelle, the spade.
retirer, to take out.
du moins, at least.
sécher, to dry.
se sécher, to get dry, to wither.
je puis, I can (from *pouvoir*).
jouir, to enjoy. *voir*, to see.

XXV. VINGT-CINQUIÈME LEÇON.

CONJUNCTIVE PERSONAL PRONOUNS.

These are *je* (I), *nous* (we), *tu* (thou), *vous* (you), *il* (he), plu. *ils* (they, m.), *elle* (she), plu. *elles* (they, f.).*

Unlike the disjunctive personal pronouns, these, except *vous* and *nous*, vary to express different cases.

Je has *me* when used either as the direct or indirect object of the verb: *tu* has *te* in the same cases.

Of him, of her, of them, of it (m. or f.), are each represented by the pronoun *en*, generally referring to things: to him, to her, each by *lui*: to them (m. or f.), by *leur*.

The objective case (direct object) of *il*, is *le* (him), and of *elle*, is *la*, (her): *les* (them) is the obj. plu. of both genders.

POSITION OF CONJUNCTIVE PRONOUNS.

General Rule. Conjunctive pronouns precede the verb except in the Imperative affirmative. In the interrogative form the subject comes after the verb.

* For *on*, of which *se* is used as the object and *soi* as the disjunctive, see Part II. L. XII.

SPECIAL RULES.

A. WITH ONE PRONOUN.

1. The nominative cases *je*, *tu*, *il*, *elle*, *nous*, *vous*, *ils*, or *elles*, usually precede the verb of which they are the subject: in an interrogative sentence, however, they are placed immediately after the verb. Ex.: —

Je pense, I think.
tu espères, thou hopest.
nous parlons, we speak.
vous jouez, you play.

Interrogative:

Finis-tu, dost thou finish?
Vient-elle, does she come?

2. The direct and indirect objects are placed immediately before the verb in a simple tense, and before the auxiliary in a compound one. Ex.: —

Tu me dis, you tell me.
Je vous donne, I give you.
Elle m'a répondu, she has answered me.
Charles nous a dit, Charles has told us.

3. If the sentence is negative, *ne* is put directly after the subject, before the governed pronoun, as:

Je ne vous donne pas, I do not give you.
Vous ne les avez pas vus, you have not seen them.
Elle ne m'a pas répondu, she has not answered me.
Charles ne nous avait pas dit, Charles had not told us.

4. In the interrogative form, the object begins the sentence, then follows the verb with its subject. If the question is a negative one, *ne* begins the sentence:

Me connaissez-vous, do you know me?
Me blâme-t-il, does he blame me?
Les vois-tu, do you see them?
Vous a-t-il répondu, has he answered you?
Ne vous a-t-il pas répondu, has he not answered you?

5. When the verb is in the Imperative affirmative, the governed pronouns are put after it, in French as in English. In this case *me*

and *te* are changed into ***moi*** and ***toi*** for the direct and indirect objects. Ex.: —

Donnez-moi, give me. *Apportez-lui*, bring (to) him.
Mangez-les, eat them. *Parlez-leur*, speak to them.

6. But when the Imperative is negative, the governed pronoun precedes the verb. Ex.: —

Ne me donnez pas, do not give me.
Ne lui apportez pas, do not bring him.
Ne les mangez pas, do not eat them.
Ne leur parlez pas, do not speak to them.

B. WITH TWO PRONOUNS.

1. When a verb, which is not in the Imperative affirmative, governs two pronouns, they are both placed immediately before the verb, so that the indirect object comes first, and the direct follows. Ex.: —

Je te le donne, I give it to thee (you).
Vous l'apporte-t-elle, does she bring it to you?
Ne nous l'apportera-t-il pas, will he not bring it to us?
On vous le dira, they will tell (it) you.
On ne vous le dira pas, they will not tell (it to) you.

2. An exception to the foregoing rule are the two indirect objects, *lui* (to him, to her), and *leur* (to them), which always follow the other governed pronoun. Ex.: —

Je le lui donne, I give it to him *or* her.
Je ne le lui donne pas, I do not give it him.
La lui donne-t-elle, does she give it him?
La leur donnera-t-il, will he give it to them?
Je ne la leur ai pas donné, I have not given it to them.
Ne le lui donnez pas, do not give it him.
Pourquoi ne la leur prêtez-vous pas, why do you not lend it to them?

3. Of two personal pronouns governed by the Imperative affirmative the indirect object always stands last:

Donnez-le-moi, give it me.
Apportez-les-lui (leur), bring them to him (to them).

4. If the Imperative is negative, both of them precede the verb

according to § 6, and *lui* and *leur* follow the direct object, according to B, § 2. Ex.: —

Ne me le donnez pas, do not give it me.
Ne la lui apportez pas, do not bring it to him.
Ne les leur envoyez pas, do not send them to them.

VOCABULARY.

Pardonner (à),* to pardon.
prêter (à), to lend.
récompenser, to reward.
corriger, to correct.
écouter, to listen to.
la vérité, the truth.
tailler, to cut, mend.
louer, to praise; to let.
accompagner, to accompany.
je promets, I promise.
l'histoire, *f.* history.
volontiers, willingly.

READING EXERCISE 25.

Je vous entends. Il me pardonnera. Elle m'a pardonné. Alfred m'a prêté un livre amusant. Prêtez-moi votre livre. Je vous le prêterai. Il me le donne. Tu me l'as donné. Elle me les donnerait, si elle les avait encore. Vous a-t-il pardonné? Lui as-tu dit (*told*) cela? Je le lui ai dit. Leur a-t-on répondu? Appelez ces écoliers. Je les récompenserai; je leur donnerai de belles images. Tu les leur donneras demain. Ne te loue pas toi-même. On ne se loue pas soi-même. Elle ne vous écoute pas. Elle ne m'a pas écouté. Nous écoutera-t-il? Vous ne me dites pas la vérité. Je vous la dis. Cette plume est trop molle; voulez-vous avoir la bonté (*kindness*) de me la tailler? Je vous la taillerai volontiers.

THEME 25.

1. I praise thee. 2. Thou praisest me. 3. Do you play? 4. Do you hear? 5. Do you hear me? 6. I hear you. 7. I do not sell my house. 8. I do not sell it. 9. Do you sell your horses? 10. I do not sell them. 11. We hear thee. 12. I call him. 13. Will you accompany me? 14. My father will accompany you.

* This mark (à) denotes that the verb after which it is placed takes an *indirect personal* object.

15. Have you mended my pen? 16. I have mended it. 17. Lend me a pencil. 18. Lend him a pen. 19. Do not give him my book. 20. Do not give it him. 21. I promise you. 22. I promise it [to] you. 23. Tell (*dites-*) him (to him). 24. Tell them. 25. Tell it him. 26. Do not tell it [to] them. 27. I should give you some money, if you were more industrious. 28. Has she given him the gloves? 29. She has given them to him. 30. She has not given them to him; she has given them to his brother. 31. Your translation is badly done (*mal faite*); correct it (*fem.*). 32. Pardon (me) my mistakes. 33. Have you corrected them? 34. Yes, I have (corrected them).

CONVERSATION.

M'entendez-vous?	Oui, je vous entends.
Ne m'entendez-vous pas?	Je ne vous ai pas entendu.
Me pardonnerez-vous?	Je ne vous pardonnerai pas.
De qui avez-vous reçu ce livre amusant?	C'est Alfred qui me l'a prêté.
Voulez-vous prêter ce livre à ma sœur?	Je le lui prêterai volontiers.
Qui veut cette plume?	Donnez-la-moi, s'il vous plaît (*if you please*).
Les aimez-vous?	Oui, je les aime beaucoup.
Dites-vous la vérité?	Je la dis toujours.
Qui vous accompagnera?	Mon cousin m'accompagnera jusqu'à (*as far as*) Bruxelles.
Vous a-t-on raconté (*told*) une histoire?	Oui, notre grand'mère nous a raconté une très-belle histoire.

READING LESSON.

SUITE DU ROSIER.

Frédéric, transporté de joie, emporta le rosier; et Charlotte le suivit plus joyeuse encore que lui.

Le jardinier avait vu le trait d'amitié de la petite fille. Il alla chercher (*he went for*) un beau sureau d'Espagne.

"Voulez-vous que je mette (*put*) ceci à la place de votre rosier?" demanda-t-il à Charlotte.

"Si vous n'en avez pas besoin."

"Non," répondit-il, "je n'en ai pas besoin." —Il le planta.

Le mois de Mai suivant, le rosier de Frédéric porta les plus belles roses, et tous les matins, Charlotte recevait un bouton à moitié ouvert, pour le mettre dans ses cheveux.

Le sureau prit (*took*) racine aussi et devint (*became*) bientôt si grand et si épais que Charlotte y trouva de l'ombrage dans la grande chaleur du jour.

Transporté, enraptured.
emporter, to carry off.
le suivit, followed him.
joyeux, joyful.
le trait, the trait.
l'amitié, friendship.
un sureau d'Espagne, a lilac-tree.
ceci, this.
demander, to ask.
un bouton, a bud.
la moitié, half.
ouvert, open, opened.
la racine, the root.
bientôt, soon.
l'ombrage, the shade.
la chaleur, the heat.

XXVI. VINGT-SIXIÈME LEÇON.

DEMONSTRATIVE PRONOUNS.

1. These are:

masculine.	feminine.
Celui,	*celle*, that.
pl. *ceux*,	*celles*, those.
celui-ci,	*celle-ci*, this, the latter.
pl. *ceux-ci*,	*celles-ci*, these.
celui-là,	*celle-là*, that (one), the former.
pl. *ceux-là*,	*celles-là*, those.

2. The pronouns *he*, *she*, *they*, preceding a relative, must be translated by *celui*, *celle*, *ceux*, *celles*. Ex.: *celui qui*, he who; *celle qui*, she who; *ceux qui*, *celles qui*, they who.

3. *Celui, celle, ceux, celles,* are used with the preposition *de*, instead of the English possessive case, when the governing noun is not expressed. Ex.: *mon chapeau et celui de mon frère,* my hat and my brother's; *ma plume et celle de ma sœur,* my pen and my sister's.

REMARK. *Celui, celle, &c.*, are used only before a relative or the preposition *de;* in all other cases *celui-ci, celle-ci, celui-la, celle-la, &c.*, must be used. Ex.: *J'ai celui-ci, je n'ai pas celui-la,* I have this one, I have not that one.

4. *Ce,* which we have seen as an adjective, is also a pronoun. It is then invariable, meaning *this, that, it.* — It is used before the relative, as: *ce qui* (subj.), *ce que* (obj.), that which (what); *ce dont,* that of which.

For the use of *ce* or *il* before the verb to be, see Rule after the vocabulary of Lesson XV. See also Lesson XXIV. 3.

5. The compounds of *ce, ceci,* this, and *cela,* that, are used absolutely, without reference to any particular noun.

Ex.: *Je ne veux pas ceci, je veux cela.*
I do not want this, I want that.

Ce que je dis, what I say.
Que dites-vous de cela, what do you say of that?
Est-ce là votre plume, is this your pen?
C'est ma plume, that is my pen.
Sont-ce là vos gants, are these your gloves?
Ce sont mes gants, these are my gloves.

6. In place of *de* and *à* with *ce, ceci, cela, ceux-ci,* and *ceux-là,* two other conjunctive pronouns are used, viz.: *en* and *y.* *En* is rendered in English by *some, of it, of them, about it, about them, etc.* *Y* corresponds to the English *to it, to them, in it, in them, there, therein, etc.* Ex.: —

Voici du jambon: en voulez-vous?
Here is ham, will you have some?

J'en prendrai un petit morceau.
I shall take a little piece of it.

Votre père est-il au jardin? —— *Oui, il y est.*
Is your father in the garden? Yes, he is there.

J'y vais aussi, I am going there also.

Donnez-m'en — donnez-lui-en.

Give me some — give him some.

Y penses-tu, do you think of that?

Je lui en ai donné, I have given him some of them (it).

VOCABULARY.

Le porte-feuille, the pocket-book.
la peur, fear.
l'âme, the soul.
la noblesse, nobility.
le corps, the body.
commode, comfortable.
le conquérant, the conqueror.
jaune, yellow.
joli, e, nice, pretty.
le commerce, the commerce.
la récompense, the reward.
bénir, to bless.
persécuter, to persecute.
souhaiter, to wish.
enrichir, to enrich.
l'agriculture, f. agriculture.
également, equally.
tout de suite, directly.
promet, promises.

READING EXERCISE 26.

Voici mon porte-feuille et celui de mon père. Voici mes gants et ceux de ma sœur. Voulez-vous ceux-ci ou ceux-là? Celui qui remplit ses devoirs est un honnête homme. Voulez-vous ceci ou cela? Ceux qui sont contents, sont toujours heureux. Heureux celui qui trouve un vrai ami! Je préfère la noblesse de l'âme à celle de la naissance (*birth*). On croit (*believes*) ce qu'on espère. Ce que vous dites me fait peur. Qui vient là? C'est moi. — Ce sont eux. Ce qui est beau n'est pas toujours utile. Ne parlez pas de ce qui ne vous regarde (*concern*) pas. Alexandre-le-Grand et Jules César furent de grands conquérants; celui-là mourut dans sa jeunesse, celui-ci fut assassiné (*murdered*).

THEME 26.

1. Here is your hat and your brother's. 2. I shall sell my house and my uncle's. 3. We speak of these, you speak of those. 4. Give me that one. 5. This is my pen. 6. These (*ce*) are your pencils. 7. Is this the garden of your aunt? 8. Are these the shoes

of your sister? 9. No, these are the shoes of my cousin Eliza. 10. This ink (*cette encre-ci*) is blacker than that. 11. These gloves are white, those are yellow. 12. I prefer the beauty of the soul to that (*f.*) of the body. 13. Agriculture and commerce are equally useful to man; the former nourishes us, the latter enriches us. 14. My mother prefers this house to that; this is smaller, but that is more comfortable. 15. Have you (any) butter? 16. Yes, I have some. 17. Give me some. 18. Here is black cloth. 19. I shall take ten yards *of it* (*j'en prendrai . . .*). 20. Were you at the theatre yesterday? 21. Yes, I was *there*. 22. Is your master in that room? 23. Yes, he is there.

XXVII. VINGT-SEPTIÈME LEÇON.

INTERROGATIVE PRONOUNS.

They are: 1. *lequel* f. *laquelle*, which (of)? 2. *qui*, who? *que* and *quoi*, what?

1. *Lequel* is used either without a noun, or is at least separated from it by *de;* but it agrees with it in gender and number. When the pronoun *which* is used interrogatively, it is always expressed by *lequel*, *laquelle*, *etc.*, as:—

> *Voici deux appartements, lequel choisirez-vous?*
> Here are two apartments, which will you choose?
>
> *Une de ses sœurs est mariée. Laquelle est-ce?*
> One of his sisters is married. Which is it?
>
> *Laquelle de vos écolières est malade?*
> Which of your pupils is ill?

The same contractions take place in the article *le* compounded with *quel*, as when used by itself: thus, by contraction with the prepositions *à* and *de*, are formed *auquel*, *auxquels*, *auxquelles*, *duquel*, *desquels*, and *desquelles*.

2. The interrogative pronoun *qui?* is only used of persons. Ex.: —

Qui est là, who is there?
A qui prêtez-vous cela, to whom do you lend this?
Qui cherchez-vous, whom are you looking for?
Pour qui est ce crayon, for whom is this pencil?

3. *Whose*, when used interrogatively, must be rendered in French by *à qui*. Ex.: —

Whose book is this? *à qui est ce livre?*

4. *Que* and *quoi* are neuter.* *Quoi*, what, is disjunctive, and used either by itself or after a preposition, as: —

De quoi parlez-vous, of what are you speaking?
Sur quoi, upon what? *Avec quoi*, with what?

5. *Que*, what, is conjunctive, and is only used before verbs: it never follows a preposition. Ex.: —

Que voulez-vous, what do you wish *or* want?
Que dit-on, what do people say?
Que demande-t-il, what does he ask?

VOCABULARY.

Marié, e, married.
levé, got up, risen.
frapper, to strike, to beat.
le cahier, the copy-book.
la nièce, the niece.
le porte-plume, the penholder.

READING EXERCISE 27.

Lequel de vos fils est malade? Laquelle de vos sœurs est mariée? Lesquels de vos écoliers n'ont pas fait leurs thèmes? Voici plusieurs canifs: lequel voulez-vous acheter? Qui est arrivé? Qui a trouvé ma bourse? De qui avez-vous parlé? A qui est la grammaire que vous avez à la main? Que souhaitez-vous, Monsieur? Qu'avez-vous porté à la poste? Quoi! vous êtes déjà levé! A quoi pensez-vous donc? Auquel de ces écoliers avez-vous promis une récompense?

* The neuter gender is recognized as existing in French only by very few grammarians. But *que* and *quoi*, the pronoun *ce*, and sometimes *le*, are certainly neither masculine nor feminine.

THEME 27.

1. Which of your horses have you sold? 2. Which of these colors is the finest? 3. Which of my copy-books will you have? 4. To which of your nieces do you write (*écrivez-vous*) a letter? 5. Which of your pupils are the most diligent? 6. Here are several pictures, which will you choose? 7. Who is at (*à*) the door? 8. Whom do you love most (*le mieux*)? 9. From whom have you received this ring? 10. To whom do you speak? 11. To whom will you give this nice pen-holder? 12. What do you carry under your arm (*bras*)? 13. With what has he beaten the dog? 14. What! are you still (*encore*) in bed (*au lit*)?

CONVERSATION.

Lequel de ces deux porte-feuilles est à vous?	Celui que vous avez à la main.
Laquelle de ces deux robes préférez-vous?	Je préfère celle-ci à celle-la.
Est-ce là votre bague?	Oui, M—, c'est ma bague d'or.
Sont-ce là vos gants?	Non, M—, ce ne sont pas mes gants, ce sont ceux de ma cousine.
Avez-vous reçu ma lettre?	Je n'ai reçu ni la vôtre (*yours*) ni celle de votre père.
Le commerce est-il utile aux hommes?	Oui, très-utile; il les enrichit.
Quelle maison vendez-vous?	J'ai deux maisons à vendre, celle de mon oncle et celle de mon grand-père.
A qui donnerez-vous ce canif?	Je le donnerai à Guillaume.
Voici du jambon et du pain, en voulez-vous?	Merci, nous en avons déjà.
Avez-vouz apporté les verres?	Non, M—, je n'y ai pas pensé.
Madame votre mère est-elle à la maison (*or* chez elle)?	Oui, M—, elle y est.

XXVIII. VINGT-HUITIÈME LEÇON.

POSSESSIVE AND RELATIVE PRONOUNS.

1. The possessive pronouns are formed from the possessive adjectives *mon, ton, son, etc.* They are :—

SING.		PLUR.		
Masc.	*Fem.*	*Masc.*	*Fem.*	
le mien,	la mienne,	les miens,	les miennes,	*mine.*
le tien,	la tienne,	les tiens,	les tiennes,	*thine.*
le sien,	la sienne,	les siens,	les siennes,	*his, hers, its*
le nôtre,	la nôtre,	les nôtres,		*ours.*
le vôtre,	la vôtre,	les vôtres,		*yours.*
le leur,	la leur,	les leurs,		*theirs.*

These are not, as in English, of the same gender as the possessor. They agree in gender and number with the object possessed. Ex. :—

Cette dame a mon crayon et le sien.
That lady has my pencil and hers.
Avez-vous ma montre ou la vôtre?
Have you my watch or yours?
J'ai la mienne, I have mine.
Ma sœur a la sienne, my sister has hers.

2. The interrogative pronouns *qui, quoi,* and *lequel,* serve at the same time as *relative* pronouns, when they have a reference to some other noun or pronoun preceding.

3. As a relative *qui* is a subject and *que* the direct object. *Qui* and *que* are used for persons and things of both genders and numbers. Ex. :—

Un enfant qui pleure, a child that cries.
La porte qui est ouverte, the door which is open.
Le voyageur que j'ai quitté, the traveller whom I have left.
Le chapeau que j'ai acheté, the hat (which) I have bought.
Les maisons que vous avez vues, the houses (which) you have seen.

The relative *que,* whom, which, *or* that, is sometimes understood in English, but it must always be expressed in French.

4. *Dont*, whose, of which, is used for persons and things of both genders and numbers; but *de qui*, from whom or of whom, which is sometimes required instead of *dont*, has only reference to persons.

REMARK. When *dont* signifies *whose* the noun which it limits must be preceded by the article; if the noun is the object of a verb it must come after that verb, and not immediately after *dont* as in English. Ex.: —

Je connais la femme dont vous avez reçu la lettre.
I know the woman whose letter you have received.

Je connais la femme de qui vous avez reçu la lettre.
I know the woman from whom you have received the letter.

L'homme — les hommes dont vous parlez.
The man — the men of whom you speak.

La lettre — les lettres dont vous parlez.
The letter — the letters of which you speak.

5. After prepositions, *qui* refers to persons, *lequel*, to things and animals. Ex.: —

Le marchand avec qui j'ai voyage.
The merchant with whom I travelled. But:

L'arbre sur lequel (not *sur qui*) *je montai.*
The tree upon which I climbed.

La clef avec laquelle on ouvrit la porte.
The key with which they opened the door.

Voilà l'homme à qui j'ai prêté mon livre.
There is the man to whom I have lent my book.

C'est le chien auquel vous avez donné à manger.
That is the dog to which you gave to eat.

6. *Lequel, laquelle, etc.*, must also be used instead of *qui* in the Nominative, when the relative is separated from its noun by another substantive to which it might seem to relate. Ex.: —

La tante de mon ami laquelle demeure à Paris.
My friend's aunt who lives at Paris.
(*qui demeure à Paris* might relate to *mon ami.*)

7. *That which*, and *what*, meaning *the thing which*, are ex-

pressed by *ce qui* for the Nominative, and *ce que* for the Objective. *All that* is rendered: Nom. *tout ce qui*, Obj. *tout ce que*. Ex.:—

What renders men miserable, is cupidity.
Ce qui rend les hommes misérables, c'est la cupidité.

I like all that is fine, *j'aime tout ce qui est beau.*
Do what I tell you, *faites ce que je vous dis.*

VOCABULARY.

L'agrément, m. the comfort, pleasure.
le tigre, the tiger.
le talent, the talent.
l'amiral, the admiral.
la victoire, the victory.
le propriétaire, the owner.
les mœurs, f. the manners.
le repas, the meal.
célèbre, celebrated.
aussi, as.
négliger, to neglect.
inviter, to invite.
châtier, to chastise.
demeurer, to live.
vanter, to praise.
fertiliser, to fertilize.
déchirer, to tear.
gagner, to win, gain.
s'appelle, is called.
tout, adv. quite.
trop, adv. too much.
maintenant, — *à présent*, now.

READING EXERCISE 28.

Mon frère est aussi grand que le tien. Ma sœur est du même âge que la vôtre. Vos roses sont très-belles, mais elles sont moins belles que les miennes. Nos chiens sont aussi fidèles que les leurs. Chaque plante a sa propriété (*peculiarity*) ; la violette a la sienne, les roses ont les leurs. Le petit garçon dont le père est mort, demeure maintenant chez nous. Les mœurs des anciens peuples étaient trés-différentes des nôtres. La ville a ses agréments, et la campagne a les siens. Le marchand que vous avez vu hier chez moi, et chez qui demeure mon ami R., est parti pour Paris.

THEME 28.

1. Your house is finer than mine, but my garden is finer than yours. 2. I have read (*lu*) your letter and his. 3. Do you prefer your knife to mine? 4. Yes, I prefer mine to yours. 5. Which bonnet is thine? 6. Your rooms are more spacious (*grandes*) than

ours, but ours are higher. 7. I think (*trouve*) your garden very small. 8. I beg your pardon (*je vous demande pardon*), Sir, it is not smaller than yours; it is quite as (*aussi*) large as that of my neighbor. 9. Where is your pen and where is mine? 10. Which one? 11. That which I have made (*taillée*) this morning. 12. The man of whom you are speaking, is dead (*mort*). 13. Is this the book (which) you have lost? 14. No, it was a French book. 15. You speak of the lady whose husband (*le mari*) has been so ill. 16. The horse to which you have given some drink (*à boire*) is mine. 17. The window upon which you lean (*vous vous appuyez*) is broken.

CONVERSATION.

Trouvez-vous mon jardin plus grand que le vôtre?	Au contraire, je le trouve plus petit que le mien.
Est-il aussi plus petit que celui de votre tante?	Non, le sien est moins grand.
Comment s'appelle cet amiral qui a remporté la victoire de Trafalgar?	Le nom de ce célèbre amiral anglais est Nelson.
Que fait le tigre?	Il déchire la main qui le châtie.
Ta sœur est-elle plus âgée que la mienne?	Elle est plus jeune que la vôtre.
Quel âge a-t-elle donc?	Elle a onze ans et demi.
Avec quoi le voleur a-t-il ouvert (*opened*) la porte?	Il l'a ouverte avec une fausse clef.
Comment s'appelle le fleuve dont les eaux fertilisent l'Égypte?	Ce fleuve s'appelle le Nil.
Avez-vous réellement une bonne intention?	Je vous assure que mon intention est aussi bonne que la vôtre.

XXIX. VINGT-NEUVIÈME LEÇON.

INDEFINITE PRONOUNS.

1. These are used by themselves, without a noun. They are: —

On or *l'on*, one, they, people.
Chacun, f. *chacune*, each, every-one.
Aucun, f. *aucune* (with *ne*), none, not one.
Quelqu'un, f. *quelqu'une*, some one, somebody, anybody. pl. *quelques-uns*, f. *quelques-unes*, some.
Personne, (with *ne*), nobody.
L'un, e — l'autre, the one — the other, pl. *les uns (unes) — les autres*, the ones — the others.
L'un (l'une) et l'autre, both.
L'un (l'une) ou l'autre, either.
Ni l'un (l'une) ni l'autre, neither.
L'un (l'une) l'autre, — pl. *les uns (les unes) les autres*, each other, one another.
Un autre, f. *une autre*, another.
D'autres, pl. others, other people.
Autrui, others, another.
Tel, f. *telle*, many a man.
Plusieurs, several.
La plupart, most, followed by *de* with the def. art., as: *La plupart des hommes*, most men.
Quiconque, whoever.
Tout, f. *toute*, all, everything. pl. *tous*, *toutes*, all.
Quelque chose, f. something, anything: when followed by *de* and an adj. it is masc.
Rien (with *ne*), nothing.
Le, la même, the same.

2. *L'on* is used for euphony instead of *on* after *et*, *ou*, *où*, *si*, unless the next word begins with *l*; also after *que* if the next word begins with a *c* or *q*. Ex.; *si l'on voit*, if one sees; *et l'on dit*, and they say. But: *si on le voit*, not *si l'on le voit*.

L'on is also sometimes used after *mais*, *ni*, *qui*, and other vowel sounds.

3. Several of the indefinite adjectives have been enumerated here again among the indefinite pronouns, because they may be used as such, viz.: *aucun*, *plusieurs*, *tout*, and *le même*. Ex.: —

Combien de plumes avez-vous, how many pens have you?
Je n'en ai aucune, I have none.
J'en ai plusieurs, I have several.
Avez-vous appelé tous les enfants, have you called all the children?
Oui, je les ai appelés tous, yes, I have called them all.

4. When *personne* and *rien* are used by themselves, they do not take *ne*, but they retain their negative meaning, as:

Qui avez-vous rencontré? *Personne.*
Whom have you met? Nobody.

VOCABULARY.

Le défaut, the fault.
le verbe, the verb.
le camarade, the comrade.
la confiance, the confidence.
venu, come (*part. p.*).
méchant, e, naughty.
jaloux, -se, jealous.
régulier, -ère, regular.
rencontrer, to meet.
chanter, to sing.
blâmer, to blame.
rire, to laugh.
arriver, to arrive.
gâter, to spoil.
secourir, to assist.
nuire, to hurt, injure.
je veux, I will.
pourri, e, rotten.

READING EXERCISE 29.

On chante, on joue et l'on danse. Tout le monde veut (*wishes*) être heureux. Chacun veut avoir raison. L'un était riche, l'autre était pauvre; l'un et l'autre étaient malheureux. Les unes dansaient, les autres jouaient. Ne blâmez pas les travaux d'autrui. Avez-vous vu quelqu'un? Je n'ai vu personne. Nous avons quelque chose de meilleur. Tel rit aujourd'hui qui ne rira plus demain. Chacun a ses défauts. Tout le monde (*everybody*) a son faible (*weakness*). La plupart de ces pommes sont pourries. Ne savez-vous (*do you know*) rien de nouveau? Nous ne savons (*know*) rien. Nous n'avons rencontré personne. Quiconque salira ses cahiers, sera puni. Donnez-moi quelques-unes de vos belles poires. Quelques-uns de mes camarades sont malades.

THEME 29.

1. One is happy when one is contented. 2. They speak of peace (*de la paix*). 3. They say so (*le*). 4. Everybody likes him. 5. Every one thinks of himself (*à soi*). 6. Everybody has his [own] faults. 7. Somebody has told (*dit*) it to me. 8. Those apples are fine, I will take some. 9. Whoever knows (*connaît*) this man, has little (*peu de*) confidence in him. 10. Nobody knows that woman. 11. Henry thinks of (*à*) nobody. 12. (The) one arrives, the other sets out (*part*). 13. These two girls love one another. 14. I do not know them all, but I know several of them (*en*). 15. Most verbs are regular. 16. The princes were jealous of one another. 17. Will you have anything? 18. I thank you, I will have (*je ne veux*) nothing. 19. These people (*gens*) speak ill (*mal*) of one another (i. e. the one of the other).

CONVERSATION.

Que fait-on là?	On joue et l'on danse.
Qui a dit cela?	Tout le monde le dit.
Qui veut ce papier?	Chacun le veut.
Vos deux neveux sont-ils riches?	L'un est riche, l'autre est pauvre.
As-tu vu quelqu'un dans ce jardin?	Non, je n'y ai vu personne.
Qu'y a-t-il de nouveau?	Je ne sais (*know*) rien du tout (*at all*).
Où sont vos deux fils?	Ils sont partis tous les deux. (Ils sont partis l'un et l'autre.)
Voulez-vous quelque chose?	Non, merci; je ne veux rien.
Avez-vous retrouvé les lettres perdues?	J'en ai retrouvé quelques-unes; la plupart sont perdues.
Avec qui êtes-vous venu?	Je ne suis venu avec personne.
Qui est là?	Personne.
Avez-vous toutes les boîtes?	Je n'en ai aucune.

Comment étaient les princes?	Ils étaient jaloux l'un de l'autre (*or* les uns des autres.)
Avez-vous d'autres plumes?	Non, ce sont encore les mêmes.
Avez-vous rencontré quelqu'un?	Je n'ai rencontré personne.

READING LESSON.

PUISSANCE DE LA CONCORDE.

Un homme qui avait douze fils, les fit (*had them*) rassembler autour de son lit de mort, et comme (*as*) ils attendaient sa dernière bénédiction, il leur montra un faisceau de flèches et ordonna à chacun d'essayer de les rompre ainsi liées, toutes à la fois. Aucun d'eux ne put (*could*) y parvenir. Il leur dit ensuite de faire le même essai, en les prenant (*by taking them*) l'une après l'autre. Ils les rompirent de cette manière avec facilité. Le père les rendit alors attentifs à cet emblême du pouvoir de la concorde. "Observez, mes enfants," leur dit-il, "qu'aussi longtemps que vous resterez unis, personne ne pourra (*will be able*) vous vaincre."

Le pouvoir, the power, might.
rassembler, to assemble.
autour de, round, about.
le lit de mort, the death-bed.
la bénédiction, the blessing.
un faisceau, a bundle.
la flèche, the arrow.
rompre, to break.
ainsi lié, thus bound together.
à la fois, at once.
parvenir, to succeed.
ensuite, at length, finally.
l'essai, the attempt.
la facilité, (the) easiness.
alors, then.
l'emblême, the emblem.
unir, to unite.
vaincre, to conquer, vanquish.

XXX. TRENTIÈME LEÇON.

PASSIVE AND NEUTER VERBS.

1. Passive verbs are formed, in French as in English, by joining the Participle past of an active verb to the auxiliary verb *être*, to be; for instance, of the verb *donner*, the passive voice is *être donné*, to be given; of *finir*; *être fini*, to be finished, etc. The Participle past varies according to the gender and number of the noun or pronoun which stands as the nominative to the verb.

CONJUGATION OF A PASSIVE VERB.

INFINITIVE.

Etre loué, to be praised.

INDICATIVE.

PRESENT TENSE.

Je suis loué *or* louée, *I am praised.*
tu es loué *or* louée, *thou art praised.*
il est loué, *he is praised.*
elle est louée, *she is praised.*
nous sommes loués *or* louées, *we are praised.*
vous êtes loués *or* louées, *you are praised.*
ils sont loués, } *they are praised.*
elles sont louées, }

IMPERFECT.

J'étais loué *or* louée, *I was praised, etc.*

PRETERITE.

Je fus loué *or* louée, *I was praised, etc.*

FUTURE.

Je serai loué *or* louée, *I shall be praised, etc.*

CONDITIONAL.

Je serais loué *or* louée, *I should be praised, etc.*

IMPERATIVE.

Sois loué *or* louée, *be praised.*
soyons loués *or* louées, *let us be praised.*
soyez loués *or* louées, *be praised.*

SUBJUNCTIVE.

PRESENT.

Que je sois loué *or* louée, *that I (may) be praised, etc.*

IMPERFECT.

Que je fusse loué *or* louée, *that I (might) be praised, etc.*

PARTICIPLE.

Étant loué *or* louée, *being praised.*

COMPOUND TENSES.

INFINITIVE.

Avoir été loué, e, *to have been praised.*

INDICATIVE.

COMPOUND OF THE PRESENT.

J'ai été loué, e, *I have been praised, etc.*

COMPOUND OF THE IMPERFECT.

J'avais été loué, e, *I had been praised, etc.*

COMPOUND OF THE PRETERITE.

J'eus été loué, e, *I had been praised, etc.*

COMPOUND OF THE FUTURE.

J'aurai été loué, e, *I shall have been praised, etc.*

CONDITIONAL.

J'aurais été loué, e,
J'eusse été loué, e, } ***I should* or *I would have been praised, etc.***

SUBJUNCTIVE.

COMPOUND OF THE PRESENT.

Que j'aie été loué, e, *that I (may) have been praised, etc.*

COMPOUND OF THE IMPERFECT.

Que j'eusse été loué, e, *that I (might) have been praised.*

PARTICIPLE.

Ayant été loué, e, *having been praised.*

2. The English preposition *by*, with the passive voice, is to be rendered by *de*, when the verb denotes a sentiment or an inward act of soul, and by *par*, when it expresses an outward action. Ex.: He is esteemed by everybody, *Il est estimé de tout le monde;* the city of Troy was taken by the Greeks, *La ville de Troie fut prise par les Grecs.*

NEUTER VERBS.

3. There are about six hundred neuter verbs in French, of which about five hundred and fifty are conjugated with *avoir* in the compound tenses. Of the remainder, some take either *être* or *avoir*, according as the idea expressed is condition or state, or action.

4. The following neuter verbs *invariably require être:*

Aller, to go.
arriver, to arrive, to happen.
choir, to fall (rarely used).
décéder, to dcease.
éclore, to hatch.
mourir, to die.
naître, to be born.
tomber, to fall.
venir, to come.
devenir, to become.
intervenir, to intervene.
parvenir, to succeed.
provenir, to arise.
revenir, to come back.
survenir, to happen.

Examples:

COMPOUND OF THE PRESENT.

Je suis arrivé *or* arrivée, *I have (am) arrived.*
tu es arrivé *or* arrivée, *etc.*

COMPOUND OF THE IMPERFECT.

J'étais arrivé *or* arrivée, *I had arrived, etc.*

COMPOUND OF THE FUTURE.

Je serai arrivé *or* arrivée, *I shall have arrived, etc.*

CONDITIONAL.

Je serais arrivé *or* arrivée, *I should have arrived, etc.*

5. Accourir, cesser, croître, déchoir, dégénérer, descendre, disparaître, échapper, échoir, empirer, entrer, grandir, monter, partir, passer, périr, rester, sortir, vieillir, and a few others, are conjugated with *avoir* when it is the *action* or *fact*, with *être* when it is the *state* or *condition* expressed by the verb, which is uppermost in the mind. Ex.: *La rivière a monté rapidement*, the river has risen rapidly. *Il est monté*, he has (is) gone up.

VOCABULARY.

La bataille, the battle.
la loi, law.
le voleur, the thief.
le voyageur, the traveller.
le flatteur, the flatterer.
la langue, the language.
la cour, the court.
le chemin, the road.
vertueux, -se, virtuous.
inconnu, unknown.
rester, to remain.
tuer, to kill.
enragé, mad.
offenser, to offend.
envoyer, to send.
mordre, to bite.
blesser, to wound.
démolir, to demolish.
rebâtir, to rebuild.
maltraiter, to treat ill, abuse.
enlever, to take away.
sauver, to save.
attaquer, to attack.
assassiné, murdered.
parce que, because.

READING EXERCISE 30.

Mon fils Théodore est aimé et loué de ses maîtres, parce qu'il est appliqué et attentif. Gustave Adolphe, roi de Suède, fut tué à la bataille de Lutzen, à l'âge de trente-sept ans. Si vous êtes vertueux, vous serez aimés et estimés de tout le monde. Ayez soin que les lois soient ponctuellement observées. Quiconque les transgresse, sera puni. Le soldat qui a été blessé, est mort. La maison qui a été démolie, a été rebâtie. Ce pauvre chien est bien maltraité par son maître. Hier je fus attaqué par un voleur. Mon argent, ma montre, tout me fut enlevé. Deux des voyageurs sont restés en chemin; ils ne sont pas encore arrivés.

THEME 30.

1. I am loved by my parents. 2. Mr. Bell is esteemed by everybody. 3. The French language is spoken at all the courts of Europe. 4. Charles was bitten by a mad dog. 5. That dog must (*doit*) be killed. 6. This ring was given me by my grandfather. 7. By whom was this letter written (*écrite*)? 8. It was written by a little boy. 9. Frederic has been punished by his teacher. 10. Have you been invited to the ball? 11. No, sir, I have not been invited. 12. I shall perhaps (*peut-être*) be invited to-morrow. 13. This letter must be sent to the post-office. 14. Flatterers are not esteemed. 15. The child has not been saved. 16. It would have been saved, if it had cried for help (*au secours*). 17. The castle was built in the year 1620. 18. Those brave soldiers will be praised and rewarded. 19. Will Mr. B.'s garden be sold? 20. It is already sold.

CONVERSATION.

Etes-vous aimés de vos amis?	Nous avons toujours été aimés de tous nos amis.
Croyez-vous que mes ordres soient exécutés?	Je ne le crois pas.
Par qui as-tu été offensé?	Par un homme inconnu.
Les bons rois sont-ils aimés?	Ils sont toujours aimés et estimés.
Ces objets seront-ils vendus?	Non, M—, ils ne seront pas vendus.
Par qui Henri IV fut-il assassiné (*murdered*)?	Il fut assassiné par Ravaillac.
Dans quelle année?	Henri IV. fut assassiné en 1610.
Quel fut le sort de Charles X?	Ce roi fut exilé (*banished*) de France en 1830.
Par qui ces jeunes gens ont-ils été blâmés?	Je crois qu'ils ont été blâmés par leur maître.

La bataille de Leipsic fut-elle sanglante (*bloody*) ?	Très-sanglante. Beaucoup de soldats et d'officiers furent tués, et encore (*still*) un plus grand nombre furent blessés.
Voyez cette pauvre fille ! Qu'a-t-elle donc ?	Elle a été mordue par un chien enragé.
N'a-t-on pas tué ce chien ?	On ne l'a pas encore tué, mais il sera tué tout de suite.
Que va-t-on (*are they going*) faire de cette vieille maison ?	Elle sera démolie et puis rebâtie à neuf (*anew*).
Avez-vous bien dormi ?	Non, je n'ai pas bien dormi.

XXXI. TRENTE ET UNIÈME LEÇON.

REFLECTIVE VERBS.

Some verbs are called reflective, because their subject and object are the same person or thing, so that the subject acts upon itself, and is, at the same time, the agent and the object of the action. Reflective verbs, therefore, have always, besides the subject, another personal pronoun, viz. : *me*, *te*, *se*, myself, thyself, himself, herself, itself, for the singular ; *nous*, *vous*, *se*, ourselves, yourselves, themselves, for the plural. But it frequently happens that in English the second pronoun is only implied, whereas it must be expressed in French. Ex. : to repent, *se repentir ;* Pres. I repent, *je me repens, etc.*

Observe that all reflective verbs, without exception, are conjugated with the auxiliary *être*, as : I have hurt myself, *je me suis blessé*, and not *je m'ai blessé*.

The conjugation of the following verb may serve as a model for all the reflective verbs.

Se réjouir, *to rejoice.*

INDICATIVE.

PRESENT TENSE.

Je me réjouis, *I rejoice.*
tu te réjouis, *thou rejoicest.*
il (elle) se réjouit, *he (she) rejoices.*
nous nous réjouissons, *we rejoice.*
vous vous réjouissez, *you rejoice.*
ils (elles) se réjouissent, *they rejoice.*

IMPERFECT.

Je me réjouissais, *I rejoiced, etc.*

PRETERITE.

Je me réjouis, *I rejoiced, etc.*

FUTURE.

Je me réjouirai, *I shall rejoice, etc.*

CONDITIONAL.

Je me réjouirais, *I should rejoice, etc.*

IMPERATIVE.

Réjouis-toi, *rejoice.*
réjouissons-nous, *let us rejoice.*
réjouissez-vous, *rejoice.*

SUBJUNCTIVE.

PRESENT.

Que je me réjouisse, *that I (may) rejoice, etc.*

IMPERFECT.

Que je me réjouisse, *that I (might) rejoice, etc.*

PARTICIPLE.

Se (me, te, etc.) réjouissant, *rejoicing.*

COMPOUND TENSES.

INFINITIVE.

S'être réjoui, e, *to have rejoiced.*

INDICATIVE.

COMPOUND OF THE PRESENT.

Je me suis réjoui, e, *I have rejoiced.*
tu t'es réjoui, e, *thou hast rejoiced.*
il s'est réjoui, *he has rejoiced.*
elle s'est réjouie, *she has rejoiced.*
nous nous sommes réjouis, ies, *we have rejoiced.*
vous vous êtes réjoui(s), ie(s), *you have rejoiced.*
ils se sont réjouis, } *they have rejoiced.*
elles se sont réjouies, }

COMPOUND OF THE IMPERFECT.

Je m'étais réjoui, e, *I had rejoiced.*
tu t'étais réjoui, e, *thou hadst rejoiced, etc.*

COMPOUND OF THE PRETERITE.

Je me fus réjoui, e, *I had rejoiced.*
tu te fus réjoui, e, *etc.*

COMPOUND OF THE FUTURE.

Je me serai réjoui, e, *I shall have rejoiced.*
tu te seras réjoui, e, *etc.*

CONDITIONAL.

Je me serais réjoui, e, *I should have rejoiced.*
tu te serais réjoui, e, *etc.*

SUBJUNCTIVE.

COMPOUND OF THE PRESENT.

Que je me sois réjoui, e, *that I (may) have rejoiced.*
que tu te sois réjoui, e, *etc.*
qu'il se soit réjoui, (qu'elle se soit réjouie), *etc.*

COMPOUND OF THE IMPERFECT.

Que je me fusse réjoui, e, *that I (might) have rejoiced.*
que tu te fusses réjoui, e, *etc.*

PARTICIPLE.

S'étant (m'étant, etc.) réjoui, e, *having rejoiced.*

WITH INTERROGATION.

PRESENT.

(Me réjouis-je), *better:* est-ce que je me réjouis, *do I rejoice?*
te réjouis-tu (*or* est-ce que tu te réjouis), *dost thou rejoice?*
se réjouit-il (*or* est-ce qu'il se réjouit)? *etc.*
nous réjouissons-nous? *etc.*
vous réjouissez-vous? *etc.*
se réjouissent-ils (elles)? *etc.*

COMPOUND OF THE PRESENT.

Me suis-je réjoui, e, *have I rejoiced?*
t'es-tu réjoui, e, *hast thou rejoiced?*
s'est-il réjoui, *has he rejoiced?*
s'est-elle réjouie, *has she rejoiced?*
nous sommes-nous réjouis, ies, *have we rejoiced?*

WITH NEGATION.

PRESENT.

Je ne me réjouis pas, *I do not rejoice.*
tu ne te réjouis pas, *etc.*
il (elle) ne se réjouit pas, *etc.*
nous ne nous réjouissons pas, *etc.*

COMPOUND OF THE PRESENT.

Je ne me suis pas réjoui, e, *I have not rejoiced.*
tu ne t'es pas réjoui, e, *etc.*
il (elle) ne s'est pas réjoui, e, *etc.*
nous ne nous sommes pas réjouis, ies, *etc.*

IMPERATIVE.

Ne te réjouis pas, *do not rejoice.*
ne nous réjouissons pas, *let us not rejoice.*
ne vous réjouissez pas, *do not rejoice.*

INFINITIVE.

Ne pas se réjouir, *not to rejoice.*
ne pas s'être réjoui, e, *not to have rejoiced.*

WITH NEGATION AND INTERROGATION.

PRESENT.

Est-ce que je ne me réjouis pas, *do I not rejoice?*
ne te réjouis-tu pas, *dost thou not rejoice?*
ne se réjouit-il pas, *does he not rejoice? etc.*

COMPOUND OF THE PRESENT.

Ne me suis-je pas réjoui, e, *have I not rejoiced?*
ne t'es-tu pas réjoui, e? *etc.*
ne s'est-il (-elle) pas réjoui, e? *etc.*
ne nous sommes-nous pas réjouis, ies? *etc.*

Many verbs, neuter or passive in English, have in French the reflective form. The principal are: —

S'affliger, *to be sorry.*
s'apercevoir, *to perceive.*
s'approcher, *to come near.*
s'arrêter, *to stop.*
s'asseoir, *to sit down.*
se baisser, *to stoop.*
se coucher, *to go to bed.*
se dépêcher, *to make haste.*
s'écrier, *to exclaim, cry out.*
s'en aller, *to go away.*
s'endormir, *to fall asleep.*
s'enrhumer, *to catch cold.*
s'entretenir, *to discourse with.*
s'étonner, *to wonder.*
s'éveiller, *to awake.*
se fier, *to trust.*
se figurer, s'imaginer, } *to fancy.*
se hâter, se dépêcher, } *to make haste.*
se lever, *to rise, to get up.*
se marier, *to marry.*
se moquer, *to mock, scoff.*
se plaindre, *to complain.*
se promener, *to take a walk.*
se repentir, *to repent.*
se reposer, *to rest.*
se soumettre, *to submit.*
se souvenir, *to remember.*
se taire, *to be silent.*
se tromper, *to be mistaken.*
se vanter, *to boast.*

Ex. — I rise, I get up, *je me lève.*
I have risen *or* got up, *je me suis levé.*
We have perceived, *nous nous sommes aperçus, etc.*

Observe also these expressions: —

How are you, *comment vous portez-vous?*
I am well, *je me porte bien.*
I am mistaken, *je me trompe.*
I have been mistaken, *je me suis trompé.*
He is silent, *il se tait.*

VOCABULARY.

La conduite, the behavior.
la forêt, the forest.
le boulet, the ball.
le titre, the right.
la Bohème, Bohemia.
vaillamment, bravely.
fondre, to cast.
bien, well; *mieux*, better.
se venger de, to revenge on.
se conduire, to behave.

tard, late.
le mal, the evil.
se rendre, to surrender.
se coucher, to go to bed.
se distinguer, to distinguish.
enfermer, to shut in.
sauver, to save.

READING EXERCISE 31.

Vous vous trompez, Monsieur. Je me suis trompé aussi. Il y a (*it is*) très-longtemps que nous ne nous (*each other*) sommes vus. Le général Ostermann s'est distingué beaucoup à l'affaire (*battle*) de Culm. S'il ne s'était pas défendu si vaillamment, l'armée alliée aurait été enfermée dans les montagnes de la Bohème.

Dans une bataille où les boulets ennemis volaient (*flew*) autour de lui, Napoléon s'écria : Le boulet qui doit (*is to*) me tuer, n'est pas encore fondu (*cast*). Pourquoi vous êtes-vous levé si tard ? Je me suis levé à sept heures. Ne vous affligez pas tant, mes amis ; habituez-vouz à souffrir avec courage les maux de la vie. Vous auriez été sauvé, si vous vous étiez réfugié au camp.

THEME 31.

1. I rejoice greatly (*beaucoup*) to see you (*de vous voir*). 2. Charles has wounded himself with a penknife. 3. The enemies have surrendered. 4. A good Christian does not revenge himself on (*de*) his enemy. 5. The soldier has distinguished himself; he will be rewarded. 6. Get up ! 7. I shall get up directly. 8. Has my brother got up ? 9. He (has) got up at six o'clock. 10. Be not sorry, children, exclaimed he, we shall all be saved ! 11. You are mistaken, Sir. 12. Yes, it is true (*vrai*), I have been mistaken. 13. Why do you rejoice at the (*du*) misfortune of others ? 14. When do you go to bed ? 15. I go to bed at eleven o'clock; but yesterday I went (have gone) to bed at ten o'clock. 16. Make haste ! 17. Where is your mother ? 18. She is not at home (*à la maison*) ; she is taking a walk. 19. I have taken a walk this morning. 20. When will you take a walk ? 21. I shall take a walk this evening. 22. How are you to-day ? 23. I am well, but my brother is not well. 24. I (have) stopped at the gate (*porte*). 25. Rest a littlo, and come near the fire (*du feu*).

CONVERSATION.

Vous vous êtes trompé, mon ami, n'est-ce pas ?	Je ne me suis pas trompé.
Quand vous coucherez-vous, mes enfants ?	Nous nous coucherons tout de suite.
A quelle heure vous êtes-vous couché hier ?	Je me suis couché à dix heures.
Et votre frère ?	Mon frère s'est couché à onze heures.
Monsieur votre père est-il déjà levé ?	Oui, il s'est levé aujourd'hui de bonne heure (*early*).
Où êtes-vous donc restés si longtemps ?	Nous nous sommes égarés (*went astray*) dans la forêt.
Ta sœur s'est-elle lavée (*washed*) ?	Je crois qu'elle ne s'est pas encore lavée.
Qui s'est lavé dans cette eau ?	Moi.
Pourquoi vous êtes-vous levés si tard ?	Nous ne nous sommes pas éveillés plus tôt (*earlier*).
Qui veut se promener avec moi ?	Ma sœur et moi.
Vous êtes-vous bien amusé ?	Oui, assez (*pretty*) bien.

READING LESSON.

LE SANSONNET.

Le vieux chasseur Maurice avait dans sa chambre un sansonnet qu'il avait élevé, et qui avait appris (*learned*) à articuler quelques mots. Quand il disait par exemple : "Sansonnet, où es-tu ?" l'oiseau répondait toujours : "Me voilà !"

Le petit Charles, fils du voisin, aimait beaucoup l'oiseau et lui faisait (*paid*) souvent des visites. Un jour il vint voir le sansonnet pendant que le chasseur était absent ; il s'empara bien vite de l'oiseau, le mit (*put it*) dans sa poche et voulait s'esquiver avec son larcin.

Mais dans ce moment le chasseur entra chez lui. Il crut (*thought*) faire plaisir au petit garçon en demandant (*by asking*) comme de coutume : " Sansonnet, où es-tu ? " — " Me voilà ! " cria de toutes ses forces (*his might*) l'oiseau qui était caché dans la poche du petit garçon.

C'est ainsi que le petit voleur fut trahi.

Le sansonnet, the starling.
le mot, the word.
me voilà, here I am.
il vint, he came.
pendant que, whilst.
s'emparer, to lay hold of
vite, quick.
la poche, the pocket.
s'esquiver, to run away.
le larcin, the larceny.
de coutume, as he used to do.
trahir, to betray.

XXXII. TRENTE-DEUXIÈME LEÇON.

IMPERSONAL VERBS.

1. Verbs which are always impersonal form their compound tenses by means of the auxiliary *avoir*. The principal are :

Neiger, to snow ;	Pres. *il neige*, it snows.
pleuvoir, to rain ;	*il pleut*, it rains.
grêler, to hail ;	*il grêle*, it hails.
tonner, to thunder ;	*il tonne*, it thunders.
faire des éclairs, to lighten ;	*il fait des éclairs*, it lightens.
geler, to freeze ;	*il gèle*, it freezes.
dégeler, to thaw ;	*il dégèle*, it thaws.
importer, to matter ;	*il importe*, it matters.

Third singular negative is *n'importe*, no matter.

2. Other verbs may become impersonal. Ex. :

Il suffit, it suffices.
il semble, it seems.
il vaut mieux, it is better.
il me tarde, I long.
il convient, it is convenient.
il arrive, it happens (takes *être*).
il s'agit, it is the question, etc.
il reste, there remains.

MODELS OF CONJUGATION.

1. Neiger, *to snow.*

	INDICATIVE.	SUBJUNCTIVE.
Present.	*Il neige.*	*Qu'il neige.*
Imperfect.	*Il neigeait.*	*qu'il neigeât.*
Preterite.	*Il neigea.*	
Future.	*Il neigera.*	
Comp. of Pres.	*Il a neigé.*	*qu'il ait neigé.*
" " Imp.	*Il avait neigé.*	*qu'il eût neigé.*
" " Pret.	*Il eut neigé.*	
" " Fut.	*Il aura neigé.*	

Interrogatively: *Neige-t-il? neigeait-il? a-t-il neigé? etc.*

CONDITIONAL.

Pres. *Il neigerait.* Comp. *Il aurait neigé.*

PARTICIPLE.

Pres. *Neigeant.* Comp. *Ayant neigé.*

2. Il y a, *there is, there are.*

INFINITIVE MOOD.

Y avoir, *there to be.*

Indic.	Present.	*Il y a*, there is, there are.
	Imperfect.	*Il y avait*, } there was, there were.
	Preterite.	*Il y eut*, } there was, there were.
	Future.	*Il y aura*, there will be.
	Comp. of Pres.	*Il y a eu*, there has *or* have been.
	" Imp.	*Il y avait eu*, } there had been.
	" Pret.	*Il y eut eu*, } there had been.
Cond.	Present.	*Il y aurait*, there would be.
	Comp.	*Il y aurait eu*, there would have been.
Interrogatively:		*Y a-t-il*, is there? are there?
Negatively:		*Il n'y a pas*, there is *or* are not.
Negat. interrogat.:		*N'y a-t-il pas*, is *or* are there not?
Subj.	Present.	*Qu'il y ait*, that there (may) be.
	Imperfect.	*Qu'il y eût*, that there (might) be.
	Comp. of Pres.	*Qu'il y ait eu*, that there (may) have been.
	" Imp.	*Qu'il y eût eu*, that there (might) have been.

NOTE 1. This verb in English is used in the *plural*, when followed by a plural substantive; in French, it remains always in the *singular*; as,

There are birds which, etc.; *il y a des oiseaux qui, etc.*

NOTE 2. It often happens that the verb *il y a* is rendered ago, these, or for these. Ex.:

I saw him two months ago.
Je l'ai vu il y a deux mois.
Il y a huit jours que je suis malade.
I have been ill these eight days.

Il est is also used impersonally, particularly in poetry, in the sense of *il y a*.

3. *Il fait froid.*

Present,	*Il fait froid*, it is cold.
Imperfect.	*Il faisait froid*, } it was cold.
Preterite.	*Il fit froid*, }
Future.	*Il fera froid*, it will be cold, etc.
Comp. of Pres.	*Il a fait froid*, it has been cold, etc.

Thus other expressions denoting the state of the weather: *Il fait beau*, it is fine weather; *il fait chaud*, it is warm; *il fait jour*, it is daylight, etc.

The English "*it is said*" is rendered in French, *on dit*.

4. Il faut.

INFINITIVE: Falloir, *to be needful, necessary.*

INDIC.	Present.	*Il faut*, it is necessary.
	Imperfect.	*Il fallait*, } it was necessary.
	Preterite.	*Il fallut*, }
	Future.	*Il faudra*, it will be necessary.
Comp. of	Present.	*Il a fallu*, it has been necessary.
"	" Imperfect.	*Il avait fallu*, } it had been necessary.
"	" Preterite.	*Il eut fallu*, }
"	" Future.	*Il aura fallu*, it will have been necessary.
COND.	Present.	*Il faudrait*, it would be necessary, (. . . ought to).
Comp.		*Il aurait fallu*, it would have been necessary.

INTERROGATIVELY.

Faut-il? fallait-il? fallut-il? a-t-il fallu? (is it necessary? was it necessary? has it been necessary?)

SUBJ.	Present.	*Qu'il faille*, that it (may) be necessary.
	Imperfect.	*Qu'il fallût*, that it (might) be necessary.
Comp. of	Present.	*Qu'il ait fallu*, that it (may) have been necessary.
"	" Imperfect.	*Qu'il eût fallu*, that it (might) have been necessary.

PARTICIPLE.

Present. wanting. Compound. *Ayant fallu.*

Rem. 1. The verb *falloir* is absolutely impersonal throughout *all* its tenses. When its subject is a personal pronoun, as: *I* must, *you* must, etc., we may add, for the first person *me*, for the second *te*, for the third *lui*, in the plural *nous, vous, leur*. More frequently, however, *que* with the Subjunctive mood is preferred. Ex.: —

I must read: *il me faut lire*, or *il faut que je lise.*
thou must read: *il te faut lire*, or *il faut que tu lises.*
he must read: / she must read: } *il lui faut lire*, or { *il faut qu'il lise.* / *il faut qu'elle lise.*
we must read: *il nous faut lire*, or *il faut que nous lisions.*
you must read: *il vous faut lire*, or *il faut que vous lisiez.*
they must read: *il leur faut lire*, or *il faut qu'ils lisent.*
I have been obliged to read: *il m'a fallu lire, etc.*

2. When the subject is a noun, *que* with the Subjunctive mood must be used. It must further be observed that, when the verb *falloir* is used in the Present or Future tense, the following verb must be put in the Present of the Subjunctive; but when it is in the Imperfect, Preterite or Conditional, the verb following it must be rendered by the Imperfect of the Subjunctive. Ex.: —

The boy must work, *il faut que le garçon travaille.*

The boy will be obliged to work.
Il faudra que le garçon travaille.

The soldiers were obliged to retire.
Il fallait or *il fallut que les soldats se retirassent.*

3. When the verb *il faut* is followed immediately by a noun substantive, it signifies *to want*; here also one of the pronouns *me, te, lui, nous, vous, leur*, according to the person, must be inserted. Ex.: —

I want (must have) a hat, *il me faut un chapeau.*
He wants some money, *il lui faut de l'argent.*
We want some bread, *il nous faut du pain.*
Did you want some books, *vous fallait-il des livres?*

VOCABULARY.

Le compte, the account, bill.
la redingote, the coat.
le départ, the departure.
la chaise, the chair.
cesser, to leave off, to cease.
quitter, to leave.

la rue, the street.
le sort, (the) fate.
la chambre, the room.
manquer, to be wanting.
gouverner, to govern.
dessiner, to draw.
partir, to set out, depart.
honnête, honest.
mécontent, e, discontented.
sagement, adv. wisely.

READING EXERCISE 32.

Il pleut. Je crois qu'il pleuvra demain. J'entends tonner. Il vaut mieux (*it is better*) qu'il pleuve. Il a neigé toute la nuit. Il y a des hommes qui sont toujours mécontents. Il fait chaud; il faisait trop chaud dans votre chambre. Il n'y avait ni hommes, ni femmes, ni enfants. Il faut partir. Il vous faut partir. Il fallait venir plus tôt (*earlier*). Ne faudra-t-il pas lui pardonner? Il faut que Charles reste à la maison. Il fallut que Charles restât à la maison. Il me fallut lui pardonner. Il y aura cette année beaucoup de cerises. Il faut que les enfants obéissent à l'instant (*instantly*). Il y a eu de (*at*) tout temps des flatteurs. Il a fallu qu'elle payât son compte. Il y a un Dieu qui gouverne tout sagement. Qu'est-ce qu'il vous faut? Il me faut une autre chambre.

THEME 32.

1. Does it snow? 2. No, it does not snow, it rains. 3. It is cold to-day. 4. I shall not leave the room. 5. Yesterday it was (has been) very cold, and it (has) snowed a great deal (*beaucoup*). 6. It thunders and lightens. 7. There are too many chairs in this room. 8. There was much wine on the table. 9. Is there money in the purse? 10. There are six francs (*francs*) [in it]. 11. There will be a great many nuts this year. 12. There are streets in London, which are very long. 13. It is necessary to begin. 14. It was necessary to set out. 15. You must begin. 16. He must read. 17. We were obliged to set out. 18. He has been obliged to speak. 19. The boy must work. 20. The girls must draw. 21. My father has been obliged to go to Paris. 22. Your uncle will be obliged to leave London. 23. The soldiers were obliged to leave the town. 24. I want a good pen. 25. Do you want an-

other room? 26. Yes, I want a larger room. 27. What do you want? 28. I want *or* I must have (*de l'*) money.

CONVERSATION.

Quel temps fait-il aujourd'hui?	Il fait beau (mauvais) temps.
Pleut-il?	Oui, il pleut très-fort.
Pleuvra-t-il?	Je ne crois pas qu'il pleuve.
La pluie a-t-elle cessé?	Pas encore; il pleut sans cesse.
Que vous faut-il?	Il me faut une redingote neuve.
Y a-t-il assez de vin?	Oui, Monsieur, il y en a assez.
Y avait-il de l'argent dans cette bourse?	Il y avait deux francs
As-tu payé le compte?	Oui, il m'a fallu le payer.
Faut-il que je me lève maintenant?	Oui, il faut vous lever tout de suite.
Vous a-t-il fallu partir de si bonne heure (*so early*)?	Le départ était fixé à quatre heures et demie.
Qui a payé le dîner?	Mon père l'a payé.
Faut-il lui rendre (*return*) l'argent?	Oui, rendez-le-lui.

READING LESSON.

PRODUCTIONS DE DIVERS CLIMATS.

La providence a si sagement arrangé toutes choses, que chaque climat fournit aux habitants ce qui leur est le plus indispensable. Dans les contrées polaires il fait si froid, qu'il ne peut y croître ni fruits, ni céréales, ni légumes. La nature y a suppléé par la grande quantité de poissons que l'on pêche dans la mer et dans les lacs, et par l'abondance des quadrupèdes qui, à la vérité (*indeed*), sont la plupart (*mostly*) sauvages et féroces, mais qui fournissent aux habitants, aguerris (*accustomed*) à les poursuivre à la chasse, de très-belles fourrures, de la chair mangeable, des os et des nerfs qu'ils emploient pour leurs arcs (*bows*) et pour divers ustensiles.

Les peuples des climats chauds ont le ver à soie (*silkworm*), qui se nourrit des feuilles du mûrier et qui leur file (*spins*) un léger tissu dont on fait des étoffes convenables à la température du pays.

Le cotonnier porte des gousses renfermant le coton dont le tissu fournit également (*likewise*) les plus beaux vêtements. Et pour préserver les habitants de la zone torride de l'inflammation d'un sang trop échauffé, leurs campagnes et leurs jardins leur fournissent les oranges, les citrons et les olives qui les rafraîchissent.

Fournir, to supply, furnish.
le besoin, the need, want.
la contrée, the region.
croître, to grow.
les céréales, corn.
les legumes, vegetables.
pêcher, to fish.
sauvage, wild.
féroce, ferocious.
aguerris, hardened.
poursuivre, to pursue.
la fourrure, fur, pelt.
la chair, the flesh, meat.
l'os, the bone.
l'ustensile, the tool.
le mûrier, the mulberry-tree.
filer, to spin. *léger*, light.
le tissu, the texture.
convenable, convenient, fit.
le cotonnier, the cotton-plant.
la gousse, the pod, husk.
le vêtement, clothing.
échauffé, heated, hot.
rafraîchir, to cool, refresh.

XXXIII. TRENTE-TROISIÈME LEÇON.

FORMATION OF ADVERBS.

Most of the French adjectives become adverbs by adding the syllable *-ment*, according to the following rules: —

1. Adjectives ending in a vowel, simply add the final syllable *-ment*, as: —

Facile, easy; adv. *facilement*, easily.
poli, polite; adv. *poliment*, politely.
vrai, true; adv. *vraiment*, truly.

2. Adjectives which do not end in a vowel, add the syllable *-ment* to their feminine termination, as: —

Haut, f. *haute*, high; adv. *hautement*, aloud.
doux, f. *douce*, soft, mild; adv. *doucement*, softly.
franc, f. *franche*, frank; adv. *franchement*, frankly, freely
heureux, f. *heureuse*, happy; adv. *heureusement*, happily.

So also the adjectives, *nouveau*, new; *fou*, foolish, and *mou*, soft; adv. *nouvellement*, *follement*, *mollement*.

3. Adjectives which end in *-ant* or *-ent*, become adverbs by changing the final *-ant* into *-amment*, and *-ent* into *-emment*, as: —

Constant, constant; adv. *constamment*.
prudent, prudent; adv. *prudemment*.
patient, patient; adv. *patiemment*.

Exceptions to this rule are: *lent*, slow, adv. *lentement*; and *présent*, present, adv. *présentement*, actually, at present.

4. The following adjectives take an *é* accented before the final *-ment*. *Profond*, deep, *profondément*; *commode*, comfortable, *commodément*; *commun*, common, *communément*; *précis*, precise, *précisément*; *énorme*, enormous, *énormément*; *exprès*, express, *expressément*; *impuni*, unpunished, *impunément*.

5. All these derived adverbs, as well as some others, are compared, as: —

	COMP.	SUP.
Facilement,	*plus facilement*,	*le plus facilement*.
commodément,	*moins commodément*,	*le moins commodément*.
souvent, often;	*plus souvent*,	*le plus souvent*.
longtemps, long;	*plus longtemps*,	*le plus longtemps*.
loin, far;	*plus loin*,	*le plus loin*.

6. The following adverbs are irregular in the formation of their comparatives and superlatives: —

	COMP.	SUP.
Bien, well;	*mieux*, better;	*le mieux*, (the) best.
mal, badly;	*pis*, worse;	*le pis*, the worst.
peu, little;	*moins*, less;	*le moins*, the least.
beaucoup, much;	*plus*, more;	*le plus*, most.

tant mieux is rendered: so much the better.
tant pis, so much the worse.

7. When either *le plus* or *le moins* qualifies a verb, adverb, or participle not used adjectively, *le* retains the masculine form. Ex.: *Une lettre écrite le plus soigneusement.*

8. The following adjectives are used adverbially without taking an additional termination, as: —

Vite, quick, fast. *fort*, very.
haut, loudly.
bas, in a low voice.
exprès, purposely.
soudain, suddenly.
droit, straightways.

VOCABULARY.

L'état, m. the state.
fâché,* sorry, angry.
égal, equal.
généreusement, generously.
éloquemment, eloquently.
éternel, eternal. *agir*, to act.
marcher, to walk.
négliger, to neglect.
occupé, occupied.
dessiner, to draw.
oublier, to forget.
ponctuellement, punctually.
avouer, to confess.
entretenu (*part.*), entertained, amused.
propre, clean.
rarement, seldom.
malheureusement, unfortunately
modestement, modestly.
probablement, likely.
extrêmement, extremely.
la fortune, property.

READING EXERCISE 33.

Vous le trouverez facilement. Les gens paresseux négligent ordinairement leurs affaires. Agissez généreusement envers vos ennemis. Dieu a sagement distribué ses dons. Parlez modestement de vos mérites. Cet homme a parlé très-éloquemment. Henri IV. etait constamment occupé de la prospérité de ses états. Le voleur marcha doucement; il avait probablement peur d'être entendu. Je suis extrêmement fâché d'apprendre cette nouvelle. Nettoyez mieux vos habits. Vous n'êtes pas proprement habillé. Ne marchez pas si lentement. Les enfants qui aiment passionnément le jeu, négligent souvent leurs tâches (*tasks*).

* When meaning, sorry, it takes *de* before its obj.: meaning, angry, *contre*.

THEME 33.

1. This pupil learns (*apprend*) easily, but he forgets as (*aussi*) easily that which he learns. 2. The king has generously pardoned (to) his enemies. 3. Nobody is constantly happy in this world. 4. The name of Shakspeare will live (*vivra*) eternally. 5. Speak frankly. 6. My brother is constantly occupied. 7. Confess freely your faults. 8. Unfortunately I have not found him at home. 9. Speak softly. 10. The artist plays admirably (well). 11. I have seldom received letters from my brother-in-law (*beau-frère*). 12. Everybody must punctually observe the laws. 13. If you fulfil faithfully your duties, you will be esteemed by (*de*) everybody. 14. You have stayed longer than your brother. 15. The little girl draws very well; she draws better than her sister.

CONVERSATION.

Comment parle cet homme ?	Il parle très-éloquemment et très-franchement.
Avez-vous des nouvelles de votre frère à Paris ?	Il m'écrit (*writes*) rarement. Heureusement je sais (*know*) par un de ses amis qu'il se porte bien.
A-t-il perdu quelque chose ?	Il a probablement perdu une partie de sa fortune.
Monsieur M. est-il fâché ?	Oui, il est extrêmement fâché.
Pourquoi est-il fâché ?	Il est fâché contre son fils qui a été méchant.
Comment faut-il agir ? (*How must people act?*)	Il faut toujours agir prudemment et honnêtement.
Charles, tu es malade ; qu'as-tu ?	J'ai mal à la tête (*head-ache*) ; mais heureusement ce n'est pas grand'chose (*consequence*).
Vous êtes probablement le frère de Monsieur Richard ?	Non, Madame, mais je suis son cousin.

Comment ce général a-t-il agi envers ses ennemis ?	Il agi très-généreusement.
Pourquoi marchez-vous si lentement ?	J'ai mal au pied.
Cette loi est-elle observée ?	Elle est ponctuellement observée de tout le monde.

XXXIV. TRENTE-QUATRIÈME LEÇON.

ADVERBS OF PLACE AND OF TIME.

1. The principal adverbs of place are :

Où, where ? whither ?
par où, which way ?
ici, here. *d'ici*, hence.
là, there. *de là*, thence.
là-bas, there below, yonder.
y, there, therein.
par ici, this way. *par là*, that way.
par-ci, *par-là*, here and there.
ça et là, to and fro.
ailleurs, elsewhere.
dessous, underneath.
dessus, above.
en haut, up, up stairs.
en bas, down stairs, below.
quelque part, somewhere.
d'où, whence ?
dedans, *en dedans*, } within, inside.
dehors, without, out of doors.
derrière, behind.
devant, before.
deça, *en deça*, on this side.
delà, *en delà*, on that side.
près, *auprès*, near.
proche, close by.
alentour, round, about.
partout, everywhere.
nulle part, nowhere.
jusqu'à, as far as.
jusqu'où, how far ?
loin, far, far off.

2. The principal adverbs of time are :

Quand, when ?
aujourd'hui, to-day.
hier, yesterday.
avant-hier, the day before yesterday.
demain, to-morrow.
un jour, one day.
autrefois, *jadis*, formerly.
auparavant, previously, before.
alors, *puis*, then.
après, after, afterwards.

après-demain, the day after to-morrow.
enfin, at last, at length.
tôt, soon. *plus tôt*, sooner.
bientôt, soon. *trop tôt*, too soon.
tantôt, by and by.
aussitôt, directly.
tard, late.
d'abord, at first.
désormais, } henceforth.
dorénavant, }
dès-lors, from then.
depuis, since.
jusqu'à, until.
ensuite, afterwards.
à présent, } now, at present.
maintenant, }
quelquefois, sometimes.
souvent, often.
longtemps, long.
toujours, always.
dernièrement, } lately, of late.
naguère, }
déjà, already.
encore, still, yet.
jamais, ever. *ne —— jamais*, never.

When and *in which* are rendered by *où*, after a noun signifying *time* or *place*.

PLACE OF ADVERBS.

REM. 1. In the simple tenses, the adverb is generally placed immediately after the verb which it modifies:

She always cries, *elle pleure toujours*.
I often take a walk with my friend.
Je me promène souvent avec mon ami.

REM. 2. When the verb is in a compound tense, the adverb generally comes between the auxiliary and the participle; as,

Je l'ai toujours respecté, I have always esteemed him.
Je me suis souvent promené avec mon maître.
I have often taken a walk with my master.

N. B. — *Hier, avant-hier, aujourd'hui, demain, après-demain, tantôt, tôt*, and *tard*, always follow the participle, unless placed before the auxiliary.

VOCABULARY.

Le temps, the weather.
le village, the village.
la grammaire, the grammar.
content, satisfied.
le chemin de fer, the railroad.
le brouillard, the fog, mist.
l'ouvrage, m. the work.
dîner, to dine.
venir, to come.
laisser, to leave.

READING EXERCISE 34.

Le temps est fort doux aujourd'hui. Mon cousin est enfin arrivé. L'autre jour je me suis égaré dans la forêt. Travaillez d'abord et ensuite jouez. Avez-vous jamais vu un enfant comme celui-là ? En effet, il est extrêmement gros. Le brouillard aura bientôt disparu. D'où venez-vous maintenant, et où avez-vous été hier ? Voyez-vous ce village là-bas ? Eh bien (*well*), j'y ai été hier et aujourd'hui. J'y vais quelquefois. M'avez-vous apporté la grammaire dont je vous ai parlé ? Voulez-vous venir dîner avec nous demain ? Demain je ne serai pas ici, mais après-demain ou plus tard. Enfin mon ouvrage est fini.

THEME 34.

1. Where is my brother ? 2. He is not here ; he is elsewhere ; he is perhaps yonder. 3. I will go (*j'irai*) that way. 4. Carry all that up stairs. 5. How far did you go yesterday ? 6. I went as far as London. 7. I shall go nowhere to-day. 8. That village is not far ; do you see (*voyez-vous*) it yonder ? 9. Where is my grammar ? 10. I have left it somewhere. 11. Is Edward here ? 12. No ; he is below. 13. My friend will not stay here long. 14. I saw (have seen) your sister yesterday at the play (*au spectacle*). 15. He will always be satisfied. 16. Come back (*revenez*) soon. 17. Did you know [have you known (*connu*)] him formerly ? 18. Yes, I have known him long. 19. Whence does the letter come ? 20. It comes from America. 21. Your dog is out of doors. 22. How is (*se porte*) your aunt to-day ? 23. She is better to-day than [she was] yesterday. 24. I hope you will dine with us to-morrow. 25. I shall go soon into the country (*à la campagne*). 26. We expected him the day before yesterday. 27. Formerly there were no railroads. 28 Henceforth I shall be very diligent.

XXXV. TRENTE-CINQUIÈME LEÇON.

ADVERBS OF NUMBER, OF QUANTITY, OF NEGATION, ETC.

The adverbs of number are:

Premièrement, firstly.
deuxièmement, *secondement*, } secondly.
troisièmement, thirdly.
quatrièmement, fourthly.
cinquièmement, fifthly.
sixièmement, sixthly, etc.
combien de fois, how often?
une fois, once.
deux fois, twice.
trois fois, three times, etc.

The principal adverbs of quantity and comparison are:

Comment, how?
combien, how much? how many?
beaucoup, much, many.
bien (with *du*, *de l'*, *des* following) a great deal *or* many.
trop, too much, too many.
tant, so much, so many.
assez,* enough, pretty.
peu, little. *un peu*, a little.
ne — guère, hardly.
bien, *très*, *fort*, } very.
plus, more.
davantage, still more.
moins, less.
tout, *tout-à-fait*, } quite, wholly, entirely.
presque, almost.
environ, *à peu près*, } about.
si, so. *ainsi*, thus.
aussi, as.
également, likewise.
autant, as much, as many.
d'autant plus, so much the more.
plutôt, rather.
surtout, above all.
au plus, *tout au plus*, } at most.
du moins, *au moins*, at least.
seulement, *ne — que*, } only.
même, even.
pas même, *pas seulement*, } not even.

The adverbs of affirmation and negation are:

Oui, yes. *si*, yes.
certes, certainly.
peut-être, perhaps.
ne — pas, not.
ne — plus, no more.
non plus, nor — either.

* Assez precedes in French the noun or adjective it limits. Ex.: Assez de vin, assez bon. See p. 32.

certainement, } certainly, to be sure.
assurément, }
non, no.
presque jamais, scarcely ever.
ne — point, not (at all).
pas du tout, } not at all.
point du tout, }
ne — rien, nothing.

There are many adverbial locutions; those most in use are:

A peine, scarcely.
en effet, really.
sur le champ, directly.
peu à peu, by degrees.
dans peu or *sous peu,* soon.
à dessein, on purpose.
en même temps, at the same time.
à la fois, at once, at a time.
de bonne heure, early.
de meilleure heure, earlier.
à bon marché, cheap.
à fond, thoroughly.
par an, yearly. *par jour,* daily.
par mois, monthly.
tout à coup, suddenly.
tout d'un coup, all at once.
à droite, to the right.
à gauche, to the left.
ensemble, together.
pêle-mêle, pell-mell.
d'avance, beforehand, in advance.
sans doute, no doubt.
tout à l'heure, } directly, immediately.
tout de suite, }
par hasard, by chance.
en attendant, meanwhile.
de temps en temps, } from time to time.
de temps à autre, }

OF NEGATION.

1. Not is translated into French by *ne,* which is placed before the verb, and *pas* or *point* after it, in simple tenses. Ex.:

Je ne veux pas, I will not, I do not wish.
Je ne sais pas, I do not know.

2. In compound tenses, *ne* comes before the auxiliary, and *pas* after it. Ex.:

Je n'*ai pas vu,* I have not seen.
Elle n'*a pas parlé,* she did not speak.

Point is merely a stronger negative than *pas,* as:

Il n'ai point parlé, I did not speak (at all).

3. *Ne* is employed without *pas,* if there is in the sentence a pronoun or adverb expressing negation, such as *personne, nul, rien, jamais, ni, ne—plus, point, guère.* Ex.:

Je ne connais personne, I know nobody.
Je ne veux rien, I wish for nothing.
Je ne sais plus, I know no more.
Elle n'a jamais dit cela, she never said so.

4. If one of the negations is followed by a noun in the partitive sense, this noun is simply preceded by *de:*

Affirmative: *J'ai du pain*, I have some bread.
Negative: *Je n'ai pas de pain*, I have no bread.
Affirmative: *Avez-vous de l'argent*, have you any money?
Negative: *Je n'ai point d'argent*, I have no money.

5. With the infinitive, *ne—pas, ne—point, ne—rien, etc.*, are generally not separated, as:

Ne pas se venger, not to revenge one's self.
Ne plus écrire, to write no more.
Ne rien manger, to eat nothing.

6. Without a verb, the negatives stand without *ne*, as:

Pas à la fois, not at once. *Pas moi*, not I.
Pas beaucoup, pas trop, pas tant, pas aujourd'hui,

7. *Non plus*, nor—either, requires the full negation *ne—pas* before it, as:

Je ne le veux pas non plus, nor will I have it either.

8. If nor—either is connected only with a noun or pronoun, without a verb, the noun or the pronoun is preceded, in French, by *ni*, as:

Nor Charles either, *ni Charles non plus.*

9. Observe the expression *ne—que* for only, as:

Je n'ai que deux sœurs, I have only two sisters.
Il n'a qu'un morceau de pain, he has only a piece of bread.
Elle n'a apporté qu'une assiette, she brought but one plate.
L'enfant n'a que dix ans, the child is only ten years old.
Il n'est que six heures, it is only six o'clock.

VOCABULARY.

La fois,* f. the time.
le crime, the crime.
travailler, to work.
laconique, laconic.
refuser, to refuse.
inouï, e, unheard of.
amicalement, friendly.
éviter, to shun.
la société, the society.
merci, thank you.

READING EXERCISE 35.

Ce crime est tout-à-fait inouï. Comment vous portez-vous? Je me porte très-bien. Combien d'aunes de ce drap vous faut-il? Il m'en faut beaucoup; il m'en faut au moins trente aunes. Vous êtes-vous promené longtemps? Je me suis promené environ deux

* When the noun *times* denotes repetition, as the number of times, it is translated by *fois*.

heures ; peut-être un peu moins. Votre tante va-t-elle souvent au spectacle ? Elle n'y va (*goes*) presque jamais, et mon oncle n'y va pas du tout. Monsieur, vous avez peu de fautes dans votre traduction. Combien en ai-je ? Vous en avez moins que votre frère ; vous n'en avez que deux ou trois, tout au plus quatre. J'ai appris (*learned*) ma leçon par cœur. Habillez-vous tout de suite. C'est en vain que vous cherchez à le sauver. Marchez à droite ; moi, je marcherai à gauche. Sans doute, cela vaut mieux. J'ai acheté ce tableau à bon marché.

THEME 35.

1. How much sugar have you bought ? 2. How many lessons a (*par*) week have you ? 3. You eat too much ; you must eat less. 4. That young man works too much. 5. Give him a little money. 6. Give me more time. 7. There were many ladies, and we had a great deal of pleasure. 8. Have you not played enough ? 9. I think (that) you will not have it. 10. Mr. A. is a very laconic man ; he always answers yes or no. 11. It is better not to refuse him. 12. I have only one brother, and my cousin has only one sister. 13. She is only five years old. 14. I have never seen her. 15. She never comes to our house (*chez nous*). 16. We certainly shall go out (*sortirons*) together. 17. My father has bought a horse very cheap. 18. Have you seen anybody ? 19. I have seen nobody. 20. The thunder-storm came on suddenly. 21. I got up early ; earlier than my brother. 22. You must always shun the society of these bad people. 23. Go (*allez*) to the right. 24. I shall go to the left ; we shall arrive at the same time.

CONVERSATION.

Comment trouvez-vous le temps aujourd'hui ?	Je le trouve fort beau (*or* bien beau).
Voici du jambon. En voulez-vous ?	Donnez-m'en un peu, s'il vous plaît (*please*).
En voulez-vous davantage ?	Non, merci, j'en ai assez.

Serez-vous chez vous (*at home*) demain matin? — Assurément, je serai chez moi toute la journée (*day*).

A quelle heure avez-vous dîné hier? — Hier j'ai dîné à cinq heures précises.

Dînerez-vous aujourd'hui à la même heure? — Non, aujourd'hui je ne dînerai qu'à six heures.

Que ferez-vous (*will you do*) pendant ce temps? — Je me promènerai en attendant.

Avez-vous fait cela à dessein? — Non, je ne l'ai pas fait exprès.

Avez-vous fini votre thème? — Je ne l'aurai guère fini avant sept heures.

Que fait cette petite fille là-bas? — Elle cherche des fraises (*strawberries*).

Connaissez-vous cet ouvrage (*work*)? — Cet ouvrage m'est tout-à-fait inconnu.

Avez-vous lu (*read*) ce livre? — Je l'ai lu plus de deux fois.

Quand voulez-vous venir jouer avec moi? — Je finirai d'abord ma tâche et après, nous jouerons.

Comment vous portez-vous? — Je me porte à merveille.

Et Monsieur votre père, comment se porte-t-il? — Il se porte assez bien. Il est sorti hier pour la première fois.

XXXVI. TRENTE-SIXIÈME LEÇON.

CONJUNCTIONS.

The principal simple conjunctions are: —

Et, and.
et — et, both — and.
ou, or.
ou — ou, either — or.
pourtant, yet, still.
néanmoins, nevertheless.
si, if, whether.
sinon, if not.

ni — ni, neither — nor.
que, that, than (after a comp.).
car, for.
mais, but.
toutefois, *cependant*, } however.
comme, as.
or, now.
donc, consequently, then.
puisque, since, as.
quoique (with the Subj.), though.

1. Among these simple conjunctions, only one governs the Subjunctive mood, viz.: *quoique*, though or although. Ex.: *quoique je sois malade*, though I am ill.

For the Subjunctive after *que*, see P. II. L. 19.

2. *Si* denotes a condition or supposition: *s'il vient*, if he comes; *si vous voulez*, if you like. When *si* is followed by an Imperfect or Pluperfect, those tenses are always in the Indicative mood. (See P. II. L. 19.)

If I had, *si j'avais;* If I were, *si j'étais;*
If I had seen him, *si je l'avais vu.*

NOTE. The *i* in *si* is cut off before *il* and *ils*, but nowhere else, as: *s'il avait*, but *si elle avait*, *etc.*

3. The conjunction *ni — ni* requires *ne* before its verb, and the noun which follows it takes no article, if used in the partitive sense, as: —

Je n'ai ni père ni mère, I have neither father nor mother.

4. The conjunction *que* serves to connect two ideas so as to form of the two one sentence, as:

Je crois que vous avez raison, I believe you are right.

In English the conjunction *that* is almost always understood, whereas *que* is not only always expressed in French, but repeated before each member of the proposition, as: —

Je crois que vous avez raison et que vous réussirez.
I think you are right and that you will succeed.

5. When a conjunction governs several verbs, it is placed before the first verb only, and *que* is used before the other verbs. Ex.: As he is diligent and takes pains, *comme il est appliqué et qu'il prend de la peine.*

6. *Donc* is often used like the English auxiliary *do*, to urge or incite. Ex.: *Taisez-vous donc*, do be silent. It is also used interrogatively: *C'est donc vous qui avez fait cela?*

VOCABULARY.

Plier, to bend.
lever, to lift up.
l'étoile, f. the star.
épuisé, e, exhausted.
avare, avaricious.
savant, learned.
rompre, to break.
habiter, to inhabit.
le bien, the good.
plus — plus, the more — the more.
plus — moins, the more — the less.
moins — moins, the less — the less.
soit — soit, be it — or.
tantôt — tantôt, sometimes — sometimes, now — then.
ni — non plus, nor — either.

READING EXERCISE 36.

L'ambition et l'avarice sont deux grandes sources du malheur humain. Les discours impies (*impious*) gâtent à la fois l'esprit et le cœur. Cette eau est froide comme de la glace. Votre tableau est précieux, mais il ne me plaît (*please*) pas. Il arriva comme je sortais. Elle n'est ni laide ni belle. Vous vous amusez, et cependant le temps fuit (*flies*). Cet homme est très-fort, et pourtant il ne peut pas lever ce fardeau (*weight*). Ou vous me paierez, ou vous irez en prison. Donnez-moi de l'eau, s'il vous plaît. Martin est encore bien jeune, néanmoins il est fort sage. Bienheureux sont ceux qui aiment la paix, car ils seront appellés les enfants de Dieu. Vous ne le savez pas? Ni moi non plus. Tantôt il veut une chose, tantôt il en veut une autre.

THEME 36.

1. Gold and silver are metals. 2. Silver is less useful than iron. 3. Mr. A. is very inconsistent (*inconséquent*); he is sometimes of one opinion (*avis*, m.) and sometimes of another. 4. I like you, as I know (*sais*) that you are always attentive. 5. This man is esteemed by everybody, even by his enemies. 6. I am very glad to see that you do not love flattery. 7. Some one has done it, either you or your brother. 8. The more you will work, the more you will gain. 9. This horse may be very strong, nevertheless it does not

please me. 10. The longer the days (are) (*constr.* the more the d. are long), the shorter (are) the nights. 11. Though he said (*dit*) (that) he had no appetite, yet he ate all the meat and bread. 12. Nobody knows whether the stars are inhabited or not. 13. The reed bends, but does not break. 14. Do not bend the bow too much, otherwise it will break. 15. The more I sang, the less embarrassed I was. 16. If you do (*faites*) it, you will be punished. 17. He appeared (*paraissait*) very modest, although he was very learned. 18. In order to be learned, you must study much. 19. I punish him as he deserves (it). 20. You must stay at home, since you are not quite well. 21. When he had done speaking (*fini de parler*), he was quite exhausted. 22. If I had had faithful friends, I should not be so unhappy. 23. You will be happy, if you do your duty (*devoir*). 24. I was sleeping when your servant entered (*entra*).

CONVERSATION.

Êtes-vous heureux, mon ami?	Je le serais, si j'avais de bons livres.
Si ce n'est que cela, je peux vous en donner. En voulez-vous?	Je vous en serais très-obligé.
Quelles sont les deux grandes sources du malheur des hommes?	L'ambition et l'avarice.
Que fait-on souvent, quand on est jeune?	On fait souvent des sottises.
Que dit Jésus-Christ de ceux qui aiment la paix?	Il dit qu'ils seront appelés "enfants de Dieu."
Que veut cet enfant?	Il veut tantôt ceci, tantôt cela.
Comment trouvez-vous cette demoiselle?	Elle n'est ni belle ni laide.
Ne pouvez-vous pas lever cette pierre?	Je ne peux pas la lever, quoique je sois très-fort.

Comment Dieu traite-t-il les hommes ?	Il les traite comme un père traite ses enfants.
Quelle propriété a le roseau ?	Il (se) plie et ne rompt pas.
Quand faut-il forger le fer ?	Quand il est chaud.

READING LESSON.

LAFITTE.

Lorsque Jacques Lafitte vint (*came*) à Paris, il se présenta chez M. Perregaux dans l'espérance d'obtenir une place ; mais le banquier lui annonça qu'il était dans l'impossibilité de satisfaire à sa demande, puisque les bureaux étaient au complet.

Lafitte, découragé par ce refus, s'éloignait tristement, lorsqu'en traversant la cour de l'hôtel, il aperçut à terre une épingle ; il la ramassa et la piqua sur sa manche. M. Perregaux ayant vu l'action du jeune solliciteur, en fut frappé (*struck*), et pensa qu'il devait être doué d'un esprit d'ordre et d'économie. Il le fit rappeler et lui dit qu'il pouvait compter sur une place dans sa maison. En effet, peu de jours après, le jeune Bayonnais entra chez le riche banquier, et chacun sait que, plus tard, il est devenu un homme riche et célèbre.

L'espérance, hope.
le bureau, the office.
s'éloigner, to retire.
une épingle, a pin.
ramasser, to pick up.
la manche, the sleeve.
doué, endowed.
en effet, indeed.

XXXVII. TRENTE-SEPTIÈME LEÇON.

CONJUNCTIVE PHRASES.

Most of these are adverbs or prepositions united with *que* or *de*. Some require the following verb in the *Indicative mood*, others in the *Infinitive*, and others again in the *Subjunctive*.

1. Conjunctive phrases with the *Indicative*: —

Ou bien, or, else.
ni — non plus, neither, nor either.
au contraire, on the contrary.
non seulement — mais encore, not only — but also.
de plus, moreover.
autant que, as much as.
après que, after, after that.
quand même, although.
si toutefois, if however.
c'est-à-dire, namely.
c'est que, *parce que*, } because.
tandis que, whereas.
pendant que, while, whilst.
tant que, as long as.
Aussi bien que, as well as.
aussitôt que, *dès que*, } as soon as.
de même que, *ainsi que*, } as.
au reste, *du reste*, } however.
de là, hence it follows.
à peine — que, scarcely — as.
c'est pourquoi, therefore.
par conséquent, consequently.
comme si, as if.
de même, thus, in the same way.
sans cela, otherwise, else.
depuis que, since.
tout — que, however — as.

2. With the *Infinitive mood*: —

Afin de, in order to, to.
à moins de, unless.
avant de, before.
au lieu de, instead of.
de peur de, *de crainte de*, } for fear of.
loin de, far from.
plutôt que de, rather than.

3. With the *Subjunctive mood*: —

Afin que, *pour que*, } that, in order that.
avant que, before.
à moins que, † *que — ne*, } unless, till.
non que, not that.
nonobstant que, notwithstanding that.
pour peu que, however little.
pourvu que, provided (that).

† Those marked with a † require *ne* before the following verb.

bien que, } though,
quoique, } although.
jusqu'à ce que, till, until.
loin que, far from.
quelque — que, however — though.
sans que, without that.
si ce n'est que, unless, till.
soit que, whether — or.

4. Besides the above-mentioned conjunctions, there are other conjunctive expressions (*locutions conjonctives*), which have been borrowed from other classes of words, and to which the conjunction *que* is added. Such are:

A condition que, on condition that. . . . .
de peur que,* † } lest.
de crainte que,*† }
de manière que, } so as to, so that. . . . .
de or *en sorte que*, }
au cas que, in case that.* . . . .
supposé que, supposing that.* . . . .
malgré que, for all that, notwithstanding.*
toutes les fois que, as often as.
peut-être que, perhaps that. . . . .
attendu que, considering that. . . . .
à ce que, according as, as far as, etc.

N. B. — Those marked with an * govern the subjunctive.

VOCABULARY.

La suite, the consequence.
la machine à vapeur, the engine.
la mémoire, the memory.
occuper, to occupy.
mettre, to put, place.
préserver, to preserve.
prêt, ready.
la princesse, the princess.
la guerre, war.
ambitieux, ambitious.
l'éducation, f. education.
regarder, to look at.

READING EXERCISE 37.

Aussitôt que la machine à vapeur fut construite (*built*), elle fut mise en mouvement (*put in motion*), pour l'essayer. Quelque grande que soit cette faute, il faut cependant la pardonner. Dès qu'il me vit (*saw*) il courut (*ran*) à moi. Pendant que nous étions occupés à faire notre tâche, on cria au feu (*fire*)! La mémoire de Henri IV. sera toujours chère aux Français parce qu'il mettait sa gloire à les rendre heureux. Que le ciel vous préserve d'un pareil (*such*) malheur ! Le malade ne boit (*drinks*) ni ne mange. Tant que ma mère sera à la campagne, je resterai avec elle. Tandis que nous parlons, le temps fuit. Depuis que j'ai perdu mon père, tout me manque.

THEME 37.

1. I am not sorry, *on the contrary*, I am very glad (*bien aise*) to (*de*) have done it. 2. I will play, *as soon as* I (shall) have finished my exercise. 3. There will always be wars among men, *as long as* they are ambitious. 4. *After* (*that*) you were gone (*sorti*), I began writing (*à écrire*). 5. *As soon as* my education is finished, I shall go to Italy. 6. *In order* to learn well, we must (*on doit*) study with a great deal of attention. 7. *In order* to gain friends, we must be honest. 8. It will be impossible to learn French, *unless* you be (*Inf.*) diligent. 9. Let us pray, *before* we begin (*Inf.*). 10. *Rather than* study, he loses his time. 11. *Far from* blaming you, I praised you. 12. Come here, *that* I may speak to you. 13. Send me your book, (*in order*) *that* I may read it. 14. I will be ready *before* they come. 15. *Unless* you accompany me, I will not take a walk. 16. Cato killed himself, *lest* he should fall into (*entre*) the hands of Cæsar. 17. *Though* that young man is not very diligent, [yet] he improves. 18. *Before* you begin an action, consider well its consequences. 19. You will never be respected *unless* you fulfil your duties. 20. He will give it to you, *on condition that* you give it back to him. 21. They beat him *so that* they almost killed him.

XXXVIII. TRENTE-HUITIÈME LEÇON.

IRREGULAR VERBS. — FIRST CLASS.

Those verbs are commonly called irregular which deviate from the three regular conjugations. This deviation is of three kinds.

1. Such verbs as take the termination corresponding to the ending of their Infinitive mood, but change their root. Ex.: Of the verb *coudre*, to sew, the radical is *coud-*, this final *d* is, in some persons and tenses, changed into *s*, for instance in the plural: *nous cous-ons*, we sew. These are the least difficult, and are therefore put in the first class.

2. Verbs which preserve their radical syllable throughout unchanged, but take flexions that do not accord with the ending of their Infinitive. For instance, the verb *cour-ir*, to run, ending in *-ir*, ought to take the flexions of the second conjugation (*finir*). But this is not the case; it takes the flexions of the third conjugation (*vendre*); the Present is not *je couris, tu couris*, etc., but *je cours, tu cours*, etc.; P. p. *couru* like *vendu*. Verbs of this kind we assign to the second class.

3. A certain number of verbs offer both these anomalies at the same time; i. e. they undergo some changes in their root, and are conjugated with other flexions than those corresponding with the ending of their Infinitive. For instance, the verb *mourir*, to die, ought, according to its Infinitive termination, *-ir*, to take the flexions of *finir*. This is not the case; it is, in most tenses, conjugated like *vendre;* and, besides, its root *mour-* is, in certain tenses and persons, changed into *meur-*, as: Pres. *je meurs, tu meurs*, etc. Such verbs, among which are included those ending in *-oir*, constitute the third class.

To facilitate the study of the irregular verbs, it is essential to distinguish the primitive tenses from the derived ones. The latter have generally a regular inflexion, whereas the former alone are subject to irregularity. As already mentioned, the primitive tenses are:

1. *The Infinitive mood.*
2. *The Participle present.*
3. *The Participle past.*
4. *The Present of the Indicative mood.*
5. *The Preterite.*

From these the other tenses and moods are derived, as it is explained, L. XX. The derivative tenses are formed regularly, and therefore seldom mentioned in the following list.

To aid the pupil's memory, the following hints will prove useful:

1. The Present of the Subjunctive may be found by dropping the final *nt* of the third person plural Indicative, as: from *ils écrivent — que j'écrive;* from *ils prennent — que je prenne;* from *ils boivent — que je boive.*

2. The plural of the Present Indicative, the Participle Present and the Imperfect of the Indicative have the same radical, as: *nous mourons,* we die; P. pr. *mourant;* Imperf. *je mourais; — nous craignons;* P. pr. *craignant;* Imperf. *je craignais; — nous allons;* P. pr. *allant;* Imperf. *j'allais, etc.*

3. The Future and Conditional are formed from the Infinitive; the following, however, have an irregular formation, — *je courrai* (instead of *courirai*), *je mourrai, je verrai, j'enverrai, j'acquerrai, je pourrai, je saurai, je voudrai, il faudra, je viendrai, je tiendrai, je ferai,* and *j'irai.*

4. When the Participle past ends with the sound of *i* (*i, is, it,*) the Preterite generally ends in *is.* Ex.: Part. p. *sorti,* gone out; Pret. *je sortis;* — Part. p. *dit,* said; Pret. *je dis;* — Part. p. *pris,* taken; Pret. *je pris, etc.*

5. But when the Participle past ends in *u,* the Preterite usually ends in *us.* Ex.: P. p. *cru,* believed; Pret. *je crus;* P. p. *lu,* read; Pret. *je lus;* — P. p. *connu,* known; Pret. *je connus, etc.*

A LIST OF ALL THE IRREGULAR VERBS ACCORDING TO THE THREE CLASSES OF IRREGULARITY.

FIRST CLASS.

Containing the verbs in *-re* which take the terminations of the third conjugation, but whose radical is somewhat changed.

a. (1—7. Insertion of an *s.*)

1. *Luire,* to shine. *Part. pres.* luisant. *Part. past,* lui.
Pres. Je luis, tu luis, il luit, nous luisons, vous luisez, ils luisent.
Subj. Pres. Que je luise. *Imperf.* Je luisais.
Pret. wanting. *Fut.* Je luirai.

Conjugate in the same manner: *Reluire,* to glitter.

2. *Suffire,* to suffice. *P. pr.* suffisant. *P. p.* suffi.
Pres. Je suffis, tu suffis, il suffit, nous suffisons, etc.

Subj. Pres. Que je suffise. *Imperf.* Je suffisais.

Pret. Je suffis, tu suffis, il suffis, nous suffîmes, etc.

Fut. Je suffirai.

In the same manner: *Confire*, to preserve, to pickle; and *circoncire*, to circumcise, except in the *Part. past*. The Participle of the former is *confit*, of the latter *circoncis*.

3. *Nuire*, to hurt. *P. pr.* nuisant. *P. p.* nui.

Pres. Je nuis, tu nuis, il nuit, nous nuisons, vous nuisez, ils nuisent. *Subj. Pres.* Que je nuise. *Imperf.* Je nuisais.

Pret. Je nuisis. *Fut.* Je nuirai.

4. *Cuire*, to boil, to bake (bread). *P. pr.* cuisant. *P. p.* cuit.

Pres. Je cuis, tu cuis, il cuit, nous cuisons, etc.

Pret. Je cuisis. *Fut.* Je cuirai.

Thus also: *Recuire*, to boil once more.

5. *Conduire*, to conduct, to lead. *Se conduire*, to behave.

P. pr. conduisant. *P. p.* conduit.

Pres. Je conduis, tu conduis, il conduit, nous conduisons, etc.

Pret. Je conduisis. *Fut.* Je conduirai.

Thus: *Reconduire*, to reconduct, to see home; *déduire*, to deduct; *enduire*, to plaster; *induire*, to lead into; *introduire*, to introduce; *produire*, to produce; *reproduire*, to produce again; *réduire*, to reduce; *séduire*, to seduce; *traduire*, to translate.

6. *Instruire*, to instruct. *P. pr.* instruisant. *P. p.* instruit.

Pres. J'instruis, tu instruis, il instruit, nous instruisons, vous instruisez, ils instruisent.

Pret. J'instruisis. *Fut.* J'instruirai.

In the same manner: *Construire*, to build; *détruire*, to destroy.

7. *Dire*, to say, to tell. *P. pr.* disant. *P. p.* dit.

Pres. Je dis, tu dis, il dit, nous disons, vous *dites*, ils disent.

Subj. Pres. Que je dise.

Pret. Je dis, tu dis, il dit, nous dîmes, vous dîtes, ils dirent.

Imperf. Subj. Que je disse.

Fut. Je dirai. *Imper.* Dis, disons, *dites*.

Conjugate in the same manner: *redire*, to say again, to object.

As for the other compounds of *dire*, viz.: *Contredire*, to contradict; *dédire*, to unsay; and *se dédire*, to retract; *interdire*, to forbid; *médire*, to slander; and *prédire*, to foretell, they do not form their second person plural of the Present Indicative with the termination *-tes*, but *-sez*, as: *vous contredisez, vous médisez, vous interdisez, etc.*— *Maudire*, to curse, takes *ss* in the following forms: Pres. plur. *nous maudissons, vous maudissez, ils maudissent.* Part. pr. *maudissant.* Imperf. *je maudissais.*

VOCABULARY.

Le soleil, the sun.
un rayon, a ray.
l'espoir, m. hope.
la dette, the debt.
moderne, modern.
la pêche, the peach.
la vérité, the truth.

THEME 38.

1. The sun shines. 2. Everything shines (glitters) in that house. 3. It is not sufficient (it does not suffice) to understand the ancient languages, it is also necessary to study the modern ones. 4. We preserve these peaches with sugar. 5. Have you pickled cucumbers (*des concombres*)? 6. Does he not hurt you in this affair? 7. All his property will not suffice to (*pour*) pay his debts. 8. Where do you conduct this blind [man]? 9. I conduct him to the physician (*chez le médecin*). 10. I instruct (the) youth. 11. We translate English into French. 12. The boys behaved very well. 13. You will hurt me more than any other person. 14. This bread is well baked. 15. What do you say? 16. I say that you are (have) right. 17. We say the truth. 18. Tell him that I am here. 19. I shall tell (it) him directly. 20. Never contradict any one (*personne*) in (*en*) public. 21. We foretold those disasters (*désastres*). 22. Let us curse nobody.

XXXIX. TRENTE-NEUVIÈME LEÇON.

IRREGULAR VERBS.—FIRST CLASS CONTINUED.

b. (8—17. Change of the final consonant.)

8. *Traire*, to milk. *P. pr.* trayant. *P. p.* trait.

Pres. Je trais, tu trais, il trait, nous trayons, vous trayez, ils traient.

Imperf. Je trayais. *Pret.* wanting. *Fut.* Je trairai.

Thus also: *Distraire*, to distract; *extraire*, to extract; *soustraire*, to subtract, to withdraw.

9. *Suivre*, to follow. *P. pr.* suivant. *P. p.* suivi.

Pres. Je suis, tu suis, il suit, nous suivons, vous suivez, ils suivent. *Subj. Pres.* Que je suive.

Pret. Je suivis. *Fut.* Je suivrai.

Imper. Suis, suivons, suivez.

Thus: *S'ensuivre*, to ensue; *poursuivre*, to pursue.

10. *Vaincre*, to conquer. *P. pr.* vainquant. *P. p.* vaincu.

Pres. Je vaincs, tu vaincs, il vainc, nous vainquons, vous vainquez, ils vainquent.

Pret. Je vainquis. *Fut.* Je vaincrai.

Imper. Vaincs, vainquons, vainquez.

In the same manner: *Convaincre*, to convince.

11. *Coudre*, to sew. *P. pr.* cousant. *P. p.* cousu.

Pres. Je couds, tu couds, il coud, nous cousons, vous cousez, ils cousent. *Subj. Pres.* Que je couse.

Pret. Je cousis. *Fut.* Je coudrai.

Thus: *Découdre*, to unsew; *recoudre*, to sew over again.

12. *Moudre*, to grind. *P. pr.* moulant. *P. p.* moulu.

Pres. Je mouds, tu mouds, il moud, nous moulons, vous moulez, ils moulent. *Subj. Pres.* Que je moule.

Pret. Je moulus. *Fut.* Je moudrai.

In the same manner: *Emoudre*, to grind (knives, etc.), to sharpen, and *remoudre*, to grind again.

13. *Résoudre*, to resolve, *P. pr.* résolvant. *P. p.* résolu (*or* résous).

Pres. Je résous, tu résous, il résout, nous *résolvons*, vous *résolvez*, ils *résolvent*. *Subj.* Que je *résolve*.

Pret. Je résolus, tu résolus, etc.

Fut. Je résoudrai. *Imper.* Résous, *résolvons*, *résolvez*.

Thus: *Absoudre*, to absolve, and *dissoudre*, to dissolve.

These two compounds have no Preterite, and make their Participles: *absous*, f. *absoute*, and *dissous*, f. *dissoute*.

14. *Peindre*, to paint. *P. pr.* peignant. *P. p.* peint.

Pres. Je peins, tu peins, il peint, nous peignons, vous peignez, ils peignent. *Subj.* Que je peigne.

Imperf. Je peignais.

Pret. Je peignis, tu peignis, il peignit, nous peignîmes, etc.

Fut. Je peindrai. *Imper.* Peins, peignons, peignez.

Thus: *Ceindre*, to gird. *Feindre*, to feign; *dépeindre*, to depict. *Teindre*, to dye; *déteindre*, to discharge color; *atteindre*, to attain, to reach; *éteindre*, to extinguish. *Restreindre*, to restrain. *Enfreindre* to infringe, to transgress.

15. *Craindre*, to fear. *P. pr.* craignant. *P. p.* craint.

Pres. Je crains, tu crains, il craint, nous craignons, etc.

Pret. Je craignis. *Fut.* Je craindrai, etc.

Thus also: *Plaindre*, to pity; *se plaindre*, to complain; *contraindre*, to compel, to constrain.

16. *Joindre*, to join. *P. pr.* joignant. *P. p.* joint.

Pres. Je joins, tu joins, il joint, nous joignons, vous joignez, ils joignent. *Subj.* Que je joigne.

Pret. Je joignis. *Fut.* Je joindrai.

Thus: *Rejoindre*, to rejoin; *enjoindre*, to enjoin; *disjoindre*, to disjoin; *Poindre*, to dawn, break; *Oindre*, to anoint.

17. *Ecrire*, to write. *P. pr.* écrivant. *P. p.* écrit.

Pres. J'écris, tu écris, il écrit, nous écrivons, vous écrivez, ils écrivent. *Subj.* Que j'écrive, etc.

Pret. J'écrivis, tu écrivis, il écrivit, etc.
Fut. J'écrirai. *Impér.* Écris, écrivons, écrivez.

Thus: *Décrire,* to describe; *circonscrire,* to circumscribe; *inscrire,* to inscribe; *prescrire,* to prescribe, to order; *récrire,* to write again, to answer; *souscrire,* to subscribe; *transcrire,* to transcribe.

VOCABULARY.

La vache, the cow.
le précepteur, the tutor.
la difficulté, the difficulty.
la vie, the life.
allemand, German.
le meunier, the miller.
partir, to set out.
la marche, course, the course.
la cendre, the ashes.
la fumée, the smoke.
la chandelle, the candle.

THEME 39.

1. We milk the cows. 2. Soldiers! follow me. 3. I will lead you to (the) victory. 4. I shall follow you. 5. This dog follows me everywhere. 6. You did not follow the lessons of your tutor. 7. The enemies were conquered. 8. You conquer all the difficulties. 9. That did not convince me. 10. They pursued (*Pret.*) the slave, but in vain (*en vain*). 11. She was sewing her gown. 12. These handkerchiefs are badly sewed. 13. I sewed them myself. 14. Does the miller grind the corn? 15. He has not ground it this morning. 16. He will grind it this evening. 17. I fear the rain. 18. We do not fear death; why should we fear it? 19. I resolved (*de*) to set out. 20. We pursued our course. 21. I have at last (*enfin*) convinced him of the greatness of his fault. 22. The wood which is burnt (*qu'on brûle*) resolves itself (*se*) into (*en*) ashes and smoke. 23. We pity the unfortunate. 24. You paint. 25. The young girl feigned to be ill. 26. Put out the candle and go to bed (*allez vous coucher*). 27. The servant feared (*de*) to displease his master (*à son maître*). 28. Charles wrote his translation last night (*hier au soir*).

XL. QUARANTIÈME LEÇON.

IRREGULAR VERBS.—FIRST CLASS CONTINUED.

c. (18—26. The vowel of the root is changed into *u*, in the *Part. past* and in the *Preterite*.)

18. *Lire*, to read. *P. pr.* lisant. *P. p. lu.*
Pres. Je lis, tu lis, il lit, nous lisons, vous lisez, ils lisent.
Pret. Je *lus*, tu lus, il lut, nous lûmes, vous lûtes, etc.
Imperf. Subj. Que je lusse.
Fut. Je lirai, tu liras, il lira, etc.

Thus also: *élire*, to elect; *réélire*, to reëlect; *relire*, to read over again.

19. *Boire*, to drink. *P. pr. buvant.* *P. p. bu.*
Pres. Je bois, tu bois, il boit, nous buvons, vous buvez, ils boivent.
Subj. Que je boive, que tu boives, qu'il boive, que nous buvions, que vous buviez, qu'ils boivent.
Imperf. Je buvais.
Pret. Je *bus*, tu bus, il but, nous bûmes, vous bûtes, ils burent.
Fut. Je boirai, tu boiras, etc.
Imper. Bois, buvons, buvez.

20. *Croire*, to believe, to think. *P. pr. croyant.* *P. p. cru.*
Pres. Je crois, tu crois, il croit, nous croyons, vous croyez, ils croient.
Subj. Que je croie, que tu croies, qu'il croie, que nous croyions, que vous croyiez, qu'ils croient.
Pret. Je *crus*, tu crus, il crut, nous crûmes, vous crûtes, ils crurent.
Fut. Je croirai, etc.

Faire accroire qch. à qn., to make one believe.
N. B. *accroire* is only used in the Infinitive.

21. *Croître*, to grow. *P. pr. croissant. P. p. crû.*

Pres. Je croîs, tu croîs, il croît, nous croissons, vous croissez, ils croissent.

Pret. Je *crûs*, tu crûs, il crût, nous crûmes, etc.

Fut. Je croîtrai, etc.

Thus: *Accroître*, to increase; *décroître*, to decrease; *recroître*, to grow again.

22. *Plaire*, to please. *P. pr.* plaisant. *P. p. plu.*

Pres. Je plais, tu plais, il plaît, nous plaisons, vous plaisez, ils plaisent. *Subj.* Que je plaise, etc.

Pret. Je *plus*, tu plus, il plut, nous plûmes, vous plûtes, ils plurent. *Fut.* Je plairai, tu plairas, etc.

Thus: *Se complaire*, to delight in . . .; *déplaire*, to displease. (*S'il vous plaît* — if you please.)

23. *Taire*, to conceal. *P. pr.* taisant. *P. p. tu.*

Pres. Je tais, tu tais, il tait, nous taisons, vous taisez, ils taisent.

Subj. Que je taise, que tu taises, qu'il taise, etc.

Pret. Je *tus*, tu tus, il tut, nous tûmes, vous tûtes, ils turent.

Fut. Je tairai.

Thus: *Se taire*, to be silent. Pres. *Je me tais*, I am silent. Imper. *Tais-toi, taisez-vous.* Pret. *Je me tus*, I was silent. Comp. of the Pres. *Je me suis tu*, I have been silent.

24. *Paraître*, to appear. *P. pr.* paraissant. *P. p. paru.*

Pres. Je parais, tu parais, il paraît, nous paraissons, vous paraissez, il paraissent. *Subj.* Que je paraisse.

Pret. Je *parus*, tu parus, il parut, etc.

Fut. Je paraîtrai.

Thus: *Apparaître*, to appear; *comparaître*, to appear before the judge; *disparaître*, to disappear; *reparaître*, to reappear.

25. *Paître*, to graze. *P. pr.* paissant.

Like *paraître*, but no *Pret.*

Thus: *Repaître*, to feed; with the Pret. *Je repus.* Part. *repu.*

26. *Connaître*,* to know. *P. pr.* connaissant. *P. p. connu.*

* *Connaître* is used in connection with knowledge obtained through one of the five senses, — *savoir* in other cases.

Pres. Je connais, tu connais, il connaît, nous connaissons, vous connaissez, etc.

Pret. Je *connus.* *Fut.* Je connaîtrai.

Thus: *Méconnaître,* to mistake, not to acknowledge; *reconnaître,* to recognize, to know again, to acknowledge.

VOCABULARY.

La conduite, the conduct.
triste, sad.
le traitement, the treatment.
le jour, the daylight.
sombre, dark.
impossible, impossible.

THEME 40.

1. What are you reading there? 2. Why did you read my letter? 3. I have not read it, and I shall not read it. 4. Read over again your lesson. 5. Dost thou drink water? 6. No, I drink wine and water. 7. When you are thirsty, what do you drink? 8. We drink fresh water. 9. Do you believe that? 10. No, I do not believe it. 11. I thought (that) you had written your exercise, but I see (*je vois*) that I am mistaken. 12. She grows every day. 13. These trees have grown rapidly (*rapidement*). 14. He did not believe what I said. 15. I (have) thought that we would be here before six o'clock. 16. The young gentleman pleased by his conduct. 17. Be silent, Frederick. 18. Tell (to) your sister, if you please, to bring me her French grammar. 19. Do you know my brother? 20. No, I do not know him. 21. You appear sad, what is the matter with you (*qu'avez-vous*)? 22. Such a treatment (has) appeared to me very cruel. 23. The daylight has disappeared.

XLI. QUARANTE ET UNIÈME LEÇON.

IRREGULAR VERBS.—FIRST CLASS CONTINUED.

27. *Faire*, to do, to make. *P. pr.* faisant.* *P. p.* fait.

Pres. Je fais, tu fais, il fait, nous faisons, vous *faites*, ils *font*.

Pres. Subj. Que je *fasse*, que tu *fasses*, qu'il *fasse*, que nous *fassions*, que vous *fassiez*, qu'ils *fassent*.

Imperf. Je faisais (fesais), tu faisais, il faisait, etc.

Pret. Je *fis*, tu *fis*, il *fit*, nous *fîmes*, vous *fîtes*, ils *firent*.

Imperf. Subj. Que je *fisse*, que tu fisses, qu'il fît, que nous fissions, que vous fissiez, qu'ils fissent.

Fut. Je *ferai*, tu feras, etc.

Imper. Fais, faisons, *faites*.

Conjugate in the same manner the compounds of *faire*, viz.: *défaire*, to undo, to loosen; *contrefaire*, to counterfeit; *refaire*, to do again; *satisfaire*, to satisfy; *surfaire*, to exact, ask too much.

28. *Mettre*, to put. *P. pr.* mettant. *P. p.* mis.

Pres. Je mets, tu mets, il met, nous mettons, vous mettez, ils mettent. *Pres. Subj.* Que je mette.

Imperf. Je mettais.

Pret. Je *mis*, tu *mis*, il *mit*, nous *mîmes*, vous *mîtes*, ils *mirent*.

Imperf. Subj. Que je *misse*, que tu misses, qu'il mît, etc.

Fut. Je mettrai, tu mettras, etc.

Thus: *Admettre*, to admit; *commettre*, to commit; *démettre*, to turn out; *omettre*, to omit; *permettre*, to permit, to allow; *promettre*, to promise; *compromettre*, to compromise, to expose; *remettre*, to put again, to replace, to hand over; *soumettre*, to submit; *transmettre*, to transmit, to send.

Se mettre à signifies to begin, as: *L'enfant se mit à pleurer*, the child began crying.

29. *Prendre*, to take. *P. pr.* prenant. *P. p.* pris.

* For the pronunciation of *faisant* and its derivatives see p. 18.

Pres. Je prends, tu prends, il prend, nous pre*n*ons, vous pre*n*ez, ils pre*nn*ent. *Pres. Subj.* Que je pre*nn*e, que tu pre*nn*es, qu'il pre*nn*e, que nous pre*n*ions, que vous pre*n*iez, qu'ils pre*nn*ent.

Imperf. Je pre*n*ais.

Pret. Je pris, tu pris, il prit, nous prîmes, vous prîtes, ils prirent. *Imperf. Subj.* Que je prisse.

Fut. Je prendrai. *Imper.* Prends, pre*n*ons, pre*n*ez.

Conjugate in the same manner the compounds of *prendre: Apprendre,* to learn; *désapprendre,* to unlearn; *rapprendre,* to learn over again; *comprendre,* to understand; *entreprendre,* to undertake; *méprendre,* to mistake; *reprendre,* to take again, to reply, to chide; *surprendre,* to surprise.

30. *Naître,** to be born. *P. pr.* naissant. *P. p. né.*

Pres. Je nais, tu nais, il naît, nous naissons, vous naissez, ils naissent. *Imperf.* Je naissais.

Pret. Je *naquis* (I was born), tu *naquis,* il *naquit,* nous *naquîmes,* vous *naquîtes,* ils *naquirent.*

Fut. Je naîtrai, tu naîtras, etc.

Thus also: *Renaître,* to be born again.

REMARK. When the person used as subject of the verb is *living,* the present instead of the past of the auxiliary is used with the past participle. Ex.: *Mon père est né en Angleterre,* My father (still living) was born in England.

31. *Vivre,* to live. *P. pr.* vivant. *P. p. vécu.*

Pres. Je vis, tu vis, il vit, nous vivons, vous vivez, ils vivent. *Subj.* Que je vive; *hence the expressions:* Vive! *pl.* vivent! *long live!*

Imper. Vis, vivons, vivez. *Imperf.* Je vivais.

Pret. Je *vécus,* tu *vécus,* il *vécut,* nous *vécûmes,* etc.

Fut. Je vivrai.

Thus also: *Survivre (à qn.),* to survive; *revivre,* to live again.

* Verbs marked thus * take *être* for an auxiliary, instead of *avoir.*

VOCABULARY.

L'après-midi, f. the afternoon.
le ruban, the ribbon.
une fois, once.
païen, pagan.
désormais, henceforward.
obéissant, obedient.
une ligne, a line.
un compagnon de voyage, a fellow-traveller.
la décision, the decision.
l'abondance, f. abundance.

THEME 41.

1. What are you doing there? 2. I am writing my exercise. 3. Have you written it? 4. Yes, I have written it. 5. Charles will write it this afternoon. 6. These pupils make a great many mistakes in their exercises. 7. Put this book on the table. 8. Where have you put your penknife? 9. I have put it in my drawer (*tiroir*, m.). 10. Did your father permit you to go to the theatre? 11. Yes, he has allowed it. 12. He allows me to go there (*d'y aller*) once a (*par*) week. 13. The servant promised henceforward to be faithful and obedient. 14. All the children began to cry. 15. I take medicine. 16. He takes coffee. 17. We take tea. 18. The children take milk. 19. I took a pen and wrote a few lines to my father. 20. Who has taken my pencil? 21. I have not taken it. 22. Take mine. 23. Do not take this chair; it is broken (*cassée*). 24. Do you understand what I say? 25. I understand every word. 26. I should undertake that journey, if I had a fellow-traveller. 27. We submit ourselves to your decision. 28. Formerly we lived in the country, but for (*depuis*) several years we have lived (*Pres. tense*) in Geneva (*Genève*). 29. Many rich people live in abundance.

XLII. QUARANTE-DEUXIÈME LEÇON.

IRREGULAR VERBS.—SECOND CLASS.

(32—41. Verbs ending in *ir*, having the flexions of the *Third* Conjugation.)

32. *Fuir*, to shun, to flee. *P. pr.* fuyant. *P. p.* fui.

Pres. Je fuis, tu fuis, il fuit, nous *fuyons*, vous fuyez, ils fuient.

Imperf. Je fuyais.

Pret. Je fuis. *Fut.* Je fuirai.

Conjugate in the same manner: *S'enfuir*, to run away. Pres. *Je m'enfuis.* Comp. of the Pres. *Je me suis enfui*, I have run away.

33. *Vêtir*, to clothe. *P. pr.* vêtant. *P. p.* vêtu.

Pres. Je vêts, tu vêts, il vêt, nous vêtons, etc.

Pret. Je vêtis. *Fut.* Je vêtirai.

Thus also: *Dévêtir*, to divest; *revêtir*, to invest.

34. *Servir* (qn.), to serve, to help. *P. pr.* servant. *P. p.* servi.

Pres. Je *sers*, tu *sers*, il *sert*, nous servons, vous servez, ils servent. *Subj.* Que je serve.

Pret. Je servis. *Fut.* Je servirai.

Thus also: *Desservir*, to clear the table; *se servir de*, to make use of, to use.

35. *Dormir*, to sleep. *P. pr.* dormant. *P. p.* dormi.

Pres. Je *dors*, tu *dors*, il *dort*, nous dormons, vous dormez, ils dorment. *Subj.* Que je dorme.

Pret. Je dormis, etc., like *servir*.

Thus: *Endormir*, to lull asleep; *s'endormir*, to fall asleep; *se rendormir*, to fall asleep again.

36. *Partir*, to set out, to leave. *P. pr.* partant. *P. p.* parti.

Pres. Je *pars*, tu *pars*, il *part*, nous partons, etc., like *servir*.

Thus: *Repartir*, to set off again, to reply. Not to be confounded with *répartir*, to distribute, which is regular.

37. *Mentir*, to lie. *P. pr.* mentant. *P. p.* menti.

Pres. Je ***mens***, tu ***mens***, il ***ment***, nous mentons, etc., like ***servir***.

Thus also: *Dementir*, to give the lie.

38. *Sentir*, to feel, to smell. *P. pr.* sentant. *P. p.* senti.

Pres. Je ***sens***, tu ***sens***, il ***sent***, nous sentons, etc., like ***servir***.

Thus: *Consentir*, to consent; *pressentir*, to foresee; *ressentir*, to feel.

39. *Se* ***repentir*** de qch., to repent. *P. pr.* se repentant. *P. p.* repenti.

Pres. Je me ***repens***, I repent, etc., like ***sentir***.

40. *Sortir*, to go out. *P. pr.* sortant. *P. p.* sorti.

Pres. Je ***sors***, tu ***sors***, il ***sort***, etc., like ***servir***.

Thus: *Ressortir*, to go out again. *Ressortir*, to resort, and *assortir*, to assort, are regularly conjugated like *finir*.

41. *Courir*, to run. *P. pr.* courant. *P. p.* ***couru***.

Pres. Je cours, tu cours, il court, nous courons, vous courez, ils courent. *Subj.* Que je coure.

Pret. Je ***courus***, tu courus, il courut, nous courûmes, vous courûtes, ils coururent.

Fut. Je ***courrai***, tu courras, il courra, nous courrons, vous courrez, ils courront. *Imper.* Cours, courons, courez.

Thus: *Accourir*, to run to; *concourir*, to compete; *discourir*, to discourse; *encourir*, to incur; *parcourir*, to run over; *recourir*, to have recourse; *secourir*, to relieve, to assist.

42. *Cueillir*, to gather. *P. pr.* cueillant. *P. p.* cueilli.

Pres. Je cueill***e***, tu cueill***es***, il cueill***e***, nous cueillons, vous cueillez, ils cueillent. *Subj.* Que je cueille.

Pret. Je cueillis. *Imper.* Cueille, cueillons, cueillez.

Fut. Je ***cueillerai***.

Thus: *Accueillir*, to receive; *recueillir*, to gather.

43. *Offrir*, to offer. *P. pr.* offrant. *P. p.* ***offert***.

Pres. J'offre, tu offr***es***, il offr***e***, nous offrons, etc.

Pret. J'offris. *Imper.* Offre, offrons, offrez. *Fut.* J'offrirai.

44. *Souffrir*, to suffer. *P. pr.* souffrant. *P. p. souffert.*

Pres. Je souffre, tu souffres, etc., like *offrir*.

45. *Ouvrir*, to open. *P. pr.* ouvrant. *P. p. ouvert.*

Pres. J'ouvre, etc., like *offrir*.

Thus: *Rouvrir*, to open again; *entr'ouvrir*, to open a little.

46. *Couvrir*, to cover. *P. pr.* couvrant. *P. p. couvert.*

Thus: *Découvrir*, to discover; *recouvrir*, to cover over.

47. *Tressaillir*, to start, to tremble. *P. pr.* tressaillant. *P. p.* tressailli.

Pres. Je tressaill*e*, tu tressaill*es*, il tressaill*e*, etc.

Pret. Je tressaillis, etc.

Fut. Je tressaill*e*rai and je tressaill*i*rai.

Thus: *Assaillir*, to assault.

48. *Saillir*, to put out, project. *P. pr.* saillant. *P. p.* sailli.

Pres. third person, il saille, *pl.* ils saillent. Like *tressaillir*; but it is used only in the *third person singular* and *plural*.

Saillir (= *jaillir*), to gush, is regular.

VOCABULARY.

Du mouton, mutton.
la voiture, the coach.
mépriser, to despise.
fatigué, tired.
la violette, the violet.
la livre, the pound.

THEME 42.

1. The enemy flee. 2. Let us shun these places. 3. We clothe the poor. 4. The young girl was clad in black. 5. I cannot meet him; he shuns me. 6. Avoid bad company. 7. Your friend, Mr. A., does not serve me well. 8. I made use of your coach. 9. Tell me what he has done to you; but, above all (*surtout*), do not lie. 10. He who lies deserves to be despised. 11. I go out every day. 12. Do not go out, Robert; it is too cold. 13. If I were as ill as you, I would not go out of my room. 14. I feel the cold. 15. Do not make any (*de*) noise, for my mother is asleep (sleeps). 16. I hope she will sleep better to-night (*cette nuit*). 17. If I do

not walk a little, I shall fall asleep. 18. Do you not repent of what (*de ce que*) you have done? 19. I always repent when I have done wrong (*mal*). 20. Do not run so fast (*vite*), you will be tired. 21. They always run when they go to see their aunt. 22. I ran faster than you. 23. If she is unhappy, I shall relieve her. 24. For whom are you gathering these violets? 25. I gather them for my mother. 26. The young lady has been received with the greatest kindness. 27. I always offer him my services. 28. He offered me a hundred pounds for my garden. 29. What are you doing there? 30. I cover the plants with (*de*) snow.

XLIII. QUARANTE-TROISIÈME LEÇON.

IRREGULAR VERBS.—THIRD CLASS.

(49—53. Verbs in *ir* changing their radical vowel and taking the flexions of the third Conjugation.)

49. *Mourir,** to die. *P. pr.* mourant. *P. p. mort.*

Pres. Je *meurs*, tu *meurs*, il *meurt*, nous mourons, vous mourez, ils *meurent*. *Subj.* Que je *meure*, que tu *meures*, qu'il *meure*, que nous mourions, que vous mouriez, qu'ils *meurent*.

Imper. Meurs, mourons, mourez.

Pret. Je mourus, tu mourus, il mourut, nous mourûmes, vous mourûtes, ils moururent.

Fut. Je mourrai, tu mourras, il mourra, etc.

Thus also: *Se mourir,* to be near dying, to be fainting. Pres. *Je me meurs*, etc.

50. *Bouillir*, to boil, *neut. v.* *P. pr.* bouillant. *P. p.* bouilli.

Pres. Je *bous*, tu *bous*, il *bout*, nous bouillons, vous bouillez, ils bouillent. *Subj.* Que je bouille.

Pret. Je bouillis.

Fut. Je bouillirai.

To boil, as an active verb, is rendered *faire bouillir*, as: To boil potatoes, *faire bouillir des pommes de terre.*

51. *Venir*,* to come. *P. pr.* venant. *P. p.* ven*u*.

Pres. Je *viens*, tu viens, il vient, nous venons, vous venez, ils viennent. *Pres. Subj.* Que je vienne, que tu viennes, qu'il vienne, que nous venions, que vous veniez, qu'ils viennent. *Imperf.* Je venais.

Pret. Je *vins*, tu vins, il vint, nous vînmes, vous vîntes, ils vinrent. *Imperf. Subj.* Que je *vinsse*, que tu vinsses, qu'il vînt, que nous vinssions, etc.

Fut. Je *viendrai*, tu viendras, etc.

Cond. Je viendrais.

Imper. *Viens*, venons, venez.

Conjugate in the same manner: *Convenir*, to agree, to suit; *devenir*,* to become; *intervenir*,* to intervene; *parvenir*,* to attain, to reach; *prévenir*, to be beforehand with, to inform; *provenir*,* to arise, spring from, to proceed; *se souvenir*, to remember; *survenir*,* to happen; *subvenir*, to relieve; *revenir*,* to come back (again).

52. *Tenir*, to hold. *P. pr.* tenant. *P. p.* ten*u*.

This verb is conjugated like *venir*, as:

Pres. Je *tiens*, tu tiens, il tient, nous tenons, vous tenez, ils tiennent. *Subj.* Que je tienne.

Pret. Je *tins*, tu tins, il tint, nous tînmes, vous tîntes, ils tinrent. *Fut.* Je tiendrai.

Imper. *Tiens*, tenons, tenez.

Thus also: *Appartenir*, to belong; *s'abstenir*, to abstain; *contenir*, to contain; *détenir*, to detain; *entretenir*, to keep up; *maintenir*, to maintain; *obtenir*, to obtain; *retenir*, to retain; *soutenir*, to sustain, uphold, support.

53. *Acquérir*, to acquire. *P. pr.* acquérant. *P. p.* acqu*is*.

Pres. J'*acquiers*, tu acquiers, il acquiert, nous acquérons, vous acquérez, ils acquièrent. *Pres. Subj.* Que j'acquière, que tu acquières, qu'il acquière, que nous acquérions, que vous acquériez, qu'ils acquièrent.

Pret. J'acqu*is*, tu acqu*is*, il acqu*it*, nous acqu*îmes*, vous acqu*îtes*, ils acqu*irent*. *Impf. Subj.* Que j'acquisse.

Fut. J'*acquerrai*, tu acquerras, il acquerra, etc.

Imper. Acqu*iers*, acquérons, acquérez.

Conjugate in the same manner: *Conquérir*, to conquer; *reconquérir*, to conquer again; *requérir*, to request, and *s'enquérir*, to inquire. *Quérir*, to seek, is used, in familiar conversation, after *aller*, *venir*, *envoyer*, as: *allez quérir*, go and seek.

VOCABULARY.

Le chagrin, grief.
maladie, f. disease, illness.
douloureux, -se, painful.
continuer, to continue.
la parole, the word.
l'assiduité, f. assiduity.
des connaissances, f. knowledge.
la chaleur, the heat.
la partie, the part.

THEME 43.

1. Your friend is dying. 2. Mrs. A. died of (*de*) grief. 3. The old general died at Paris of a very painful disease. 4. Take the water off the fire; it boils. 5. Boil that meat again, it has not boiled long enough. 6. Miss Emily is coming. 7. Dost thou come? 8. Yes, I come. 9. Why do you not come when I call you? 10. He came to see me every morning. 11. Come back soon. 12. I shall be (come) back in an hour. 13. Mrs. B. would have come to us if it had not rained (*plu*). 14. I hope you will keep your word and (will) come to-morrow. 15. I maintain, and will always maintain, that you will not be happy without virtue. 16. I agree that Miss L. is the prettiest of the family; but she is so proud, that I know (*sais*) not what will become of her (*ce qu'elle* . . .). 17. My uncle will not come back to-day. 18. Mr. S. will not obtain that situation (*place*). 19. If you study much, you will acquire knowledge. 20. I do not think (that) this color suits (to) your sister. 21. That hat would suit you very well, if you were a little taller. 22. Alexander the Great conquered the greatest part of Asia. 23. Your uncle has acquired a great name in America. 24. The young man did not survive (outlive) (to) that misfortune. 25. You will become a great man, if you continue to study with the same assiduity.

XLIV. QUARANTE-QUATRIÈME LEÇON.

IRREGULAR VERBS.—THIRD CLASS CONTINUED.

(54—66. Verbs in *-oir*. Contraction of the root and the terminations, *Part. past and Pret.* in *u*.)

54. *Devoir*, to owe, (ought to). *P. pr.* devant. *P. p. dû.*

Pres. Je *dois*,* tu *dois*, il *doit*, nous devons, vous devez, ils *doivent*. *Pres. Subj.* Que je *doive*.

Pret. Je dus, tu dus, il dut, nous dûmes, vous dûtes, ils durent. *Imperf. Subj.* Que je dusse.

Fut. Je devrai, tu devras, etc. *Cond.* Je devrais.*

Thus also: *redevoir.*

55. *Recevoir*, to receive. *P. pr.* recevant. *P. p. reçu.*

Pres. Je *reçois*, tu *reçois*, il *reçoit*, nous recevons, vous recevez, ils reç*oi*vent.

Pret. Je reç*us*, tu reç*us*, il reç*ut*, nous reç*ûmes*, vous reç*ûtes*, ils reç*urent*.

Fut. Je recevrai, tu recevras, etc.

Thus also: *Décevoir*, to deceive; *apercevoir*, to perceive; *concevoir*, to conceive; *percevoir*, to collect.

56. *Déchoir*, to fall, to decay. (No *P. pr.*) *P. p. déchu.*

Pres. Je *déchois*, tu déchois, il déchoit, nous décho*y*ons, vous décho*y*ez, ils déchoient. *Subj.* Que je déchoie.

Pret. Je déchus, tu déchus, il déchut, nous déchûmes, vous déchûtes, ils déchurent.

Fut. Je déch*errai*, tu déch*erras*, ils déch*erra*, nous déch*errons*, vous déch*errez*, ils déch*erront*.

Thus: *Echoir*, to fall to, to expire; P. pr. *échéant*; P. p. *échu*. It is now only used in the third pers. sing.: *il* or *elle échoit, il échut, etc.* *Choir* is only used in the Infinitive mood.

* Je dois, followed by a verb, corresponds to the English; *I am to*, *I must*. Je devrais, *I ought to, I should*.

57. *Faloir*, to be necessary, is an impersonal verb, the conjugation of which has been given p. 147.

Pres. Il *faut*. *Imperf*. Il fallait, etc.

58. *Mouvoir*, to move. *P. pr*. mouvant. *P. p. mu.*

Pres. Je *meus*, tu *meus*, il *meut*, nous mouvons, vous mouvez, ils *meuvent*. *Subj*. Que je *meuve*, que tu *meuves*, qu'il *meuve*, que nous mouvions, que vous mouviez, qu'ils *meuvent*.

Pret. Je mus, tu mus, il mut, nous mûmes, vous mûtes, ils murent.

Fut. Je mouvrai.

Thus also: *Émouvoir*, to move, to excite, stir up; *s'émouvoir*, to be moved, affected.

59. *Pleuvoir*, to rain (*impers.*). *P. pr*. pleuvant. *P. p. plu.*

Pres. Il pleut. *Subj*. Qu'il pleuve. *Imperf*. Il pleuvait.

Pret. Il plut. *Subj. Imperf*. Qu'il plût.

Fut. Il pleuvra.

60. *Pourvoir*,* to provide. *P. pr*. pourvoyant. *P. p. pourvu.*

Pres. Je *pourvois*, tu pourvois, il pourvoit, nous pourvoyons, vous pourvoyez, ils pourvoient.

Pret. Je *pourvus*. *Fut*. Je pourvoirai.

Thus: *Prévoir*, to foresee, which makes in the Pret. *je prévis*.

61. *Pouvoir*, to be able. *P. pr*. pouvant. *P. p. pu.*

Pres. Je *peux* (or je *puis*), tu *peux*, il *peut*, nous pouvons, vous pouvez, ils *peuvent*. *Pres. Subj*. Que je *puisse*, que tu *puisses*, qu'il *puisse*, que nous *puissions*, que vous *puissiez*, qu'ils *puissent*.

Impf. Je pouvais.

Pret. Je pus, tu pus, il put, nous pûmes, vous pûtes, ils purent.

Imperf. Subj. Que je *pusse*.

Fut. Je *pourrai*, tu pourras, il pourra, nous pourrons, vous pourrez, ils pourront. *Cond*. Je pourrais.

NOTE. May, expressing a wish, is rendered by the Present tense of the Subjunctive. Ex.: *Puisse-t-il être heureux*, may he be happy!

* Like 65 — Voir, except the *Pret*. and *Fut*.

62. *Savoir*, to know. *P. pr.* sachant. *P. p.* su.

Pres. Je *sais*, tu *sais*, il *sait*, nous savons, vous savez, ils savent. *Subj.* Que je *sache*, que tu sa*ches*, qu'il sa*che*, que nous sa*ch*ions, que vous sa*ch*iez, qu'ils sa*ch*ent. *Imperf.* Je savais, tu savais, etc.

Pret. Je sus, tu sus, il sut, nous sûmes, vous sûtes, ils surent.

Fut. Je *saurai*, tu *sauras*, etc.

Imper. Sache, sachons, sachez.

When the word *can* means *to know how*, it is rendered in French by *savoir*, instead of *pouvoir*. Ex.: *Saves-vous parler français?* Can you speak French?

Note. There is also an old form of the Pres. Ind. *Je sache.* The Cond. *Je ne saurais* (without *pas*) signifies, I cannot, as: *Je ne saurais vous dire*, I cannot tell you.

63. *Valoir*, to be worth. *P. pr.* valant. *P. p.* valu.

Pres. Je *vaux*, tu *vaux*, il *vaut*, nous valons, vous valez, ils valent. *Subj.* Que je *vaille*, que tu *vailles*, qu'il *vaille*, que nous valions, que vous valiez, qu'ils *vaillent*.

Imperf. Je valais.

Pret. Je valus, tu valus, il valut, nous valûmes, etc.

Fut. Je *vaudrai*, tu *vaudras*, etc.

Cond. Je *vaudrais*.

Observe the expression: *Il vaut mieux*, it is better, etc. Conjugate in the same manner: *prévaloir*, to prevail; but it makes the Subj. pres.: *Que je prévale* (not *prévaille*), *que tu prévales, qu'il prévale, que nous prévalions, que vous prévaliez, qu'ils prévalent.*

64. *Vouloir*, to be willing. *P. pr.* voulant. *P. p.* voulu.

Pres. Je *veux*, tu *veux*, il *veut*, nous voulons, vous voulez, ils *veulent*. *Subj.* Que je *veuille*, que tu *veuilles*, qu'il *veuille*, que nous voulions, que vous vouliez, qu'ils *veuillent*. *Imper.* (*Veuille*), *veuillez*, be so kind as.

Imperf. Je voulais.

Pret. Je voulus, tu voulus, il voulut, nous voulûmes, etc.

Fut. Je voudrai, tu voudras, etc.

Cond. Je voudrais, *I should like to.*

The first person, *je veux*, is mostly used to imply authority, command. *Je désire* is substituted as a more polite expression for the *affirmative*. Je ne veux pas, is used, however, for the *negative*.

65. *Voir*, to see. *P. pr.* voyant. *P. p. vu.*

Pres. Je *vois*, tu vois, il voit, nous voyons, vous voyez, ils voient.

Imperf. Je voyais, tu voyais, etc.

Pret. Je *vis*, tu vis, il vit, nous vîmes, vous vîtes, etc.

Fut. Je *verrai*, tu *verras*, il *verra*, etc.

Imper. Vois, voyons, voyez.

Thus: *Revoir*, to see again; *entrevoir*, to have a glimpse of. For *pourvoir* and *prévoir* see No. 60. *Aller voir* and *venir voir qn.* are rendered: to call upon a person.

66. *S'asseoir*, to sit down. *P. pr.* s'asseyant. *P. p. assis.*

Pres. Je m'*assieds*, tu t'*assieds*, il s'*assied*, nous nous *asseyons*, vous vous *asseyez*, ils s'*asseient*. Or, je m'assois, etc.

Imperf. Je m'asseyais. Or, je m'assoyais, etc.

Pret. Je m'assis, tu t'assis, il s'assit, nous nous assîmes, vous vous assîtes, ils s'assirent.

Fut. Je m'*assiérai*, tu t'*assiéras*, il s'*assiéra*, etc. Or, je m'as*seierai*, tu t'asse*ieras*, il s'asse*iera*, etc.

Imper. Assie*ds*-toi, assey*ons*-nous, assey*ez*-vous.

VOCABULARY.

Un panier, a basket.
le danger, the danger.
le ressort, the spring.
le beau-frère, the brother-in-law.
répéter, to repeat.
coupable, criminal.
la glace, the looking-glass.
épais, thick.
l'herbe, f. the grass.
humide, damp.
le bruit, *la nouvelle*, the report.
arrêter, to stop.
l'adresse, f. the direction.

THEME 44.

1. I am to copy my exercise. 2. We must set out. 3. You ought to come at two o'clock. 4. I receive a letter every day. 5. We receive our money from the banker (*du banquier*). 6. My friend received a basket filled with grapes (*de raisins*). 7. The

hunter perceived a bird on a tree. 8. They did not perceive the danger. 9. The spring which moves the whole machine is very ingenious (*ingénieux*). 10. Does it rain? 11. No, it does not rain; but it will rain this evening. 12. If men do not provide for it (*y*), God will provide for it. 13. Before he left (*avant de partir*), he provided for (*à*) all. 14. Can you come? 15. I cannot come, but my brother can (come). 16. We could see nothing, for it was dark (*il faisait nuit*). 17. I could do it myself, if I had time. 18. *May* you be happy! I could do no better. 19. I know that he is your friend, but I did not know that he was your brother-in-law. 20. Do you know why he has (is) not come? 21. No, I do not know (it). 22. When you know (*Fut.*) your lesson, come and repeat it to me. 23. These pens *are worth* nothing. 24. It is (*vaut*) better to be unfortunate than guilty. 25. Can't you see that star? 26. I do not see it. 27. Sit down there a minute. 28. Why do not you sit down? 29. Let us sit upon the grass. 30. I would sit down upon the grass, if it were not so damp. 31. *Can* you speak French? 32. I *can* read, but I *cannot* speak [it]. 33. Is this report true? 34. I *cannot* (*Cond.*) tell (it) you. 35. He does not choose to (will not) eat. 36. If I chose (would), I should tell you where he lives. 37. What would you have me do (that I should do) (*Imperf. Subj.*)? 38. We could have stopped him, if we had *chosen*. 39. I send you herewith (*ci-joint*) the direction of Mr. L. 40. I have found the ring which my cousin has lost, and I shall send it to her.

XLV. QUARANTE-CINQUIÈME LEÇON.

IRREGULAR VERBS. — THIRD CLASS CONTINUED.

67. *Rire*, to laugh. *P. pr.* riant. *P. p.* ri.
Pres. Je ris. *Imperf.* Je riais.
Pret. Je ris, tu ris, il rit, etc. *Fut.* Je rirai.

68. *Envoyer*, to send. *P. pr.* envoyant. *P. p.* envoyé.
Pres. J'envoie. *Imperf.* J'envoyais. *Pret.* J'envoyai.
Fut. J'en*verrai*, tu en*verras*, etc. *Cond.* J'enverrais.

69. *Aller*,* to go. *P. pr.* allant. *P. p.* allé.
Pres. Je *vais*, tu *vas*, il *va*, nous allons, vous allez, ils *vont*.
Pres. Subj. Que j'*aille*, que tu *ailles*, qu'il *aille*, que nous allions, que vous alliez, qu'ils *aillent*.
Imperf. J'allais, tu allais, il allait, etc.
Pret. J'allai, tu allas, il alla, nous allâmes, vous allâtes, ils allèrent.
Imperf. Subj. Que j'allasse, que tu allasses, etc.
Imper. Va, allons, allez. *Perf.* Je suis allé, *I have gone.*
Fut. J'irai (*I shall go*), tu iras, il ira, nous irons, vous irez, ils iront. *Cond.* J'irais, tu irais, etc.

Conjugation of *S'en aller*, to go away.

We give the reflective verb *S'en aller*, to go away, at full length, because its conjugation is rather difficult on account of its two pronouns. Observe that *en* is never separated from the objective *m', t', s', nous, etc.;* hence it follows, that the compound or Perfect must not be written: *Je me suis en allé*, but *je m'en suis allé, tu t'en es allé, etc.*

INDICATIVE MOOD.

PRESENT TENSE.

Je m'en vais, *I go away.*		nous nous en allons, *we go away.*	
tu t'en vas,	etc.	vous vous en allez,	etc.
il s'en va,	etc.	ils s'en vont,	etc.

Neg. Je ne m'en vais pas.	M'en vais-je, *do I go away?* etc.
tu ne t'en vas pas, etc.	Ne m'en vais-je pas? etc.

IMPERFECT.

Je m'en allais, tu t'en allais.	M'en allais-je, *did I go away?*
Je ne m'en allais pas.	Ne m'en allais-je pas?

PRETERITE.

Je m'en allai.	M'en allai-je?
Je ne m'en allai pas.	Ne m'en allai-je pas?

FUTURE.

Je m'en irai.	M'en irai-je?
Je ne m'en irai pas.	Ne m'en irai-je pas?

IMPERATIVE.

AFFIRMATIVE.	NEGATIVE.
Va-t'en.	Ne t'en va pas.
(qu'il s'en aille).	(qu'il ne s'en aille pas).
allons-nous-en.	ne nous en allons pas.
allez-vous-en.	ne vous en allez pas.
(qu'ils s'en aillent).	(qu'ils ne s'en aillent pas).

COMPOUND OF THE PRESENT.

Je m'en suis allé, *I have gone away.*	nous nous en sommes allés.
tu t'en es allé.	vous vous en êtes allé(s).
il s'en est allé.	ils s'en sont allés.
elle s'en est allée.	elles s'en sont allées.

NEGATIVELY.

Je ne m'en suis pas allé.	nous ne nous en sommes pas allés.
tu ne t'en es pas allé.	vous ne vous en êtes pas allé(s).
il ne s'en est pas allé.	ils ne s'en sont pas allés.

INTERROGATIVELY.

M'en suis-je allé ?	nous en sommes-nous allés ?
t'en es-tu allé ?	vous en êtes-vous allé(s) ?
s'en est-il allé ?	s'en sont ils allés ?

NEGATIVE-INTERROGATIVE.

Ne m'en suis-je pas allé ?	ne nous en sommes-nous p. allés ?
ne t'en es-tu pas allé ?	ne vous en êtes-vous pas allés ?
ne s'en est-il pas allé ?	ne s'en sont-ils pas allés ?

COMPOUND OF THE IMPERFECT.

Je m'en étais allé.	M'en étais-je allé ?
Je ne m'en étais pas allé.	Ne m'en étais-je pas allé ?

SUBJUNCTIVE.

PRESENT.

Que je m'en aille.	que nous nous en allions.
que tu t'en ailles.	que vous vous en alliez.
qu'il s'en aille.	qu'ils s'en aillent.

IMPERFECT.	PERFECT.
Que je m'en allasse.	Que je m'en sois allé.
que tu t'en allasses.	PLUPERFECT.
qu'il s'en allât, etc.	Que je m'en fusse allé.

INFINITIVE.

S'en aller.	S'en être allé.

PARTICIPLES.

S'en allant.	S'en étant allé.

VOCABULARY.

Obligé, obliged.	*sonner*, to strike.
Jeudi dernier, last Thursday.	*la santé*, health.
la musique, music.	*importuner*, to importune.
le pavillon, the flag.	*hissé*, hoisted.

THEME 45.

1. I go to London. 2. Thou goest to Paris. 3. He goes to Berlin. 4. My brother has also gone to Berlin. 5 Where are you going? 6. I am going to the play (*au spectacle*). 7. I would go with you, if I had time. 8. Why are they going away so soon? 9. They are obliged to go away. 10. Will not your mother be angry (*fâchée*), if you go away before her? 11. I told her that I would go away before her, and she has permitted (it to) me. 12. My sister and I (we) went to the concert last Thursday. 13. If you had gone (there, *y*) also, you would have heard fine music. 14. These men went yesterday from house to (*en*) house. 15. At what o'clock will you go (away)? 16. I should have already gone, if it had not rained so fast (*fort*). 17. Is he really gone (away)? Yes, he went (has gone) away this morning. 18. Let us go (away), it is going to (*il va*) strike three o'clock. 19. How is (*va*) your health? 20. Thank you, it is not very good. 21. I wish (should like that) the boy would go (away) (*Imperf. Subj.*). 22. I wish they would go away. 23. Begone (go away), you importune me.

XLVI. QUARANTE-SIXIÈME LEÇON.

DEFECTIVE VERBS.

Verbs whereof some tenses or persons are wanting are defective verbs. They are as follows:—

70. *Braire*, to bray.
Pres. Il brait, ils braient. *Fut.* Il braira.
Cond. Il brairait.

71. *Bruire*, to roar. *P. pr.* bruyant.
Imperf. Il bruyait, *pl.* ils bruyaient.

72. *Choir*, to fall. *P. p.* chu.

73. *Clore*, to close. *P. p.* clos.

Pres. Je clos, tu clos, il clôt.

Fut. Je clorai, tu cloras, etc. *Cond.* Je clorais.

74. *Éclore*,* to be hatched. *P. p.* éclos.

Pres. Il éclôt, *pl.* ils éclosent. *Subj.* Qu'il éclose, *pl.* qu'ils éclosent.

Fut. Il éclôra, *pl.* ils éclôront. Its compound tenses are formed with *être*.

75. *Faillir*, to fail. *P. pr.* (faillant.) *P. p.* failli.

Pres. Il faut.

Pret. Je faillis, tu faillis, il faillit, nous faillîmes, vous faillîtes, ils faillirent.

Perf. J'ai failli, *I had nearly.*

Thus : *Défaillir*, to faint.

76. *Férir* is used only in the expression: *Sans coup férir*, without striking a blow.

77. *Frire*, to fry. *P. pr. wanting.* *P. p.* frit.

Pres. Je fris, tu fris, il frit. *Plur. wanting.*

Fut. Je frirai. *Cond.* Je frirais. *Perf.* J'ai frit, etc.

78. *Gésir*, to lie. *P. pr.* gisant.

Pres. ci-gît, *here lies ; pl.* ci-gisent (*used on tombstones*). *Further:* nous gisons, vous gisez, ils gisent.

Imperf. ci-gisait ; *pl.* ci-gisaient.

79. *Issir*, to be born, is used only in the *P. p. issu.*

80. *Ouïr*, to hear. *P. p.* ouï.

Pret. J'ouïs, tu ouïs, etc. *Imperf. Subj.* Que j'ouïsse, etc.

Further the compound tenses, as : *J'ai ouï, etc.*

81. *Sourdre*, to rush out of the ground, as water, has only the Infinitive and the Present, *elle sourd, elles sourdent.*

82. *Seoir*, to fit. *P. pr.* séant. *P. p.* sis.

Ind. pres. Il sied. *Fut.* Il siéra. *Cond.* Il siérait.

83. *Surseoir*, to put off. *P. p.* sursis.

Pres. Je surseois. *Pret.* Je sursis.

NOTE.—Most of these verbs are not much in use.

AN ALPHABETICAL LIST OF ALL THE FRENCH IRREGULAR AND DEFECTIVE VERBS.*

CONTAINING THEIR FIVE PRIMITIVE TENSES.

Infinitive.	*Pres.*	*Part. pr.*	*P. p.*	*Pret.*	*No.*
Absoudre	j'absous	absolvant	absous, te	*wanting*	13.
Acquérir	j'acquiers	acquérant	acquis, e	j'acquis	53.
Aller	je vais	allant	allé, e	j'allai	69.
Assaillir	j'assaille	assaillant	assailli, e	j'assaillis	47.
S'asseoir	je m'assieds	s'asseyant	assis, e	je m'assis	66.
Atteindre	j'atteins	atteignant	atteint, e	j'atteignis	14.
Battre, *see* L. XXIII., Rem. 1.					
Boire	je bois	buvant	bu, e	je bus	19.
Bouillir	je bous	bouillant	bouilli, e	je bouillis	50.
Braire	il brait	—	*wanting*	*wanting*	70.
Bruire *Imp.*	il bruyait	bruyant	—	—	71.
Ceindre	je ceins	ceignant	ceint, e	je ceignis	14.
Choir, *see* déchoir		—	—	—	56.
Circoncire	je circoncis	—	circoncis	je circoncis	2.
Clore	je clos	—	clos	—	73.
Conclure	je conclus	concluant	conclu, e	je concl*us*	*L.* 23.
Concevoir	je conçois	concevant	conçu, e	je conçus	55.
Conduire	je conduis	conduisant	conduit, e	je conduisis	5.
Confire	je confis	confisant	confit, e	je confis	2.
Connaître	je connais	connaissant	connu, e	je connus	26.
Coudre	je couds	cousant	cousu, e	je cousis	11.
Courir	je cours	courant	couru, e	je courus	41.
Couvrir	je couvre	couvrant	couvert, e	je couvris	46.
Craindre	je crains	craignant	craint, e	je craignis	15.
Croire	je crois	croyant	cru, e	je crus	20.
Croître	je croîs	croissant	crû, e	je crûs	21.
Cueillir	je cueille	cueillant	cueilli, e	je cuellis	42.
Cuire	je cuis	cuisant	cuit, e	je cuisis	4.
Déchoir	je déchois	—	déchu, e	je déchus	56.
Devoir	je dois	devant	dû	je dus	54.
Dire	je dis	disant	dit, e	je dis	7.
Dormir	je dors	dormant	dormi	je dormis	35.

* The *derivatives* which are not in this table will be found with the primitives under their respective number.

Échoir	il échoit	échéant	échu	il échut	56.
Éclore	il éclôt	—	éclos	—	74.
Ecrire	j'écris	écrivant	écrit, e	j'écrivis	17.
Envoyer	j'envoie	envoyant	envoyé	j'envoyai	68.
Faire	je fais	faisant	fait, e	je fis	27.
Faillir	—	faillant	failli	je faillis	75.
Falloir	il faut	—	fallu	il fallut	57.
Feindre	je feins	feignant	feint, e	je feignis	14.
Férir	—	—	—	—	76.
Frire	je fris	—	frit, e	—	77.
Fuir	je fuis	fuyant	fui	je fuis	32.
Gésir	il gît	gisant	—	—	78.
Joindre	je joins	joignant	joint, e	je joignis	16.
Issir	—	—	issu, e	—	79.
Instruire	j'instruis	instruisant	instruit, e	j'instruisis	6.
Lire	je lis	lisant	lu, e	je lus	18.
Luire	je luis	luisant	lui	—	1.
Mentir	je mens	mentant	menti	je mentis	37.
Mettre	je mets	mettant	mis, e	je mis	28.
Moudre	je mouds	moulant	moulu, e	je moulus	12.
Mourir	je meurs	mourant	mort, e	je mourus	49.
Mouvoir	je meus	mouvant	mu, e	je mus	58.
Naître	je nais	naissant	né, e	je naquis	30.
Nuire	je nuis	nuisant	nui	je nuisis	3.
Offrir	j'offre	offrant	offert, e	j'offris	43.
Oindre	j'oins	—	oint	j'oignis	16.
Ouïr	—	—	ouï	j'ouïs	80.
Ouvrir	j'ouvre	ouvrant	ouvert, e	j'ouvris	45.
Paître	je pais	paissant	pu	—	25.
Paraître	je parais	paraissant	paru	je parus	24.
Partir	je pars	partant	parti	je partis	36.
Peindre	je peins	peignant	peint	je peignis	14.
Plaindre	je plains	plaignant	plaint	je plaignis	15.
Plaire	je plais	plaisant	plu	je plus	22.
Pleuvoir	il pleut	pleuvant	plu	il plut	59.
Prendre	je prends	prenant	pris	je pris	29.
Poindre	je poins	poignant	(point)	(je poignis)	16.
Pourvoir	je pourvois	pourvoyant	pourvu, e	pourvus	60.
Pouvoir	je peux (puis)	pouvant	pu	je pus	61.
Repentir, se	je me repens	repentant	repenti	je me repentis	39.
Restreindre	je restreins	—	restreint	je restreignis	14.
Rire	je ris	riant	ri	je ris	67.

Rompre, *see* **L. XXIII., Rem. 2.**

Saillir	**il saille**	**saillant**	**sailli**	**il saillit**	**48.**
Savoir	**je sais**	**sachant**	**su, e**	**je sus**	**62.**
Sentir	**je sens**	**sentant**	**senti, e**	**je sentis**	**38.**
Seoir	**il sied**	**séant**	**sis, e**	**—**	**82.**
Servir	**je sers**	**servant**	**servi, e**	**je servis**	**34.**
Sortir	**je sors**	**sortant**	**sorti**	**je sortis**	**40.**
Souffrir	**je souffre**	**souffrant**	**souffert, e**	**je souffris**	**44.**
Sourdre	**elle sourd**	**—**	**—**	**—**	**81.**
Suivre	**je suis**	**suivant**	**suivi, e**	**je suivis**	**9.**
Suffire	**je suffis**	**suffisant**	**suffi**	**je suffis**	**2.**
Surseoir	**je surseois**	**sursoyant**	**sursis**	**je sursis**	**83.**
Taire	**je tais**	**taisant**	**tu, e**	**je tus**	**23.**
Teindre	**je teins**	**teignant**	**teint, e**	**je teignis**	**14.**
Tenir	**je tiens**	**tenant**	**tenu, e**	**je tins**	**52.**
Traire	**je trais**	**trayant**	**trait**	**—**	**8.**
Tressaillir	**je tressaille**	**tressaillant**	**tressailli**	**je tressaillis**	**47.**
Valoir	**je vaux**	**valant**	**valu**	**je valus**	**63.**
Vaincre	**je vaincs**	**vainquant**	**vaincu, e**	**je vainquis**	**10.**
Venir	**je viens**	**venant**	**venu, e**	**je vins**	**51.**
Vêtir	**je vêts**	**vêtant**	**vêtu**	**je vêtis**	**33.**
Vivre	**je vis**	**vivant**	**vécu**	**je vécus**	**31.**
Voir	**je vois**	**voyant**	**vu, e**	**je vis**	**65.**
Vouloir	**je veux**	**voulant**	**voulu, e**	**je voulus**	**64.**

XLVII. QUARANTE-SEPTIÈME LEÇON.

HOW TO RENDER *DO*, *DID*, *SHALL*, *WILL*, ETC.—SUPPLEMENTARY TENSES.

The auxiliaries *do*, *will*, *shall*, *etc.*, in answers, are often used in English in an elliptical manner, when in French the principal verb must be repeated, and a noun or pronoun supplied.

Si, "yes," is generally used in answers instead of *oui* in replying to a question in which there is a negation, or in contradiction to a negative statement.

EXAMPLES :

Avez-vous du pain ? Oui, *j'en* ai.	*Have you any bread ? Yes*, I have.
Avez-vous répondu ? Oui, j'ai *répondu ?*	*Have you answered ? Yes*, I have.
Achèteront-ils ce beurre ? Oui, ils *l'achèteront.*	*Will they buy that butter ? Yes, they* will.
Voulez vous le lui demander ? Oui, *je veux bien.*	*Will you ask him for it ? Yes*, I will.
Etes-vous Anglais ? Non je ne *le* suis pas.	*Are you an Englishman ? No*, I am not.
Avez-vous été à Rome ? Non, je *n'y ai pas été.*	*Have you been in Rome ? No*, I have not.
Est-ce vous qui êtes venu hier soir ? Non, *ce n'est pas* moi.	*Was it you who came last night ? No, it* was not I.
Ce n'est pas ce peintre qui a fait votre portrait ? *Si, c'est lui.*	*That painter did not take your likeness, did he ?* Yes, he did.
Lui rendrez-vous son portrait ? *Cela va sans dire.*	*Will you return her likeness to her ?* Of course I will.
Partira-t-il ? Oui, *il partira.*	*Will he set out ?* Yes, he will.
Iriez vous s'il y *allait ?* Mais oui, *je le ferais.*	*Should you go there if* he did ? Why, yes, I should.
Est-ce la mode ? Oui, c'est la mode.	Is it the fashion ? Yes, it is.
Pourquoi vous plaignez-vous ? Je ne me plains pas ; c'est mon frère qui se plaint. Il se plaint ! Oui, vraiment, et il y a longtemps qu'il se plaint.	Why do you complain ? I do not complain ; my brother does. — Does he ? Indeed he does, and he has complained for a long time.
J'ai faim. Vraiment ? Oui, bien faim.	I am hungry. Are you ? Yes, very.
Doit-elle venir ce soir ? Oui, elle *doit venir.*	Does she intend to come this evening ? Yes, she does.

In exclamations the auxiliary must be translated by some words expressive of the meaning implied by the English ellipsis. Ex. : —

Son associé est revenu des Indes. Est-ce possible, vous me surprenez, *or simply*, Ah ! vraiment !	His partner has returned from India. Has he ?
J'ai sommeil. Ah ! vraiment ? *or*, Allons donc, vous plaisantez.	I am sleepy. Are you ?

SUPPLEMENTARY TENSES.

The verbs *aller*, *devoir*, and *venir de* are idiomatically used, forming, with an infinitive, what some grammarians have called "Supplementary Tenses."

Aller and *devoir* before an infinitive form idiomatic futures, and correspond to the English verbs *to go* and *to be* (to be about to), in a like position.

Venir de forms idiomatic past tenses, and corresponds to the English *to have just*.

CONJUGATION OF THE SUPPLEMENTARY TENSES.

Je vais	avoir,	*I am going*	*to have.*
Tu vas	chanter,	*Thou art going*	*to sing.*
Il va	danser,	*He is going*	*to dance.*
Nous allons	finir,	*We are going*	*to finish.*
Vous allez	rendre,	*You are going*	*to render.*
Ils vont	recevoir,	*They are going*	*to receive.*

J'allais avoir, etc. — *I was going to have, etc.*

Je dois	avoir,	*I am*	*to have.*
Tu dois	chanter,	*Thou art*	*to sing.*
Il doit	danser,	*He is*	*to dance.*
Nous devons	finir,	*We are*	*to finish.*
Vous devez	rendre,	*You are*	*to render.*
Ils doivent	recevoir,	*They are*	*to receive.*

Je devais avoir, etc. — *I was to have.*

Je devrais avoir, etc. — *I should* or *ought to have.*

J'aurais dû avoir, etc. — *I should* or *ought to have had.*

Je viens de (d')	avoir,	*I have just*	*had.*
Tu viens "	chanter,	*Thou hast just*	*sung.*
Il vient "	danser,	*He has just*	*danced.*
Nous venons "	finir,	*We have just*	*finished.*
Vous venez "	rendre,	*You have just*	*rendered.*
Ils viennent "	recevoir,	*They have just*	*received.*

Je venais d' avoir, etc. — *I had just had, etc.*

These last tenses may be expressed by *faire* preceded by *ne* and followed by the conjunctive *que*, with an infinitive preceded by *de* (*ne faire que de*). e. g. *Il ne fait que d'arriver.* He has but just arrived. *Je ne fais que de sortir.* I have but just gone out.

N. B. The particle *de* is here indispensable, because, without it the expression would have quite another sense, and would denote a continuation or a frequent repetition of the action. Ex.: *Vous ne faites que sortir.* You do nothing but go out. *Elle ne fait que jouer.* She does nothing but play.

PART II.

ELISION.

The vowels *a*, *e*, *i*, when final, are sometimes elided before a word beginning with a vowel or *h* mute; thus: *l'âme*, *l'homme*, *s'il*, instead of *la âme*, *le homme*, *si il*.

ELISION OF *a*. A is elided only in the word *la*. Ex.: *l'amitié*.

ELISION OF *e*. E is elided in the nine monosyllables *je*, *me*, *te*, *le*, *de*, *ne*, *ce*, *se* and *que*. Ex.: *j'aime*; *c'est l'homme qu'il n'estime pas*.

EXCEPTIONS. — 1. The vowels of the pronouns *le*, *la*, *je*, and *ce* are never elided when they come after the verb. Ex.: *Ai-je un livre*; *est-ce elle*. The *e* in *je* and *ce* is not pronounced, however, though the *e* and *a* of *le* and *la* are in *voyez-la aujourd'hui*, *voyez-le aujourd'hui*.

2. Before *oui* and *onze* no elision takes place: *je crois que oui*; *le onze*.

The E is elided in *lorsque*, when; *puisque*, since; *quoique*, though, only before *il*, *elle*, *on* and *un*. Ex.: *lorsqu'il*, *puisqu'on*, etc. In *quelque* the *e* is elided only before *un*, *une*, and *autre*. Ex.: *quelqu'un*; *quelqu'autre*. In *entre* and *presque*, *e* is elided only when they form part of a compound word. Ex.: *entr'acte*, *presqu'île*.

ELISION OF *i*. I is elided only in the conjunction *si* before *il* and *ils*. Ex.: *s'il*, *s'ils*.

I. PREMIÈRE LEÇON.

ON THE GENDER OF SUBSTANTIVES.

I. RULES ON THE GENDER OF SIMPLE NOUNS.

§1. MASCULINE BY THEIR SIGNIFICATION ARE:

1. The names of all masculine beings, as: *Henri*, Henry; *l'empereur*, the emperor; *le maître*, the master; *le Français*, the Frenchman; *le taureau*, the bull, etc.

2. The names of metals, trees, shrubs, seasons, months, and days, as: *le fer*, iron; *le chêne*, the oak; *le printemps*, spring; *le joli Mai*, (the) fine May; (*le*) *lundi*, Monday, etc.

3. All words that are made substantive by prefixing the article, as: *le vert*, the green (color); *le bien*, the good; *le boire et le manger*, drinking and eating; *le oui et le non*, the yes and no.

4. Nouns expressing professions, titles, or qualities which belong generally to men: *philosophe*, *orateur*, etc.

5. The names generally used in natural history to designate the different species of animals: *un quadrupède, un mammifère, un herbivore*, etc.

6. The names employed in Chemistry to designate simple bodies and most of their compounds: *l'or, le cuivre, l'hydrogène, l'oxygène.*

7. The names of the decimal nomenclature: *le mètre, le franc, le centime*, etc.

§2. MASCULINE BY TERMINATION:

1. Nouns ending in a consonant (except those in *aison*, *ion*, and *eur*).

2. Nouns ending in any vowel except *e* mute and *é* preceded by *t* or *ti*.

3. Nouns ending in *e* mute preceded by *b*, *g*, *l* (not double), *m*,

r (except *rr* not preceded by *u*), *s*, *t* (not double), or *u* (except those in *ique*).

To any rules for terminations, there will be found many exceptions. These rules are general. Most of the exceptions in common use, the pupil will learn as they occur in this grammar.

§ 3. FEMININE BY SIGNIFICATION:

1. All names of female persons and animals, as: *Marie*, Mary; *la reine*, the queen; *la fille*, the girl; *la jument*, the mare, etc.

2. The names of fruits, flowers, and herbs, as: *la poire*, the pear; *la pomme*, the apple; *la rose*, the rose; *l'herbe*, the grass.

Except: *Le marron*, the chestnut; *le citron*, the lemon; *le raisin*, the grape; *un abricot*, an apricot; *un œillet*, a pink; *le lis*, the lily, and a few more, on account of their masculine termination.

3. The names of countries, places, and rivers ending in *e* mute, as: *la France, la Prusse, l'ancienne Rome, la Loire, la Seine*, etc.

Except: *Le Hanovre, le Mexique, le Danube, le Rhône.*

§ 4. FEMININE BY TERMINATION:

1. Nouns ending with *e* mute, not included in the masculine terminations, as: *la vie*, life; *l'épée*, the sword.

2. Those ending in *aison*, *ion*, and *eur*, as: *la maison*, the house; *la religion, la grandeur.*

3. Those ending in *é* preceded by *t* or *ti*, as: *la beauté*, beauty.

4. These five words ending in *i* are feminine: *la foi*, faith; *la loi*, law; *la fourmi*, the ant; *la merci*, mercy; *l'après-midi*.

5. Most nouns ending in *oire* (not *oir*) are feminine, as: *la gloire*, glory; *l'histoire*, history; *la victoire*, victory; *la machoire*, the jaw.

6. *Gens.* This word presents an anomaly in gender. It is masculine, but when an adjective *precedes* it, that adjective takes the feminine form, if its termination is not *e* mute. If a definitive, as *tout* or *certain*, precedes this adjective, the definitive also takes

the feminine form. In all other cases, *gens* takes a masculine adjective, as: *Toutes les vieilles gens sont soupçonneux*, all old people are suspicious. But, *Tous les jeunes gens.*

II. GENDER OF COMPOUND SUBSTANTIVES.

This depends upon the manner of their composition.

1. When the first component is a noun, it determines the gender of the whole, as: *Le chou-fleur*, the cauliflower; *un arc-en-ciel*, a rainbow; *la fête Dieu.*

2. When they consist of a preposition or an adjective and a noun, the gender of the noun remains for the whole, as: *Le contre-coup*, the counter-buff; *l'avant-bras*, m. the fore-arm.

3. Those nouns compounded with a verb and noun are always of the masculine gender, as: *Le porte-manteau*, the portmanteau: *le tire-bouchon*, the corkscrew; *le porte-feuille*, the portfolio (though *feuille* is feminine).

THEME 1.

Indicate the gender of the following nouns, by placing an article, either the definite or the indefinite, before them:

The horse, — *cheval.* The pear, — *poire.* The metal, — *métal.* A winter, — *hiver.* Italy, — *Italie.* The cherry, — *cerise.* The cherry-tree, — *cerisier.* The house, — *maison.* The vapor, — *vapeur.* The walnut, — *noix.* A leaf, — *feuille.* The truth, — *vérité.* The van-guard, — *avant-garde.* The cart, — *charette.* The work, — *travail.* The shell, — *coquille.* The hat, — *chapeau.* The shoe, — *soulier.* The honey, — *miel.* The carpenter, — *charpentier.* The nurse, — *nourrice.* The sun, — *soleil.* The earth, — *terre.* A year, — *année.* The life, — *vie.* The feast, — *fête.* The treaty, — *traité.* The master-key, — *passe-partout.* The spit, — *tourne-broche.* Christianity, — *christianisme.*

III. DOUBLE GENDER OF SOME NOUNS.

1. The following nouns have a double gender:

L'aide, m. the assistant.	*L'aide*, f. the help, support.
l'aigle, m. the eagle.	*l'aigle*, f. the standard.

l'aune, m. the alder-tree.	*l'aune*, f. the ell, yard.
un couple, a couple, husband and wife.	*une couple*, a brace, two of a sort.
un enseigne, an ensign.	*une enseigne*, a sign.
le garde, the keeper.	*la garde*, the guard, watch.
le guide, the guide.	*la guide*, the rein in driving.
le livre, the book.	*la livre*, the pound.
le manche, the handle.	*la manche*, the sleeve.
le mémoire, the memorandum.	*la mémoire*, the memory.
le mousse, the cabin-boy.	*la mousse*, the moss.
l'orgue, m. sing, the organ.	*les orgues*, pl. organ, *or* organs.
le page, the page (of a prince).	*la page*, the page (of a book).
un paillasse, a merry andrew.	*une paillasse*, a straw-bed.
Pâques, pl. m. Easter.	*la pâque*, the Passover.
le poêle, the stove.	*la poêle*, the frying-pan.
le poste, the post, military post.	*la poste*, the post-office.
un somme, a nap, slumber.	*la somme*, the sum.
le tour, the trick, turn.	*la tour*, the tower.
le trompette, the trumpeter.	*la trompette*, the trumpet.
un voile, a veil.	*une voile*, a sail.

2. There are in French some nouns which have no particular form for the feminine, and remain always *masculine*, even when applied to a woman. Such are:

Un auteur, } m. and f. an author, a writer.
Un écrivain, }
Un orateur, m. and f. an orator.
Un peintre, m. and f. a painter.
Un sculpteur, m. and f. a sculptor.
Un témoin, m. and f. a witness.

NOTE. Sometimes the word *femme* may precede, as: *Une femme auteur*, *les femmes poètes*.

3. On the contrary, there are a few feminine nouns which apply also to male individuals:

La caution, the bail.	*la basse*, the base.
la pratique, the customer.	*la sentinelle*, the sentry.

IV. FORMATION OF FEMININE APPELLATIONS.

1. Male appellations which are originally adjectives, form their feminine according to the rules on the adjectives (see Part I., L. XVI.), as:

MASCULINE.	FEMININE.
Le Français, the Frenchman.	*La Française*, the Frenchwoman.
un Russe, a Russian.	*une Russe*, a Russian lady.
un Juif, a Jew.	*une Juive*, a Jewess.
l'époux, the husband.	*l'épouse*, the wife.
le veuf, the widower.	*la veuve*, the widow.

2. Those ending in one of the nasal sounds *an*, *on*, *ien* (not *in*), and those in *t* double their *n* or *t* before the feminine *e*, as:

Le paysan, the peasant.	*La paysanne*, a peasant woman.
le lion, the lion.	*la lionne*, the lioness.
le chrétien, the Christian.	*la chrétienne*, the Christian woman.
le baron, the baron.	*la baronne*, the baroness.

3. Many nouns ending in *e* mute form their feminine in *esse*, as:

Le comte, the count.	*La comtesse*, the countess.
le nègre, the negro.	*la négresse*, the negress.
le maître, the master.	*la maîtresse*, the mistress.
le prince, the prince.	*la princesse*, the princess.

4. Those in *-eur* change this termination into *-euse:*

Le danseur, the dancer.	*La danseuse*, the dancer, *f.*
le chasseur, the hunter.	*la chasseuse*,* the huntress.

5. Many in *-teur* change it into *-trice*, as:

L'acteur, the actor.	*L'actrice*, the actress.
le bienfaiteur, the benefactor.	*la bienfaitrice*, the benefactress.
le tuteur, the guardian.	*la tutrice*, the guardian, *f.*

6. The following nouns form their feminine in an irregular way:

Le dieu, the god.	*La déesse*, the goddess.
le duc, the duke.	*la duchesse*, the duchess.
l'empereur, the emperor.	*l'impératrice*, the empress.
le roi, the king.	*la reine*, the queen.
le héros, the hero.	*l'héroïne*, the heroine.
le gouverneur, the tutor.	*la gouvernante*, the governess.
le serviteur, the man-servant.	*la servante*, the maid-servant.
le pécheur, the sinner.	*la pécheresse*, the sinner *f.*
le compagnon, the companion.	*la compagne*, the companion *f.*
le loup, the he-wolf.	*la louve*, the she-wolf.
le mulet, the mule.	*la mule*, the mule *f.*
le dindon, the turkey-cock.	*la dinde*, the turkey-hen.

* *Chasseresse* is a poetical form.

THEME 2.

Form and write the feminine of the following masculine nouns, according to the above rules:

The neighbor, *le voisin;* f. —. The hunter, *le chasseur;* f. —. The dwarf, *le nain;* f. —. The talker, *le bavard;* f. —. The prisoner, *le prisonnier;* f. —. The dumb man, *le muet;* f. —. The teacher, *l'instituteur*; f. —. The patient, *le malade;* f. —. The husband, *l'époux;* f. —. The master, *le maître;* f. —. A musician, *un musicien;* f. —. The founder, *le fondateur;* f. —. The Englishman, *l'Anglais;* f. —. The German, *l'Allemand;* f. —. The actor, *l'acteur;* f. —. The inventor, *l'inventeur;* f. —. The liar, *le menteur* (root *ment-*, termination *-eur*); f. —. The traitor, *le traître;* f. —. The singer, *le chanteur;* f. —. The idler, *le paresseux;* f. —. The lion, *le lion;* f. —. The tiger, *le tigre*; f. —.

READING LESSON.

Un honnête père de famille, chargé[1] de biens et d'années, voulut régler d'avance[2] sa succession entre ses trois fils, et leur partager ses biens, le fruit de ses travaux et de son industrie. Il en fit trois portions égales, et assigna à chacun son lot. — Puis il leur dit: "Il me reste encore un diamant de grand prix; je le destine à celui de vous qui saura le mieux le mériter par quelque action noble et généreuse, et je vous donne trois mois pour vous mettre en état de l'obtenir."

Aussitôt les trois fils se dispersent, mais ils se rassemblent au temps prescrit.[3] Ils se présentent devant leur juge, et voici ce que raconte l'aîné[4]: "Mon père, un étranger s'est trouvé dans des circonstances qui l'ont obligé de me confier[5] toute sa fortune: il n'avait de moi aucune sûreté, par écrit,[6] et n'aurait pu produire contre moi aucune preuve du dépôt; mais je lui ai tout remis fidèlement. Cette fidélité n'est-elle pas quelque chose de louable[7]?" "Tu as fait, mon fils," lui répondit le viellard, "ce que tu devais faire. Il serait honteux d'en agir autrement, car la probité est un devoir."

1. Laden. 2. Beforehand. 3. Prescribed, appointed. 4. The eldest. 5. To trust. 6. In writing. 7. Laudable.

CONVERSATION.

Qui voulut régler sa succession?	Un honnête père de famille.
Que fit-il à cet effet (*for this purpose*)?	Il partagea ses biens entre ses trois fils.
Que lui restait-il?	Un diamant de grand prix.
A qui le destina-t-il?	A celui d'entre eux qui ferait une action noble et généreuse.
Combien de temps leur donna-t-il pour cela?	Il leur donna trois mois pour obteuir ce prix.
Que firent ensuite les fils?	Ils se dispersèrent, mais au bout du temps prescrit, ils revinrent à la maison.
Quelle avait été l'action de l'aîné?	Il avait remis fidèlement à un étranger la fortune que celui-ci lui avait confiée sans reçu (*receipt*).
Que lui dit le viellard?	Tu n'as fait, mon fils, que ce que tu devais faire.

FIN.

Le second fils plaida[1] sa cause à son tour, à peu près en ces termes: "Je me suis trouvé, pendant mon voyage, sur le bord d'un lac; un enfant venait[2] imprudemment de s'y laisser[2] tomber; il allait se noyer;[3] je l'en ai tiré, et je lui ai sauvé la vie, aux yeux des habitants d'un village situé au bord de ce lac; ils pourront attester la vérité du fait."[4]—"A la bonne heure," interrompit[5] le père; "mais il n'y a point encore de noblesse dans cette action; il n'y a que de l'humanité."

Enfin, le dernier des trois frères prit la parole. "Mon père," dit-il, "j'ai trouvé mon ennemi mortel, qui, s'étant égaré la nuit, s'était endormi, sans le savoir, sur le penchant[6] d'un abîme;[7] le moindre mouvement qu'il eût fait, au moment de son réveil,[8] ne pouvait manquer[9] de le précipiter; sa vie était entre mes mains; j'ai pris soin de l'éveiller[10] avec les précautions convenables, et l'ai tiré de cet endroit[11] fatal."

"Ah! mon fils," s'écria le bon père avec transport, et en l'embrassant tendrement, "c'est à toi, sans contredit,[12] que la bague[13] est due."

1. To plead. 2. Had just fallen. 3. To be drowned. 4. The fact. 5. To interrupt. 6. The slope. 7. Abyss. 8. Of his awakening. 9. Fail. 10. To wake. 11. Place, spot. 12. Without doubt. 13. The ring.

CONVERSATION.

Qu'avait fait le second fils?	Il avait sauvé un enfant qui allait se noyer.
Qui avait vu cela?	Les habitants d'un village situé au bord du lac.
Enfin, quelle avait été l'action du dernier des trois frères?	Il avait retiré son ennemi endormi au bord d'un abîme, où le moindre mouvement l'eût précipité.
Laquelle de ces trois actions était la plus noble?	Celle du plus jeune fils.
Les actions des deux autres n'étaient-elles pas nobles et généreuses?	Non, la première était une action de justice, la seconde une action d'humanité.
Et qu'est-ce que lui dit le père?	Il s'écria avec transport: "Mon fils, c'est à toi, sans contredit, que la bague est due."

II. DEUXIÈME LEÇON.

PLURAL OF NOUNS.

(See Part I. Lesson 2, p. 30.)

The general rules on this subject have already been given in the second lesson of Part I. We have to add here the following particulars.

1. Nouns of two and more syllables, ending in *-ant* and *-ent*, are spelled by some French writers in the plural *-ens* and *-ans*, instead of *-ents* and *-ants*, as: *momens* for *moments*, *enfans* for *enfants*. This orthography, however, is not to be recommended.

2. The following nouns in *al* and *ail* do not form their plural in *aux*, but take an *s*.

Le bal, the ball.
le cal, callus.
le narval, the narwhal.
le carnaval, the carnival.
le régal, the regale, treat.
le détail, the particulars.
le gouvernail, the helm, rudder.
l'éventail, m. the fan.
l'épouvantail, m. the scarecrow.
un portail, a portal, front gate.
le poitrail, the poitrel.
le serail, the seraglio.
l'ail, garlic (has in Plur. both *les ails* and *les aulx*).

Plural: *Les bals, les cals, les détails, les éventails, etc.*

Note. *Le bétail*, cattle, makes in the plural *les bestiaux*.

3. The usual plural of *ciel* is *cieux*, the heavens; there is, however, a regular plural, *les ciels*, meaning: 1, the testers; 2, the climats; 3, the skies of pictures.

4. *L'œil*, the eye, has in the plural *les yeux*. *Des œils de bœuf* are oval or round windows. *Aïeul*, has *aïeuls* when it means grandfathers, and *aïeux* in the sense of ancestors.

5. How compound words form their plural: —

1. When a word is composed of a substantive and an adjective, or of two substantives, both take the mark of the plural. Ex.: —

Les beaux-frères, the brothers-in-law.
Les belles-sœurs, the sisters-in-law.
Les choux-fleurs, the cauliflowers.
Les chefs-lieux, the chief-towns (of counties).

2. But when a word is composed of two substantives separated by a preposition, the first alone takes the plural termination. Ex.: —

Les chefs-d'œuvre, the masterpieces.
Les arcs-en-ciel, the rainbows.

3. When a word consists of a substantive and a verb or preposition, the substantive alone can take the sign of the plural, if required by the sense. Ex.: —

Les tire-bottes, the boot-jacks.
Les essuie-mains, the towels.
Les garde-fous, the balusters.

4. When there is no substantive in the compound word, none of the components can take the mark of the plural. Ex.: —

Les passe-partout (not *passe-partouts*), the master-keys.
Les forte-piano, the pianos.

5. The words: *la grand'mère*, the grandmother; *la grand'tante*, grand-aunt; *la grand'rue*, the main street; *la grand'route*, the highway, — have, in the plural, *les grand'mères, les grand'tantes, etc.*

6. The following nouns take in the plural another meaning than in the singular :—

SINGULAR.	PLURAL.
Le ciseau, the chisel.	*les ciseaux*, the scissors.
la lunette, the telescope.	*les lunettes*, the spectacles.
le fer, iron.	*les fers*, the fetters, chains.
la grâce, grace, pardon.	*les grâces*, grace, charms.
le gage, the pawn, pledge.	*les gages*, the wages.
la mesure, the measure.	*les mesures*, the measures.
la viande, meat.	*les viandes*, food.
la troupe, the troop.	*les troupes*, the troops.
la lumière, the light.	*les lumières*, knowledge.
l'aboi, the barking.	*les abois*, agony.
la défense, the defence.	*les défenses*, the tusks, fangs.

7. Substantives which have no singular in French : —

Les annales, f. annals. *les gens*, m. people.
les ancêtres, m. ancestors. *les hardes*, f. clothes.

les alentours, m. } the environs.
les environs, m. }
les broussailles, f. brushwood.
les décombres, m. rubbish.
les débris, m. the remains.
les dépens, m. cost.
les entrailles, f. the entrails.
les frais, m. expenses.
les funérailles, f. funeral rites.
les légumes, m. vegetables.
les mathématiques, f. mathematics.
les matériaux, materials.
les mœurs, f. the manners.
les mouchettes, f. the snuffers.
des mouchettes, a pair of snuffers.
les pleurs, f. the tears.
les ténèbres, f. darkness.
les vivres, m. victuals.

THEME 3.

1. We had many balls last winter.[1] 2. Are these fans dear? 3. No, they are not dear. 4. The heavens declare[2] the glory of God. 5. The great portals of those churches are beautiful. 6. We honor[3] the virtues of our ancesters. 7. The eyes of (*de l'*) man are the mirror[4] of his soul. 8. The eyes of a mother watch[5] over her child's life. 9. I have two brothers-in-law and three sisters-in-law. 10. Those pictures are masterpieces. 11. I want[6] two or three towels. 12. These master-keys must be very old. 13. Both my (*mes deux*) grandaunts are dead; but my grandmothers are still alive (*en vie*). 14. Lend me your scissors, if you please. 15. The fetters are made of iron. 16. Do you know the environs* of London? 17. Yes, I know them. 18. Bring me a pair of snuffers. 19. Do you like vegetables? 20. I like them, when they are dry. 21. I found this ring[7] under the rubbish in my garden. 22. The little humming-birds (*oiseaux-mouches*) are the jewels[8] of nature* (*Def. art.*). 23. I study[9] mathematics.

1. Use the article, see Lesson 3. 2. To declare—*Annoncer*. 3. *Honoror*. 4. *Miroir*, m. 5. *Veiller*. 6. *Il me faut* (see Part I. p. 148, 3). 7. *Bague*, f. 8. *Bijou*, m. 9. *Étudier*.

READING LESSON.

LE CASTOR. *The Beaver.*

Dans le nord de l'Amérique, sur les bords des fleuves et des grands lacs du Canada, loin des grand'routes, habite le castor. La

*In these Themes, words, the last letter of which is printed in *italics*, are the same in French and English.

partie la plus singulière de son corps est sa queue.[1] Ses pattes de devant (*fore-feet*) sont des espèces de mains, dont il se sert fort adroitement[2]. Les castors entreprennent des travaux très-considérables pour se construire des habitations solides et commodes. Ce sont des cabanes (*huts*) ou plutôt des espèces de maisonnettes bâties dans l'eau, avec deux issues, l'une pour aller à terre, l'autre pour se jeter à l'eau. La forme de cet édifice[3] est presque toujours ovale ou ronde ; il y en a depuis quatre ou cinq pieds jusqu'à huit ou dix de diamètre et de deux ou trois étages.[4] Les murailles[5] ont jusqu'à deux pieds d'épaisseur ;[6] elles sont élevées à plomb[7] sur un pilotis,[8] qui sert en même temps de fondement et de plancher à la maison.

Les castors aiment à ronger[9] continuellement de l'écorce (*bark*), et ils en font ample provision pour se nourrir pendant l'hiver. Chaque cabane a son magasin, et ils ne vont jamais piller[10] leurs voisins. Ces cabanes contiennent quelquefois jusqu'à trente castors, qui vivent toujours en paix ensemble. Si quelque castor aperçoit un ennemi, il donne un grand coup, de sa queue, sur l'eau. A ce signal, tous les autres plongent dans l'eau, ou se réfugient dans les cabanes.

1. Tail. 2. Skilfully. 3. Building. 4. Floor, story. 5. The walls. 6. Thickness. 7. Perpendicularly. 8. Pale, post. 9. To gnaw. 10. To plunder.

CONVERSATION.

Où habite le castor.	Il habite dans le nord de l'Amérique, sur les bords des fleuves et des lacs.
Quelle est la partie la plus remarquable de son corps ?	C'est sa queue.
Comment sont ses pattes de devant ?	Ce sont des espèces de mains dont il se sert fort adroitement.
Les castors que font-ils de curieux ?	Ils bâtissent des cabanes dans l'eau.

De quelle manière les bâtissent-ils ?	Ils font deux issues, l'une pour aller à terre, l'autre pour se jeter à l'eau.
Quelle est la forme de ces maisonnettes ?	La forme en est ordinairement ronde ou ovale.
Y a-t-il plusieurs étages ?	Oui, les cabanes sont de deux ou trois étages.
Les murailles sont-elles solides ?	Très-solides ; elles ont jusqu'à deux pieds d'épaisseur.
Y a-t-il plusieurs castors dans un tel édifice ?	Ces cabanes contiennent quelquefois jusqu'à trente castors qui vivent ensemble en paix.
Que font-ils quand un ennemi approche ?	Ils se jettent tous dans l'eau, ou se réfugient dans les cabanes.

III. TROISIÈME LEÇON.

USE OF THE ARTICLE.

I. THE DEFINITE ARTICLE IS USED IN FRENCH AND NOT IN ENGLISH : —

1. Before abstract nouns, when taken in their whole extent, as :

L'amitié, f. friendship.	*la bonté*, goodness.
la paresse, idleness.	*l'occupation*, f. employment.
l'amour, m. love.	*la patience*, patience.
la vieillesse, old age.	*la jeunesse*, youth.

Examples :—

Le temps est précieux, time is precious.
Le vice est odieux, vice is odious.
La modestie est une belle vertu, modesty is a fine virtue.
L'*occupation est le meilleur remède contre* l'*ennui*.
Occupation is the best remedy against wearisomeness.

2. Before collective names of corporations, bodies, governments, sciences, religious creeds, seasons, metals, etc., as:

La noblesse, nobility.
le gouvernement, government.
la monarchie, monarchy.
l'histoire, f. history.
la géographie, geography.
le christianisme, Christianity.
le judaïsme, Judaism.
l'hiver, m. winter.
l'or, m. gold.
le fer, iron.

3. Before words which represent a whole genus or species, as:

L'homme est mortel, man is mortal.
Les voix des animaux sont très-différentes.
The voices of animals are very different.

4. Before the following and other nouns taken in a general sense:

L'homme, man.
les hommes, men.
le ciel, heaven.
la terre, earth.
la vie, life.
la mort, death.
le temps, time.
le malheur, misfortune.
la loi, law.
le sort, fate.
l'usage, la coutume, custom.
les mœurs, manners.
la faim, hunger.
la soif, thirst.
le dîner, dinner.
le déjeuner, breakfast.

5. When particular parts or qualities of an organic body are mentioned, as:

Ce garçon a la tête très-petite.
This boy has a very little head.
Cette femme a la bouche petite et les yeux bleus.
This woman has a little mouth and blue eyes.
Le loup a la tête longue, le nez effilé et les oreilles étroites.
The wolf has a long head, a thin nose, and small ears.
La fille aux yeux bleus, the blue-eyed girl.

6. When in English the possessive case is used, as:

My father's house, *la maison de mon père.*
The king's palace, *le palais du roi.*

7. Before adjectives used substantively, as:

J'aime le vert, I am fond of green.
Les riches ne donnent pas toujours.
Rich men do not always give.

8. Before proper names of countries, provinces, rivers, mountains, and winds, as:

L'Angleterre est riche, England is rich.
Le mont Vésuve, Mount Vesuvius.
La France est plus grande que l'Italie.
France is larger than Italy.

NOTE. Further particulars on proper names will be found in the sixth lesson.

9. Before nouns of dignity, and titles, followed by proper names, as:

Admiral Nelson, l'*amiral Nelson.*
Professor A., le *professeur A.*

10. The definite article replaces the English indefinite article, when the price of things is indicated, as:

Three francs *a* pound, *trois francs la livre.*
Five francs *a* yard, *cinq francs le mètre.*

11. In the following phrases the definite article is used:

A l'école—à l'église, at *or* to school; at *or* to church.
Il s'est cassé la jambe, he has broken his leg.
L'épée à la main, a sword in his hand.
Je vous souhaite le bon jour, I wish you good morning
Je n'ai pas le temps, I have not time.
Il n'a pas le sou, he has not a farthing.
J'ai mal à la tête, I have *a* headache.
J'ai mal aux dents, I have *a* toothache.
Soyez le bienvenu,—la bienvenue, etc., be welcome.
La semaine passée (*dernière*), last week.

12. After *dont* between nouns, as:

Un homme dont la réputation est perdu, est malheureux.
A man whose good reputation is lost is unhappy.

II. REPETITION OF THE ARTICLE.

The article must be repeated in French before every substantive. Examples:

The mind and heart, *l'esprit et le cœur.*
The shoemaker, hatter, and tailor.
Le bottier, le chapelier, et le tailleur.
I have bought meat, cheese, and fruits.
J'ai acheté de la viande, du fromage et des fruits.

THEME 4.

1. Virtue is the highest[1] good (*bien*, m.). 2. Men are mortal. 3. Modesty adorns[2] youth. 4. Human life is short. 5. Man is liable[3] to a variety of (*à bien des*) changes.[4] 6. Gold and silver cannot render[5] man happy. 7. Men of (*d'un*) real genius[6] are scarce. 8. Black and white are two opposite[7] colors. 9. Beauty and wit[8] are valuable[9] endowments (*avantages*), when heightened (*relevés*) by modesty. 10. Iron and steel are more useful than gold and silver. 11. How much *a* pound? 12. The love of glory (*Def. art.*), the fear of shame,[10] are often the cause of great valor. 13. Summer is warm, but winter is cold. 14. The instructions of adversity are wholesome (*salutaires*), though unpleasing;[11] the lessons of prosperity are pleasing, but often pernicious. 15. Geography is a very useful science. 16. Painting,[12] sculpture, and poetry[13] belong to the imagination. 17. Good and bad seem to be blended (*mêlés*) together through all nature. 18. Hypocrisy is an homage which vice pays (*rend*) to virtue. 19. Do you know General Knox? 20. Yes, I know him. 21. White garments[14] are the symbol of innocence. 22. The knife and fork are broken. 23. Let us go to church. 24. The boys were at school this morning. 25. Fear[15] and ignorance are the sources of superstition. 26. Good wine is sold (*se vend*) [for] four shillings *a* bottle.

1. *Grand*. 2. *Orner*. 3. *Sujet*. 4. *Changement*, *m*. 5. *Rendre*. 6. *Vrai génie*. 7. *Opposé*. 8. *Esprit*. 9. *Précieux*. 10. *La honte*. 11. *Désagréable*. 12. *La peinture*. 13. *La poésie*. 14. *Vêtements*. 15. *Peur*, *f*.

III. THE DEFINITE ARTICLE IS OMITTED:—

1. Before the ordinal numbers which come after the names of sovereigns, as:

Henry the Fourth, *Henri quatre*.
Louis the Eighteenth, *Louis XVIII* (*dix-huit*).
George the Third, *George trois*.

2. Before the ordinal numbers used in quotations, as:

Book the first, chapter the fifth.
Livre premier, chapitre cinq.

3. Before *plus*, used in the sense of *the more*. Ex.:

Plus je la vois, plus je l'aime, the more I see her, the more I love her.

IV. THE INDEFINITE ARTICLE IS OMITTED IN FRENCH:—

1. Before national and professional names, when the subject is a noun or personal pronoun, as:

Je suis Anglais, I am an Englishman.

Mon père était médecin, my father was a physician.

NOTE. But it is expressed after *c'est* and *voici* or *voilà,* and also when the noun is qualified.

C'est un Anglais, he is an Englishman.

Voici un officier, here is an officer.

M. Dubois était un médecin distingué, Mr. Dubois was a distinguished physician.

2. It is also omitted in appositions, that is, when a substantive is used to qualify another, as:

L'avare, comédie par Molière, the Miser, a comedy by Molière.

Auguste, fils de M. S., Augustus, a son of Mr. S.

Munich, ville d'Allemagne, Munich, a city of Germany.

3. In the title of a book:

A French grammar, *Grammaire française.*

A history of England, *Histoire d'Angleterre.*

4. After the word *quel*, used to express surprise:

What a noise you make! *quel bruit vous faites!*

5. Before the words, *quantité*, a quantity; *nombre*, a number; *force*, a great number, when they are used adverbially. Ex.:

Je l'ai vu nombre de fois, I have seen him many times.

Il m'a donné quantité de jolies choses.

He gave me a great many pretty things.

6. The indefinite article is left out in French and supplied by *par*, before substantives that denote time, or in mentioning what is paid for salary, wages, etc.:

Five guineas *a* month, *cinq guinées par mois.*

So much *a* lesson, *tant par leçon.*

7. Sometimes after *jamais*, never, as:

Jamais général ne s'est plus distingué.

Never has a general distinguished himself more.

8. In the following and other expressions, in which the noun and verb are inseparably connnected:

Trouver moyen, to find (a) means.
Faire signe, to make a sign.
Faire présent, to make a present.
Mettre fin, to put an end *or* stop.
Livrer bataille, to fight a battle.
Prendre exemple, to take an example.
Rendre service, to render a service.
Ne dire mot, to say not a word.

THEME 5.

1. Book the tenth, chapter the third. 2. Charles the Second, king of (*d'*) Spain, son of Philip the Fourth, left his kingdom (*royaume*) to Philip the Fifth. 3. William the Third, king of England, married (*épousa*) the princess Mary, daughter of James (*Jacques*) the Second. 4. Apelles was *a* painter.[1] 5. Socrates[2] was *a* philosopher, Cicero[3] *an* orator (*-teur*). 6. Is your father *a* physician? 7. No, sir; he is a lawyer (*avocat*). 8. Henry's uncle is a skilful[4] physician. 9. Who is that gentleman?[5] 10. He is (*c'est*) an officer. 11. How much do you charge (*demandez-vous*) for your lessons? 12. I charge ten francs *a* lesson. 13. A German Grammar. 14. A Roman history, from the foundation[6] of Rome to (*jusqu'a*) the destruction of the Roman empire. 15. What *an* unhappy situation! 16. How much does the bookseller[7] pay you for your novels?[8] 17. He pays me five crowns (*écus*) *a* sheet.[9] 18. We went to Caen, *a* large town of Normandy.[10] 19. The Duke of York, *a* prince of the blood royal. 20. I am reading the "Misanthrope," *a* comedy by Molière. 21. I shall find *a* means to satisfy[11] him. 22. He said not a word. 23. Our neighbor made us *a* sign to leave[12] the room.

1. *Peintre.* 2. *Socrate.* 3. *Cicéron.* 4. *Habile.* 5. *Monsieur.* 6. *Fondation.* 7. *Libraire.* 8. *Roman, m.* 9. *Feuille.* 10. *De Normandie.* 11. *Satisfaire.* 12. *Quitter.*

V. THE ARTICLE IS OMITTED IN BOTH LANGUAGES:—

1. In many proverbs, as:

Contentement passe richesse, content surpasses wealth.
Pauvreté n'est pas vice, poverty is no disgrace.
Mauvaise herbe croît toujours.

2. In enumerating several substantives in the partitive sense, when summed up by *tous* or *rien*, as:

Hommes, femmes, enfants, tous voulaient le voir.
Men, women, children, all wished to see him.

3. After *ni — ni, soit — soit*, when the nouns are taken in the partitive sense, as:

Ni or ni argent, neither gold nor silver.
Ni prières, ni menaces ne pouvaient l'engager à, etc.
Neither prayers nor threats could induce him to, etc.
Soit crainte, soit ignorance, il ne voulait rien dire.
Be it fear or ignorance, he would say nothing.

4. The partitive article is further omitted after prepositions when the noun following forms with them an adverbial phrase, as:

Avec plaisir, with pleasure.
avec patience, with patience.
avec soin, with care.
avec élégance, elegantly.
sans argent, without money.
sans façons, without ceremonies.
sans peine, without trouble.
sans péril, without danger.
par jour, daily, a day.
par an, yearly, a year.
par mois, monthly, a month.
sur mer, *par mer*, } by water, by sea.
sur terre, *par terre*, } by land.
sous peine de mort, on pain of death.

5. No article is used before a substantive which is repeated with a preposition, as:

Promesses sur promesses, promises upon promises.
De temps en temps, from time to time.
De siècle en siècle, from age to age.

6. In the following expressions, where the noun forms but one idea with the verb antecedent, as:

Avoir faim, to be hungry.
avoir soif, to be thirsty.
prendre patience, to have patience.
prendre soin, to take care.

avoir soin, to take care.
avoir peur, to be afraid.
avoir bonne mine, to look well.
avoir pitié, to have pity.
avoir honte, to be ashamed.
avoir raison, to be right.
avoir tort, to be wrong.
avoir sujet, to have occasion for.
avoir dessein, to intend.
avoir envie, to have a desire, a mind.
avoir besoin, to want.
avoir coutume, to be in the habit, to use.
prendre part, to join.
prendre garde, to take care.
prendre congé, to take leave.
faire grâce, to grant pardon.
faire attention, to pay attention.
faire grand cas, to value.
faire peur, to frighten.
faire mention, to mention.
faire fortune, to make one's fortune.
rendre compte, *rendre raison*, } to account for.
rendre visite, to visit.
porter envie, to envy.
courir risque, to run risk.
demander pardon, to beg one's pardon.
demander grâce, to beg for grace.
ajouter foi, to give credit.

7. Further, after many verbs which are followed by *de*, *à*, or *en*, as: —

Combler de bienfaits, to load with benefits.
Vivre de pain, to live upon bread.
Monter à cheval, to mount (get) on horseback.
Monter en voiture, to enter a carriage.
Tomber de cheval, to fall from horseback.
Descendre de cheval, to alight.
Se mettre à table, to go to dinner.
Se lever de table, to rise from dinner.
Perdre de vue, to lose sight of.
Mourir de faim, to die of hunger.
Mourir de froid, to die of cold, to freeze.
Trembler de peur, to tremble with fear.
Être malade de chagrin, to be ill with grief.

THEME 6.

1. Charity[1] begins at home (*par soi-même*). 2. Necessity has no law (*loi*). 3. Games,[2] conversation, theatre, nothing diverts (*distrait*) him. 4. Nobody was satisfied; father, uncles, aunts and brothers, all thought themselves (*se crurent*) neglected.[3] 5. This man has neither vices nor virtues; neither talents nor defects.[4] 6.

15

We expected our friend from day to day. 7. It does not suffice to heap (*d'entasser*) facts[5] upon facts to load[6] your memory; you must exercise[7] also your judgment.[8] 8. I shall do it with pleasure. 9. One florin *a* day. 10. Ten pounds a year. 11. The poor woman was starving with hunger and (with) cold. 12. You *are* always right; I have been wrong. 13. Have pity on (*de*) my weakness.[9] 14. The least noise[10] frightens me. 15. Those who speak without reflection, are exposed to many (*à bien des*) errors. 16. I must take leave of you. 17. Many poor people live on (*de*) bread and potatoes only. 18. The king has granted (*fait*) him [his] pardon.

1. *Charité.* 2. *Jeu*, m. 3. *Négligés.* 4. *Défaut.* 5. *Le fait.* 6. *Charger.* 7. *Exercer.* 8. *Jugement.* 9. *Faiblesse.* 10. *Bruit*, m.

READING LESSON.

DÉMOSTHÈNE.

Démosthène, jeune homme d'Athènes, avait grande envie de devenir orateur habile; mais la nature semblait lui en avoir refusé tous les moyens.

D'abord il bégayait[1] à l'excès; puis il ne pouvait prononcer la lettre R.; ensuite il avait une voix désagréable et glapissante,[2] et de faibles poumons.[3] D'autres ajoutent qu'il avait encore la mauvaise habitude de lever l'épaule[4], quand il avait prononcé trois ou quatre mots. Aussi, la première fois qu'il harangua le peuple, il s'en tira si mal, qu'il fut sifflé[5].

Tout autre que lui aurait à jamais perdu courage. Mais Démosthène prit patience et résolut, en dépit[6] de la nature, de devenir bon orateur, et il le devint. Écoutez comment il s'y prit.[7]

Quelquefois il allait au bord de la mer, dans l'endroit où les vagues[8] venaient se briser (*break*) avec fracas.[9] Là, il débitait[10] un discours à haute voix, pour s'accoutumer à dominer le tumulte d'une assemblée populaire.

D'autres fois, il mettait dans sa bouche de petits cailloux (*pebbles*); puis il courait en gravissant[11] une montagne et en déclamant, afin de se contraindre[12] à prononcer clairement jusqu'à la moindre syllabe.

Enfin, on dit qu'il s'exerçait à parler dans une chambre souterraine,[13] et que pour se mettre dans la nécessité de rester longtemps enfermé, il s'était fait raser[14] la moitié de la tête.

Il se plaçait des heures entières devant un miroir, pour se donner une bonne contenance et des gestes convenables. On dit qu'il se mettait aussi l'épaule nue immédiatement sous la pointe d'une épée,[15] afin qu'elle le piquât,[16] toutes les fois que, d'après sa mauvaise habitude, il ferait son mouvement d'épaule.

C'est par des exercices soutenus[17] de ce genre, joints à une étude profonde des sciences, qu'il se rendit enfin le plus grand orateur qui ait existé ; et aujourd'hui encore, après tant de siècles,[18] ses harangues sont admirées comme des chefs-d'œuvre d'éloquence.

1. To stammer. 2. Shrill. 3. Lungs. 4. Shoulder. 5. To hiss. 6. In spite of. 7. To manage. 8. The waves. 9. Noise. 10. To deliver. 11. To climb. 12. To force. 13. Subterranean. 14. To shave. 15. A sword. 16. To sting. 17. Continued. 18. Century.

CONVERSATION.

La nature avait-elle favorisé Démosthène ?	Au contraire, elle semblait lui avoir refusé tous les moyens de devenir orateur.
Quels défauts avait-il donc ?	Il bégayait et ne pouvait prononcer la lettre *r*.
Comment était sa voix ?	Elle était désagréable et glapissante.
Comment s'en tira-t-il, lorsqu'il prononça son premier discours ?	Il s'en tira si mal qu'il fut sifflé (*hissed*).
Fut-il découragé par ce résultat ?	Non, il ne perdit pas courage ; au contraire, il persista dans son dessein.
Et comment s'y prit-il ?	Il s'exerçait continuellement et de différentes manières.

Dites-moi comment.	Il mettait de petits cailloux dans sa bouche pour se défaire (*rid of*) de l'habitude de bégayer.
Est-ce qu'il réussit dans ses efforts ?	Il réussit si parfaitement qu'il devint à la fin le plus grand orateur qui ait existé.
Ses harangues existent-elles encore ?	Oui, elles ont été conservées, et elles sont encore aujourd'hui admirées comme des chefs-d'œuvre d'éloquence.

IV. QUATRIÈME LEÇON.

SPECIAL USE OF *DE* AND *A*.

In general we may say *de* is used when *made of, composed of, coming from, belonging to,* can be understood; whereas *à* is employed when *for the purpose of* is meant.

I. DE IS USED : —

1. After adverbs of quantity, as : *beaucoup, peu, plus, moins, tant,* etc. (See Part I. L. 6, p. 42.)

2. Before a limiting word which follows a noun used partitively and preceded by a word denoting quality. Ex.: —

Il y eut deux hommes DE *tués,* there were two men killed.
Voici quelque chose DE *plus,* here is something more.
Voici un homme DE *trop,* here is a man too many.
J'ai deux chambres DE *louées,* I have two rooms let.

NOTE. The noun may be understood. Ex.: *J'en ai une de louée.* Or *rien* or *personne* may supply the place of the noun and its preceding word. Ex.: *Il n'y a personne de malade chez nous,* there is no one sick at our house. *Rien de bon,* nothing good.

3. As in English, after nouns expressing *quantity*, *number*, *measure*, *weight*, etc., as: —

Une quantité de noix, a quantity of walnuts.
Une paire de bas, a pair of stockings.
Une livre de beurre, a pound of butter.
Une pièce de toile, a piece of linen.
Un morceau de fromage, a piece of cheese.
Une main de papier, a quire of paper.
Une bouteille de vin, a bottle of wine.

4. After adjectives denoting *dimension* or *age*, as: —

A wall twenty feet high: *un mur haut de vingt pieds* or *un mur qui a vingt pieds* DE *haut* or DE *hauteur*.

A boy ten years old, *un (petit) garçon de dix ans*.

A table six feet long, *une table longue de six pieds* or *de six pieds de longueur*.

NOTE. It may be observed here that with adjectives of dimension, the verb *to be* may be rendered in French by *avoir*, as: —

This tower is 120 feet high.
Cette tour A *cent vingt pieds* DE *hauteur*.

5. When an English adjective is rendered in French by a noun, the order of the substantives is inverted in English. In French the latter is preceded by *de*. Ex.: —

A witty man, *un homme* d'*esprit*.
A gold watch, *une montre* d'*or*.
Silk stockings, *des bas de soie*.
The Russian Ambassador, *l'ambassadeur de Russie*.
Irish linen, *la toile* d'*Irlande*.
Spanish wool, *la laine* d'*Espagne*.
Burgundy wine, *le vin de Bourgogne*.

6. *De* is used, as in English, after a common noun followed by its proper name. Ex.: —

Le royaume d'Espagne, the kingdom of Spain.
L'île de Malte, the island of Malta.
La ville de Londres, the city of London.
Le lac de Genève, the lake of Geneva.

Except the combinations with *mont*, *rue*, *place*, and *église*, as: *le Mont Blanc*, *le Mont Etna*, *rue Richelieu*, *place Vendôme*, *l'église Saint-Sulpice*, *etc.*

7. After many adjectives it takes the place of the English *with*, *from*, *of*, *by*, *in*, etc. (See L. 8, compl. of adj. 1.) Ex.: —

Full of ardor, *plein de feu*.
Greedy after money, *avide d'argent*.
Dressed in black, *vêtu de noir*.

I am pleased with my situation.
Je suis content de ma position.

I am deprived of everything, *je suis privé de tout*.

8. *De* is used for *than*, instead of *que*, after *plus*, more, and *moins*, less, when these adverbs are followed by a numeral adjective or substantive: —

Il a plus de six ans, he is more than six years old.

9. For *in*, after a superlative, before the name of a place: —

Une des meilleures institutions DE *Boston*, one of the best institutions *in* Boston.

Les garçons DE *notre école*, the boys in our school.

FRENCH COMPOUND NOUNS WITH DE.

10. English nouns compounded with two substantives are generally rendered in French by two separate substantives joined by *de*, when one expresses the *nature*, *species*, or *quality* of the other. (Compare p. 240, 2.) In French the order must be altered, the last coming first, and a preposition inserted. Westminster bridge, for instance, must be translated as if it were bridge of Westminster: *le pont de Westminster*.

1. *De* is used when *coming from*, *belonging to*, *made of* can be understood, as: —

A toothache, *un mal de dents*.
A headache, *un mal de tête*.
The town-hall, *l'hôtel de ville*.
A sea-fish, *un poisson de mer*.
A feather-bed, *un lit de plumes*.
A holiday, *un jour de fête*.
A gold mine, *une mine d'or*.
The moon-light, *le clair de lune*.
A masterpiece, *un chef-d'œuvre*.

2. When in the English word the second component denotes a person or an animal, in French *de* is always used, as: —

A schoolmaster, *un maître d'école.*
A chambermaid, *une femme de chambre.*
The dancing-master, *le maître de danse.*
The music-mistress, *la maîtresse de musique.*
A saddle-horse, *un cheval de selle.*
A sea-fish, *un poisson de mer.*

THEME 7.

1. Give me much bread and little meat. 2. You must use more prudence. 3. I have bought a quantity of apples and pears. 4. You make too much noise. 5. How many children has your aunt? 6. She has four children. 7. You have eaten too many cherries. 8. We have not bread enough.* 9. Mr. Henry has a great many friends. 10. We had a great deal of pleasure. 11. I bought a pound of cheese. 12. We want a dozen pens, a bottle of ink, and two quires of paper. 13. A great number of friends remained attached[1] to me. 14. They have built a wall eighty feet long and ten feet high. 15. How many boys were there killed? 16. There were six killed (see § 2). 17. How many soldiers were there wounded? 18. There were six books lost. 19. How many were there found? 20. How many rooms are there let in that house? 21. Have you anything good? 22. I have nothing bad. 23. When my sister was a girl of seven years, she lived with my mother in Italy. 24. Have you a gold or a silver watch? 25. My watch is of gold. 26. Irish linen is as[2] good as Dutch[3] linen. 27. I prefer Burgundy wine to Spanish wine. 28. The kingdom of Spain is larger than the kingdom of Portugal. 29. The city of Paris is older than the city of Berlin. 30. Is that gentleman[4] your music-master? 31. No; he is my writing[5]-master.

1. *Attachés.* 2. *Aussi.* 3. *D'Hollande.* 4. *Monsieur.* 5. *Écriture,* f.

* *Assez,* enough, is placed after the substantive in English, and always before in French.

THEME 8.

1. To-morrow is (*c'est*) a holi[1]day; it will be a day of happiness.[2] 2. Human life is full of disappointments.[3] 3. Mr. E. is a young man endowed[4] with (*d'*) wit[5] and judgment. 4. We were very much pleased with his behavior.[6] 5. I was in England, but I have not seen Westminster bridge. 6. Burgundy wine is very dear. 7. Spanish wool is better than German wool. 8. I have sold my gold watch. 9. Mr. B. always wears[7] silk stockings. 10. My sisters and I (we) have taken[8] a walk by (*au*) moonlight. 11. The battle-field was covered with the dead and dying. 12. This girl is the chambermaid of the Duchess of L. 13. Who are these gentlemen? 14. One is my music-master, and the other is my sister's dancing-master. 15. Let us go to (*allons dans*) the dining-room; dinner is served (*servi*). 16. I shall not dine to-day; I have a bad[9] headache.

1. *Fête.* 2. *Bonheur.* 3. *Revers.* 4. *Doué.* 5. *Esprit.* 6. *Conduite*, f. 7. *Porter.* 8. To take a walk = *se promener.* 9. *Violent.*

II. SPECIAL USE OF *à*.

1. The preposition *à* alone (without article) is used after a verb in the following expressions:

Condamner à mort, to condemn to death.
Fermer à clef, to lock.
Tomber à terre, to fall to the floor *or* ground.
Aller à pied, to go on foot, to walk.
Aller à cheval, to ride, to go on horseback.
Monter à cheval, to get *or* mount on horseback.
Tomber à genoux, } to kneel down.
Se mettre à genoux, }
Se mettre à table, to sit down to dinner.

2. When two substantives make a compound word in English, their order is inverted in French, and the preposition *à* intervenes, when the one expresses the use of the other, or when *for the purpose of*, *by means of*, may be understood:

The silk-worm, *le ver à soie*.

A milk-pot, *un pot à lait.**
A teacup, *une tasse à thé.*
A repeater, *une montre à répétition.*
A windmill, *un moulin à vent.*
A paper-mill, *un moulin à papier.*
A powder-mill (a mill for powder), *un moulin à poudre.*
Gunpowder, *de la poudre à canon.*
A dining-room, *une salle à manger.*
A bedroom, *une chambre à coucher.*
A wineglass, *un verre à vin.**
A coffee-cup, *une tasse à café.*
A steam-engine, *une machine à vapeur.*
A steamboat, *un bateau à vapeur.*
Fire-arms, *des armes à feu.*

3. If the second word begins with a vowel or *h* mute, the article is commonly inserted, as:

An ink-bottle, *une bouteille à l'encre* (or *à encre*).
A water-jug (pitcher), *une cruche à l'eau* (or *à eau*).

4. When the compound word denotes a place where certain things are sold or kept in quantities, the article is also used with *à*, as:

The horse-market, *le marché aux chevaux.*
The fish-market, *le marché aux poissons.*
The corn-market, *la halle aux blés.*

5. *A* together with the article is further used to call a dish or drink after its principal ingredient, as:

A milk-soup, *une soupe au lait.*
Coffee with milk, *du café au lait.*
A cream-tart, *une tarte à la crême.*
A pancake with herbs, *une omelette aux fines herbes.*

NOTE. But we say *du syrop de groseille*, not *syrop à groseille*, currant-syrup, because this is made entirely of currants.

6. To denote the different kinds of hunting, shooting, etc., as:

A deer-hunt, *la chasse aux chevreuils.*
Fox-hunting, *la chasse aux renards.*

7. *A* is generally employed to translate expressions in which *with*

* *Un pot de lait, un verre de vin*, signify a pot of milk, a glass of wine; *pot au lait* refers both to the vessel and to its contents.

is expressed or could be employed, or when *having* could be used. Ex.:

Une maison à deux étages, a two-story house.
Un chapeau à grands bords, a broad-brimmed hat.
Une voiture à deux places, a double-seated carriage.

THEME 9.

1. I have bought six *teacups;* take[1] them into the dining-room. 2. Where is the *oil[2]-bottle?* 3. Who has broken this *flower-pot?* 4. Bring me a *wineglass* and two *teaspoons*. 5. Why has he been condemned *to* death? 6. He has committed[3] a murder. 7. Your room is locked. 8. Is this an *ink-bottle?* 9. No; it is a *vinegar[4]-bottle*. 10. Let us sit down (*mettons-nous*) to dinner. 11. Did you observe[5] that man *with*[6] black hair? 12. You must buy another *milk-pot*. 13. Is this the *corn-market?* 14. I always keep (keep always) *fire-arms* in my *bedroom* for my safety[7] during the night; but I have no *gunpowder* at present, thus (*ainsi*) my *fire-arms* are useless.[8]

1. *Portez*. 2. *Huile*, f. 3. *Commis*, P. p. of *commettre*. 4. *Vinaigre*. 5. *Remarquer*. 6. *Aux*, pl. 7. *Sûreté*, f. 8. *Inutile*.

THEME 10.

1. Whom have you called? 2. I have been to the fish-market; however I have bought no fish, because it was too dear.[1] 3. I went *fox-hunting* yesterday, and to-morrow I shall see a *deer-hunt*. 4. What had you for dessert? 5. We had *cherry-pie*[2] and a *cream*[3] *tart*.[4] 6. Can you tell me where the *hay-store* is? 7. It is near the *horse-market*. 8. Who invented *gunpowder?* 9. Berthold Schwarz, a German monk.[5] 10. The poor girl has broken a *milk-pot*, two *wineglasses*, and several *teacups*. 11. The Great Eastern is the largest steamship in the (*au*) world. 12. Call the milk-woman;[6] I must buy a pot *of* milk.

1. *Cher*. 2. *Gâteau*. 3. *Crême*, f. 4. *Tourte*, f. 5. *Moine*. 6. *Laitière*.

V. CINQUIÈME LEÇON.

PECULIARITIES IN THE USE OF NAMES OF COUNTRIES, TOWNS, ETC.

(See Part I., L. VII.)

1. As mentioned in the *First Part* (7th lesson), the definite article is put before the names of countries, provinces, rivers, and mountains. But the names of countries and islands, which have the same name as cities situated in them, such as *Naples*, *Bade*, *Gènes* (Genoa), *Malte*, *Candie*, etc., are used without the article.

Except, however: *le Hanovre* and *le Luxembourg.*

2. Further, the definite article is always retained with names of countries which are only used in the plural, and in those which are compounded with an adjective. Ex.: —

The productions of India, *les productions des Indes.*

The governor of the Netherlands.
Le gouverneur des Pays-bas.

The queen of Great Britain.
La reine de la Grande-Bretagne.

3. In the following cases *de* only, without the article, is used before names of countries: —

1. When sovereigns, courts, and titles are spoken of. Ex.: —

La reine d'*Angleterre,* the queen of England.
Le Grand-duc de Bade, the grand-duke of Baden.

NOTE. With the names of some countries that are not European, the article is generally used, as: —

L'empereur de la Chine, du Brésil, etc.
The emperor of China, of Brazil, etc.

However, with Persia, *la Perse,* and Egypt, *l'Egypte,* only *de* is used: —

Le roi de Perse, the king of Persia.

2. Where the names of countries have the meaning of an adjective (see also L. IV. 4), as:—

L'argent de France, French money.
La soie d'Italie, the silk of Italy.
Du fromage de Suisse, Swiss cheese (*de* may be omitted).

3. After the verbs: *venir*, to come; *revenir*, to come back, to return; *arriver*, to arrive, and the noun *le retour*, if the name of the country is feminine, as:—

Il est venu de France, he has come from France.
Lorsque je revins d'Espagne, when I returned from Spain.
A mon retour d'Italie, on my return from Italy.

But if the same is masculine, the definite article is used, as:—

J'arrive du Tyrol, du Mexique, du Portugal, etc.

4. After words, such as *empire*, *royaume* (kingdom), *duché*, *ville*, *île* (isle), as in English (see L. IV. 6):—

L'empire d'Autriche, the Empire of Austria.
La ville de Paris, the city of Paris.

4. Both *to* and *in* used after a word signifying *going*, *coming*, *sending*, *living*, *being*, etc., before names of countries in the singular, must be rendered in French by the preposition ***en***, without any article. Ex.:—

We are going to America, *nous allons en Amérique*.
He is to go back to Belgium, *il doit retourner en Belgique*.
I send him to Switzerland, *je l'envoie en Suisse*.
My brother is in America, *mon frère est en Amérique*.
Rouen is in France, *Rouen est située en France*.

5. If the name of the country be accompanied by an adjective, *dans* with the definite article must be used:

Dans la Suisse française, in French Switzerland.
Dans l'Allemagne méridionale, in southern Germany.

6. The article is omitted before names of towns, villages, etc., as:—

Anvers, Antwerp.
Athènes, Athens.
Bruxelles, Brussels.
Douvres, Dover.
Genève, Geneva.
Livourne, Leghorn.
Lisbonne, Lisbon.
Londres, London.
Lyon, Lyons.
Venise, Venice.

NOTE. A few names of towns are preceded by the article:—

Le Havre, Havre.
la Haie, the Hague.
la Rochelle, Rochelle.
le Caire, Cairo, etc.

7. The names of rivers and mountains are preceded by the definite article, as in English:

La Seine, the Seine.
le Rhône, the Rhone.
le Rhin, the Rhine.
les Alpes, the Alps.
le Tibre, the Tiber.
le Danube, the Danube.
la Moselle, the Moselle.
le Righi, the Righi.

8. Both *to* and *at* or *in* before names of places are rendered by *à*. Ex.:—

Are you going to Brussels, *allez-vous à Bruxelles?*
He was at Rome and Naples, *il était à Rome et à Naples.*

9. After *partir*, to set out, to leave, the preposition *pour* must be used before names of countries *with* the article, before names of cities *without* it:—

Nous partirons pour l'Espagne et le Portugal.
We will set out (*or* leave) for Spain and Portugal.
Elle est partie pour Paris et Lyon.
She left for Paris and Lyons.

THEME 11.

1. I prefer the wines of Germany to the wines of France. 2. We shall soon go to Switzerland and Italy. 3. Naples may (*peut*) be called a paradise,[1] from its (*à cause de sa*) beauty and fertility.[2] 4. This merchant has bought Italian silk, Spanish wool, and French wines. 5. My grandfather lives in the West Indies.[3] 6. I set out for Egypt to-morrow. 7. This cheese comes from Switzerland. 8. Cologne is situated[4] on (*sur*) the Rhine. 9. The Alps are higher than the Pyrenees. 10. The emperor of Russia, Peter[5] the Great, died at St. Petersburgh in the year (*en*) 1725. 11. Sicily is the granary[6] of (§ 1) Italy, and Italy the garden of Europe.

1. *Paradis*, m. 2. *Fertilité.* 3. *Les Indes occidentales.* 4. *Située.* 5. *Pierre.* 6. *Grenier*, m.

READING LESSON.

CHARLES XII. (*Douze.*)

Charles XII, roi de Suède, naquit[1] à Stockholm le 27 Juin 1682. Il perdit sa mère dans sa onzième année, et avait à peine quinze ans lorsque son père mourut. Selon[2] le testament du feu[3] roi, il ne devait être majeur[4] qu'après avoir passé sa dix-huitième année, mais sur la proposition du ministre Piper, les états lui déférèrent[5] le gouvernement déjà en 1697. L'an 1700, Pierre I, empereur de Russie, Frédéric IV, roi de Danemark, et Auguste, électeur de Saxe, lui déclarèrent la guerre.

Il les attaqua l'un après l'autre et remporta d'abord[6] des victoires éclatantes,[7] entre autres celle de Narva, où il défit[8] avec moins de[9] 8,000 Suédois, quatre-vingt mille Russes, dont il resta plus de vingt mille sur le champ de bataille, tandis qu'il ne perdait que six cents hommes. Mais plus tard, lorsqu'il pénétra en Russie, il perdit la bataille décisive de Pultawa, et fut contraint de se réfugier sur le territoire turc avec une faible escorte de deux cent cinquante Suédois.

1. Was born. 2. According to. 3. Late. 4. Of age. 5. To transfer. 6. At first. 7. Splendid. 8. To defeat. 9. Than.

CONVERSATION.

Où naquit Charles XII?	Ce roi naquit à Stockholm.
Dans quelle année?	En 1682, le 27 Juin.
Perdit-il ses parents de bonne heure?	Oui, il perdit sa mère, quand il avait 11 ans, et son père, quand il avait 15 ans.
Quand fut-il déclaré majeur?	En 1697, à l'âge de quinze ans et demi.
Qu'arriva-t-il trois ans après?	Pierre I, empereur de Russie, Frédéric IV, roi de Danemark, et Auguste, électeur de Saxe, lui déclarèrent la guerre.
Que fit Charles XII?	Il les attaqua l'un après l'autre et les défit.

Quelle est sa plus éclatante victoire ?	Celle de Narva, où il battit 80,000 Russes.
Avait-il beaucoup de soldats ?	Il n'avait que 8,000 Suédois.
Y eut-il beaucoup de tués ?	Les Russes perdirent plus de vingt mille hommes, lés Suédois à peine six cents.
A-t-il toujours été heureux dans ses batailles ?	Non, il perdit la bataille de Pultawa.
A quoi fut-il contraint ?	Il fut contraint de se réfugier sur le territoire turc, avec une faible escorte.

VI. SIXIÈME LEÇON.

POSSESSIVE ADJECTIVES.

(See the First Part, L. XII.)

1. Possessive adjectives must be repeated :—

1. Before every noun of the same sentence, as :—

My brothers and sisters have arrived.
Mes frères et mes sœurs sont arrivés.

2. Before two or three adjectives qualifying different things :—

I love your great and your little children.
J'aime vos grands et vos petits enfants.

NOTE. But when the two substantives relate to the same person, and when the two or three adjectives are of the like signification* and qualify the same object, the possessive adjective is not repeated. Ex.:—

My teacher and friend, *mon précepteur et ami.*
His good and useful advice, *ses bons et utiles conseils.*

* If they have a contrary signification, the possessive adjective must be repeated, as : *Ses bonnes et ses mauvaises pensées* (thoughts).

2. Custom requires the use of the possessive adjective before the names of relations in addressing them or speaking of them. Ex.: —

Aunt, when do you leave?
Ma tante, quand partez-vous?

Cousin, will you go with me?
Mon cousin (ma cousine), voulez-vous aller avec moi?
Father is not at home, *mon père n'est pas à la maison.*

3. When in English the possessive pronouns *mine*, *thine*, *his*, *hers*, etc., preceded by the preposition *of*, are placed after a noun to which they relate, they are rendered in French by *mes*, *tes*, *ses*, etc., before the noun, which is put in the plural. Ex.: —

A book of mine, *un de mes livres.*
A friend of yours, *un de vos amis.*

4. When the verb *to be* is found before a possessive adjective followed by a noun in the possessive case, and signifies *to belong*, in French *à* must be used. Ex.: —

This book is my father's, *ce livre est* à *mon père.*
That house is our uncle's, *cette maison-là est* à *notre oncle.*

5. When parts of the body, or physical and intellectual faculties are spoken of, the French generally use the definite article where in English the possessive adjective is used (see L. III. 5.) Ex.: —

I have a pain in my head, *j'ai mal à la tête.*
He has lost his senses, *il a perdu* l'*esprit.*

NOTE 1. If, however, there were an ambiguity to be feared, the *possessive adjective* should be used in French as in English.

NOTE 2. When a habitual complaint is spoken of, the possessive adjective is also properly used. Ex.: —

His headache has returned, *sa migraine l'a repris.*

6. After the verbs *changer* and *redoubler* the possessive adjective is dropped and replaced by the preposition *de*, as: —

He has changed his religion, *il a changé de religion.*
We have changed our opinion.
Nous avons changé d'*opinion* or d'*avis.*

They redoubled their activity, *ils redoublèrent* d'*activité.*

THEME 12.

1. My father, mother and sisters are in the country. 2. His uncle and aunt know it. 3. I thank you for (*de*) your good and useful services. 4. He is a friend of mine. 5. I found a pencil of yours. 6. Where are you, daughter? 7. Here I am, mother. 8. Come, friend, let us work. 9. He will never betray[1] me, for he is my friend and protector.[2] 10. We changed our mind[3] when we heard that news. 11. He tells[4] a falsehood[4] as often as (*toutes les fois qu'*) he opens *his* mouth. 12. A cousin of ours came yesterday to see us. 13. Give me my dictionary and grammar.[5] 14. My mother has [a] pain in (*à*) *her* head. 15. I have [a] pain in *my* ear.[6] 16. The man who fell from the roof[7] of our house, dislocated (*se démit*) *his* wrist.[8] 17. In (*à*) the last battle[9] our general lost *his* right leg, and I was wounded[10] in *my* shoulder.[11]

1. *Trahir.* 2. *Protecteur.* 3. *Avis*, m. 4. *Dire un mensonge.* 5. *Grammaire*, f. 6. *Oreille.* 7. *Toit*, m. 8. *Poignet*, m. 9. *Bataille*, f. 10. *Blesser*, reg. v. 11. *Epaule*, f.

---

7. When in English the word *own* is found alone, i. e. without a noun, after a possessive adjective, the latter is rendered by a possessive pronoun: *le mien, le tien, le sien* (*propre*), etc., or in the feminine by *la mienne, la tienne, la sienne* (*propre*), etc. Ex.: —

The daughter of his friend and his own.
La fille de son ami et la sienne (propre).

8. The indefinite pronoun *one's* denoting a possession is translated in French *son, sa, ses.* Ex.: —

One is glad to find one's money again.
On est content de retrouver son argent.

9. When *its* and *their* refer to a thing which is not the subject of a preposition they are rendered by *en* unless preceded by a preposition, in which case *son, sa, ses, leur, leurs* must be used. Ex.: —

I like this country, its air (*Nom.*) is healthy, its soil fruitful, etc.
J'aime ce pays; l'air en est sain, le sol en est fertile.

What plant is this? — I do not know its name.
Quelle est cette plante? — Je n'en connais pas le nom.

16

Look at these trees; what is their height?
Voyez ces arbres; quelle en est la hauteur (not *leur h.*)?

But we must say:

Paris a ses beautés.
Paris has its beauties.

J'admire la grandeur de ses rues.
I admire the size of its streets.

Ces arbres sont remarquables par leur hauteur.
These trees are remarkable for their height.

10. Observe the following gallicisms: —

Let me soon hear of you.
Donnez-moi bientôt de vos nouvelles.

I shall go to meet you, *j'irai à votre rencontre.*
They are cousins of mine, *ce sont de mes cousins.*

With regard to me, — to you, — to us.
A mon égard, à votre égard, à notre égard.

THEME 13.

1. He has worked much more for our good[1] than for *his* own. 2. Paris is a large city, *its* streets are too narrow.[2] 3. I particularly[3] admire (I adm. p.) its rich stores.[4] 4. Windsor is a fine town; I admire its situation, walks[5] and streets. 5. London *has its* beauties. 6. I like the size[6] *of its* streets. 7. This illness[7] is dangerous; I know *its* origin[8] and effects.[9] 8. This is (*voici*) a fine tree; *its* fruit is delicious.[10] 9. Every science has *its* principles. 10. An illustrious (*—tre*) birth[11] receives from virtue *its* most shining[12] lustre. 11. Mr Dubois has sold his father's house and *his own.*

1. *Le bien.* 2. *Etroit, e.* 3. *Surtout.* 4. *Magasin.* m. 5. *Promenade,* f. 6. *Grandeur,* f. 7. *Maladie,* f. 8. *Origine,* f. 9. *Effet,* m. 10. *Délicieux.* 11. *Naissance,* f. 12. *Beau.*

READING LESSON.

EUDAMIDAS.

Eudamidas de Corinthe fit, en mourant, un testament qui semblerait ridicule à tout autre qu'à un ami. Il touchait à sa dernière heure, et laissait sa mère et sa fille exposées à la plus cruelle indigence, n'ayant pour tout bien que deux fidèles amis, Carixène et Aréthus. Eudamidas ne fut point alarmé ; il jugea des cœurs de ses amis par le sien propre, et il fit ce testament qui ne doit jamais être oublié. "Je lègue[1] à Aréthus le soin de nourrir ma mère, et de l'entretenir dans sa vieillesse ; à Carixène le soin de marier ma fille, et de lui donner une dot[2] convenable."

Carixène étant mort quelque temps après, Aréthus exécuta la commission de tous les deux ; et, pour rendre son action plus illustre, il maria la fille de son ami et la sienne en un même jour, et leur donna à toutes deux une même dot. Quant à (*as to*) la mère, il la nourrit jusqu'à la mort. Si la générosité d'Aréthus est digne d'admiration, la noble hardiesse[3] et la confiance du testateur[4] l'est encore davantage ; car celui qui a la résolution de faire un semblable[5] testament, est capable non-seulement de l'exécuter, mais de quelque chose encore de plus, et il n'est pas douteux qu'il n'eût nourri la mère de son ami, et marié sa fille, aussi bien que la sienne propre, même sans en être prié.

1. I bequeath. 2. Dowry, portion. 3. Boldness. 4. Testator. 5. Such, similar.

CONVERSATION.

Que fit Eudamidas de Corinthe en mourant?	Il fit un testament remarquable.
Était-il riche?	Au contraire, il était très-pauvre, mais il avait deux fidèles amis.
Que légua-t-il donc à ses amis?	Il légua à son ami Aréthus le soin de nourrir sa vieille mère, et à Carixène le soin de marier sa fille.
Devait-il la marier sans dot?	Non, avec une dot convenable.
Les deux amis exécutèrent-ils ce que le testament leur imposa?	L'un d'eux, Carixène, mourut quelque temps après.
Et l'autre que fit-il?	Aréthus exécuta la commission de tous les deux.

De quelle manière l'exécuta-t-il ?	Il maria la fille de son ami et la sienne en un même jour, et leur donna à toutes deux une dot égale.
Et comment agit-il envers la mère d'Eudamidas ?	Il la nourrit jusqu'à la mort.
Comment trouvez-vous la générosité d'Aréthus ?	Elle est digne d'admiration.

VII. SEPTIÈME LEÇON.

NUMERALS.

(See the First Part, L. XIII.)

1. When the cardinal numbers are used substantively they take the masculine article, as :

Un un, a one. *Le trois,* the three.
Ce huit est mal fait, this eight is badly made.

2. *A* and *one* before hundred and thousand are not translated. Ex. :

A hundred and twenty horses, *cent vingt chevaux.*
In the year one thousand one hundred and sixty.
L'an (or simply *en*) *mil cent soixante.*

3. Observe the following expressions with numerals :

Un à un, one by one.
Deux à deux, two by two.
L'un après l'autre, one after the other.
Vers six heures or *vers les six heures,* by about six o'clock.
Vers midi or *vers le midi,* towards (by) twelve o'clock.
Une heure et demie, one hour and a half *or* half-past one.
Deux heures moins un quart, a quarter to two.
Trois heures (et) un quart, a quarter past three.

Tous les deux jours, every other day.
D'aujourd'hui en huit, to-day week.
D'aujourd'hui en quinze, to-day fortnight.
Dans quinze jours, in a fortnight.
Il y a huit jours, a week ago.
Il y a un an, a year *or* a twelvemonth ago.

4. More than, and less than, before numbers are rendered *plus de* and *moins de*, instead of *plus que* and *moins que*. Ex.:

I have spent more than a hundred francs.
J'ai dépensé plus de cent francs.
You have not less than ten mistakes in your exercise.
Vous n'avez pas moins de dix fautes dans votre thème.

5. Nearly, before a number, is translated *près de*. Ex.:

It is nearly five o'clock, *il est près de cinq heures.*

THEME 14.

1. This six is well made, but this nine is badly made. 2. Henry the Fourth was one of the greatest kings of France. 3. Numa was one of the seven kings of Rome. 4. America was discovered[1] in the year one thousand four hundred and ninety-two. 5. The shepherd[2] has sold a hundred sheep. 6. When do you dine? 7. I dine at twelve o'clock, sometimes at one o'clock. 8. I sup[3] at half-past eight, and I go to bed[4] at midnight. 9. Is it four o'clock? 10. No, sir; it is a quarter to four. 11. I must go out at a quarter past four. 12. We went in (*entrâmes*) one by one. 13. My brother will set out this day week, and will come back in a fortnight. 14. Has Mr. L. three children? 15. No; he has (*en a*) more than three: he has four or five. 16. This book costs less than ten francs. 17. How old is your son Charles? 18. He is nearly fourteen years old. 19. I have a French lesson[5] every other day.

1. *Fut découverte.* 2. *Le berger.* 3. *Souper.* 4. *Se coucher.* 5. *Une leçon de français.*

VIII. HUITIÈME LEÇON.

ADJECTIVES.

See Part I., Lesson XVI.

AGREEMENT OF THE ADJECTIVE WITH THE NOUN.

1. In French, the adjective agrees in gender and number with the noun to which it relates:

Une feuille verte, a green leaf.
De bons amis, good friends.
Les prunes sont mûres, the plums are ripe.

1. If it belongs to two or more nouns in the singular, it must be in the plural:

Le pauvre et le riche sont égaux devant Dieu.
The poor and the rich are alike before God.
J'ai trouvé la porte et la fenêtre fermées.
I found the door and the window shut.
La clemence et la majesté étaient peintes sur son front.
Clemency and majesty were imprinted on his brow.

2. If the substantives are of different genders, and joined by *et*, and, the adjectives must be in the *masculine* plural:

Mon frère et ma sœur sont très-heureux.
My brother and sister are very happy.

3. When the two adjectives are joined by *ou*, or, or when the conjunction is left out, the adjective agrees only with the latter noun:

Un château ou une maison ruinée.
A ruined castle or house.
Le fer, la flamme était toute prête.
The sword, the flame was quite ready.

2. The adjectives *demi*, half; *nu*, bare; *excepté*, except; *y compris*, included; *supposé*, supposed; *ci-joint*, inclosed, annexed, are invariable when they precede the noun; *demi* and *nu* are then joined with their noun by a hyphen. Ex.:

Une demi-heure, half an hour

Marcher nu-pieds, to walk barefooted.
Marcher nu-tête, to walk bareheaded.
Excepté les deux premières pages.
Except the two first pages.
Y compris la somme de cent francs.
The sum of a hundred francs included.
Supposé ces faits, these facts supposed.

But they must agree with their noun when they follow it, as:

Une heure et demie, an hour and a half.
Avoir les jambes nues, to have bare legs.
Les deux premières pages exceptées.
The two first pages excepted.
Copie de ma lettre est ci-jointe.
A copy of my letter is annexed.

3. ***Feu***, late, is invariable, like the preceding ones, when it is before the article or possessive pronoun; when it follows, it varies, as:

Feu la reine or *la feue reine*, the late queen.
Feu mes tantes or *mes feues tantes*, my late aunts.

4. Some adjectives, as *bon*, *vite*, *bas*, etc., may be used adverbially: then, of course, they are invariable. Ex.:

Ces roses sentent très-bon (not *bonnes*).
These roses smell very sweet.
Les cerfs courent très-vite, the stags run very fast.

5. If the expression *avoir l'air*, to look, is followed by an adjective, this latter remains unchanged when a moral or intellectual quality is spoken of, as:

Ces dames ont l'air bon.
These ladies look good-natured.

But if a bodily or organic quality is mentioned, or when the adjective refers rather to the subject than to the word *air*, the adjective agrees with the subject of the sentence. In this latter case, the verb *être* is understood, as:

Ces pierres ont l'air très-dures.
These stones seem to be very hard.
Madame F. a l'air mecontente (i. e. *d'être mécontente*).
Mrs. F. appears to be discontented.

6. If a noun is accompanied by an adjective in the superlative,

the latter always agrees with it in gender and number. When the superlative follows, the article must be repeated :

La plus belle femme, the handsomest woman.
Les gens les plus riches, the richest people.

THEME 15.

1. I have a good friend. 2. The leaves are green. 3. These pears are riper than those apples. 4. His brother and cousin have arrived. 5. Charles and Louisa are very industrious. 6. Men and women are mortal. 7. My son and daughter are happy. 8. His uncle and aunt are dead. 9. Louis XIV. had in France an absolute[1] power[2] and authority (*autorité*). 10. She left her room and her trunk[3] open. 11. I found the windows and the shutters[4] shut. 12. Give these presents to the most industrious pupils. 13. Miss Emma is the daughter of the richest man in (*de*) this town. 14. I remained there (*y*) [for] half an hour. 15. The child slept two hours and a half. 16. I have read the whole book, except the two last chapters.[5] 17. The late queen was opposed[6] to that measure.[7] 18. Why do you go barefooted ? 19. These pears appear to be ripe.

1. *Absolu.* 2. *Pouvoir,* m. 3. *Coffre,* m. 4. *Volet,* m. 5. *Chapitre,* m. 6. *S'opposait.* 7. *Mesure.*

B. PLACE OF THE ADJECTIVE.

The principal rules have already been given in the seventeenth Lesson of Part I. We have to add here only the following.

When two adjectives refer to the same noun, we should examine what kind of adjectives they are.

1. If both of them are such as precede, when single, they may both remain before the noun if one of them forms with the noun, as it were, but one idea. Ex. :

*Une jolie petite fille,** a pretty little girl.
Un beau jeune homme,† a handsome young man.

* In Latin *filiola.*

† Youth (juvenis).

2. If both preceding adjectives are taken in their full sense, they must be joined by *et*, and, as :

Un grand et beau jardin, a large, beautiful garden.

3. An adjective usually placed before the noun, when connected by a conjunction with another adjectivo which is to be put after it, is itself placed after the noun. Ex. :

Une action belle et courageuse.*
A fine, courageous action.
Une femme petite, mais bien faite.
A short but well-made woman.

4. In English, two or more adjectives may qualify a substantive, without a conjunction; but in French, *et* (or sometimes *mais*) is always placed before the last of the adjectives, if these *follow* their noun. Ex. :

Une dame riche, jeune et aimable.
A young, rich, amiable lady.
Un homme instruit, modeste et estimé de tout le monde.
A well-instructed, modest, and generally-esteemed man.

THEME 16.

1. Charles is a handsome young man. 2. Henry is a pretty little boy. 3. This is a long (and) tedious[1] book. 4. My friend is an amiable and virtuous man. 5. He has a large and beautiful house. 6. This is a drowned[2] man or woman. 7. For this place I want an aged man or woman. 8. Is it the elder brother or sister? 9. The savage lived in a large, damp[3] cavern. 10. Spain is a fertile country, but badly cultivated.[4] 11. A plain,[5] simple, and natural style is the only one *to be recommended.*[6] 12. Brave and trusty[7] men are generally humane[8] and merciful.[9] 13. This is an interesting[10] and instructive study.[11]

1. *Ennuyeux.* 2. *Noyé e.* 3. *Humide.* 4. *Cultivé e.* 5. *Uni.* 6. *Recommandable.* 7. *Constant.* 8. *Humain.* 9. *Miséricordieux.* 10. *Intéressant.* 11. *Etude*, f.

* "A fine action" would be, *Une belle action.*

C. COMPLEMENT OF ADJECTIVES.

The complement of an adjective is either a substantive or a verb, preceded by one of the prepositions *de*, *à*, *en*, etc.

1. Adjectives and participles which denote *plenty*, *desire*, *scarcity* or *want*, and most of those followed in English by *of*, *with* and *from*, govern in French by means of the preposition *de*, as:

La vie est pleine de misères, life is full of miseries.
Le jeune homme fut comblé d'honneurs, (loaded with honors).

2. The following adjectives govern also by means of *de*:

Capable, capable.
content, contented, pleased.
digne, worthy.
exempt, free.
honteux, ashamed.
jaloux, jealous.
las, tired, wearied.
libre, free.
mécontent, discontented.
satisfait, satisfied.
sûr, sure, etc.

Ex.: *Il est digne de récompense*, he is worthy of reward.

3.* Adjectives denoting fitness, unfitness, disposition, inclination, readiness, or any habit, require *à* before the object. Ex.:

Il est propre à tout, he is fit for anything.
Le cheval est utile à l'homme, the horse is useful to man.

NOTE 1. The following adjectives are followed by *à* in French and *of* in English:

Attentif à, heedful of; *sensible à*, sensible of; *insensible à*, insensible of *or* to.

Ex.: *Soyez attentifs au danger*, be heedful of (the) danger.
Je suis sensible à votre bonté, I am sensible of your kindness.

NOTE 2. Some adjectives are followed in French by the preposition *à*, and in English by *in*; such are:

Habile à, skilful in.
exact à, punctual in.
patient à, patient in.
impatient à, impatient in.

Ex.: *Il est habile à tout*, he is skilful in doing all.
Elle est exacte à son service, she is punctual in her service.

4. The following adjectives, which are followed in English by *to* or *towards* when they express *behavior*, require in French the preposition *envers*:

* To this rule must be excepted some words in the preceding list, § 2.

Affable envers, affable to.
bon envers, (or *pour*) kind to.
juste envers, just to.
cruel envers, cruel to.
honnête envers, civil to.
poli envers, polite to.
reconnaissant envers, thankful to.
respectueux envers, respectful to.
généreux envers, generous to.
libéral envers, liberal to.

Ex.: *Il a été très-bon envers moi* (or *pour moi*).
He has been very kind to me.
Soyez poli envers tout le monde.
Be polite (civil) to everybody.

5. All others not mentioned in the foregoing sections, and which take in English the preposition *to*, are followed in French by *à*. Ex.:

That is easy to say, *cela est facile à dire.*
Religion is necessary to man, *la religion est nécessaire à l'homme.*
He was deaf to my prayers, *il était sourd à mes prières.*

THEME 17.

1. We were loaded[1] *with* honors. 2. The basket[2] is full *of* fruit. 3. Do not be so greedy *of* (after) riches. 4. My cousin is worthy *of* your friendship. 5. Are you pleased *with* your horse? 6. Human life[3] is never free *from* troubles.[4] 7. Voltaire was always greedy of praise and insatiable of glory. 8. I am not satisfied *with* your exercise. 9. That old man is not fit *for* that place; he is not punctual *in* his engagements. 10. My servant is always ready *to* do his duty.[5] 11. Nature[3] is content *with* little. 12. Many people are dissatisfied *with* their condition. 13. Let us be kind *to* everybody. 14. These children are inclined[6] *to* idleness.[7] 15. That is easy *to* say, but difficult *to* do. 16. Scipio Africanus[8] was respectful *to* his mother, liberal *to* his sisters, good *to* his servants, just and affable *to* everybody. 17. Children must[9] not be cruel *to* animals. 18. He is insensible to all the remonstrances[10] of his friends.

1. *Comblé.* 2. *Le panier.* 3. Put the article. 4. *Peine*, f. 5. *Devoir*, m. 6. *Enclin.* 7. *Paresse*, f. 8. *Scipion l'Africain.* 9. *Doivent.* 10. *Remontrance*, f.

D. ADJECTIVES OF DIMENSION.

1. Adjectives relating to the *dimenson* or *size* of objects are expressed in French either by an adjective or a substantive. Thus

long can be rendered by the adjective *long* or *longue* (f.) *de*, or by the noun *de longueur*. Observe that in the first case *de* follows, in the second precedes, and that these adjectives are placed after the substantive and before the dimension. Ex.:

A table ten feet long, } *une table longue de dix pieds.* / *une table de dix pieds de longueur.*

A tower a hundred feet high, } *une tour haute de cent pieds.* / *une tour de cent pieds de hauteur.*

2. The verb *to be* connected with such adjectives, must be expressed by *être* when, in French, the adjective of dimension is preferred to the noun, as:

This table is ten feet long.
Cette table est longue de dix pieds.
That tower is a hundred feet high.
Cette tour-là est haute de cent pieds.

3. But the verb *to be* must be rendered by *avoir* when the dimension is expressed by a noun. Ex.:

This table is ten feet long.
Cette table a dix pieds de longueur.
That tower is a hundred feet high.
Cette tour-là a cent pieds de hauteur.

4. In a similar manner *age* is expressed either with *âgé de* and the verb *être*, or with the verb *avoir* without the verb *âgé*. Ex.:

A boy eight years old, *un garçon âgé de huit ans.*

I am twenty years old, } *je suis âgé de vingt ans.* / *j'ai vingt ans.*

(The latter is much preferred.)

5. The word *by*, which is sometimes used in English after a comparative, to denote how much a thing exceeds another, is rendered by *de*, not by *par*. Ex.:

Charles is taller than I by three inches.
Charles et plus grand que moi de trois pouces.

THEME 18.

1. I have seen a tree ninety feet high. 2. We have a house eighty feet long and forty-five high. 3. This stick is three feet long. 4. This plank[1] is two inches[2] thick.[3] 5. This tree is fifty feet high. 6. London bridge[4] is nine hundred and twenty feet long, fifty-five high, and fifty-six wide.[5] 7. The monument of London stands (*est placé*) on a pedestal[6] twenty feet high. 8. This ditch *is* twelve feet deep.[7] 9. The famous mine of Potosi in (*dans le*) Peru is more than (*de*) fifteen hundred feet deep.[7] 10. My room is forty feet long and thirty wide. 11. The walls of Algiers[8] are fourteen feet thick and thirty feet high. 12. King Street[9] is about[10] a mile[11] and a half long and sixty-five feet wide. 13. My brother is elder than I by two years. 14. I am taller than Robert by seven inches. 15. Westminster bridge is forty-four feet broad;[5] the free-way[12] under the arches of this bridge is eight hundred and seventy feet; it consists[13] of fourteen piers,[14] thirteen large arches, and two small ones; the two middle[15] piers are each (*chacun*) seventeen feet wide, and contain two hundred tons[16] of solid stones.

1. *Planche*, f. 2. *Pouce*, m, 3. *Epais*, *épaisse*. 4. *Le pont de Londres*. 5. *Large* or —*largeur*. 6. *Piédestal*. 7. *Profondeur*. 8. *Alger*. 9. *La rue royale*. 10. *Environ*. 11. *Mille*, m. 12. The free-way = *le passage*. 13. *Il consiste*. 14. *Pile*, f. 15. *Du milieu*. 16. *Tonneau*, m.

READING LESSON.

L'ÉLÉPHANT.

L'éléphant est le plus gros des quadrupèdes; il habite les forêts épaisses,[1] les bords des fleuves et les lieux humides. Ses jambes informes soutiennent un corps épais et lourd.[2] On aperçoit à peine sa petite queue,[3] tandis que de larges oreilles ombragent[4] les deux côtés de sa tête. Ses yeux sont petits en proportion de son corps énorme. Son nez, qui se prolonge de plusieurs pieds et qui est très-flexible, lui sert de main. A l'aide de ce nez, qu'on appelle trompe,[5] il puise (*draws*) de l'eau, cueille les herbes et les fleurs, dénoue[6] les cordes, ouvre et ferme les portes, débouche les bouteilles, ramasse par terre la plus petite pièce de monnaie ; en un mot, il fait presque tout ce que nous faisons avec nos doigts. Quand il a soif, il remplit d'eau cette trompe, et boit ensuite comme s'il vidait[7] une bouteille. Il se nourrit d'herbes, de feuilles, de fruits et de riz (*rice*). Il mange environ cent cinquante livres d'herbes par jour.

De chaque côté de sa trompe sortent deux énormes dents qu'on appelle défenses. Ces défenses sont des armes terribles, dont il épouvante[8] les plus féroces animaux. Elles fournissent une matière précieuse, qu'on appelle ivoire, et pèsent[9] jusqu'à cent livres chacune.

1. Thick. 2. Heavy. 3. Tall. 4. To shade, over-shade. 5. Trunk *or* proboscis. 6. To untie. 7. To empty. 8. To terrify. 9. To weigh.

CONVERSATION.

Que savez-vous de l'éléphant ?	L'éléphant est le plus gros des quadrupèdes.
Où habite-t-il ?	Il habite les forêts épaisses, les bords des fleuves et les lieux humides.
Qu'est-ce qu'il a de particulier ?	Il a une trompe, à l'aide de laquelle il puise de l'eau, cueille les herbes et les fleurs, dénoue des cordes, etc.
De quoi se nourrit-il ?	Il se nourrit d'herbes, de feuilles, de fruits et de riz.
Quand il a soif, que fait-il ?	Il remplit d'eau sa trompe et boit ensuite.
Combien mange-t-il par jour ?	Environ 150 livres d'herbes.
D'ou vient l'ivoire ?	L'ivoire se fait des défenses de l'éléphant qui pèsent jusqu'à cent livres chacune.

IX. NEUVIÈME LEÇON.

I. PERSONAL PRONOUNS.

(See Part I., L. XXIV.)

1. Conjunctive pronouns, in the first and second persons, should be repeated before every verb in a simple tense. Ex.: —

Je vous aime et je vous aimerai toujours.
I love you and (I) shall always love you.

Vous dites et vous direz toujours.
You say and (you) will always say.

Je le vois et je l'entends.
I see and hear it.

Il nous ennuie et nous obsède sans cesse.
He wearies (us) and besets us unceasingly.

NOTE. With a compound tense, or when the pronouns are in the third person, they are rarely repeated, though more frequently than in English, as: —

Je l'ai vu et entendu.
I have seen and heard it.
Il écoute et ne peut comprendre, etc.
He listens and cannot conceive, etc.

2. When an emphasis is laid upon the personal pronoun, it must be repeated in French, but then, the first is *disjunctive*. Very often it is then preceded by *c'est*, or for the third person plural, by *ce sont*. Ex.: —

I say so, { *moi, je le dis.* / *c'est moi, qui le dis.* }

He has pretended this, { *lui, il a prétendu cela.* / *c'est lui qui a prétendu cela.* }

We have not said so,
It is not we who said so, { *nous n'avons pas dit cela, nous.* / *nous, nous n'avons pas dit cela.* / *ce n'est pas nous qui avons dit cela.* }

They have done it, { *eux, ils l'ont fait.*
ce sont eux qui l'ont fait.

NOTE. Observe that in such cases the verb is put in the same number and person as the pronoun which is the antecedent of the relative *qui*, as: —

Is it I who told this news?
Est-ce moi qui ai dit cette nouvelle?

3. When a verb relates to subjects of different persons, it is put in the plural with *nous*, if one of the several subjects is in the first person, — or with *vous*, if the subjects are in the second and third persons. Ex.: —

My brother and *I* shall go into the country.
Mon frère et moi, nous irons à la campagne, or,
Nous irons à la campagne, mon frère et moi.

I told you and him *or* both you and him.
Je vous l'ai dit à toi et à lui.

You and your friend will come with me.
Vous et votre ami, vous viendrez avec moi.

4. When the verb governs two pronouns (both being persons) one in the Direct Objective, the other in the Indirect, the Indirect is a disjunctive (see p. 110). Ex.: —

Je vais vous présenter à lui.
I am going to introduce you to him.

5. A personal pronoun, used as subject, may follow the verb after *aussi*, *peut-être*, *encore*, *toujours*, *en vain*, *du moins*, or *au moins*.

THEME 19.

1. I believe and shall always believe that you were (*avez eu*) wrong. 2. He says so, but he does not believe it. 3. I honor and respect him, but I do not love him. 4. We come and go. 5. A passionate[1] temper[2] renders a man unfit[3] for business,[4] deprives[5] him of his reason, and makes him unfit (makes that he is not fit) (*propre*) for society.[4] 6. I have always loved and esteemed her. 7. They (*on*) flatter[6] and praise us. 8. It is I who have written it.

9. It is they who have seen it. 10. They and my brother have come. 11 You like the town and I the country.

1. *Passionné.* 2. *Caractère.* 3. *Inepte.* 4. Put the definite article. 5. *Priver.* 6. *Flatter.*

6. When *two* personal pronouns limit a verb, both should be disjunctive, and therefore after the verb. Ex.: —

I forgive both you and her.
*Je pardonne à vous et à elle.**

I speak to him and not to you.
Je parle à lui et non à vous.

7. The pronouns himself, herself, themselves, when with a reflective verb, are expressed in French by *se;* otherwise by *lui-même, elle-même, eux-mêmes, elles-mêmes.* Ex.: —

He (she) does not know himself (herself).
Il (elle) ne se connaît pas.

They highly distinguished themselves.
Ils (elles) se distinguèrent beaucoup. But:

Has he done it himself? Yes, himself.
L'a-t-il fait lui-même? Oui, lui-même.

8. *Soi*, self, is of both genders, and is used of things as well as of persons. Ex.: —

Il est sage de parler rarement de soi.
It is wise to talk seldom of one's self.

9. The pronoun *itself*, preceded by a preposition and relating to an inanimate object, is expressed by *soi*, when the antecedent noun is taken in an abstract sense. Ex.: —

L'aimant attire le fer à soi.
The loadstone attracts iron to itself.

La vertu est aimable en soi.
Virtue is amiable in itself.

* This sentence may better be translated thus: *Je vous pardonne ainsi qu'à elle*, and the following, *c'est à vous que je parle, etc.*

10. But it is rendered by *elle*, when the inanimate object is of an individual nature and of the feminine gender. Ex.: —

La rivière entraîna tout avec elle.
The river carried everything away with itself.

Ces raisons sont solides en elles-mêmes.
Those reasons are solid in themselves.

11. The English personal pronouns are always rendered by the *disjunctive* (*moi*, *toi*, *lui*, *etc.*), when they are used alone, or when after a preposition or after *que*, than. Ex.: —

Qui a fait cela? Moi, lui, elle, etc.
Who has done that? I, he, she, etc.

Voulez-vous aller avec moi, avec lui, avec eux? etc.
Will you go with me, with him, with them? etc.

Je parle de toi, d'elle, d'elles, de vous, etc.
I am speaking of thee, of her, of them, of you, etc.

Il est plus jeune que moi.
He is younger than I.

THEME 20.

1. I speak to you and to him. 2. I forgive [both] you and him, because I hope (that) you will behave[1] better for the future (*à l'avenir*). 3. The governor is your enemy; if you apply[2] to him, you will never succeed.[3] 4. I do not trust[4] (to) him, but I should trust (to) his brother. 5. That man works for himself. 6. Each acts for himself. 7. If you do this for him and for her, you will greatly oblige me. 8. One ought not[5] [to] speak of one's self, unless (*qu'*) with modesty. 9. That man is too proud; he does not know himself. 10. The moon brought[6] a change[7] of weather with it (§ 10).

1. *Se conduire.* 2. *S'addrsser à qn.* 3. *Réussir.* 4. *Se fier à qn.* 5. *On ne doit pas.* 6. *Amena.* 7. *Changement*, m.

II. PARTICULAR USE OF *EN* AND *Y*.

1. The pronouns *it* and *them*, used with regard to inanimate objects, are rendered by *en*, when the French verb requires *de* before an object which follows, whatever preposition may be used in English. Ex.: —

A-t-on parlé de mon ouvrage? Oui, on en a parlé.
Did they speak of my work? Yes, they spoke of it.

Vous m'avez rendu service. Je vous en remercie.
You have done me a service. I thank you for it.

2. *En* is further used to express the words *some* and *any*, when they come after a verb, and supply the place of an antecedent substantive, as: —

Voici du jambon; en veux-tu? Donnez-m'en, s'il vous plaît.
Here is ham, will you have some? Give me some, if you please.

J'ai des noix, en voulez-vous? Donnez m'en trois.
I have some walnuts; will you have any? Give me three of them.

Donnez-lui-en, give him some.

Offrez-leur-en, offer them some.

NOTE. Observe 1, that when used with another personal pronoun, *en* follows that pronoun; and 2, that, in the affirmative Imperative, *moi* and *toi* are changed into *m'* and *t'* before *en*, as: *donnez-m'en.*

3. *Y* stands for *in it, into it, at it, to it, there,* and, with the verb *penser*, for *of it, about it, of them.* Like the other conjunctive pronouns, it is placed immediately before the verb, except with the affirmative Imperative, where it follows it.* Ex.: —

Votre père est-il au jardin? Oui, il y est.
Is your father in the garden? Yes, he is in it (there).

Allez-vous au spectacle? Non, Monsieur, je n'y vais pas.
Are you going to the theatre? No, sir, I am not.

Y pensez-vous? Je n'y pense plus.
Do you think of it? I do no more think of it.

Allez-y, go there.

N'y allez pas, do not go there.

NOTE. *Y* must always refer to an antecedent.

* Except *moi* and *toi* which follow the word *y*, with the affirmative Imperative, as: *Conduisez-y-moi, rends-y-toi* (go there), whereas we say: *Conduisez-nous-y.* When both *en* and *y* happen to be governed by the same verb, *y* stands before *en.* Ex.: *Je vous y enporterai,* I will bring you some there. But *conduisez-moi là* is preferable to *conduisez-y-moi.*

THEME 21.

1. We speak of it. 2. You speak of them. 3. I am sorry for it. 4. I have heard that your uncle has arrived, and I am very glad of it. 5. She spoke to him of it. 6. Talk[1] no more of it, for I will not hear of it. 7. Have you [any] books? 8. Yes, I have. 9. Have you bought some flowers? 10. Yes, I have bought some. 11. Give me three of them, if you please. 12. You have bread, give some to the poor. 13. I thank you for it. 14. Do not thank me for it. 15. I study that language,[2] I know its rules well. 16. Since[3] you have no apples in your garden, I will send you some. 17. If I had money, I would give you some. 18. Send us some. 19. Send me none. 20. Mr. A. is a true friend; I shall never forget the services which I have received[4] from him. 21. Is your father in his garden? 22. Yes, he is (in it). 23. Do you agree[5] to it? 24. Yes, I agree to it. 25. Have you[6] just returned from the country? 26. No, I am going there. 27. We shall think of it. 28. We have forced[7] them to it. 29. There is a ditch,[8] take care[9] [not] to fall into it. 30. Our orchard[10] is very fruitful, we see all sorts[11] of fruits in it. 31. It is (*c'est*) a good book, one (*on*) reads excellent things in it.

1. *Parler.* 2. *Langue,* f. 3. *Puisque.* 4. *Reçu.* 5. *Consentir.* 6. *Revenez-vous?* 7. *Forcés.* 8. *Un fossé.* 9. *Prenez garde.* 10. *Verger.* 11. *Toutes sortes de.*

III. THE SUPPLYING PRONOUNS *LE, LA, LES.*

1. The pronouns *le, la, les* are used in French to supply the place of an antecedent substantive or adjective, or of a phrase. In such case, their equivalent in English is *so* or *it*, either expressed or understood.

2. When *le* refers to a noun with the definite article or possessive adjective, it takes the gender and number of that noun. Ex.: —

Etes-vous la mère de ces enfants. Oui, je la suis.
Are you the mother of these children? Yes, I am.
Mesdemoiselles, êtes-vous les nièces de Madame B.? Oui, Madame, nous les sommes.

Ladies, are you Mrs. B.'s nieces? Yes, madame, we are.
Sont-ce là vos domestiques? *Oui, ce les sont.*
Are those your servants? Yes, they are.
Sont-ce là vos gants neufs? *Non, ce ne les sont pas.*
Are those your new gloves? No, they are not.

3. But when *le* supplies the place of an adjective, of a noun used adjectively, or of a phrase, it remains unchanged. Ex.: —

Depuis quand êtes-vous malade? *Je le suis depuis huit jours.*
How long have you been ill? I have been (so) these eight days.
Ces dames sont-elles mariées? *Oui, elles le sont.*
Are these ladies married? Yes, they are (it *or* so).
Etes-vous chrétiens? *Oui, nous le sommes.*
Are you Christians? Yes, we are.
Il le fera, s'il le peut, he will do it, if he can.

NOTE. *Le, la, les* must be used (§ 2) when the adjective is used substantively, as:

Mademoiselle, êtes-vous la malade? *Oui, je la suis.*
Miss, are you the sick one? Yes, I am (she).

4. *Le* should also be inserted in sentences containing a comparative, after *que — ne*, as:

Il est maintenant plus actif qu'il ne l'était auparavant.
He is now more active than he was before.
Elle est moins riche qu'on ne le pense.
She is not so rich as one would think.

THEME 22.

1. Is that your book? 2. Yes, it is. 3. Are those your books? 4. Yes, they are. 5. Are you the mistress of the house? 6. No, I am not. 7. Are these boys the pupils of Mr. M.? 8. Yes, they are. 9. Are you my friend's sisters? 10. Yes, we are. 11. You want some men of good will?[1] 12. We are all *so*. 13. Are these your horses? 14. Yes, they are. 15. Are the brothers rich? 16. No, they are not. 17. Are the house and garden large? 18. Yes, they are. 19. Is not this pretty girl your gardener's daughter? 20. Yes, madam, she is. 21. We need[2] only think ourselves happy, and we shall be *so*. 22. Young ladies, are you English? 23. Yes, we are. 24. Are you physicians? 25. Yes,

sir, we are. 26. Are you the physicians? 27. Yes, sir, we are. 28. Is he sad?[3] 29. No, he is not. 30. Is she rich? 31. Yes, she is. 32. Are those gentlemen brothers? 33. Yes, they are. 34. Are you still my friend? 35. Yes, I am. 36. Are you the sister of Mrs. A.? 37. Yes, I am. 38. Are you the ladies whom my mother expects? 39. Yes, we are. 40. Because she is pretty, she must not imagine[4] that she will always be *so*. 41. We were embarrassed,[5] and are *so* yet (*encore*). 42. Children ought to (*doivent*) apply[6] themselves to their studies as much as they can.

1. *De bonne volonté.* 2. *Nous n'avons qu'à nous croire.* 3. *Triste.* 4. *Il ne faut pas qu'elle s'imagine.* 5. *Embarrassés.* 6. *S'appliquer.*

READING LESSON.

L'ÉLÉPHANT. (*Continuation.*)

L'éléphant vit (*lives*) au delà de cent cinquante ans, quand il est libre. Ces animaux marchent ordinairement de compagnie; le plus âgé conduit la troupe; le second d'âge marche le dernier; les jeunes et les femelles sont au milieu des autres; les mères portent leurs petits et les tiennent embrassés de leurs trompes.

L'éléphant dompté[1] est le plus doux et le plus patient de tous les animaux. Il s'attache à celui qui le soigne;[2] il le caresse, et semble deviner[3] tout ce qui peut lui plaire. En peu de temps il comprend les signes et même la parole. Il reçoit les ordres de son maître avec attention et les exécute avec prudence. Un éléphant domestique rend autant de service que six bons chevaux.

Ils ne cassent rien de ce qu'on leur confie. Ils posent doucement les paquets qu'ils portent, et les rangent dans l'endroit[4] qu'on leur montre. Ils essaient avec leurs trompes flexibles, s'ils sont bien situés, et quand un tonneau[5] commence à rouler, ils vont d'eux-mêmes chercher des pierres pour l'établir solidement.

1. To tame. 2. To take care. 3. To guess. 4. Place. 5. Cask.

CONVERSATION.

Quel âge l'éléphant atteint-il ?	Il vit au delà de 150 ans.
Se laisse-t-il dompter ?	Oui; et quand il est dompté, il est le plus doux de tous les animaux.
L'éléphant est-il intelligent ?	Très-intelligent ; il comprend les signes et même la parole.
Se rend-il utile aux hommes ?	Un seul éléphant rend autant de service que six bons chevaux.
Les éléphants sont-ils maladroits (*awkward*) ?	Non, pas du tout ; ils ne cassent rien de ce qu'on leur confie.
Que font-ils quand un tonneau commence à rouler ?	Ils vont chercher des pierres pour l'établir solidement.

X. DIXIÈME LEÇON.

INTERROGATIVE PRONOUNS.

See Part I., Lesson xxv.

In regard to the interrogative pronouns *lequel? qui? que?* and *quoi?* the following observations are to be made: —

1. *Lequel*, which? always refers to some noun either preceding or immediately following, and agrees with it in gender and number. Ex.: —

Voici deux routes, laquelle prendrez-vous?
Here are two routes; which will you take?
Lesquels de vos souliers sont déchirés?
Which of your shoes are worn out?

NOTE. The interrogative adjective *what* joined to a noun is always expressed by *quel*, f. *quelle*. Ex.: —

What book do you read? *quel livre lisez-vous?*
What are your reasons? *quelles sont vos raisons?*

2. The interrogative pronouns *who? whose? to whom? whom?* are expressed by *qui? de qui?* (not *dont?*) *à qui?* and for the objective *qui?* (*que* as an interrogative means *what*, never *whom*). Ex.: —

Who comes? *qui vient?*
Of whom do you speak? *de qui parlez-vous?*
Whom do you seek? *qui cherchez-vous?*

3. Instead of the simple *qui?* the form *qui est-ce qui*, who? is often used for the Nom., and *qui est-ce que*, whom? for the Dir. Obj. Ex.: —

Qui est-ce qui vient là, who comes there?
Qui est-ce que vous cherchez, whom are you looking for?

4. The same is the case with *que?* for which *qu'est-ce qui?* is often used in the Nom., and *qu'est-ce que?* in the Dir. Obj. The latter has a still stronger form, *qu'est-ce que c'est que* . . ? This compound form is generally used in the expression *what is that?* and also when a simple noun follows, e. g.: —

Qu'est-ce que cela?
Qu'est-ce que c'est que cela? } what is that?
Qu'est-ce que la vie?
Qu'est-ce que c'est que la vie? } what is life?

5. The pupil must be careful, however, not to confound *qui est-ce qui*, who? with *qu'est-ce qui*, what? The latter is used for the wanting Nominative of the conjunctive pronoun *que*. We say: —

Who has offended you? { *qui est-ce qui vous a offensé?*
qui vous a offensé?

Whereas:

What (*Nom.*) makes you so sad?
Qu'est-ce qui vous rend si triste?

What are you doing there? { *qu'est-ce que vous faites là?*
que faites vous là?

What is the news? { *qu'y a-t-il de nouveau?*
qu'est-ce qu'il y a de nouveau?

6. *Que*, what? as the conjunctive form, can only be used before the verb or in close connection with it; but the disjunctive form *quoi*, what? stands either alone or after a preposition, or is even used as an interjection. Ex.: —

Vous cherchez quelque chose; quoi donc?
You are looking for something; what is it?
À quoi pense-t-il, of what does he think?
De quoi parle-t-on, of what do people talk?
Quoi! vous êtes marié! what! you are married!
NOTE. *Quoi* is also used instead of *qu'y a-t-il*, as: —
Quoi de plus magnifique qu'une belle nuit d'été! (instead of *qu'y a-t-il de plus magnifique!*)
What is there more splendid than a beautiful summer's night?

7. In antithetical questions with *or* (as *you or I?*), the French usage departs very widely from the English, inasmuch as the contrasted persons or objects, instead of standing in the Nominative as in English, usually follow *de*. Ex.: —

Qui de vous ou de moi remportera le prix?
Who will take the prize, you or I?
Qui a été le plus appliqué de toi ou d'Emile? or
Qui de toi ou d'Emile a été le plus appliqué?
Who has been the most diligent, you or Emil?

8. *De* may be omitted, however, when two or more *ou*'s occur, and also when *de* or *des* with *lequel* precedes. Ex.: —

Laquelle des deux nations était la plus vertueuse, les Grecs ou les Romains?
Which of the two nations was the more virtuous, the Greeks or the Romans?

THEME 23.

1. Which of your brothers is married? 2. Which of your sisters has (*est*) gone to England? 3. Of all these pictures, which should you like best?[1] 4. Which of your daughters learns Italian?[2] 5. Here are two pencils; which will you take? 6. What countries did Alexander the Great conquer?[3] 7. What are your terms?[4] 8. Who goes there? 9. To whom do you speak? 10. For whom does a miser[5] hoard[6] riches?[7] 11. Who will be bold[8] enough to attack him? 12. Who are these women? 13. Whose[9] gloves are these?

14. Here are two grammars; to which do you give the preference? 15. Who sustains[10] this globe in the air? 16. What is more pleasant than to do good?[11] 17. What is human life? 18. What should prevent[12] your father from buying (*d'acheter*) this house? 19. A little more fame,[13] a little more wealth, — what does all this signify?[14] 20. What are you speaking of? 21. Of what do you accuse me? 22. On (*sur*) what will you interrogate[15] him? 23. What! Charles has been arrested![16] 24. Which of you has been sick, Emily or Emma? 25. Which was the greatest man, Alexander, Cæsar, or Napoleon the First?

1. *Le mieux*. 2. Put the article. 3. Put has conquered, *a conquis*. 4. *Condition*, f. 5. *L'avare*, m. 6. *Amasser*. 7. *Richesse*. 8. *Hardi*. 9. See p 264, § 2, 2, *à qui*. 10. *Soutenir*. 11. *Du bien*. 12. *Empêcher*. 13. *Gloire*. 14. *Signifier*. 15. *Interroger*. 16. *Arrêté*.

READING LESSON.*

SERVILIUS SE DÉFEND DEVANT LE PEUPLE.

"Si l'on m'a fait venir ici pour me demander compte[1] de ce qui s'est passé dans la dernière bataille où je commandais, je suis prêt à vous en instruire; mais si ce n'est qu'un prétexte pour me faire périr, comme je *le* soupçonne,[2] épargnez-moi[3] des paroles inutiles: voilà mon corps et ma vie que je vous abandonne, vous pouvez en disposer.

"*Quel* est donc mon crime? *Quelle* faute ai-je commise jusqu'ici? On m'accuse d'avoir perdu beaucoup de monde dans le dernier combat. Mais *quel* est le général qui puisse livrer des batailles contre une nation aguerrie,[4] qui se défend courageusement, sans qu'il y ait de part et d'autre[5] du sang de répandu? *Quelle* divinité s'est engagée envers le peuple romain, à lui faire remporter des victoires sans aucune perte?[6] *A qui* fera-t-on croire que la gloire s'acquiert[7] autrement que par de grands périls? J'en suis

* The Conversation on this Reading Lesson will be found at the end of the following lesson.

venu aux mains avec des troupes plus nombreuses que celles que vous m'aviez confiées ; j'ai mis en déroute leurs légions, qui, à la fin, ont pris la fuite. *Que* me restait-il à faire ? *Qui* d'entre vous eût pu se refuser à la victoire qui marchait devant moi ? Etait-il même[8] en mon pouvoir de retenir vos soldats, que leur courage emportait, et qui poursuivaient avec ardeur un ennemi effrayé ? Que dis-je ? Si j'avais fait sonner[9] la retraite, si j'avais ramené nos soldats dans leur camp, de *quoi* ne m'accuserait-on pas aujourd'hui ? *Lequel* de vos tribuns aurait approuvé ma conduite ? Ne m'accuseraient-ils pas d'intelligence avec les ennemis ?"

1. Account. 2. Suspect. 3. Spare. 4. Warlike. 5. On both sides. 6. Loss. 7. Can be gained. 8. Even. 9. To sound.

XI. ONZIÈME LEÇON.

RELATIVE PRONOUNS.

(See Part I., L. XXIV.)

1. The relative pronouns *who*, *which* and *that* are rendered by *qui*, when they are in the Nominative case, whether they refer to persons or things, as :—

The man who works, *l'homme que travaille.*

The pen which is on the table.
La plume qui est sur la table.

2. The same pronouns when in the Direct Objective, *whom*, *which*, *that*, are expressed by *que*, as :—

The man whom you know, *l'homme que vous connaissez.*
The book which I have lost, *le livre que j'ai perdu.*

NOTE. Sometimes, however, *lequel* must be employed instead of *qui* or *que*, when by the use of the latter an ambiguity might arise. In such a case as this for instance : *Le frère de Madame Lebeau qui habite Paris,* where two persons being mentioned, it would be doubtful whether we mean to say that the brother or the lady lives in Paris. In the first case, we must say: —

Le frère de Mad. Lebeau lequel habite Paris,

or if the lady is meant:

Le frère de Mad. Lebeau laquelle or *qui habite Paris.*

For the latter of the two persons *qui* can generally be used.

3. When the relative pronouns *whom* or *which* follow a preposition, they are usually expressed by *qui* in speaking of persons,* and by *lequel* or *laquelle* (pl. *lesquels, lesquelles*) in speaking of animals and things, as: —

The little boy to whom I give the book, is diligent.
Le petit garçon à qui je donne le livre, est appliqué.

The Englishman with whom I travelled.
L'Anglais avec qui j'ai voyagé.

The glory to which heroes sacrifice, etc.
La gloire à laquelle les héros sacrifient, etc.

The cane with which he struck me, etc.
La canne avec laquelle il me frappe, etc.

4. The relative pronouns *whose, of whom* or *of which* are commonly expressed in French by *dont*, both for persons and for objects, as: —

The Frenchman whose brother arrived yesterday.
Le Français dont le frère est arrivé hier (see L. III., 12).

I have seen the garden of which you speak.
J'ai vu le jardin dont vous parlez.

5. But *lequel* must be employed when the noun which follows *whose* is governed by a preposition.

We can consequently say: —

The man whose merits are known.
L'homme dont les mérites (Nom.) *sont connus.*

The author whose works you have read.

* After *entre*, between, and *parmi*, among, we must always write *lesquels* or *lesquelles* whether persons or things be spoken of.

L'auteur dont vous avez lu les ouvrages (Dir. Obj.).*

But we must say:

The man of whose modesty people talk so much.
L'homme de la modestie duquel on parle tant.

The friend to whose honesty I have trusted, has deceived me.
L'ami à la probité duquel je me suis fié, m'a trompé.

6. The relative pronouns *whom*, *which*, and *that*, are often left out in English, but in French *qui* and *que* are never omitted. Example: —

The boy I saw with you yesterday.
Le garçon que j'ai vu hier avec vous.

I shall send you the books you have chosen.
Je vous enverrai les livres que vous avez choisis.

THEME 34.

1. The man who has done this is generally[1] esteemed. 2. The flocks[2] which graze[3] in those meadows[4] are mine (*à moi*). 3. The watch which I had is broken. 4. The books which you read are good, but difficult[5] to be understood. 5. The sister of my friend who arrived here last week, is very ill. 6. The physician's daughter of whom I spoke to you the other day, has married Mr. B. 7. A bird whose wings have been clipped,[6] cannot fly any more. 8. Bees[7] among which we find such admirable order,[8] are very useful insects. 9. The professor[9] to whom I write, is very learned. 10. The man you respect is my friend. 11. Idleness is a vice to which young people are much inclined. 12. The country we inhabit[10] is beautiful and fruitful. 13. The reasons upon which I rely,[11] are unanswerable.[12] 14. Mr. B. is a man to whose discretion I dare[13] not trust. 15. He who gets[14] riches, knows not for whom he gets them. 16. The daughter of Minos gave a thread[15] to Theseus,[16] by means (*au moyen*) of which he went out[17] of the labyrinth (*le labyrinthe*).

* Observe here the position of the noun. If the word depending upon *dont* is a Direct Objective, it must stand *after* the active verb.

1. *Généralement.* 2. *Troupeau*, m. 3. *Pâtre*, (see p. 178, No. 25). 4. *Prairie*, f. 5. *Difficiles à comprendre.* 6. *Rognés.* 7. *Les abeilles.* 8. *Ordre*, m. 9. *Professeur.* 10. *Habiter.* 11. *Je me fonde.* 12. *Sans réplique.* 13. *Je n'ose me fier.* 14. *Amasser.* 15. *Un fil.* 16. *Thésée.* 17. *Sortir.*

7. *Quoi*, what, is also used as a relative, but only in connection with a preposition, as: —

C'est à quoi je pense le moins.
This is the thing of which I think the least.

Savez-vous à quoi il s'occupe à présent?
Do you know what he busies himself with now?

Après quoi, after which. *Sans quoi*, otherwise.
C'est pourquoi, on that account, therefore.

8. The adverbs of place *où*, *d'où* and *par où*, are also often employed instead of the relative pronouns *dans lequel*, *duquel*, *par lequel*, *etc.*, when things are spoken of, as: —

L'embarras où (for *dans lequel*) *se trouve mon père.*
The embarrassment in which my father finds himself.

Le village par où (for *par lequel*) *nous venons de passer.*
The village through which we have just passed.

9. The correlative pronouns *he who*, fem. *she who*, pl. *they who* or *those who*, are rendered by *celui qui*, fem. *celle qui*, pl. masc. *ceux qui*, pl. fem. *celles qui*. Ex.: —

He who is contented, is happy.
Celui qui est content est heureux.

They (or those) who are discontented, are unhappy.
Ceux qui sont mécontents, sont malheureux.

NOTE 1. Both or either may vary according to the verb they depend on, (*celui qui*, *celui que*, *etc.*) as: —

I shall give it to him whom I love most.
Je le donnerai à celui que j'aime le mieux.

NOTE 2. In French both pronouns must be joined, and no inversion can take place as in English. Ex.: —

He is a bad citizen who rebels against his country.
Celui qui se révolte contre sa patrie est un mauvais citoyen.

10. The English *what*, when not an interrogative pronoun, but a

compound relative in the sense of *that which*, is translated by *ce qui* for the Nominative, *ce que* for the Direct Objective, and by *ce dont*, when the verb takes the preposition *de*, as:—

What is fine, is not always good.
Ce qui est beau n'est pas toujours bon.

I shall do what I have promised.
Je ferai ce que j'ai promis.

I have sent him what he needed.
Je lui ai envoyé ce dont il avait besoin.

11. When *ce qui*, *ce que* or *ce dont* begins the sentence, *c'est* must be placed before the second clause, except (as in the first sentence above) when an adjective or a participle follows, as:—

Ce que vous pouvez faire de mieux, c'est de partir tout de suite.
The best thing for you to do, is to leave immediately.

Ce qui me chagrine, c'est la perte de mon domestique.
What grieves me, is the loss of my servant.

12. Proverbial and general expressions usually commence with *qui*, whoever, instead of *celui qui*. Ex.:—

Qui court deux lièvres, n'en prend aucun.
He who chases two hares catches none.

Qui casse les verres, les paie.
Who(ever) breaks the glasses must pay for them.

Sauve qui peut! let him save himself who can!

THEME 25.

1. This is the object[1] at which he aims.[2] 2. The study to which I am devoted,[3] gives me great pleasure. 3. Nature, whose beauty we daily[4] admire, is an inexhaustible[5] source of enjoyment[6] for us. 4. Your pupil's mother, with whom I was speaking yesterday, left[7] this morning. 5. What sort of a book is that in which you are reading? 6. It is a Roman History. 7. There is nothing upon (*à*) which I think more frequently[8] than the sad fate[9] of my poor friend. 8. What is true is also good. 9. Virtue and freedom are the conditions without which we cannot be happy. 10. Is the house in which you live on the highway?[10] 11. No, it is tolerably

far[11] from it (*en*). 12. That is the thing about which I would speak with you. 13. The thing the miser thinks least about (*à*) is to aid[12] the poor. 14. That is the thing with which he struck me. 15. It is an illness to the progress[13] of which (§ 5) one cannot apply[14] too prompt remedies.[15] 16. He who cannot keep a secret, is incapable of governing.[16] 17. That which most deserves our respect is virtue. 18. What I most wish, is to see you happy. 19. What I like most, is to be alone.

1. *Le but.* 2. *Tendre.* 3. *Dévoué.* 4. *Journellement.* 5. *Inépuisable.* 6. *Le plaisir.* 7. *Est partie.* 8. *Souvent.* 9. *Le sort.* 10. *La route.* 11. *Assez éloigné.* 12. *Assister.* 13. *Progrès*, m. 14. *Apporter.* 15. *De trop prompts remèdes.* 16. *De gouverner.*

READING LESSON.

SUITE DE "SERVILIUS."

"Si vos ennemis se sont ralliés, s'ils ont été soutenus par un corps de troupes qui s'avançait à leur secours; enfin, s'il a fallu recommencer tout de nouveau le combat, et si, dans cette dernière action, j'ai perdu quelques soldats, n'est-ce pas le sort[1] ordinaire de la guerre? Trouverez-vous des généraux qui veuillent se charger du commandement de vos armées, à condition de ramener à Rome tous les soldats qui en seraient sortis sous leur conduite? N'examinez donc point si, à la fin d'une bataille, j'ai perdu quelques soldats, mais jugez de ma conduite par ma victoire.

"S'il est vrai que j'ai chassé[2] les ennemis de votre territoire, que je leur ai tué beaucoup de monde dans deux combats, que j'ai forcé les débris[3] de leurs armées de s'enfermer dans leurs places,[4] que j'ai enrichi Rome et vos soldats du butin[5] qu'ils ont fait dans le pays ennemi: que (*let*) vos tribuns s'élèvent, et qu'ils me reprochent en quoi j'ai manqué[6] contre les devoirs[7] d'un bon général.

"Mais ce n'est pas ce que je crains: ces accusations ne servent que de prétexte pour pouvoir exercer impunément leur haine[8] et leur animosité contre le sénat et contre l'ordre des patriciens. Faut-il que vous ne demandiez jamais rien au sénat qui ne soit préjudiciable au bien commun de la patrie, et que vous ne le demandiez que par des séditions ? Si un sénateur ose[9] vous représenter l'injustice de vos prétentions, si un consul ne parle pas le language séditieux de vos tribuns ; s'il défend avec courage la souveraine puissance dont il est revêtu, on crie au tyran.[10] A peine est-il sorti de charge, qu'il se trouve accablé d'accusations. C'est ainsi que, par votre injuste plébiscite, vous avez ôté la vie à Ménénius, aussi grand capitaine que bon citoyen. Ne devriez-vous pas mourir de honte d'avoir persécuté si cruellement le fils de ce Ménénius Agrippa, à qui vous devez vos tribuns et ce pouvoir qui vous rend à présent si furieux ?

"On m'en voudra peut-être de la liberté avec laquelle je vous parle dans l'état où je me trouve à présent ; mais je ne crains point la mort : condamnez-moi, si vous l'osez ; la vie ne peut être qu'à charge à un général qui est réduit à se justifier de ses victoires. Après tout, un sort pareil à celui de Ménénius ne peut me déshonorer."

1. The fate. 2. Driven out. 3. Remains. 4. Fortresses. 5. Booty. 6. To fall. 7. Duties. 8. Hatred. 9. Dare. 10. Behold the tyrant.

CONVERSATION.

Qui était Servilius ?	Un fameux général romain.
Pourquoi l'a-t-on fait venir à Rome ?	Pour se justifier devant le peuple.
De quoi l'avait-on accusé ?	On l'avait accusé d'avoir perdu trop de soldats dans un combat.
Est-il possible de livrer (une) bataille, sans qu'il y ait du sang de répandu ?	Non, ce n'est pas possible. Il doit y avoir de part et d'autre du sang de répandu.
Peut-on remporter une victoire sans aucune perte ?	Il est impossible de défaire un ennemi nombreux et aguerri sans perdre du monde.
Comment se justifia Servilius du reproche qu'on lui faisait ?	Il rappela aux Romains qu'il avait remporté une victoire décisive, et mis en déroute les légions des ennemis.

Etait-il en son pouvoir de retenir ses soldats?	Non, leur courage les emportait, et ils poursuivaient avec ardeur l'ennemi effrayé.
Avait-il manqué contre les devoirs d'un bon général?	Non, on ne lui put rien reprocher.
Si Servilius avait fait sonner la retraite, de quoi l'aurait-on accusé?	Les tribuns du peuple l'auraient accusé d'intelligence avec les ennemis.
Quels services avait-il rendus à (*to*) Rome?	Il avait chassé les ennemis du territoire romain et enrichi Rome du butin qu'il rapportait du pays ennemi.
Quand un sénateur était sorti de charge, que faisaient les tribuns du peuple?	Ils l'accablaient d'accusations.
Quel exemple d'injustice leur reprocha-t-il?	Celui de Ménénius.
Servilius s'attendait-il à un sort semblable à celui de Ménénius?	Oui, mais il dit qu'un sort pareil à celui de Ménénius ne pourrait le déshonorer.

XII. DOUZIÈME LEÇON.

INDEFINITE PRONOUNS.

In regard to the indefinite pronouns treated of in Lesson XXIX., Part I., the following peculiarities are to be observed: —

1. The word *on* derived from *homme*, man (Latin *homo*), serves to render all vague and general reports expressed in English by *they say*, *people say*, *it is said*, *we say*, etc. The verb which follows is always in the third person singular, as: —

People say, it is said, *on dit.*

One cannot have everything, *on ne peut pas avoir tout.*

NOTE 1. When in English the passive voice is used in this sense, the verb must be changed in French into the active voice with *on*, as: —

It is said, *on dit.* It is believed, *on croit.*

I was told, *on m'a dit.* I am deceived, *on me trompe.*

Letters have been received, *on a reçu des lettres.*

NOTE 2. For the cases where *l'on* is used instead of *on*, see Lesson XXIX., 2.

2. *Chacun, e*, each, has for the English *his, her*, or *its*, which follows it, *son, sa, ses*, and *leur, leurs*, for their, as: —

Put these books each in its place.

Remettez ces livres chacun à sa place.

The judges have given sentence each according to his conscience.

Les juges ont opinés chacun selon sa conscience.

The bees build each their cells.

Les abeilles bâtissent chacune leur cellule.

When *chacun* means *every one, everybody* (including *all*), it is always masculine. Example: *Chacun à son tour.* But when used relatively, i. e., in reference to a part of mankind, it may be feminine. Example: *Chacune de nous (femmes) se prétendait supérieure aux autres.*

3. *Aucun, personne*, and *rien* do not require *ne* before the verb, in a sentence interrogative or of doubt: *aucun* then stands for any, *personne* for anybody, and *rien* for anything. Ex.: —

Je ne crois pas qu'il y ait aucun homme sans défaut.

I do not think there is any man without a fault.

Je doute qu'il y ait rien de plus beau.

I doubt whether there is anything more beautiful.

NOTE. *Aucun* and *nul* are not used in the plural, except before nouns which have no singular, or which are used in a different sense in the plural.

5. When, however, these three pronouns serve to answer a question without repeating the verb used by the inquirer, they retain their negative meaning, as: —

Qu'avez vous ?	*Rien.*	*Rien du tout.*
What is the matter with you ?	Nothing.	Nothing at all.

5. *None, not one*, are rendered by *aucun ne* and *pas un ne*. Examples: —

None of you were there, *aucun de vous* n'*y était.*
I have four sisters; none (not one) of them is married.
J'ai quatre sœurs, aucune or *pas une n'est mariée.*

6. *Somebody, some one, anybody*, and *any one*, are expressed by *quelqu'un* singular and masculine. Ex.: —

Somebody told me so, *quelqu'un me l'a dit.*
Do you know any one here? *Connaissez-vous quelqu'un ici?*

7. *La plupart*, most, is properly a collective noun, and like most other collective nouns takes the plural after it. This requires the verb and attribute which follow to be put in the plural. Ex.: —

La plupart de ces pommes ne sont pas encore mûres.
Most of these apples are not yet ripe.

8. *Another* is usually expressed by *un autre*, and *others* (Nom. and Direct Obj.) by *d'autres* or *les autres*. Ex.: —

Another would not have acted so.
Un autre n'aurait pas agi ainsi.

Charity is contented that others be preferred.
La charité est contente que les autres soient préférés.

Buy some others, *achetez-en d'autres.*

9. *Autrui*, others, only applies to persons; it is, however, also taken as a singular in the sense of *another*. It is employed only after a preposition. Consequently, when in English the indefinite pronoun *others* occurs in the *Nom.* or *Dir. Obj.*, it must not be translated by *autrui*, but by *d'autres* or *les autres* (§ 8). Ex.: —

Charity rejoices in the happiness of others.
La charité se réjouit du bonheur d'autrui.

Attendez d'autrui ce que vous faites à autrui.
Expect from others the same treatment which you give them.

10. When, however, the verb in the latter clause governs the Dir. Obj., *en* is used instead of *son* or *ses*. Ex.: —

Souvent nous blâmons les défauts d'autrui sans en reconnaître les bonnes qualités (without acknowledging their good qualities).

11. *Tel* has two significations: *such* and *many a* (*man*). In the

former, it is an adjective and agrees with its noun, in the latter it is often a pronoun, i. e. is used without a substantive. Ex.: —

Telle était la difficulté du terrain que, etc.
Such was the difficulty of the ground, etc.

Tel parle de choses qu'il n'entend pas.
Many a man speaks of things which he does not understand.

12. *Such a* must be rendered by *un tel, une telle.* Ex.: —

Un tel homme, such a man.
Une telle femme, such a woman.

Un tel has also the meaning of *so and so*, as : —

Chez Monsieur un tel ; Madame une telle.

13. *Tel que* has the meaning *such as* or *just as*, and agrees in gender and number with the noun to which it refers. Ex.:—

Telles que vous les voyez, such as you see them (*fem.*).

14. Notice also the expression : *Il n'y a rien de tel que . . .* or *il n'est rien tel que . . .*, there is nothing like. Ex.: —

Il n'y a rien de tel que d'avoir une bonne conscience.
There is nothing like having a good conscience.

THEME 26.

1. They speak of peace. 2. People are not always fortunate. 3. French is spoken here. 4. The invention of gunpowder is attributed[1] to to Berthold Schwarz of Friburg.[2] 5. It is said that the queen is in London. 6. Everybody has his faults. 7. What is the price of each of these medals ?[3] 8. My children have each a good place. 9. Every one has his [own] manner of thinking[4] and acting. 10. I do not know *any* of his friends. 11. Would anybody dare[5] deny[6] it ? 12. None of the judges were against you. 13. Of all the nations of the earth, there is none (not one) but has (*qui n'ait*) an idea[7] of God. 14. I expect somebody. 15. Those apples are fine, I will take some. 16. When we are in (*en*) town, we have almost every day somebody to dine[8] with us. 17. I have lost my stick, I must buy another. 18. Most of my books are

new. 19. Do not speak ill (*mal*) of others. 20. Do not unto (*à*) others what thou wouldst not they should[9] do unto thee. 21. Many a man sows[10] who does not reap.[11] 22. There is nothing like being (*que d'être*) an honest man. 23. You must take them such as they are.

1. *Attribuer*. 2. *Fribourg*. 3. *Médaille*, f. 4. *De penser et d'agir*. 5. *Oser*. 6. *Nier*. 7. *Idée*, f. 8. *A dîner*. 9. *Qu'ils te fassent à toi même*. 10. *Semer*. 11. *Récolter*.

XIII. TREIZIÈME LEÇON.

INDEFINITE PRONOUNS, CONTINUED..

1. *L'un et l'autre*, fem. *l'une et l'autre* (plur. *les uns et les autres*, fem. *les unes et les autres*), *both*. These pronouns agree in gender and number with the noun to which they refer; if they are preceded by a preposition in English, that preposition must be repeated in French before each part. Ex.: —

Both are gone, *l'un et l'autre sont partis*.

I will do it for them both.
Je le ferai pour l'un et pour l'autre.

NOTE 1. When in English the word *both* is followed by a noun, it is rendered in French by *les deux*. Ex.: —

I use both hands, *je me sers des deux mains*.

NOTE 2. *Both* followed by *and* is a conjunction and is commonly omitted in French, as: —

She is both handsome and rich, *elle est belle et riche*.

2. *L'un ou l'autre*, fem. *l'une ou l'autre*, *either*, also requires the repetition of the preposition, as: —

I will do it for either.
Je le ferai pour l'un ou poúr l'autre.

3. *Ni l'un ni l'autre,* fem. *ni l'une ni l'autre, neither,* requires *ne* before the verb, as: —

Neither has obtained the prize.
Ni l'un ni l'autre n'a gagné le prix.

I will do it for neither of them (*fem.*).
Je ne le ferai ni pour l'une ni pour l'autre.

4. *L'un l'autre,* fem. *l'une l'autre* (plur. *les uns les autres,* fem. *les unes les autres*), *one another, each other.* The first of the two pronouns is always the subject and consequently stands in the Nominative in French. Active verbs then require *se, nous* or *vous* to be prefixed, although no reflective pronoun appears in English. When they are preceded by a preposition in English, that preposition must come between them in French. Ex.: —

These two girls love each other tenderly.
Ces deux jeunes filles s'aiment (l'une l'autre) tendrement.

Charles and Henry speak ill of each other.
Charles et Henri parlent mal l'un de l'autre (not *de l'un l'autre.*)

5. The word *the same* is expressed by *le même* or *la même* for the singular and by *les mêmes* for the plural of both genders, whether it be connected with a noun or not, as: —

Is that the same pencil which I have lent you.
Est-ce le même crayon que celui que je vous ai prêté?

Yes, it is the same, *oui, c'est le même.*

6. *The same,* meaning the *same thing,* is expressed by *la même chose.* Ex.: —

He did the same, *il a fait la même chose.*

7. When *même* signifies *even,* it is an adverb and invariable. It may be placed before or after the nouns. Ex.: —

Vos frères, vos amis, vos ennemis même.
Your brothers, your friends, your enemies even.

8. *Everything, all,* are expressed by *tout* without any article, placed, in compound tenses, between the auxiliary and the participle, as: —

I have lost everything, *j'ai tout perdu.*
Everything falls, *tout tombe.*
All have perished there, *tous y ont péri.*
I have seen them all, *je les ai toutes vues.*

9. *Le tout* stands for a substantive singular and masculine, and answers to the English *the whole*, as: —

Le tout est plus grand que la partie.
The whole is greater than a part.
Je prendrai le tout, I will take the whole.

10. The English words *all that*, *everything that* and *whatever*, are rendered in French by *tout ce qui* (Nom.), or *tout ce que* (Dir. Obj.), always singular and masculine. Ex.: —

I like all that is fine, *j'aime tout ce qui est beau.*
All that he says is true, *tout ce qu'il dit est vrai.*

11. In the sense of *quite, entirely*, before an adjective or a participle masculine of both numbers, and before an adjective feminine beginning with a vowel or *h* mute, *tout* remains uninflected; but it is declinable before an adjective or a participle feminine which begins with a consonant, and agrees with it in gender and number. Examples: —

Nous fûmes tout surpris, we were quite surprised.
Ma sœur était tout étonnée.
My sister was quite astonished.
Elle fut toute surprise, she was quite surprised.

12. When *tout* in connection with *que* stands for . . . *as*, *although*, *however*, it is used as a *conjunction* with the Indicative mood; and in this use the above-mentioned rule (§ 11) also holds good (see also § 13). Ex.: —

Tout riches que vous êtes, rich as you are.
Toutes savantes que sont ces dames.
Learned as these ladies are (however learned these ladies are, etc.).

THEME 27.

1. Both are (*ont*) right. 2. Both serve the same purpose.[1] 3. Do you speak of my brother or of my sister? 4. I speak of both.

5. Both his uncle and aunt are dead. 6. Either of you can do me a great favor. 7. Yesterday I expected my two best friends, but neither of them came. 8. Both suspect[2] him, but neither will say why. 9. Fire and water destroy[3] each other. 10. Love[4] one another, said our Lord.[5] 11. They speak ill of one another. 12. It is rare to hear two authors[6] speak well of each other. 13. This poem is the same that[7] I was mentioning[8] to you. 14. How much do you ask for the whole? 15. I will not sell the whole; I must keep[9] a part for myself. 16. All is mutable[10] in this world. 17. Everything displeases[11] you. 18. He has taken everything for himself. 19. All is not gold that glitters[12] (*transl.:* All that (L. XI., § 10) glitters is not gold). 20. Whatever is good in itself (*en soi*), is not always approved.[13] 21. His mother was (*fut*) quite cast down[14] at that news; however, sorry[15] though she was, she received me kindly, and desired[16] me to dine with her. 22. This fashion[17] is quite new. 23. My friend, however learned he may be, is sometimes mistaken.[18]

1. *Usage*, m. 2. *Soupçonner.* 3. *Se détruisent.* 4. *Aimez-vous.* 5. *Seigneur.* 6. *Auteur.* 7. *Que celui dont.* 8. *Parle.* 9. *Garder.* 10. *Variable.* 11. *Déplaire.* 12. *Brille.* 13. *Approuver.* 14. *Abattue.* 15. *Affligée.* 16. *Prier.* 17. *Mode*, f. 18. *Se tromper.*

---

13. *Quelque — que, however, though — ever so,* is used in the same sense as *tout — que*, with this difference, that *tout — que* supposes something more true or real, whereas *quelque — que* implies something as possibly assumed, and on this account always governs the Subjunctive. *Quelque*, when before an adjective or participle, remains unchanged. The construction of the sentence is as follows: *quelque* begins the clause, the second place is taken by the adjective or participle, then follows *que*, then the pronoun, then the verb in the Subjunctive mood. Ex.: —

Quelque[1] *habiles*[2] *que*[3] *vous*[4] *soyez*[5].
However skilful you may be.

But when the subject is not a pronoun, but a substantive, then the verb takes the fourth place and the noun the fifth. Ex.: —

Quelque[1] *louable*[2] *que*[3] *soit*[4] *votre*[5] *conduite, elle sera condamnée.*

However praiseworthy your conduct may be — *or* though your conduct be ever so praiseworthy, — it will be condemned.

14. *Quelque*, followed by a substantive and any other verb than *to be*, is an adjective, and therefore takes an *s* before a noun plural. It corresponds with the English *whatever*. The construction is: 1, *quelque*(*s*); 2, the substantive; 3, *que;* 4, the pronoun; 5, the verb in the Subjunctive mood; the rest as in English. Ex.: —

Quelques[1] *richesses*[2] *qu'*[3]*ils*[4] *aient*[5] *amassées, ils ne sont pas heureux.*

Whatever riches they may have collected, they are not happy.

Quelques fautes qu'il ait commises, je lui pardonnerai.

Whatever faults he has committed, I will forgive him.

15. *Quel que*, fem. *quelle que*, must be divided when it is immediately followed by the verb *to be;* it agrees in gender and number with the noun to which it relates; it likewise requires the verb to be put in the Subjunctive mood. Ex.: —

Quelle que soit votre faute, on vous pardonnera.

Whatever your fault may be, they will forgive you.

Quels que soient les talents de votre frère, il ne réussira pas.

Whatever your brother's talents may be, he will not succeed.

16. The English *whoever* and *whosoever* are usually rendered by *quiconque* when they mean *every one who* or *all those who.* Examples: —

Quiconque n'observera pas cette loi, sera puni.

Whoever does not observe this law, will be punished.

Je parle à quiconque veut m'entendre.

I speak to whomsoever will hear me.

17. The same two pronouns *whoever* and *whosoever* are expressed in French by *qui que ce soit* (or *fût*) *qui*, when they mean *whatever may be the person who.* The verb is in the Subj. mood. Examples:

Whoever has done that, he is a man of talent.

Qui que ce soit qui ait fait cela, c'est un homme de talent.

Whomsoever you meet with, do not say what you have seen.
Qui que ce soit que (Dir. Obj.) *vous rencontriez, ne dites pas ce que vous avez vu.*

18. A shorter expression for *qui que ce soit que* (not *qui*) is *qui que*, which is often used, except before *il* and *ils:*

Qui que vous soyez, vous êtes le bienvenu.
Whoever you may be, you are welcome.
Qui que vous rencontriez, ne dites pas, etc.
Whomsoever you meet with, do not say, etc.

19. *Nobody whatever*, is expressed by *qui que ce soit* and *ne* before the verb. Ex.: —

Let nobody whatever enter my room.
Ne laissez entrer qui que ce soit dans ma chambre.
I trust nobody whatever.
Je ne me fie à qui que ce soit.

NOTE. But when *nobody whatever* begins the sentence, *personne* is used, as: —

Nobody whatever has spoken ill of you.
Personne n'a parlé mal de vous.

20. When the English indefinite pronoun *whatever* does not mean *all that which* or *everything which*, but *whatever may be the thing which*, it is rendered into French by *quelque chose qui*, *quoi que*, or *quoi que ce soit* (or *fût*) *qui* or *que*. Ex.: —

Whatever may be said to you, do not believe it.
Quelque chose qu'on vous dise, ne le croyez pas. Or:
Quoi qu'on vous dise, ne le croyez pas. Or:
Quoi que ce soit qu'on vous dise, ne le croyez pas.
Whatever you may order, I will do it.
Quelque chose que vous commandiez, je le ferai. Or:
Quoi que ce soit que vous commandiez, je le ferai.

21. *Nothing whatever, not anything whatever*, is translated by *quoi que ce soit* or *fût*, and *ne* before the verb. Ex.: —

Without application, it is impossible to succeed in anything whatever.
Sans application on ne peut réussir en quoi que ce soit.

THEME 28.

1. The wise man does not fear men, however powerful they may be. 2. Men, however great or small they may be, are never sufficiently[1] sensible how necessary they are to each other. 3. Whatever wealth[2] you may have, you will never be happy, unless you[3] restrain your passions. 4. Do not lose [your] courage, whatever may happen to you. 5. Distrust[4] every one who (§ 16) speaks ill of his friends. 6. The laws condemn[5] all criminals,[6] whoever (§ 15) they may be. 7. I tell it to every one who will hear. 8. I hope that you will not tell my secret to anybody whatever. 9. Regulus did not allow himself to be moved,[7] whatever the promises were that the Carthaginians[8] made him. 10. Unfortunate [man]! whoever (§ 18) you are, I will not betray[9] you. 11. Whatever (§ 20) may happen to you in this world, never murmur[10] against Divine Providence; for whatever we may suffer, we deserve[11] it. 12. Of whomsoever you speak, always speak the truth. 13. I have found nothing whatever. 14. I complain[12] of nothing whatever. 15. Young men![13] whatever the destiny[14] may be that awaits[15] you, in whatever region of the earth your days may be[16] spent, nature will continually offer to you her products[17] and her wonders;[18] you will continually be surrounded[19] with the objects of your study.

1. *Assez.* 2. *Richesse*, f. 3. *A moins que vous ne réprimiez.* 4. *Méfiez-vous de.* 5. *Condamner.* 6. *Criminel.* 7. *Ne se laissa pas ébranler.* 8. *Carthaginois.* 9. *Trahir.* 10. *Murmurer.* 11. *Mériter.* 12. *Se plaindre de.* 13. *Gens.* 14. *Le sort* 15. *Attendre.* 16. *Doivent s'écouler.* 17. *Produits*, m. 18. *Merveilles.* 19. *Entourés de.*

XIV. QUATORZIÈME LEÇON.

ADVERBS.

See Part I., Lessons XXI and XXXII.

1. As already observed, the manner or mode of the action is expressed by the adverbs of quality or manner, as:

Il agit sagement (not *sage*), he acts wisely.
Il écrit mal (not *mauvais*), he writes badly.

2. There are certain adjectives, however, which are used instead of the adverb. This is the case in the following expressions: —

Aller vite, to walk fast.
coûter cher, to be expensive.
vendre cher, to sell dear.
sentir bon, to smell sweet.
sentir mauvais, to smell badly.
trouver bon, to approve.
trouver mauvais, to take ill.
voir clair, to see clearly.
tenir ferme, to hold fast.
rester court, *demeurer court*, to stop short.
payer comptant, to pay cash.
marcher droit, to walk straight.
chanter juste, to sing correctly.
chanter faux, to sing false.
parler haut, to speak loud.
parler bas, to speak low.
faire exprès, to do on purpose.

3. The adjectives in this case remain, of course, unchanged. Examples: —

Cette montre coûte trop cher (not *chère*).
This watch is too dear.
Les enfants parlent trop haut (not *hauts*).
The children speak too loud.
La chanteuse a chanté faux (not *fausse*).
The songstress has sung false.

NOTE 1. In speaking of the state of the health, however, the adverb *bien* or *mal* is employed. Ex.: —
Je suis bien, I am well.
Elle se trouve mal, she finds herself ill.

NOTE 2. Observe also the expressions, *Elle est bien*, she is pretty; and *elle n'est pas mal*, she is not bad-looking.

4. Some adverbs take after them an object with *de* or *à*, in case the adjective from which they are derived also takes one. Ex: —

Conformément à vos ordres.
In conformity with your orders.
Indépendamment de mes instructions.
Independently of my instructions.
Cette rivière coule parallèlement à la Vistule.
That river flows parallel with the Vistula.

THEME 29.

1. Do not go so fast. 2. The night is approaching; I no longer (*plus*) see clearly. 3. The rose smells sweet, but the pink[1] smells

better. 4. Do not speak low (in a whisper) in the presence of others. 5. How does the singer[2] sing? 6. She sings false (incorrectly). 7. Do not speak so low; speak louder, so that you can[3] be understood. 8. You do not read well, and you write no (*pas*) better. 9. To-day I am not very well. 10. Do not eat so fast. 11. This merchant sells his goods[4] very dear. 12. It is dark; I do not see clearly. 13. I have distributed[5] the money according to (in conformity with) your orders.

1. *L'œillet.* 2. *La chanteuse.* 3. *Qu'on puisse vous comprendre.* 4. *Marchandises.* 5. *Distribuer.*

ADVERBS OF TIME, ETC.

1. Observe the distinction between the following adverbs: — 1. *Plutôt* means rather (of inclination); *plus tôt*, sooner (of time). 2. *Tout à coup* means at once, suddenly, unexpectedly; *tout d'un coup* means at once, i. e., at one time; *à la fois* means altogether. 3. Immediately is translated by *tout de suite*, *tout à l'heure*, and also by *sans délai*. *De suite* means successively, one after the other. 4. *L'autre jour* means the other day, lately, synonymous with *dernièrement*. On the next day is *le lendemain*. 5. A little while ago is *tantôt;* just is expressed by the verb *venir* (see Part I. Lesson XLVI.). Ex.: —

He has just gone out, *il vient de sortir*

2. *Très*, *fort*, and *bien*, all mean very, right; and whether one or the other is to be used before the adjective depends upon euphony alone. *Very much*, with verbs is generally translated by *beaucoup*, and sometimes also by *bien;* but never by *très* or *très beaucoup*. *Bien*, with a noun in the sense of much or a great many, must be followed by *de* with the definite article (see Lesson IV., § 1).

3. *When*, in interrogative phrases, is rendered by *quand*. In other cases, *quand* refers to a possible, probable fact; *lorsque* to a positive, real fact. *Quand* is vague; *lorsque* is precise, as its etymology shows, *alorsque*, i. e., *à l'heure que*.

4. *Plus* and *davantage* both mean more. The latter always stands at the end of a sentence, and consequently can be followed neither by a noun nor by a comparison with than. Than after *plus* and *moins* is usually *que*, but before a numeral it is translated by *de*.

5. Adverbs follow the simple verb. Do not say, *Ma sœur rarement sort le matin ;* but, *ma sœur sort rarement le matin*, my sister seldom goes out in the morning. *Je pense souvent à vous*, I often think of you.

In connection with the compound tenses of the verb, the adverb is generally placed between the auxiliary and the Participle Past. Ex.:

Ma sœur a beaucoup voyagé.
My sister has travelled a great deal.

6. But adverbs of time can also be placed at the beginning of the sentence, when an emphasis it laid upon them. Ex.: —

Bientôt je le vis reparaître, I saw him soon reappear.

THEME 30.

1. We often put off[1] till the next day what we ought to do at once. 2. Fortune is so fickle[2] that she often suddenly deserts[3] those that she has favored[4] the most. 3. A single[5] drop of vinegar contains more than a hundred animalculæ.[6] 4. This man has a great many faults. 5. Children must obey immediately. 6. This man has been very much regretted.[7] 7. One does not arrive at once at the highest pinnacle[8] of fame. 8. Mr. M. (has) won a thousand dollars at one time. 9. He undertakes too many things at once. 10. Did you believe this man? 11. At first (*d'abord*) I was not willing to believe him. 12. Good taste[9] is rather a gift[10] of nature, than an acquirement[11] of art. 13. How much money have you lent him? 14. I have lent him more than eighty florins.

1. *Renvoyer* or *différer*. 2. *Inconstant*. 3 *Abandonner*. 4. *Favorisés*. 5. *Une seule goutte*. 6. *Animalcule*, m. 7. *Regretter*. 8. *Degré*, m. 9. *Goût*, m. 10. *Don*, m. 11. *Acquisition*, f.

READING LESSON.

LE CONNÉTABLE DE BOURBON ET BAYARD.

(Dialogue.)

Le Connétable. N'est-ce pas le pauvre Bayard que je vois au pied de cet arbre, étendu sur l'herbe,[1] et percé d'un grand coup? Oui, c'est lui-même. Hélas! je le plains. En voilà deux qui périssent aujourd'hui par nos armes: Vandenesse et lui. Ces deux Français étaient deux ornements de leur nation par leur courage. Je sens que mon cœur est encore touché pour sa patrie. Mais avançons pour lui parler. Ah! mon pauvre Bayard, c'est avec douleur que je te vois en cet état.

Bayard. C'est avec douleur que je vous vois aussi.

Le Con. Je comprends bien que tu es fâché de te voir dans mes mains par le sort[2] de la guerre; mais je ne veux point te traiter en prisonnier, je te veux garder comme un bon ami, et prendre soin de ta guérison,[3] comme si tu étais mon propre frère. Ainsi tu ne dois point être fâché de me voir.

Bay. Hé! croyez-vous que je ne sois point fâché d'avoir obligation au plus grand ennemi de la France? Ce n'est point de ma captivité, ni de ma blessure,[4] que je suis en peine:[5] je meurs dans un moment, la mort va me délivrer de vos mains.

Le Con. Non, mon cher Bayard, j'espère que nos soins réussiront à te guérir.

Bay. Ce n'est point là ce que je cherche, et je suis content de mourir. (*To be continued.*)

1. Grass. 2. Fate. 3. Recovery. 4. Wound. 5. Sorry.

XV. QUINZIÈME LEÇON.

SYNTAX OF NEGATIONS.

(See P. I., L. XXXII.)

1. It is necessary in the first place to distinguish whether the negation belongs to a *verb* or not; if not, the negative particle stands without *ne*. *Not*, without a verb, before nouns, is translated by *non* or *non pas*. Ex.: —

His cruelty and not his pride.
Sa cruauté et non (or *non pas*) *son orgueil.*

Not in connection with other words is simply *pas*: —

Not much, *pas beaucoup*. Not I, *pas moi*.
Not so much, *pas tant*. Why not, *pourquoi pas*.
Not at all, *pas du tout* or *point du tout*.

N. B. Observe the following expressions: —

Not (nor) — either, *non plus*.
Nor his brother either, *ni son frère non plus*.
Nor I either, *ni moi non plus*.
Not only — but, *non-seulement — mais*. (See § 4.)

2. But if the negation belongs to the verb the negative particle, whatever it may be, is invariably accompanied by *ne*. Ex.: —

Ne lui parlez pas, do not speak to him.
Je n'ai rien vu, I have seen nothing.
Je ne l'ai plus, I have it no more.
Aucun de vous n'y était, none of you were there.
Le pauvre homme n'a point d'argent.
The poor man has no money.
Je ne connais personne ici, I know nobody here.
Ni prières ni * *menaces ne purent l'attendrir.*
Neither prayers nor threatenings could move him.

* If *neither — nor* come before two verbs in the *Indicative* mood, the former is expressed simply by *ne* before the first, and *nor* by *ni ne* before the second. Ex.: —
I neither praise nor blame him.
Je ne le loue, ni ne le blâme.

Il ne sait ni lire ni écrire.
He knows neither how to read nor write.

Nous n'approuvons nullement votre dessein.
We by no means approve of your design.

NOTE. When the verb is in the simple Infinitive *ne pas* or *ne point* (also *ne jamais*) are not separated, as: —

Not to study, *ne pas étudier* or *ne point étudier.*

But when it is in the compound Infinitive it is optional to separate them or not, as: —

Not to have studied, { *ne pas (point) avoir étudié.* / *n'avoir pas (point) étudié.* }

3. The words *no more* or *not any more* (meaning *not more*) are expressed by *ne* before the verb and *pas plus* after, when *more* is followed by *than:* —

He is no more than fifteen years of age.
Il n'a pas plus de quinze ans.

But they are rendered by *ne — plus* without *pas,* when *more* is not followed by *than.* Ex.: —

I shall read no more (no longer), *je ne lirai plus.*

4. *Non seulement, not only,* takes no *ne* with the verb. Ex.: —

Je l'ai fait non seulement pour lui, mais aussi pour ses enfants.
I have done it not only for his sake, but also for his children's.

THEME 31.

1. I do not speak. 2. I have not spoken. 3. Have you bought this book? 4. No, sir, I have not (P. I., L. XLVII.). 5. It is your friendship which I seek, *not* my interest.[1] 6. Not I. 7. Not we. 8. Are you tired? 9. Not at all. 10. I was not there; nor my sister either. 11. This peasant[2] can neither read nor write. 12. The boy has neither paper[3] nor pens. 13. I have never had such a (*un si*) good book. 14. We have no desire at all[4] to do it. 15. The speaker[5] has convinced[6] not only his friends but also his adversaries. 16. Charles XII. persisted in[7] never speaking (never to speak) French. 17. I have no more hope.

1. *Intérêt,* m. 2. *Paysan,* m. 3. See p. 224, § 3. 4. *Nullement envie.* 5. *L'orateur.* 6. *Convaincre.* 7. *S'obstina à.*

NE USED ALONE WITHOUT *PAS*.

5. The negative *not* is expressed by *ne* without *pas* or *point* with the three verbs: *cesser*, to cease; *oser*, to dare; *pouvoir*, to be able; when followed by an Infinitive, as: —

Elle ne cesse de pleurer, she does not cease crying.
Il n'ose revenir, he dares not come back.
Je ne puis le croire, I cannot believe it.

NOTE 1. *Cesser* takes *pas*, however, when a time is specified, as: —

Il ne cesse pas de travailler avant huit heures du soir.

NOTE 2. In regard to *pouvoir*, use in the first person of the Present tense either: —

Je ne puis (without *pas*), or: *Je ne peux pas.*

6. When the negative use of *savoir* means *to be uncertain*, i. e. in doubt, it does not take *pas*. In the same way *pas* is always omitted in the expression *je ne saurais*, I cannot. Ex.: —

Je ne savais que dire, I did not know what to say

Je ne saurais vous donner une garantie.
I cannot give you a security.

But if "not know" has the signification of *not to have learned*, not to know (a language, etc.), then *savoir* always takes *ne* and *pas*. Ex.: —

Je ne sais pas nager, I cannot swim.
Ne savez-vous pas l'allemand, do you not know German?

7. In sentences depending upon *prendre garde*, to take care, there is no *pas*. Ex.: —

Prenez garde qu'il ne vous trompe.

Pas is used however if an infinitive follows. Ex.: —

Prenez garde de ne pas tomber.

8. Of two negative sentences standing in immediate connection with each other, the latter loses its *pas*. Ex.: —

Je ne connais personne qui ne fasse quelquefois des fautes.

NOTE 1. Also *peu* and *sans* are here regarded as a negation, as: —

Peu s'en faut qu'il ne soit tombé, he was very near falling.
Sans rien faire, without doing anything.

Note 2. The former sentence may also be interrogative if only the idea of negation be contained in it, as: —

Y a-t-il (or *est-il*) *un homme qui ne croie en Dieu?*

9. Do not put *pas* after *que ne*, when used instead of *pourquoi pas*. Ex.: —

Si vous avez froid, que ne mettez-vous votre manteau?
If you are cold, why not put on your cloak?

10. Nor after *voilà*, *il y a* and *depuis que*, when the verb which has the idea of negation is in the compound of the Present or in the compound of the Imperfect. Ex.: —

Il y a deux mois que je ne lui ai parlé.
Il a bien changé depuis que je ne l'ai vu.

11. *Pas* is not used when *ne* is connected with *d'autre* followed by *que*, as: —

Je n'ai d'autre ambition que de vous rendre heureux.
I have no other ambition than to make you happy.

12. Further in the following idioms: —

N'avoir garde, to take care not to, to be on one's guard.
N'importe, it does not matter.
Ne voir goutte, to see nothing (at all).
Ne dire mot, to say not a word.
à Dieu ne plaise que, etc., God forbid, etc.

13. *A moins que* and conjunctions expressing fear, take *ne* before the following verb (in the subjunctive). Ex.: —

A moins que vous ne le fassiez, Unless you do it.

THEME 32.

1. Alcibiades could not suffer that his country should obey[1] a rival.[2] 2. I dare not enter[3] his room. 3. It is no more than a week[4] since I saw (*que j'ai vu*) your uncle; he has gone to America, you will see him no more. 4. I cannot (§ 6) tell you whether (*si*) my father is at home or not (*non*); I have not seen him this morning. 5. Take care lest (*que*, § 7) he steal your money. 6.

Take care not to be (to come) too late. 7. We dare not tell him this news. 8. There is no enemy who is (*soit*) not able[5] to injure.[6] 9. God forbid that I should betray[7] your secret.

1. Imperf. Subj. 2. *A une rivale.* 3. *Entrer dans.* 4. *Huit jours.* 5. *En état.* 6. *De nuire.* 7. *Trahir.*

NEGATION USED IN FRENCH, AND NOT IN ENGLISH.*

14. *Ne* is moreover often employed in French when in English no thought of negation is to be discovered. This is the case: —

With the affirmative verb of a comparative clause introduced by *que*, than, when the verb closely follows *que*. Also after verbs, nouns, and conjunctions expressing fear and apprehension. Ex.: —

Il est plus âgé que je ne croyais.
He is older than I thought.

Je crains qu'il ne vienne.
I fear he may come.

Il parle autrement qu'il n'agit.
He speaks otherwise than he acts.

A moins que vous ne le fassiez.
Unless you should do it.

NOTE. But if the first clause of the sentence be negative, *que* of the latter clause is not followed by *ne*, if the compared action is not doubtful, as:

Il n'écrit pas mieux qu'il parle.

15. The verbs *douter*, to doubt; *nier* and *disconvenir*, to deny; *contester*, to contest, require *ne* before the verb (in the Subjunctive) of the dependent sentence, yet only when these verbs themselves are used simply negatively or simply interrogatively. Ex.: —

Je ne doute pas / *Doutez-vous* } *que cela ne soit vrai. (?)*
I do not doubt (do you doubt) that this is true.

Niez-vous / *Je ne nie pas* } *qu'il ne soit coupable. (?)*
Do you deny (I do not deny) that he is guilty?

* The pupil should learn, in connection with this lesson, § 6, L. XIX.

16. But when these verbs are affirmative, or negative-interrogative, *ne* is not inserted in the second clause. Also when *ne pas douter* has the force of *être sûr*. Ex.:—

Je doute que cela soit vrai (without *ne*).
Ne niez-vous pas qu'il soit coupable?

17. If the dependent sentence in English is negative, it takes, of course, *ne—pas*. Ex.:—

I fear he will not come, *je crains qu'il ne vienne pas.*
They fear the fortress will not have ammunition enough.
On craint que la forteresse n'ait pas assez de munition.

18. *Empêcher*, to prevent, to hinder, requires *ne* before the following verb in the Subjunctive mood, as:—

J'empêcherai qu'il ne sorte.
I will hinder him from going out.

Empêchera-t-il } *que vous ne le fassiez.*
Il n'empêchera pas }
Will he prevent you (he will not prevent you) from doing it?

THEME 33.

1. He is more wicked than I thought. 2. Henry is stronger than he was last year. 3. Ireland is more powerful, at present, than were the three kingdoms at (*à*) the death of queen Elizabeth. 4. A traveller often relates[1] things otherwise than they are. 5. I fear lest (*que*) some misfortune has befallen[2] my son. 6. I fear our master will come; do you not fear he will come? 7. He denies that his brother is mixed up[3] in that affair. 8. The city of Paris has become much more beautiful since[4] you saw (have seen) it. 9. Do you fear he will write to your father? 10. I do not fear it. 11. We do not fear that the battle is lost. 12. Do you deny that you have procured [for] him the means of flight?[5] 13. I do not deny that I have given him some clothes and some money. 14. I will hinder him from coming back. 15. I doubt whether the letter has been sent to him (see p. 275, § 1, Note 1). 16. I cannot prevent him from loving (that he loves) pleasure[6] better than work.[6]

1. *Rapporter.* 2. *Etre arrivé à.* 3. *Mêler.* 4. *Depuis que.* 5. *Fuite,* f. 6. Put the def. article.

READING LESSON.

Le Connétable de Bourbon et Bayard.

(Suite.)

Le Con. Qu'as-tu donc? Est-ce que tu ne saurais te consoler d'avoir été vaincu et fait prisonnier dans la retraite de Bonnivet? Ce n'est pas ta faute, c'est la sienne: les armes sont journalières (*changing*). Ta gloire est assez bien établie par tant de belles actions. Les Impériaux[1] ne pourront jamais oublier cette vigoureuse défense de Mézières contre eux.

Bay. Pour moi, je ne puis jamais oublier que vous êtes ce grand connétable, ce prince du plus noble sang qu'il y ait dans le monde, et qui travaille à déchirer[2] de ses propres mains sa patrie et le royaume de ses ancêtres.

Le Con. Quoi! Bayard, je te loue, et tu me condamnes! Je te plains, et tu m'insultes!

Bay. Si vous me plaignez, je vous plains aussi; et je vous trouve bien plus à plaindre que moi. Je sors de la vie sans tache; j'ai sacrifié la mienne à mon devoir, je meurs pour mon pays, pour mon roi, estimé des ennemis de la France, et regretté de tous les bons Français. Mon état est digne d'envie.

Le Con. Et moi, je suis victorieux d'un ennemi qui m'a outragé, je me venge de lui; je le chasse du Milanais;[3] je fais sentir à toute la France combien elle est malheureuse de m'avoir perdu, en me poussant à bout.[4] Appelles-tu cela être à plaindre?

Bay. Oui, on est toujours à plaindre quand on agit contre son devoir. Il vaut mieux périr en combattant pour la patrie, que de la vaincre et de triompher d'elle. Ah! quelle horrible gloire que celle de détruire[5] son propre pays! (*To be continued.*)

1. The Imperialists, Austrians. 2. To tear. 3. From the Milanese territory. 4. To the extreme. 5. Destroy.

XVI. SEIZIÈME LEÇON.

REMARKS ON SOME PREPOSITIONS.

The use of the prepositions is of too various a nature to allow of its being determined by definite rules. Their departure from the original signification can only be shown by examples.

Prepositions must generally be repeated before every noun. *A*, *de*, and *en* must always be repeated.

All prepositions except *en* govern the infinitive; *en* is followed by the present participle. Ex.: —

Pour aller, in order to go. *En allant*, in going.

I. ON THE USE OF SOME FRENCH PREPOSITIONS.

à.

A denotes 1st place, and is used before names of places (not countries), and common names; (in English *at* or *in*): —

à Paris, at Paris. *à l'église*, at church.
à la campagne, in the country. *à l'ombre*, in the shade.
au théâtre or *au spectacle*, at the theatre.
à la poste, at the post-office.
frapper à la porte, to knock at the door.
à la main, in the hand. *à droite*, to the right.

2. Time: —

à quelle heure, at what o'clock?
à deux heures, at two o'clock. *a midi*, at twelve o'clock.
au commencement de la leçon, at the beginning of the lesson
à temps, in time. *à mon arrivée*, on my arrival.
à la pointe du jour, at daybreak.

3. Manner and instrument: —

à la mode, in fashion, fashionably.
à pied, on foot. *à cheval*, on horseback.
à bras ouverts, with open arms.
travailler à l'aiguille, to work with the needle.

peindre à l'huile, to paint in oil
mesurer à l'aune, to measure by the ell (yard).
deux à deux, two and two.
goutte à goutte, drop by drop.
à bon marché, cheap.
à cinq pour cent, at five per cent.
à l'anglaise, after the English style.

4. Destination: —

Une cuiller à thé, a teaspoon.
Une montre à répétition, a repeater (watch).

5. Direction, especially with the verb *aller* or *se rendre*, to go (the English *to*): —

Aller à Vienne, to go to Vienna.
Nous allons à la campagne, we are going into the country.
Aller au théâtre, to go to the theatre.
Aller à la chasse, to go hunting, etc.

Dans, en.

Dans means both in and into a (closed) place; it is used in a more determinate sense than *en*, and is always followed by the article or another determinate word (such as, this, my, which, etc.). Ex.: —

Dans la (ma, votre) chambre, in the (my, your) room.
Dans ma poche, in my pocket.
Dans l'hiver de 1850, in the winter of 1850.
Dans une colère affreuse, in a dreadful passion.
Il est dans la prison, he is in (the) prison (of that place).
Etre dans la ville, to be within the town (not in the country).

Observe also the difference in the following expressions: —

Il est au jardin and *il est dans son jardin.*
Je suis à la maison (at home) and *je suis dans ma maison.*

En is used in a more vague sense, and is followed by no article. It is used for *in* or *to* before the name of a kingdom, republic, country, county, or province. Ex.: —

En liberté, in liberty. *En colère*, in a passion.
En France, in or to France.
En Avril or *au mois d' avril*, in April.
En été, in summer. *En hiver*, in winter.

En automne, in autumn (but *au printemps*, in spring.)
Etre en voyage, to travel about.
En ces termes, in these words.
Vivre en paix, to live in peace.
Etre en ville, to be out, to be from home.
Il est en prison, he is in prison (he is a prisoner).

NOTE. There are a few expressions in which the article is retained after *en*; such are, *en l'absence*, in the absence; *en l'honneur*, in honor. Only *l'* and *la* are thus found after *en*, never *le*.

Dans and *en*, relating to time, are differently used. *Dans* denotes the point of time, *en* the duration. Ex.: —

Dans dix minutes, ten minutes hence.
En dix minutes, within the space of ten minutes.
Je partirai dans huit jours, I shall set out in a week.
M. B. reviendra dans deux mois, Mr. B. will return in two months.
J'ai appris le français en dix mois, I learned French in ten months.

Entre, parmi.

Entre answers in general to the English between, betwixt, and is said of two objects only. Ex.: —

Entre la porte et la fenêtre, between the door and the window.
Entre autres, among others.
La mère tenait l'enfant entre ses bras.
The mother held her child in her arms.

Parmi is said of several objects, as: —

Parmi les rochers, among the rocks.
Votre grammaire se trouva parmi mes livres.
Your grammar was found among my books.

Devant, avant.

Devant is a local preposition, and is also used for *in presence of*, as: —

Nous jouerons devant la maison, we will play before the house.
Il a paru devant le juge, he appeared before the judge.
Sur le devant, in the front; *la porte de devant*, the front door.

Avant denotes priority of time and order, as: —

Je suis arrivé avant vous, I arrived before you.
L'article se met avant le nom, the article is put before the noun.

Avant tout, above all.

Avant is also used before an infinitive with *de* : —

Avant de partir, before leaving.

Envers, vers.

Envers, *towards*, *to*, is used for *with regard to*, in a moral sense, as : —

Soyez charitables envers les pauvres, be charitable towards the poor.

Comportez-vous bien envers lui, behave well towards him (with regard to him).

Vers expresses motion and is put before names of places and persons : —

Vers la colline, towards the hill.

Il s'avança vers moi, he advanced towards me.

Chez.

Chez might be rendered in English by *at the house of*, *with*, *among*, etc. Ex. : —

Chez votre père, at your father's.

Chez les Romains, among the Romans.

Chacun est maître chez soi, everybody is master in his own house.

Je viens de chez vous, I come from your house.

Hors de, hors.

1. *Hors de* denotes an exclusion from a place, *out of*, *outside of*, *without*. Ex. : —

Hors de la maison, out of the house.

Hors du royaume, out of the kingdom.

Note. In this signification *de* may be left out, as : *Hors la maison*, *hors la barrière*, etc.

2. *Hors de* is also used in a figurative or temporal sense, as : —

Il est hors de danger, he is out of danger.

Hors d'état, out of condition, unable.

3. *Hors* (without *de*) signifies except, besides : —

Hors cela nous sommes d'accord, with the exception of that we are agreed.

Note. In this sense *hormis* is sometimes used for *hors*, more frequently *excepté*.

D'avec, d'entre, de dessous, etc.

Some prepositions are preceded by *de*, which serves to indicate the point from which an action proceeds, as :—

Ma séparation d'avec mon père.
My separation from my father.
On arracha l'enfant d'entre les bras de sa mère.
They tore the child from the arms of its mother.
On le tira de dessous le lit.
They drew him from under the bed.

Sans.

Sans, without, is sometimes expressed in English by *but for*. Example : —

Sans lui, je serai mort de faim.
But for him, I should have starved.

Es.

This word is a contraction for *en les*. It is used for university degrees. Ex. : —

Bachelier ès lettres, bachelor of arts.

THEME 34.

1. Where are you going? 2. I am going into the country. 3. My friend arrived in the beginning of summer; he was received with open arms. 4. Is this book to (*à*) your taste?[1] 5. No, I do not like it. (*It does not please me*). 6. I met that gentleman on my journey in Italy. 7. Is Mr. A. at home? 8. Yes, sir; he is in the garden. 9. In the absence of the king, who is now in Italy, these affairs must be suspended.[2] 10. The poor man had to choose between slavery[3] and death. 11. Why has she been so unjust towards her parents? 12. Did you arrive before or after four o'clock? 13. Before the church there are three high poplars.[4] 14. My neighbor was kindly disposed towards me. 15. I found this letter among my papers. 16. Brandy (*l'eau de vie*) is the source of great evils among that people.

1. *Goût*, m. 2. *Suspendre*. 3. *L'esclavage*, m. 4. *Peuplier*, m.

THEME 35.

1. They (*on*) told me amongst other things, that the ship had been taken by the enemy (*pl.*). 2. The old man was unable (*not in a condition*) to do anything for her. 3. He has sold all his horses, except one or two. 4. Now we turn to (towards) the south. 5. Among the merchants in London, there are many beneficent[1] men. 6. He lives with his brother. 7. The tailor will come to your house to-morrow. 8. Where do you come from? 9. I come from my aunt's. 10. The wooden horse was outside the walls[2] of Troy. 11. The patient[3] is at present out of danger. 12. Nobody besides myself was present. 13. Out of (*sur*) sixty soldiers who tried the attack, twenty-five fell into (*entre*) the hands of the enemy (*pl.*). 14. One must distinguish true friendship from (*d'avec*) (the) false. 15. The dog sprang out[4] from under the table.

1. *Bienfaisant.* 2. *Les murs de Troie.* 3. *Le malade.* 4. *Sauter.*

II. HOW TO EXPRESS SOME ENGLISH PREPOSITIONS.

Above.

Above, when it expresses time or number, so as to signify *more than* or *longer than*, is rendered in French by *plus de*. Ex.: —

The fight lasted above four hours.
Le combat dura plus de quatre heures.
It is above twenty miles from here.
Il y a plus de vingt lieues d'ici.

About.

1. *About*, in the sense of *around*, is to be rendered by *autour de*. 2. In the signification of *concerning*, it is *touchant*, *concernant*, *sur*, or simply *de*. 3. In speaking of things which people carry about them, it is translated with *sur*. Ex.: —

1. All thronged about the prince.
   Tout le monde se pressa autour du prince.
2. I will speak to him about our affair (business).
   Je lui parlerai touchant (or *sur* or *de*) *notre affaire.*
3. I have no money about me, *je n'ai pas d'argent sur moi.*

At.

1. *At* is most commonly rendered by *à* with or without an article. 2. After nouns or verbs denoting derision, anger, surprise, sorrow, etc., at is rendered by *de*. 3. It is translated *chez* when, in English, it precedes the word *house*, either expressed or understood. Ex.:—

1. We were at dinner, *nous étions à dîner.*
   Do you play at cards, *jouez-vous aux cartes?*
2. She laughed at him, *elle se moqua de lui.*
   I am surprised at what you say.
   Je suis surpris de ce que vous dites.
3. We were at your aunt's, *nous étions chez votre tante.*

By.

1. *By* denoting the agent or cause is translated *de* or *par* (see p. 135, 2). Ex.:—

Mr. Bell is respected by everybody.
M. Bell est respecté de tout le monde.
Troy was destroyed by the Greeks.
Troie fut détruite par les Grecs.

2. In affirmations and swearing by is translated *par:*

He swears by his honor, *il en jure par son honneur.*

3. *By*, after the verbs to sell, to buy, to work, etc., preceding a noun of weight or measure, day, week, month, or year, is rendered in French by *à* with the definite article. Ex.:—

I sell the tea by the pound, *je vends le thé à la livre.*
We work by the hour *or* by the day.
Nous travaillons à l'heure ou *à la journée.*

4. When preceding a numeral immediately followed by an adjective of dimension, *by* is rendered in French by *sur*. Ex.:

This room is fifteen feet long by ten wide.
Cette chambre a quinze pieds de longueur sur dix de largeur.

5. *By*, immediately following the verbs to kill, to wound, etc., is translated in French by *d'un coup de*, when it expresses the blow, wound, firing, etc., of an instrument by which a man was wounded, killed, etc. Ex.:—

The officer was wounded by a bullet.
L'officier fut blessé d'un coup de fusil.
Achilles was killed at the siege of Troy by an arrow.
Achille fut tué au siège de Troie d'un coup de flèche.

NOTE. If the blows have been repeated, *à coups de* is used, in which case it is most commonly rendered in English by *with*. Ex.: —

They knocked him down with a stick.
Ils l'assommèrent à coups de bâton.

THEME 36.

1. My father was not above twenty-two years old when he was married.[1] 2. My uncle's country-house[2] is very handsome; but it cost him above eighty thousand francs. 3. It is above a year since my friend set off for[3] America. 4. Rome was built by Romulus. 5. The poor man has been driven out[4] of his house by his creditors.[5] 6. I will get up to-morrow at six o'clock. 7. Were you at Mrs. D.'s ball last night? 8. I will pay you at the end of this month. 9. I rejoice greatly at your good luck.[6] 10. She always smiles[7] at everything that is said. 11. Where was your sister this morning? 12. She was at her aunt's. 13. My box[8] is a foot and a half deep by two wide and four long. 14. Harold was wounded by an arrow.[9] 15. William the Second was killed by an arrow in the New-Forest. 16. He is so strong that with his fist[10] (5, *Note*) he could knock down[11] an ox. 17. They killed the dog with stones. 18. The soldiers kill one another with bayonets.[12]

1. To be married, *se marier*. 2. *La maison de campagne*. 3. *Pour*. 4. *Chassé*. 5. *Créancier*, m. 6. *Bonheur*. 7. *Sourire*. 8. *Le coffre*. 9. *Flèche*, f. 10. *Le poing*. 11. *Abattre*. 12. *La baïonette*.

From.

1. *From*, preceding the name of a person, or a possessive adjective, or a personal or interrogative pronoun after the verbs to go, to come, to send, etc., is generally rendered by *de la part de*. Ex.: —

Many compliments from Dr. O.
Bien des compliments de la part de Monsieur le docteur O.
I come from him *or* her (from them), etc.
Je viens de sa part (*de leur part*).

2. *From*, meaning from some one's house, is in French *de chez*. Example: —

I come from my uncle's, aunt's, etc.
Je viens de chez mon oncle, — de chez ma tante, etc.

3. *From — to* is rendered by *de — en*. Ex.: —

He went from street to street, from town to town, etc.
Il alla de rue en rue, de ville en ville, etc.

NOTE. When two names of towns or villages are mentioned, *to* is rendered by *à*. Ex.: —

From Paris to Rouen, *de Paris à Rouen.*

4. *From* is rendered by *depuis*, and *to* by *jusqu'à*, when speaking of extent or time. Ex.: —

From Easter to Christmas, *depuis Pâques jusqu'à Noël.*

In.

1. *In — dans* or *en*, see these words in the first part of this Lesson.

2. *In*, after words denoting pain, hurting, etc., and preceding a possessive adjective with any part of the body, is to be rendered by *à* with the definite article. Ex.: —

I have constantly a pain in my head.
J'ai toujours mal à la tête.

3. In adverbial expressions of time, *in* is not expressed in French. Ex.: —

In the morning, *le matin.* In the evening, *le soir.*

On or *upon.*

1. *On* or *upon* is most generally *sur*. Ex.: —

He climbed upon the tree, *il grimpa sur l'arbre.*

2. After the verbs to play, to live, to depend, and the like, *on* or *upon* is rendered by *de*. Ex.: —

You play on the violin, and I play on the flute.
Vous jouez du violon et moi, je joue de la flûte.
A good end often depends on a good beginning.
Une bonne fin dépend souvent d'un bon commencement.
The prisoner lives on bread and water.
Le prisonnier vit de pain et d'eau.

3. The preposition *on*, before the days of the week and with dates, is dropped in French. Ex. : —

Come on Sunday, *venez dimanche.*
On the twelfth of May, *le douze mai.*

4. *On*, denoting time, in other cases is translated by *en*.

Over.

This preposition is commonly rendered in French by *sur*, but it must be expressed by the Part. Past of the verbs *passer*, *finir*, *achever*, when it denotes an action ended. Ex. : —

As soon as the rain will be over.
Dès que la pluie sera passée.
Is dinner over, *le dîner est-il fini?*

With.

1. *With* is rendered by *de* after such verbs as, to die, to meddle, to do, to dispense, to load, to cover, to fill, and after some adjectives, as: pleased, contented, etc. (see p. 250, § 1 and 2). Ex.: —

He died with cold, *il mourut de froid.*
The wagon is loaded with goods, *la voiture est chargée de marchandises.*

2. *With* is expressed by *à* and the article before nouns denoting in what manner a thing is done or made. Ex. : —

To draw with a pencil, *dessiner au crayon.*
To fight with pistols, *se battre au pistolet.*

NOTE. *Charger* takes *à*, and *se battre, au, à la, à l'* (as the noun may require), before the names of materials or weapons *generally used* for loading fire-arms or for fighting; otherwise, *with* is rendered by *avec*. Ex. : —

Charger un fusil à balles, avec des pierres. Se battre à l'épée, au pistolet, avec des haches, avec des martaux.

The ambiguous English sentence, He struck the man with a wooden leg, would be translated into French by *Il frappa l'homme à la jambe de bois,* if the man was crippled; but if the wooden leg is the weapon of attack, *avec* is used.

3. *With* must not be expressed after the following verbs : to meet with, *rencontrer* ; to trust with, *confier qch. à qn.* ; to supply

with, *fournir qch. à qn.;* to reproach with, *reprocher qch. à qn.* Examples: —

We will supply him with everything.
Nous lui fournirons tout.
I reproached him with his ingratitude.
Je lui reprochai son ingratitude.

REMARK. Prepositions are placed in French *before* the words they govern, though in English they are sometimes placed after. Ex.: —

Whom do you speak to, *à qui parlez-vous?*
What's that for, *pour quoi cela?*
The man whom you are interested in.
L'homme pour qui vous vous intéressez.

THEME 37.

1. Go from me to Mr. S., and tell him that I am expecting him. 2. From whom do you come? 3. I come from Miss B. 4. Charles was wounded in his arm, and not (*non*) in his leg. 5. I have very often a pain in my teeth. 6. I will call upon you in the afternoon, and in the evening (I will) go to the play. 7. Upon what instrument does your sister play? 8. She plays the piano. 9. That happened[1] on the 12th [of] March. 10. I am in the habit[2] of taking a cup of coffee as soon as dinner is over. 11. Do not meddle[3] with my affairs; attend to your own. 12. Is that house covered with slate[4] or tiles?[5] 13. It is covered with tiles. 14. This picture seems to be done with chalk.[6] 15. When you meet a poor man, never reproach him [with] his poverty. 16. France extends[7] from the Rhine to the Atlantic[8] Ocean. 17. What does he complain[9] of? 18. We have travelled from Switzerland to Italy. 19. You spend all the day in going (*à aller*) from house to house, from street to street, from place to place. 20. Those laborers[10] work from (*depuis*) morning[11] to night.[11] 21. I walk every day from twelve (*midi*) to three.

1. *Se passa.* 2. To be in the habit of, *avoir l'habitude de.* 3. *Se mêler.* 4. *Ardoise,* in singular. 5. *Tuile,* in plural. 6. *Craie,* f. 7. *S'étendre.* 8. *l'Océan Atlantique.* 9. *Se plaindre de qch.* 10. *Ouvrier,* m. 11. Put the article.

XVII. DIX-SEPTIÈME LEÇON.

DIFFERENT USES OF THE CONJUNCTION *QUE.*

I. *QUE* WITH THE INDICATIVE.

1. The conjunction *que* is used 1. to join the two terms of a comparison; 2. in a restrictive sense, for but or only, as:

Elle n'a que deux frères, she has only two brothers.

2. The *que* of admiration or exclamation expresses wonder or surprise; it answers to the English words how, how much, how many. Ex.: —

Que vous êtes heureux! how happy you are!
Que la terre est petite en comparaison avec le soleil!
How small is the earth compared with the sun!
Que de peine vous prenez pour moi!
How much trouble you take for me!

3. In short exclamations *que* is inserted after the noun when the verb is omitted. Ex.: —

Quel beau pays que l'Italie!
What a beautiful country Italy is!
Quel homme que ce Fénélon!
What a man that Fenelon is (*or* was)!

4. It stands for *pourquoi* in negative exclamations, as: —

Que ne puis-je vous aider! why can I not assist you!

5. The French paraphrase of a sentence with *c'est* is followed by *que*, whereas in English this is not expressed. Ex.: —

C'est une belle chose que la discrétion.
Discretion is a good thing.
C'est une chose détestable que la haine.
Hatred is a detestable thing.

If, however, an Infinitive follows, *que* need not be used: —

C'est une honte (que) d'ignorer sa langue maternelle.
It is a shame not to know one's mother tongue.

6. *Que* must be inserted after *c'est-à-dire*, that is to say, when a verb follows. *Que* is also frequently used after *voilà* and *peut-être*. Example: —

Vous serez parfaitement libres, c'est-à-dire que vous ne dépendrez de personne.
You will be perfectly free, that is to say, you will depend upon nobody.

7. In the expressions: *que oui*, yes; *que si!* O yes! *que non*, no; *que* is used pleonastically. Ex.: —

Je dis que oui, I say yes.

8. *Que* stands for *since* instead of *depuis que:*

Combien y a-t-il que votre sœur est morte?
How long is it since your sister died?

9. *Que* is used for *when* after *à peine*, scarcely, and in the signification of *as* or *when*, after the specification of a time, in which case the use of *lorsque* would be incorrect. Ex.: —

A peine était-il sorti, que la maison s'écroula.
Scarcely was he gone out, when the house fell.

Un matin que je sortais de très-bonne heure.
One morning as I went out early.

Maintenant que vous êtes en France, etc.
Now that you are in France. . . .

10. *Que* corresponds to the English *that* after all verbs of *thinking*, *feeling*, *saying*,* as: *dire*, *affirmer*, *répondre*, *déclarer*, *croire*, *penser*, *sentir*, *etc.*, and usually takes the Indicative when these words are used affirmatively. In English the *that* is often omitted, but in French it must always be employed. Ex.: —

Dites-lui que je l'attends.
Tell him that I am waiting for him.

Il m'a répondu qu'il n'en savait rien.
He answered me that he knew nothing of it.

On croit qu'elle est très-riche.
She is supposed to be very rich.

* Where in Latin the *Acc.* is used with the *Infinitive.*

Note. *Que* is not only always expressed in French, but repeated before each member of the proposition. Ex.: —

Je crois que vous vous trompez et que vous ne réussirez pas.
I think you are mistaken, and that you will not succeed.

11. In many cases where the conjunction is repeated in English, the French, instead of repeating it, put *que* in the place of it. This is the case with *lorsque*, *quand*, *pendant que*, *tandis que*, *parce que*, *tant que* and *dès que*. Ex.: —

Lorsque l'empereur fut revenu et qu'il (and when he) *eut visité le camp, il résolut de livrer bataille.*

Tandis que Charles XII donnait un roi à la Pologne soumise, que le Danemark n'osait le troubler, et que le roi de Prusse recherchait son amitié, le czar devenait de jour en jour plus redoutable.

THEME 38.

1. I am much younger than you. 2. Caroline is only seventeen years old. 3. How pretty she is! 4. How I hate flatterers![1] 5. How small is the part of the world which we inhabit![2] 6. What (*que de*) misfortunes you have undergone![3] 7. If you are (*avez*) cold, why (§ 4) don't you put on your cloak? 8. It is a very difficult thing to know (§ 5) [how to] keep what one has. 9. Look, it rains! 10. Perhaps he will come. 11. I believe (that) you are right. 12. He told me that he had not yet received a letter from his uncle. 13. Are you ready? 14. O no! (§ 7) I cannot finish before an hour. 15. Have you not been there? 16. O yes! 17. How long is it since you lost your father? 18. One day when the two sparrows[4] had flown out,[5] the children took away[6] their nest. 19. Tell me the day (on which, § 9) you think[7] of leaving. 20. I think he is not at home. 21. Scarcely is he out of bed before he beings to work. 22. Why (§ 4) did you not tell it? 23. When you have acknowledged your faults, and (§ 11) have repaired[8] them, I will forgive you.

1. *Flatteur*. 2. *Habiter*. 3. *Éprouvés*. 4. *Le moineau*. 5. *Étaient sortis*. 6 *Enlever*. 7. *Vous comptez partir*. 8. *Réparés*.

II. *QUE* WITH THE SUBJUNCTIVE MOOD.

1. *Que*, in a conditional sense, is used in the beginning of a sentence for the word *whether*, and in the middle, to avoid the repetition of *si*; in both cases it governs the Subjunctive mood. Ex.: —

Whether he come or not, I do not care.
Qu'il vienne ou non, je ne m'en soucie pas.

If somebody calls and I am out, send for me.
Si quelqu'un vient me voir et que je sois sorti, envoyez-moi chercher.

If you meet her, and (if) you have time to speak to her.
Si vous la rencontrez et que vous ayez le temps de lui parler.

2. For *till*, instead of *jusqu'à ce que* after *attendre*, to wait. Example: —

Wait till it gets less cold.
Attendez qu'il fasse moins froid.

You must wait till I am back.
Il faut attendre que je sois de retour.

3. For the English third person of the Imperative, *let him* or *let them*. Ex.: —

Let him come, *qu'il vienne.*
Let them do it, *qu'ils (qu'elles) le fassent.*

4. For *that*, instead of *pour que, afin que*: —

Come here that I may speak to you.
Venez ici que je vous parle.

5. *Que* is used with *ne* for the English *but* (or *but that*) after verbs expressing *doubt, fear, etc.* (see p. 293, § 15). Ex.: —

I don't doubt but that you are right.
Je ne doute pas que vous n'ayez raison.

6. In the same manner *que* is used for *before*, instead of *avant que*; for *unless*, instead of *à moins que*; for *without*, instead of *sans que*, and for *yet*, instead of *et cependant*. Ex: —

I shall not go out before you are in.
Je ne sortirai pas que vous ne soyez rentré.

I shall not pardon you unless you acknowledge your faults.
Je ne vous pardonnerai pas que vous ne reconnaissiez vos fautes.

He takes no trip without some accident befalling him.
Il ne fait pas de voyage qu'il ne lui arrive quelque accident.

Though he should have all the gold in the world, yet he would not be satisfied.
Il aurait tout l'or du monde, qu'il ne serait pas content.

(For the use of *que* instead of repeating compound conjunctions, and after verbs governing the Subjunctive, see Lesson 19, on the Subjunctive Mood, § 12).

THEME 39.

1. Whether it rain or not, I must go out directly. 2. If I were rich and had children, I would give them a good education. 3. Whether you be rich or poor, you should (*devez*) be a man of probity. 4. He had not a doubt (*did not doubt*) but that this was his pursuer.[1] 5. Wait till the rain is over. 6. A miser[2] might have all the gold in the world, he would never be satisfied. 7. You shall not go out before it is light.[3] 8. Let him have his share.[4] 9. Come that I may tell you the reason of that thing (*en*). 10. May heaven bless[5] you! 11. May the earth lie lightly on him (*be light*[6] *to him*). 12. Let him employ his time well. 13. I shall not leave the house (*go out*) before you pay me. 14. He cannot play but he hurts[7] himself. 15. If you go to Paris and (§ 1) will take me with you, I shall be most happy.[8] 16. My friend says he will not pay the bookseller[9] before he has received all the books (which) he (has) ordered. 17. I shall put off[10] my journey;—I shall wait till your time allows you to accompany me.

1. *Persécuteur.* 2. *Avare*, f. 3. To be light—*faire jour.* 4. *Part*, f. 5. *Bénir.* 6. *Légère.* 7. *Se faire mal.* 8. Most happy—*Enchanté.* 9. *Le libraire.* 10. *Remettre.*

READING LESSON.

LE CONNÉTABLE DE BOURBON ET BAYARD.

(Fin.)

Le Connét. Mais ma patrie a été ingrate après tant de services que je lui avais rendus. Le roi m'a fait une injustice énorme. En me dépouillant[1] de mon bien, on a détaché de moi jusqu'à (*even*) mes domestiques, Matignon et d'Argouges. J'ai été contraint, pour sauver ma vie, de m'enfuir presque seul. Que voulais-tu que je fisse ?

Bay. Que vous souffrissiez toutes sortes de maux, plutôt que de manquer à la France et à la grandeur de votre maison. Si la persécution était trop violente, vous pouviez vous retirer : mais il valait mieux être pauvre, obscur, inutile à tout, que de prendre les armes contre nous. Votre gloire eût été au comble[2] dans la pauvreté et dans le plus misérable exil.

Le Conn. Mais ne vois-tu pas que la vengeance s'est jointe à l'ambition pour me jeter dans cette extrémité ? J'ai voulu que le roi se repentît de m'avoir traité si mal.

Bay. Il fallait l'en faire repentir par une patience à toute épreuve, qui n'est pas moins la vertu d'un héros que le courage.

Le Conn. Mais le roi, étant si injuste et si aveuglé[3] par sa mère, méritait-il que j'eusse de si grands égards pour lui ?

Bay. Si le roi ne le méritait pas, la France entière le méritait. La dignité même de la couronne, dont vous êtes un des héritiers, le méritait. Vous vous deviez[4] à vous-même d'épargner[5] la France, dont vous pouviez être un jour roi.

Le Conn. Eh bien ! j'ai tort, je l'avoue ; mais ne sais-tu pas combien les meilleurs cœurs ont de peine à résister à leur ressentiment ?

Bay. Je le sais bien : mais le vrai courage consiste à résister. Si vous connaissez votre faute, hâtez-vous de la réparer. Pour moi, je meurs, et je vous trouve plus à plaindre dans vos prospérités, que moi dans mes souffrances. Quand l'empereur ne vous tromperait pas, quand même il vous donnerait sa sœur en mariage, et qu'il partagerait la France avec vous, il n'effacerait point la tache[6] qui déshonore votre vie. Le connétable de Bourbon rebelle ! ah ! quelle honte ! Écoutez Bayard mourant comme il a vécu, et ne cessant de dire la vérité.

1. Strip. 2. The highest. 3. Blinded. 4. To owe. 5. To spare. 6. The stain.

XVIII. DIX-HUITIÈME LEÇON.

USE OF THE TENSES OF THE INDICATIVE.

I. PRESENT TENSE.

1. The *Present* of the Indicative corresponds to the English present. In French there is only one form of this tense, as: *Je lis*, I read; *j'aime*, I like. The English forms: I am reading, I do read, etc., must therefore always be translated as if they were: I read, *je lis*. Ex.: —

The children are playing in the garden.
Les enfants jouent au jardin.

Nous dînons toujours à deux heures.

2. The *Present tense* is sometimes employed for the Future, when speaking of actions which are to be done at a time proximate or near, as: —

Je pars demain, I (shall) set out to-morrow.

3. It is also used in a narrative, instead of the Preterite, in order to give more vivacity to the description, and to make the event, as it were, present. For this reason it is called also the *historical* or *narrative Present*. Ex.: —

A cette nouvelle, qu'il repousse avec irritation, Napoléon descend de la montagne du Salut et s'approche de la Moskwa et de la porte Dorogomilow. Il s'arrête (stops) *encore à l'entrée de cette barrière, mais inutilement. Murat le presse, etc.*

Here *repousse, descend, s'approche, s'arrête, presse* are *historical Presents* (instead of *repoussa, descendit, s'approcha, s'arrêta, pressa*). It is particularly liked for euphony, when several Preterites of the first conjugation would be used. Example: —

Mentor range les soldats, il marche à leur tête et s'avance vers les ennemis (instead of *rangea, marcha, s'avança*).

4. The *Present tense* must also be used for the English *Perfect,* when a duration of time is expressed in which the condition is still continuing: —

How long have you been here?
Depuis quand êtes-vous ici?

Have you had this dog long?
Y a-t-il longtemps que vous avez ce chien?

I have had him these two years.
Je l'ai depuis deux ans.

If the Compound of the Present were used in these sentences, it would imply that the condition no longer existed. *Il y a deux ans qu'il a été mort,* would be absurd in French, as it would imply that *he was alive again.*

THEME 40.

1. Do you speak French? 2. Yes, sir, I do. 3. Is it raining? 4. No, it does not rain. 5. I do not like lazy boys. 6. I cannot write with a bad pen. 7. I see a man who is asleep.[1] 8. What are you doing? 9. I am reading a very amusing book; you must read it also; to-morrow I shall send it to you. 10. I set out to-morrow for Germany. 11. I shall be ready in a moment. 12. How long have you been (§ 4) in Paris? 13. I have been here for (*depuis*) three months. 14. Have you had this stick[2] long? 15. I have had it for more than (*de*) four years. 16. Has your father known that gentleman long? 17. I think he has known him for a year or two.

1. *Qui dort.* 2. *Canne,* f.

II. PAST TENSES.

5. The *Imperfect tense* denotes *continuity* of an action or condition, in past time. It is therefore used to express what was customary or habitual. It is also used in descriptions of persons and of things, in expressing physical and moral qualities, traits of character etc.* Ex.: —

* Hence it is called by some grammarians the *simultaneous past*, and by some the *descriptive tense.*

Henri IV était un bon prince, il avait de belles qualités, il aimait son peuple et en était aimé.

Je ne savais pas cela.

Pendant mon séjour à la campagne je me levais tous les matins à cinq heures et je faisais de longues promenades.

Calypso ne pouvait se consoler du départ d'Ulysse. Sa grotte ne résonnait plus de son chant. Les nymphes qui la servaient, n'osaient lui parler. Elle se promenait souvent seule, etc.

Lorsque j'étais en pleine mer, je m'amusais quelquefois à dessiner les beaux nuages, semblables à des groupes de montagnes, qui voguaient à la suite les uns des autres, sur l'azur des cieux.

La grotte de la déesse était sur le penchant d'une colline: de là on découvrait la mer; d'un autre côté on voyait une rivière où se montraient des îles bordées de hauts peupliers qui portaient leurs têtes superbes jusque dans les nues. Les divers canaux qui formaient ces îles, semblaient se jouer dans la campagne: les uns roulaient leurs eaux claires avec rapidité; d'autres avaient une eau paisible et dormante. On apercevait de loin des collines et des montagnes qui se perdaient dans les nues. Les montagnes voisines étaient couvertes de pampres verts qui pendaient en festons: le raisin, plus éclatant que la pourpre, ne pouvait se cacher sous les feuilles, et la vigne était accablée sous son fruit.

6. When two occurrences take place, that which is interrupted by the other and which was lasting before the other happened, must be in the *Imperfect* tense: —

Je dormais (I was sleeping) *lorsqu'il entra.*

Je le surpris pendant qu'il écrivait.

From this we see that whenever in English the *Imperfect*, I was, with the *Part. pres.* is used (I was sleeping, I was writing, etc.), in French the Imperfect tense must be employed.

7. In longer narrations, *all those parts which do not form the thread of the narrative*, but serve only to illustrate the principal facts, and which are only explanatory additions or observations of the writer, are in the *Imperfect* tense. Ex.: —

Au temps que l'Italie était française, une sédition éclata (broke out) *dans un des régiments en garnison à Livourne. C'était une affaire grave: c'était beaucoup plus qu'une mutinerie de soldats. L'empereur parut extrêmement irrité, lorsqu'il apprit cette nouvelle. Ses ordres étaient précis et terribles; il ne voulait pas de conseils de guerre, etc.*

Etait, étaient and *voulait* serve as illustrative additions and explanatory observations of the writer on the facts expressed by the verbs *éclata, parut, apprit.*

8. After the conjunction *si*, if, the *Imperfect* is used to denote a condition or supposition (see § 18). Ex.: —

Si j'avais de l'argent. Si mon frère venait, etc.

Il me demanda si j'avais des heures libres.

He asked me if I had some hours to spare.

9. Sometimes the Imperfect is used instead of the Conditional, to denote that something would have happened, had not another occurrence prevented it, as: —

J'étais perdu, s'il ne m'avait pas retenu.

I should have been lost, if he had not held me.

NOTE. In a similar manner the expressions: *should have, ought to have,* and *could have,* are often rendered in French by the Imperfects: *Il fallait, je devais, il pouvait, etc.* Ex.: —

Vous deviez me le dire tout de suite.

You ought to have told me directly.

THEME 41.

1. Cæsar was a great general. 2. Henry the Fourth was a good king, he loved his people. 3. We were at dinner when the courier[1] arrived (*Pret.*). 4. Tranquillity reigned throughout (*dans*) the whole country. 5. The general was waiting for troops[2] which were to (*devaient*) come. 6. My father studied (used to study) much when he was young. 7. If he came now, he would find me prepared. 8. When I was at Paris, I went every morning to take a walk in the *Champs-Elysées*, or in the *Bois de Boulogne;* afterwards[3] I came home, where I employed[4] myself till dinner, either in reading[5] or writing, and [in] the evening, I generally went [for] amusement[6] to the French Theatre or the Opera. 9. If I were in France, I would learn French. 10. If he had something, he would give it to you. 11. I asked him if his father was at home. 12. He answered that he did not know it. 13. I thought you were wrong. 14. I observed that he was quite pale.[7]

1. *Le courier.* 2. *Troupes,* pl. f. 3. *Après cela.* 4. *S'occuper.* 5. *A lire.* 6. *M'amuser.* 7. *Pâle.*

THE PRETERITE.

10. This tense (as: *J'allai, je vis, je reçus, etc.*) is used in French to express a particular fact or event entirely elapsed, which has happened but once, or very seldom, at a definite time. It is the narrative or historical tense. Ex.: —

Je fus à Rome l'été passé.
Il partit le 20 *Octobre.*
Les Romains chassèrent Tarquin de Rome.
Après la mort d'Aristide, Cimon prit les rênes du gouvernement.
Ce fut l'époque où la Grèce commença à produire les grands hommes.
Quand les ordres de Criton furent exécutés, un domestique apporta la coupe (cup, goblet) *fatale.*

Le premier Octobre 1714 *Charles XII quitta enfin la Turquie. Les Turcs accompagnèrent le roi jusqu'à la frontière et comblèrent ce monarque de tous les signes de leur respect et de leur admiration. Pendant cinq jours Charles supporta la lenteur qu'entraîne naturellement un long cortége; le sixième jour il perdit patience et conçut l'idée de continuer le voyage avec deux compagnons. Accompagné de deux colonels suédois, il abandonna le cortége. Tous trois franchirent la frontière et continuèrent le voyage à cheval avec une vitesse extraordinaire. Après* 22 *jours Charles arriva devant les portes de Stralsund.*

11. In longer narrations all the facts which form the thread of the relation, are expressed in the Preterite, whereas explanatory remarks serving only to elucidate or complete the relation of the facts, are in the Imperfect (see § 7) or in the Pluperfect. Ex.: —

Les onze magistrats qui veillaient à l'exécution des criminels se rendirent à la prison de Socrate pour lui annoncer le moment de son trépas (death). *Plusieurs de ses disciples entrèrent ensuite; ils étaient à peu près au nombre de vingt; ils trouvèrent auprès de lui Xantippe, son épouse, qui tenait le plus jeune de ses enfants entre ses bras. Dès qu'elle les aperçut, elle s'écria: Ah! voilà vos amis. Socrate pria Criton de la faire remener chez elle* (to take her home).

Here the Preterites *rendirent, entrèrent, trouvèrent, aperçut, s'écria* and *pria*, express the facts, whereas *qui veillaient, ils étaient, qui tenait*, etc., are incidental additions.

12. When two facts occur together so that one is interrupted by the other, the verb which expresses the interruption is in the Preterite, the other in the Imperfect. Ex.: —

Je dormais quand il entra.

Je déjeûnais quand vous vîntes me demander.

I was breakfasting when you came to ask for me.

THEMÉ 42.

1. I saw the queen of England last year. 2. My aunt died the day before yesterday. 3. Cato killed himself lest he should (*de peur de*) fall into the hands of Caesar. 4. Marius was ill-treated by (*de*) fortune; however he did not lose [his] courage. 5. Rome was, for (*pendant*) more than two hundred years, the mistress[1] of the world. 6. King Pepin died in 768; Charlemagne, his son, succeeded (him). 7. We set off as soon as we had[2] the order for it (*en*). 8. My brother's servant brought me a letter this morning before I was up.[3] 9. Epaminondas refused the presents of Darius. 10. The Duke of Bouillon was obliged to give the town of Sedan to Henry the Fourth; but this prince, satisfied with his submission,[4] gave[5] it him back[5] soon. 11. Napoleon was born[6] in Corsica.[7] 12. When some one represented to Napoleon that a thing was impossible, he declared that this word was not French.

1. *La maîtresse.* 2. Pret. of *recevoir.* 3. *Levé.* 4. *Soumission*, f. 5. *Rendre.* 6. Pret. of the verb *naître*, p. 181. 7. *En Corse.*

THE COMPOUND OF THE PRESENT.

13. The Compound of the Present (*j'ai vu, j'ai reçu, etc.*) is used to express a thing as having taken place at a time not specified, or in a period not fully elapsed. Ex.: —

J'ai perdu tous mes enfants.

M. Laurent a beaucoup voyagé.

Nous avons renoncé (given up) *à nos droits.*

Alexandre le Grand a détruit l'empire des Perses.

L'avez vous vu aujoud'hui? — Oui je l'ai vu ce matin.

Nous avous eu beaucoup de pluie cette année.

NOTE. The French Perfect corresponds to the same form in English in all cases, except that given under the Present tense, § 4, in such phrases as *Depuis quand êtes vous ici*, how long have you been here? But the French tense is much more frequently used than the English, as will be seen in the following paragraphs.

14. The Compound of the Present translates the English Imperfect, whenever this does not denote continuous or habitual state or action (see §§ 5, 6, 7), or is not strictly a *historical* past. It is the tense most frequently used in conversation. Ex.: —

Did you see him yesterday?
L'avez-vous vu hier (not *le vîtes-vous*)?
No, sir, I did not see him.
Non, Monsieur, je ne l'ai pas vu.
Did they tell him to come at six?
Lui a-t-on dit de venir à six heures?
Yes they told him to come at six o'clock precisely.
Oui, on lui a dit de venir à six heures précises.
Les Français ont gagné la bataille de Marengo.

In this last sentence, *gagnèrent* would be perfectly correct, but would refer merely to an historical event in the past, with no bearing upon the present. *Ont gagné* connects the fact stated with something present, either in the speaker or in the hearer.

15. The Compound of the Present is idiomatically used in familiar conversation, instead of the Compound of the Future, as:

Avez-vous bientôt fini votre thème? Oui, je l'ai fini dans un moment.

Will you soon have done your exercise? Yes, I shall have finished it in a moment; instead of the more formal *Aurez-vous fini. . . . . J'aurai fini.*

THEME 43.

1. The horse, when he has run[1] his course; the bee, when it has made its honey;[2] and the good man, when he has done good[3] to others, do not make a noisy boast[4] about it, but go on[5] repeating the action; as the vine,[6] in its season, produces new clusters[7] again. 2. Fénelon preached with success from the age of nineteen, and wrote many works which are admired for their beauty of style; but that which has gained[8] him the greatest reputation is his "Telmachus,"[9] where he has displayed[10] all the riches of the French language. 3. No work had ever a greater reputation; it is written in a lively,[11] simple, natural, and elegant manner; its fictions are well imagined, the moral[12] sublime, and the political maxims (which) it contains, all[13] tend to the happiness of mankind.[14]

1. *Achevé.* 2. *Miel*, m. 3. *Du bien.* 4. *Ne s'en vantent pas.* 5. *Continuer.* 6. *Vigne*, f. 7. *Grappe*, f. 8. *Lui a fait.* 9. *Télémaque.* 10. *Déployer.* 11. *Animé.* 12. *La morale.* 13. *Tendre à.* 14. *Des hommes.*

THE COMPOUNDS OF THE IMPERFECT AND OF THE PRETERITE.

16. These tenses are formed from the Imperfect and Preterite, and correspond to them fully; only that they represent their action as having taken place previous to some other event referred to, and cannot be used entirely independently, but usually stand connected with a conjunction or an adverb of time. If this conjunctive clause expresses a definite past time, the Compound of the Preterite is employed, especially after the conjunctions ***aussitôt que***, ***lorsque***, ***quand***, ***dès que***, ***à peine***, ***bientôt***, ***en un moment***, ***un jour que***, *etc.* Example: —

Aussitôt que j'eus terminé mes affaires, je repartis.
A peine eut-il prononcé ce mot, qu'il s'en repentit.
Dès que le parlement se fut assemblé, l'émeute cessa.
As soon as the parliament was assembled, the riot ceased.

It is here not to be overlooked that in the use of the Compound Preterite a more immediate relation, a closer connection must exist between the two past events.

17. With the Compound of the Imperfect, this close connection fails, and this is the distinguishing feature of this tense, which is also used like the Imperfect for descriptions, for continuous events, and frequently repeated or customary previous actions. Ex.; —

Platon avait reçu de la nature un corps robuste.
J'avais déjà terminé mes affaires, quand je reçus votre lettre.
A la campagne, quand j'avais dîné, je faisais une promenade de deux lieues.

18. The Compound of the Imperfect is also used after the conjunction *si*, if, the same in French as in English (see § 9). Ex.:

Si vous étiez venu plus tôt, vous m'auriez trouvé à la maison.
S'il avait parlé plus haut (louder), *je l'aurais compris.*

THEME 44.

1. The Tyrians had, by their pride,[1] offended the great Sesostris, who ruled in Egypt, and who had conquered so many kingdoms. 2. The wealth which they had acquired[2] by commerce, and the strength

of the impregnable[3] city of Tyre, lying[4] in the sea, had lifted up[5] the heart of these people. 3. They had refused to pay Sesostris the tribute[6] which he had imposed upon them (*leur*) on his return from his conquests;[7] and they had furnished troops to his brother, who had attempted[8] to kill him in the midst of the festivities[9] of a great banquet. 4. As soon as Sesostris learned[10] this, he determined[11] to humiliate their pride and to destroy their commerce upon all seas. 5. Julius Cæsar, having disembarked[12] in Africa, fell [down] as he was leaving the vessel; this appeared to his soldiers a very inauspicious[13] omen:[13] he, however, turned the feelings of the army to his advantage by exclaiming (*en s'écriant*), "It is now, O Africa, that I hold thee."

1. *Orgueil*, m. 2. *Acquises*. 3. *Imprenable* (before the noun). 4. *Située dans*. 5. *Enflé*. 6. *Le tribut*. 7. *Conquête*, f. 8. *Voulu*. 9. *Joies*. 10. *Apprendre*. 11. *Il résolut d'humilier*. 12. *Ayant débarqué*. 13. *Un présage de mauvaise augure*.

III. THE FUTURE TENSES.

19. The Future (*je parlerai*, *je ferai*, *etc.*) denotes in general future events or circumstances, as: —

Charles partira demain.

20. It must sometimes be used in French after adverbs of time (*quand*, *lorsque*, *etc.*) where the English use the Present, when the idea is one of future time. Ex.: —

Vous pouvez venir quand vous voudrez.
You may come when you like.

21. It is used as a softened form of the Imperative, implying the expectation of fulfilment. Ex.: —

Vous m'écrirez demain, (do) write to me to-morrow.
Vous ne tuerez point, thou shalt do no murder.
Quand vous viendrez, vous apporterez mon livre.
When you come you will bring my book.

NOTE 1. When *shall* and *will* imply determination, they are rendered by *vouloir*, as: —

I will do it, *je veux le faire.*
You shall do it, *je veux que vous le fassiez.*

22. It sometimes has the sense of the Imperative in sentences like the following: —

Croira qui voudra l'historien Capitolin et quelques autres écrivains qui font danser les éléphants sur la corde.

Believe who will the historian Capitolinus and several other writers, who make elephants dance on a rope.

NOTE. To be on the point of doing something is expressed in French by *aller*, which corresponds precisely with the English to be going, etc. (See Part I., Lesson XLVI.) Ex.: —

Are you going to write to him? *allez-vous lui écrire?*

I am coming, *je vais venir.*

Napoléon dit à ses soldats, "Nous allons entreprendre la conquête de l'Egypte. Les peuples avec lesquels nous allons vivre, sont Mahométans," etc.

23. The Compound of the Future indicates an event which is to precede another future event specified. Ex: —

Quand j'aurai terminé mes affaires, je partirai tout de suite.
Aussitôt que je serai arrivé, j'irai le voir.

24. When the conjunction *si* signifies *whether*, expressing uncertainty, the future can be used after it, in French as in English. *Si* is never followed by the future, unless it means whether. Ex.: —

Je ne sais si mon frère viendra.
I do not know if my brother will come.

25. When *si* signifies *on condition that*, the English Future must be rendered by the Present. Ex.: —

Vous deviendrez savant, si vous étudiez bien.
You will become a learned man, if you will study.

26. The Future is sometimes used to imply surmise. Ex.: —

Où est mon argent? L'aurai-je peut-être perdu?
Where is my money? Have I perhaps lost it?

27. The Conditionals, *je parlerais, j'aurais parlé*, are used in French as in English, in conditional sentences: —

Je serais heureux si j'avais des amis.
I should be happy if I had some friends.

NOTE. The English I wish, when it does not relate to something past, is often translated by the Conditional of *vouloir, je voudrais.* Ex.: —

I wish he would come soon, *je voudrais qu'il vînt bientôt.*

28. After *si*, when it means *suppose that*, the English Conditional must be rendered by the Imperfect (see § 8). Ex. : —

Si je continuais mon commerce, je deviendrais riche.
If I should continue my trade, I should become rich.

But when *si* means *whether*, the Conditional is also used in French : —

Je ne sais si mon oncle viendrait, en cas que vous l'invitassiez.

29. The compound Conditional of *devoir*, *pouvoir*, and *vouloir*, followed by the simple Infinitive, must be used when, in English, the auxiliaries should, ought, could, might, are followed by a compound Infinitive Ex. : —

Vous auriez dû écrire une lettre.
You ought to have written a letter.
J'aurais pu lui donner de l'argent.
I could have given him some money.

THEME 45.

1. I shall go to London. 2. The bookseller will send you the book to-morrow. 3. When I am in the country, will you come to see me? 4. I shall play as soon as I have finished my lesson. 5. There will always be wars among men, as long as they are (§ 20) ambitious. 6. I hope you will not refuse me this favor. 7. When you are ready, we will go [and] take a walk. 8. I do not know if my sister will consent to it (*y*). 9. If your person were as gigantic[1] as your desires, the whole[2] world could not contain you; your right hand would touch the east[3] and your left the west[4] at the (*en*) same time, said the Scythian[5] ambassador to Alexander. 10. I could have kept[6] the book; nobody would have known it.

1. *Gigantesque.* 2. *Entier* (after the noun). 3. *L'orient*, m. 4. *L'occident*, m. 5. *L'ambassadeur des Scythes.* 6. *Garder.*

THEME 46.

1. My country has been ungrateful[1] to me, although I have rendered it (*lui*) great service (*pl.*). 2. The king has done me great injustice; he has robbed[2] me of my entire fortune, he has even

taken[3] from me my two servants. 3. I have been compelled to flee, in order to preserve[4] my life, which was seriously threatened. 4. What was to be done?[5] 5. You should rather have endured[6] (§ 29) all injuries than to offend[7] against France and the greatness of your house. 6. If you were persecuted, you could have retired;[8] it would have been (*valu*) better to be poor and unknown[9] than to take up[10] arms against your country. 7. Even in poverty and in the most wretched[11] exile, your fame[12] would not have been lost.

1. *Ingrat.* 2. *Privé.* 3. *M'a dépouillé jusqu'à.* 4. *Pour sauver.* 5. *Que voulez-vous que je fasse?* 6. *Souffrir.* 7. *Que de manquer à.* 8. *Vous retirer* (reflective verb). 9. *Obscur.* 10. *Prendre les armes.* 11. *Misérable.* 12. *Gloire, f.*

READING LESSON.

ALEXANDRE SELKIRK.

Pendant la guerre pour la succession d'Espagne, quelques particuliers[1] équipèrent en Angleterre deux vaisseaux armateurs, destinés à faire des prises[2] dans la mer du sud. Le capitaine Rogers fut nommé pour les commander. Ils levèrent[3] l'ancre de Bristol le 2 Août, 1708. Au mois de Janvier de l'année suivante ils se trouvaient du côté du pôle antarctique.[4] Rogers doubla le Cap-Horn sans prendre terre en aucun lieu de ces parages[5] jusqu'à l'île de Juan Fernandès, située dans la mer du sud, à la distance de cent-dix lieues du Chili. Il y envoya une pinasse,[6] qui revint au vaisseau avec quantité d'écrevisses,[7] et un homme vêtu de peaux de chèvres[8] qui paraissait plus sauvage que ces animaux mêmes. C'était un Écossais, nommé Alexandre Selkirk, qui avait été maître à bord du vaisseau "Les Cinq-Ports," et que le capitaine Stradling avait abandonné sur cette île depuis quatre ans et quatre mois. Voici le récit que ce malheureux fit de ses aventures au capitaine Rogers.

"Dès mon enfance j'ai été élevé[9] dans la marine. Ayant suivi le capitaine Stradling dans son expédition, j'eus un démêlé[10] avec lui, ce qui l'engagea à me débarquer sur cette île. Je résolus d'abord d'y rester, plutôt que[11] de m'exposer à de nouveaux chagrins, d'autant plus que le vaisseau était en mauvais état. Cependant revenu à moi même, je souhaitai d'y retourner, mais le capitaine n'y voulut pas consentir."

(*To be continued.*)

1. Private men. 2. Capture. 3. To weigh. 4. South. 5. Parts of the sea. 6. Pinnace. 7. Crab. 8. Goat-skins. 9. Brought up. 10. Quarrel. 11. Rather than.

QUESTIONNAIRE.

Que firent quelques particuliers anglais pendant la guerre de la succession d'Espagne ?

Qui commanda les deux vaisseaux ?

Où prit-il terre pour la première fois ?

Où est située cette île ?

Qui trouva-t-on là ?

Qui était cet homme ?

Comment y était-il venu ?

Combien de temps y était-il resté ?

Pourquoi avait-il été débarqué par le capitaine ?

XIX. DIX-NEUVIÈME LEÇON.

THE SUBJUNCTIVE MOOD.

1. The Subjunctive is in most cases dependent, and is therefore used in subordinate clauses. Whenever in French a subordinate clause is dependent upon a leading clause which contains the idea of something not yet having an actual existence for the speaker, consequently of something possible or uncertain, its verb will be in the Subjunctive. This unreality can apply as well to something external, i. e. to actions and events, as to something internal, i. e. to conceptions and emotions. This is the general

ground of distinction in the application of the French Subjunctive. The two languages by no means agree in this point. Many verbs in English are put in the Future, the Conditional, or the Present Indicative, which, in French, must be in the subjunctive. Thus for instance: —

Je ne pense pas qu'il soit si âgé.
I do not think he is so old.

Nous craignions qu'il ne s'en allât.
We feared he would go.

2. But before passing to the rules concerning the use of the Subjunctive, it will be indispensably necessary to understand the relation of the tenses of the Subjunctive to those of the Indicative and Conditional, without which the clause, dependent upon them, cannot be properly translated. The following rules are here applicable: —

1. If the verb of the leading clause is in the Present or Future Indicative, that of the dependent clause will be in the Present or Compound of the Present of the Subjunctive. Ex.: —

*Je veux qu'il vienne,** I wish him to come.
Connaissez-vous quelqu'un qui sache faire cela?
Do you know anybody who knows how to do this?

Je ferai en sorte que tout soit prêt.
I will have everything ready.

J'attendrai que mon père soit parti.
I will wait till my father has departed.

2. If the verb of the leading clause be in a past tense of the Indicative, or in the Conditional, the Imperfect of the Subjunctive must follow in the subordinate clause; or if the subordinate clause contain an event which has already taken place, the Compound Imperfect of the Subjunctive must be employed, according to the following scheme: —

Je craignais
Je craignis
J'ai craint
J'avais craint
Je craindrais
J'aurais craint
} *qu'elle n'arrivât demain — aujourd'hui, — trop tard, — trop tôt, etc.*

*Observe that the Present and Future are the same in the Subjunctive Mood in French; the context alone shows of which of the two we speak. Ex.: —

Je ne crois pas qu'elle vienne.
I do not think she is coming.

Je ne crois pas qu'elle vienne.
I do not think she will come.

Je craignais
Je craignis
J'ai craint *
J'avais craint
Je craindrais
J'aurais craint
} *qu'ils ne fussent arrivés hier — avant-hier, — la semaine dernière, etc.*

3. There are a great many verbs which govern the verb of the subordinate clause in the Subjunctive mood; they may be divided into four classes, viz.: —

1. Verbs of wishing, willing, desiring, commanding or permitting.
2. Verbs of thinking, believing, and saying.
3. Verbs expressing fear, doubt, sorrow, astonishment, denial, duty, necessity, joy, or delight.
4. Impersonal verbs which do not express certainty or probability.

4. Verbs of wishing, willing, commanding, etc. Such are: —

Aimer, to like.
aimer mieux, to prefer.
défendre, to forbid.
demander, to ask.
désirer, to wish for, to desire.
exiger, to demand.
ordonner, to order.
permettre, to permit, allow.
prier, to beg, to ask.
recommander, to recommend.
souhaiter, to wish.
souffrir, to suffer.
supplier, to beg, request.
vouloir, to be willing, etc.

Examples: —

J'ordonne qu'il sorte, I order him to go out.

J'aime qu'il soit courageux, I like him to be brave.

Il veut que je dise la vérité (*Pres. Subj.*, § 2, 1).
He wishes me to say the truth.

Il voulait que je lui disse la vérité (*Imperf.*, § 2, 2).
He desired me to tell him the truth.

Le roi exigea que je partisse tout de suite.
The king demanded that I should leave directly

* As the Compound of the Present belongs to Present as well as to Past time, it can be followed also by the Present of the Subjunctive, when the dependent clause refers to Present time. Ex.: —

Dieu nous a donné la raison pour que nous nous en servions.
God has given us reason that we may make use of it.

5. Verbs of thinking, believing, saying, etc.

These verbs, and, in general, all those which express the intellectual faculties of the mind, govern the Indicative when they are affirmatively used, and most commonly the Subjunctive when they are used negatively, interrogatively, or are preceded by the conjunction *si*. If I say, for instance: *Je crois que Charles est malade*, I represent Charles's illness to myself as a reality, and consequently the Indicative is required. But in the sentences: *Je ne crois pas que Charles soit malade*, or, *croyez-vous que Charles soit malade?* an uncertainty is expressed in regard to Charles's illness, and the Subjunctive must be used. Ex.: —

Je ne crois pas que le concert ait lieu ce soir.
I do not think that the concert will take place to-night.
Pensez-vous qu'il puisse apprendre tout cela.
Do you think he can learn all that?
Je ne dis pas qu'il ait tort.
I do not say that he is wrong.
Partons, si vous pensez qu'il fasse beau temps.

NOTE 1. If however we ask a question, less to be informed of a thing than to inform others of it, the second verb (having the sense: Do you know?) is put in the Indicative, and not in the Subjunctive. Ex.: —

Vous ai-je dit que mon frère est arrivé?

NOTE 2. Observe that the verbs of knowing, being sure, resolving, etc., are not comprised among those which govern the Subjunctive. They generally require the Indicative, even when used interrogatively or negatively: —

Je savais } *qu'il était ici.*
Je ne savais pas }
Je ne sais s'il le fera, I do not know if he will do it.

THEME 47.

1. I wish him to come (that he c.). 2. The law requires that thieves[1] [should] be punished. 3. I demanded that he should pay me. 4. Has he demanded that you should pay the bill?[2] 5. I forbid that he should go there. 6. God wills that we love our enemies. 7. Caligula wished that the Romans should render him divine honors.[3] 8. Your father expects that you should give[4] an ac-

count of what you have done. 9. My aunt wishes that I should set out to-morrow. 10. Tell him to wait. 11. Augustus commanded in his will[5] that they should not seek to[6] extend the empire. 12. Allow me to tell you (allow that I tell y.) the truth. 13. I will be obeyed (that one ob. me). 14. Do you think your aunt will come by herself?[7] 15. If I find that you frequent bad company, you will lose my friendship. 16. Do you hope they (*on*) will make peace?[8]

1. *Les voleurs.* 2. *Le compte.* 3. *Des honneurs divins.* 4. To give an account, *rendre compte.* 5. *Testament*, m. 6. *A étendre.* 7. *Seule.* 8. *La paix.*

---

6. The Subjunctive is used after verbs of fear, doubt, sorrow, joy, denial or hinderance, astonishment, etc. Such are: —

Avoir peur, } to fear.
craindre, }
douter, to doubt.
s'étonner, to wonder.
empêcher, to hinder, prevent.
nier, to deny.

And likewise after:

Être bien aise, to be glad.
être charmé, } to be very glad.
être enchanté, }
être content, to be satisfied.
se réjouir, to rejoice.
trembler, to tremble.
être affligé, to be afflicted.
être fâché, to be sorry.
être étonné, to be astonished.
être surpris, to be surprised.
regretter, to regret.
se plaindre, to complain.

Examples: —

Je crains que ma mère ne soit malade.
I fear my mother is ill.

Je ne doutais pas qu'il n'arrivât avant vous.
I did not doubt that he would arrive before you.

J'empêcherai qu'il ne sorte.*
I will hinder him from going out.

Je regrette qu'il soit venu trop tard.
Mon père est fâché que je ne lui aie pas écrit plus tôt.
Je suis charmé que vous soyez venu me voir.
Je m'étonne qu'il n'ait pas reçu ma lettre.

* Concerning the particle *ne*, see L. XV. § 15–18.

Note 1. The verbs *avoir peur, appréhender, craindre* and *trembler* require the particle *ne* before the verb in the Subjunctive mood, but only when these verbs themselves are affirmative or negative-interrogative. Ex.: —

Je crains qu'il ne vienne.
Ne craignez-vous pas qu'il ne vienne?

But if the sentence be simply negative or simply interrogative, *ne* is not used, as: —

Je ne crains pas qu'il vienne.
Craignez-vous qu'il vienne?

Note 2. If after those verbs mentioned in § 6, we wish to express ourselves with definiteness, *de ce que* is used instead of the simple *que*, and this is followed by the Indicative: —

Il est fâché de ce que vous ne lui avez pas écrit.
Je me plains de ce qu'elle m'a oublié.

Note 3. If the second verb is negative in English, *ne — pas* must be used in French, as: —

Je tremble qu'il n'arrive pas à temps.
I tremble lest he may not arrive in time.

7. Subjunctive after Impersonal verbs.

A verb preceded by *que* is always put in the Subjunctive after the following Impersonals: —

Il est surprenant, it is surprising.
il convient, it is proper.
il faut, it must.
il importe, it is important, it matters, it concerns.
il suffit, it is sufficient.
il vaut mieux, it is better.
il plaît, it pleases, suits.
il est fâcheux, it is sad.
il est juste, it is just, right.
il est difficile, it is difficult.
il est possible, it is possible.
il est naturel, it is a matter of course.
il se peut, il peut se faire, it may be.

And likewise after: —

Il est temps, it is time.
c'est dommage, it is a pity.
c'est un malheur, it is a misfortune, *etc., etc.*

Examples: —

Il faut que vous partiez tout de suite.
You must leave directly.

Il est possible qu'il revienne.
It is possible that he come back.

C'est dommage que vous ne soyez pas venu plus tôt.
It is a pity that you have not come earlier.

Il suffit qu'il ait avoué sa faute.
It is enough that he has confessed his fault.

Il est juste que vous soyez puni.
It is right that you be punished.

Further, after *il y a*, and all impersonal verbs with an adjective denoting evidence, certainty, or probability, when they are used in a negative, interrogative, or conditional manner. Ex.:—

Y a-t-il un mortel qui puisse dire qu'il est toujours heureux?
Is there a mortal who can say that he is always happy?

Est-il sûr qu'il ait tort?
Is it certain that he is in the wrong?

Il n'est pas sûr qu'il ait tort.
It is not certain that he is in the wrong.

THEME 48.

1. I doubt whether that is true. 2. I doubt whether your uncle will arrive to-morrow. 3. The Egyptians did not doubt (see Lesson XV., § 15) that certain plants and animals were divinities.[1] 4. We question whether riches can afford[2] happiness. 5. I did not know that you were to come. 6. Do you doubt that I am your friend? 7. I do not doubt that you are my friend. 8. He denies that he had been told that. 9. He does not deny that he has been told that. 10. It is time for us to go (that we go) home, for it begins to (*à*) rain. 11. It is evident that Greece could no more defend herself, so much was she at that time sunken.[3] 12. It is sufficient if you tell him this. 13. It is a pity that you did not go with us; you would have enjoyed yourself much. 14. It is not probable that they will do it. 15. I must go to (*en*) town.

1. *Des divinités.* 2. *Accorder.* 3. *Déchue.*

---

8. The Subjunctive is used in relative dependent clauses beginning with *qui*, *que*, *lequel* or *où*, which depend upon a leading clause in which a wish, doubt, or condition is implied, especially after an Imperative. Ex.:—

Lisez des ouvrages qui puissent former votre goût.
Read such books as can form your taste.
Choisissez un appartement où vous soyez à votre aise.
Choose an apartment where you may be comfortable.
Ils envoyèrent des députés qui consultassent Apollon.
They sent deputies who were to consult Apollo.

If, however, no such requirement or expectation is contained in the leading clause; if, on the contrary, the matter is rather regarded as something which is actual, or which has already taken place, then, of course, the Indicative is used. Ex.:—

J'ai loué un appartement où je suis bien à mon aise.
Ils envoyèrent des députés qui consultèrent Apollon.

9. A verb preceded by the relative *qui* or *que* is put in the Subjunctive after the Superlative, when the relative clause only expresses an *opinion*, as:—

C'est le plus beau jardin que je connaisse.
This is the most beautiful garden I know.
C'est une des dernières lettres que St. Paul ait écrites.
This is one of the last letters St. Paul has written.
La meilleure garde qu'un roi puisse avoir, c'est le cœur de ses sujets.
The best guard a king can have is the hearts of his subjects.

If, however the thing is represented as certain or as a matter of fact, the Indicative follows. Ex.:—

Souviens-toi que je suis le seul qui t'a déplu (displeased).
Néron est le premier empereur qui a persécuté l'Église.

10. The Subjunctive is used further after the ordinal numbers (as, *le premier*, *le second*, *le dernier*, etc.), and after *unique*, *seul*, *peu*, *rien*, and *personne*. Ex.:—

Vous êtes le premier ami que j' aie rencontré à Paris.
You are the first friend I have met with in Paris.
C'est l'unique espoir qui me soit resté.
This is the only hope that remains to me.
Il y a peu d'hommes qui sachent supporter l'adversité.
There are few men who know how to bear adversity.
Je ne connais personne qui soit aussi heureux que lui.
I know nobody who is so happy as he is.

NOTE. *Qui* and *que* do not govern the Subjunctive, when they are preceded by *de* and its object, to which they refer. Ex.:—

Ne dites rien de ce que je vous ai confié (Ind.).

THEME 49.

1. You are the most learned man I know in this town. 2. Robert is the only friend on whom I can depend.[1] 3. Nero was the first emperor that (has) persecuted the Christians. 4. I seek a servant who is faithful. 5. The diamond is the most valuable[2] stone we know. 6. You are the first German I have met with in China. 7. There is no one who does it more easily[3] than she. 8. Is this the first time you have been mistaken?[4] 9. I wish it were the first time. 10. Lucretius[5] and Pliny were the only natural philosophers[6] whom the Romans had.

1. *Compter.* 2. *Précieux.* 3. *Aisément.* 4. *Se tromper.* 5. *Lucrèce et Pline.* 6. *Naturalistes.*

11. Subjunctive after conjunctions. A verb is put in the Subjunctive after the following conjunctions: —

Avant que, before.
à moins que (ne), unless.
afin que, in order that.
bien que, although.
de peur que (ne), lest.
de crainte que (ne), for fear that.
de manière (sorte) que, so that.
en attendant que, till.
en (au) cas que, in case.
encore que, although.
jusqu'à ce que, until.
loin que, far from,
malgré que, for all that, notwithstanding that.
nonobstant que, notwithstanding.
non que, / *non pas que,* } not that.
pour que, in order that.
pour peu que, / *si peu que,* } if ever so little.
pourvu que, provided.
que — ne, till, before.
quel — que, / *quelque — que,* } however. (See p. 282.)
quoique, although.
sans que, without.
sinon que, but that.
si tant est que, if so be that.
soit que — soit que, / *soit que — ou que,* } whether — or. be it that — or.
supposé que, suppose that.

EXAMPLES.

Rentrons avant qu'il fasse nuit.
Let us go home before it gets dark.
Afin que (pour que) vous le sachiez.
That you may know it.
Je ne sortirai d'ici que je ne sois payé.
I shall not go away from here before I am paid.

Quoiqu'il me l'ait promis.
Although he has promised me.
Pourvu qu'il y consente.
Provided he consent to it.
Quelque effort que fassent les hommes, leur néant paraît partout.
Whatever effort men may make, their nothingness appears everywhere.
A moins que vous ne me demandiez pardon.
Unless you ask me for pardon.
Au (en) cas qu'il mourût.
In case he should die.

NOTE. The Indicative can sometimes be used after *avant que, jusqu'à ce que, sinon que, de sorte que, si ce n'est que, tellement que,* and *de manière que,* when all doubt and uncertainty are excluded, and the clause expresses a fact. Ex.: —

Je gardai mon sang froid, jusqu à ce que je l'entendis calomnier mon frère.
Il s'est occupé de cette affaire de manière (de sorte) qu'on n'a pu le blâmer.

12. In the same manner the Subjunctive is employed after the simple *que*, when used instead of one of the conjunctions mentioned in § 11. Ex.: —

Je ne puis vous pardonner avant que vous me fassiez l'aveu de vos fautes et que vous me promettiez de vous corriger.
I cannot pardon you before you confess your faults and promise me to improve.
Venez que (instead of *afin que*) *je vous en dise la raison.*
Come, that I may tell you the reason of it.
Son esprit est toujours actif, quoiqu'il soit malade et qu'il ne puisse travailler.
His mind is always active, although he is sick and cannot work.

13. The conjunction *que*, used to avoid the repetition of *si*, governs the Subjunctive. Ex.: —

Si je ne suis pas rentré à quatre heures et qu'on vienne me demander, etc.
If I am not at home at four o'clock, and somebody comes for me, etc.

14. The Subjunctive is also used after *attendre; till* is translated by *que*, and not by *jusqu'à ce que*, as: —

Attendez qu'il revienne, wait till he comes back.

15. Aside from the instances above-mentioned, the Subjunctive also occurs in a few expressions which appear either the expression of a wish or as a kind of third person Imperative. Notice espe-

cially: *Dussé-je!* should I! *Puissiez-vous!* would that you! *Puissent-ils!* may they . . . . ! Further:—

Dieu veuille or *plût à Dieu,* would to Heaven.
Vive le roi, long live the king!
Puissiez-vous être heureux, may you be happy!
Qu'on amène l'accusé, let the culprit be brought here!
Qu'ils viennent, let them come!
Que Dieu vous bénisse, God bless you!
Que la terre lui soit légère, may the earth lie lightly upon him!
A Dieu ne plaise que, may heaven not permit, etc.

THEME 50.

1. Before war was declared, the Carthaginians sent once more ambassadors to Rome. 2. I cannot depend on your promise, unless you give me the necessary security.[1] 3. Cæsar went by forced[2] marches to Vienne, on the Rhône, before the enemy (*plur.*) became aware[3] of his approach. 4. Get up early to-morrow morning, that we may start[4] in good time (*à temps*). 5. I shall not yet pass to the perusal[5] of this author, unless you advise[6] me [to] it. 6. Keep a strict watch[7] over all your senses, lest intemperance get[8] the better of you. 7. Though he is lazy, yet he improves a little (*fait quelques progrès*). 8. I shall wait until (§ 14) you have done. 9. Wait till the rain be over (*passée*). 10. Although Homer,[9] according to[10] Horace, slumbers[11] at times,[12] he is nevertheless (*il n'en est pas moins*) the first of all poets. 11. You will succeed,[13] provided you act with vigor. 12. I shall soon speak French, though I am convinced that it is a difficult language. 13. I shall not leave the house before (*que — ne*) you sign[14] this paper. 14. May God protect[15] you. 15. May Heaven preserve us from war.

1. *Garantie,* f. 2. *A marches forcées.* 3. *S'apercevoir de.* 4. *Partir.* 5. *Lecture,* f. 6. *Conseiller.* 7. *Veillez avec soin.* 8. To get the better of, *maîtriser qn.* 9. *Homère.* 10. *Selon.* 11. *Sommeiller.* 12. *Quelquefois.* 13. *Réussir.* 14. *Signer.* 15. *Protéger.*

THEME 51.

1. A thoughtless[1] man knows nothing, though he have read a great many books; in the same manner a great many persons[2] re-

main ignorant, though they have travelled through the most civilized countries. 2. She will forgive you, provided you make her an apology.[3] 3. If somebody comes, and I am not at home, send for me. 4. I shall be obliged[4] to do it. 5. We should be obliged to do it. 6. I feared you would have complained of me. 7. Our cousin set out without our knowing (w. that we knew) [of] his intentions. 8. I do not believe he has studied history. 9. Do you think they would refuse me, if I requested it of them (*si je les en priais*)? 10. May all nations be convinced[5] of this truth! 11. I do not think he is so old. 12. Get in[6] without his seeing you (w. that he s. y.). 13. Go gently,[7] lest he should hear you. 14. Make haste,[8] lest they should set off without you. 15. I do not deny that it may be so. 16. We do not fear that it will give you pain.[9] 17. Do not let[10] that child ride this horse; I am afraid he will throw[11] him off. 18. We ought to practise what the gospel[12] teaches us. 19. Shall[4] I read the letter aloud? 20. Yes, if you please. 21. I doubt whether the young man would have succeeded, *had it not been for*[13] your assistance.

1. *Insouciant.* 2. *Gens.* 3. *Vos excuses.* 4. *Falloir.* 5. To be convinced, *se convaincre.* 6. *Entrez.* 7. *Doucement.* 8. *Dépêchez-vous.* 9. *Faire de la peine.* 10. *Permettre.* 11. *Jeter à bas.* 12. *L'évangile*, m. 13. *Sans*, see p. 300.

READING LESSON.

ALEXANDRE SELKIRK.

(Suite.)

"Abandonné sur cette île déserte avec mes habits, un lit, un fusil,[1] une livre de poudre, des balles, du tabac, une hache, un couteau, un chaudron,[2] une bible et quelques autres livres; je m'amusai et pourvus[3] à mes besoins[4] le mieux qu'il me fut possible. Mais durant les premiers huit mois j'eus beaucoup de peine à vaincre la mélancolie et à surmonter l'horreur que me causait une si affreuse solitude.

"Je fis deux cabanes[5] à quelque distance l'une de l'autre, avec du bois de piment;[6] je les couvris d'une espèce de jonc[7] et les doublai[8] de peaux de chèvres que je tuais à mesure que j'en avais besoin, tant que ma poudre dura. Lorsqu'elle approchait de sa fin, je trouvai le secret de tirer du feu avec deux morceaux de bois que je frottais[9] l'un contre l'autre. Je faisais la cuisine[10] dans la plus petite de mes huttes, et dans la grande je dormais, chantais des psaumes et priais Dieu. Le malheur m'avait fait connaître le prix de la religion.

"Accablé de tristesse, manquant de pain et de sel, je ne mangeais qu'à l'extrémité, lorsque la faim me pressait, et je n'allais me coucher que lorsque je ne pouvais plus soutenir la veille.[11] Le bois de piment me servait à cuire la viande, et à m'éclairer, et son odeur[12] aromatique récréait[13] mes esprits abattus.

"Je ne manquais pas de poissons, mais je n'osais en manger sans sel, parce qu'ils m'incommodaient, à la réserve[14] des écrevisses de rivière, qui sont ici d'un goût exquis, et aussi grosses que celles de mer. Tantôt je les mangeais bouillies, et tantôt grillées,[15] de même que la chair des chèvres, qui n'a pas le goût si fort que celle des nôtres, et qui donne un excellent bouillon.[16] J'en avais tué jusqu'à cinq cents. Quand ma poudre fut finie, je les prenais à la course. Par un exercice continuel je m'étais rendu si agile que je courais à travers les bois, sur les rochers et les collines avec une vitesse incroyable. Peu s'en fallut un jour que mon agilité ne me coûtât la vie. Je poursuivais une chèvre avec tant d'ardeur que je la pris sur le bord d'un précipice que des buissons[17] me cachaient, et je culbutai[18] de haut en bas avec elle. Cette chute[19] terrible me fit perdre toute connaissance. Enfin revenu à moi-même, je trouvai la chèvre morte sous moi, et j'eus assez de peine à me traîner[20] à ma cabane, qui en était à un mille,[21] et à en sortir au bout de dix jours."

(*To be continued.*)

1. Gun. 2. Kettle. 3. From *pourvoir*, to provide. 4. Need, want. 5. Hut. 6. Pimenta. 7. Rush. 8. To line. 9. To rub. 10. To cook. 11. Watch, watching. 12. Smell. 13. To revive. 14. Exception. 15. Broiled. 16. Broth. 17. Bushes. 18. To tumble. 19. Fall. 20. To drag. 21. A mile.

QUESTIONNAIRE.

Quels effets (*things*) lui avait-on laissés ?
N'avait-il pas de nourriture spirituelle ?
Quel fut le premier soin de Selkirk ?
De quoi couvrit-il les cabanes ?
D'où tira-t-il ces peaux ?
Est-ce qu'il priait aussi Dieu ?
Avait-il de quoi faire du pain ?
Que mangeait-il donc ?
N'avait-il pas de poisson ?
N'y avait-il pas d'écrevisses ?
Comment les mangeait-il ?
Eut-il toujours assez de poudre ?
Comment prenait-il alors les chèvres ?
Etait-il donc si agile ?
N'eut-il pas d'accident fâcheux ?
N'avait-il pas remarqué le précipice ?
Se blessa-t-il par suite de cette chute ?
Quand il revint à lui, dans quel état se trouvait-il ?

XX. VINGTIÈME LEÇON.

THE INFINITIVE.

1. The Infinitive sometimes takes the place of a noun. It is used as the subject of a sentence, where in English the Part. Pres. is often found. Ex.: —

Secourir les pauvres est une action louable.
To relieve the poor is a praiseworthy action.
Médire est une infamie.
Calumniating is shameful.

NOTE 1. In some instances it becomes properly a noun and takes the article with it, as: *le manger, le boire, les vivres* (victuals). If such an Infinitive is amplified by means of other words, it is better to write *c'est* or *c'était* instead of *est* or *était*, and sometimes also *voilà*. Ex.: —

N'aimer que soi, c'est aimer peu de chose.
To love no one but one's self is to love very little.

NOTE 2. When this amplification is somewhat long, the Infinitive cannot remain at the beginning of the sentence, but must be placed after the the predicate, and takes *de* before it. In order, however, not to confuse the sense and the construction of the sentence, *ce* or *il* is employed as a merely introductory subject; *ce*, if a substantive follows, *il*, if an adjective. Examples: —

C'est un honneur d'être utile à sa patrie.
Il est glorieux de mourir pour sa patrie.

NOTE 3. If this antecedent predicate have several or long amplifications the subject-infinitive is commonly introduced by an expletive *que*. Ex.: —

C'était une grand nouveauté pour le roi que d'entendre parler si naturellement.

2. Where two imperatives are connected in English by *and*, if the first is a verb of motion the second must be translated in French by the Infinitive, and the conjunction omitted. Ex.: —

Go and see my brother, *allez voir mon frère.*
Go and do it, *Allez le faire.*

3. A verb immediately preceded by and depending on another verb (auxiliaries excepted), or following a preposition, other than *en*, must be put in the Infinitive: —

Je vous le ferai savoir, sans être pressé.

4. *Comment*, how; *que*, what; *où*, where; *pourquoi*, why, and a few other words similarly used in interrogations, are often followed by the Infinitive instead of the Indicative, when the sense will not thereby be rendered obscure. Thus "*Pourquoi aller?*" may mean "Why do you go?" "*Que faire?*" "What is to be done?" "*Que dire?*" "What shall I say?"

5. The Infinitive without a preposition is used in French after

verbs of motion, as: *aller*, *envoyer*, *etc.;* after verbs that denote a perception of the senses, as: *entendre*, *sentir*, *voir*, *etc.*, and after the following verbs: —

Affirmer, to affirm.
assurer, to assure.
avouer, to confess.
compter, to reckon, intend.
croire, to believe.
daigner, to deign.
déclarer, to declare.
désirer,* to wish.
devoir, to be obliged.
dire, to say.
espérer,* to hope.
faillir, to miss.
faire, to do.
falloir (*il faut*), it must.
s'imaginer,* to imagine.
jurer, to swear.
laisser, to let, to permit.
nier, to deny.
oser, to dare.
paraître, to appear.
penser, to think.
prétendre, to pretend.
pouvoir, to be able.
reconnaître, to acknowledge.
savoir, to know.
sembler, to appear, to seem.
souhaiter,* to wish.
soutenir, to maintain.
témoigner, to testify.
vouloir, to be willing.

Examples: —

Venez nous voir demain.
Come and see us to-morrow.

Je cours lui apprendre cette nouvelle.
I hasten to tell him this news.

Il faut envoyer chercher le médecin.
We must send for the doctor.

Vous osez, — daignez, — désirez, etc. lui parler!
You dare, — deign, — wish, etc. to speak to him!

Je croyais —, je désirais, etc. lui rendre un service.
I thought —, I wished —, etc. to render him a service.

Je compte —, j'espère, etc. aller à Paris.
I intend —, I hope, etc. to go to Paris.

Je ne sais pas nager.
I cannot swim.

Croyez-vous avoir raison?
Do you believe you are in the right?

Je l'entends venir.
I hear him coming.

Note 1. After the above four verbs marked,* *de* is sometimes used, especially when they themselves stand in the Infinitive. Ex.: —

Peut-on espérer de vous voir demain?
Personne ne doit s'imaginer de tout savoir.

Note 2. The verb *faire* is used for *to do, to make* and *to get, to cause*; in all these cases it is immediately followed, in French, by the Infinitive *active* without a preposition: —

Je ferai bâtir une maison.
I will cause a house to be built.

Voulez-vous faire laver vos gants?
Will you have your gloves washed?

Je lui ferai faire un thème.
I will make him write an exercise.

6. The simple Infinitive is governed further by the verbs: *aimer*,* when used in the Conditional, I should like; *préférer*, to prefer; *aimer autant*, to like as much; *il vaut mieux*, it is better. Examples: —

J'aimerais le voir, I should like to see him.
Il vaut mieux céder, it is better to yield.
Je préfère rester à la maison, I prefer staying at home.

Note. When, however, in the second member of a comparison a second Infinitive follows *que*, this latter takes *de* before it. Ex.: —

J'aime mieux mourir que de trahir mon secret.
I will rather die than betray my secret.

7. The Infinitive is used after every preposition except *en*. Examples: —

Au lieu de jouer, instead of playing.
Sans aller, without going.
Pour voir, for the purpose of seeing.

THEME 52.

1. To speak too much is dangerous. 2. To clothe[1] the poor is a good work.[2] 3. To lie is to disregard[3] God and to fear men. 4. To purchase peace of an enemy is to give him the means of carry-

* In regard to *aimer* with *à* consult § 15 of this lesson.

ing on[4] war. 5. Can you inform me whether the courier has arrived? 6. He has not yet arrived. 7. One must know [how] to keep[5] a secret. 8. This man thinks he knows (*Inf.*) everything. 9. We hope to see the queen. 10. When do you intend to return? 11. I do not know precisely;[6] but I hope to see you again soon. 12. The king caused the brave soldiers to be rewarded. 13. It is much better to keep silent[7] than to say such things. 14. The most unfortunate of men is he who thinks himself to be such (*l'*). 15. He assured us that he had been there. 16. To yield[8] to necessity is not to be [a] coward.[9] 17. Eating, drinking, and sleeping were his only occupations. 18. I hastened to communicate[10] to him this intelligence.[11] 19. He came to tell me that he had won nothing in the lottery. 20. Who would not rather (like to) be poor than possess unjustly acquired wealth?[12] 21. Bayard said to the Constable de Bourbon: "It is better to perish fighting (*en combattant*) for one's (*sa*) country,[13] than to conquer and (to) triumph[14] over it (*d'elle*).

1. *Vêtir.* 2. *Œuvre*, f. 3. *Mépriser.* 4. *Continuer.* 5. *Taire.* 6. *Au juste.* 7. *Se taire.* 8. *Céder à.* 9. *Lâche.* 10. *Communiquer.* 11. *Nouvelle*, f. 12. *Des richesses mal acquises.* 13. *Patrie.* 14. *Triompher.*

THE INFINITIVE PRECEDED BY *DE*.

8. After a substantive which the verb limits, the English preposition *of* with a Pres. Participle (of going, of seeing, etc.) is generally expressed by *de* with the Infinitive. Ex.: —

Le désir de vous voir, the desire of seeing you.
Sa manière de penser et d'agir (of thinking and acting).
Il est temps de partir, it is time to set out.
J'ai l'honneur de vous saluer.

9. The preposition *de* is placed before a verb in the Infinitive, after the adjectives: *avide, content, mécontent, las, digne, capable, incapable, etc.*, and in general after an adjective, whenever, by inverting the sentence, the clause containing the Infinitive might

be made the leading term of an assertion expressed as subject to some tense of *to be.* Ex.:—

Je suis curieux de savoir.
I am anxious to know.
Etes-vous las de travailler?
Are you tired with working?
Cet homme est capable de vous tromper.
That man is capable of deceiving you.
Vous êtes très-adroit d'avoir si bien réussi.
You are very clever to have succeeded so well.

10. *De* is used before the Infinitive after impersonal verbs, such as: *il convient*, it is proper; *il importe*, it concerns; *il s'agit*, it is the question; *il suffit*, it is enough; *il me tarde*, I long, and after *il est*, *il était* or *it semble* followed by an adjective, as: *il est facile*, *il était nécessaire*, *etc.* Ex.:—

Il m'importe beaucoup de lui dire cela.
It concerns me much to tell him this.
Il est beau de pardonner à son ennemi.
It is a good thing to pardon one's enemy.
Il suffira de lui parler.
It will be enough to speak to him.

11. *De* is used after *que*, than, in a comparison of predicates. See Note, § 6, of this lesson.

THEME 53.

1. You have no cause[1] to be angry with (*contre*) me. 2. Were you at the concert yesterday? 3. I did not have the pleasure of seeing you. 4. The way[2] to be happy is to be virtuous. 5. Have you the intention of selling your horse? 6. Not at all; I intend to keep it. 7. I fear losing (to lose) your confidence.[3] 8. It is too late; it is time to go to bed. 9. The art of dancing was known to the ancients. 10. It is disgraceful[4] to obey (*à*) one's passions. 11. The desire of appearing clever often prevents one becoming so.[5] 12. We rejoice greatly to see you. 13. It is agreeable to hear the twitter[6] of the birds. 14. It is useless to warn[7] him. 15. It is a

beautiful thing to forgive one's enemies. 16. It is pleasant to live with one's friends. 17. It is the fate[8] of all human things to be of short duration.[9] 18. The great secret of being happy is to work and to be virtuous. 19. I don't approve [of] your project of going to Europe. 20. Gentleness[10] is the surest means of escaping every offence. 21. It is sad to have no friends and to be forsaken.[11]

1. *Avoir sujet.* 2. *Le moyen.* 3. *Confiance,* f. 4. *Honteux.* 5. *De le devenir.* 6. *Le gazouillement.* 7. *Avertir.* 8. *Le sort.* 9. *De n'avoir qu'une courte durée.* 10. *La douceur.* 11. *Abandonné.*

12. *De* is further used before the Infinitive, when the latter is immediately preceded by any of the following verbs: —

Abstenir (s'), to abstain.
accuser, to accuse.
achever, to finish.
affecter, to affect.
agir (s') (unip.), to be the question.
ambitionner, to aspire to.
appartenir, to pertain, to become.
applaudir (s'), to rejoice, exult.
appréhender, to apprehend.
avertir, to warn.
aviser (s'), to determine.
blâmer, to blame.
brûler, to wish ardently.
censurer, to censure.
cesser, to cease.
chagriner (se), to grieve.
charger, to commission.
choisir, to choose.
commander, to command.
conjurer, to entreat.
conseiller, to advise.
convenir, to become, to suit.
convaincre, to convince.
corriger, to correct.
craindre, to fear.
décourager, to discourage.
dédaigner, to disdain, scorn.
défendre, to forbid.
défendre (se), to decline.
défier, to challenge.
dépêcher (se), to hasten.
désaccoutumer (se), } to leave off.
déshabituer (se), }
désespérer, to despair.
désirer, to desire. *De* is often omitted after this verb.
désoler (se), to be grieved.
détester, to detest. *De* may be omitted.
détourner, to dissuade.
devoir (se), to owe it to one's self.
différer, to put off.
dire, to tell.
disconvenir, to disown, deny.
discontinuer, to discontinue.
disculper, to exculpate.
dispenser, to excuse from.
dispenser (se), to forbear.
dissuader, to dissuade.
douter, to doubt.
écrire, to write.
efforcer (s'), to endeavor.
effrayer (s'), to be frightened.
empêcher, to hinder.
empresser (s'), to hasten.
enrager, to be enraged.

entreprendre, to undertake.
épouvanter (s'), to be frightened.
essayer, to try.
étonner (s'), to wonder.
éviter, to avoid.
excuser (s'), to excuse one's self.
feindre, to feign.
féliciter, to congratulate.
finir, to finish.
flatter (se), to flatter one's self.
frémir, to shudder.
garder (se), to take care.
gemir, to moan, lament.
glorifier (se), to pride one's self.
hasarder, to hazard, to risk; *se hasarder* requires *à*.
hâter (se), to hasten.
imputer, to impute.
indigner (s'), to be indignant.
ingérer (s'), to intermeddle.
inspirer, to inspire.
jurer, to swear.
manquer, to fail.
méditer, to contemplate.
mêler (se), to concern one's self.
menacer, to threaten.
mériter, to deserve.
moquer (se), to laugh at.
mourir (fig.), to long.
négliger, to neglect.
nier, to deny.
offrir, to offer.
omettre, to omit.
ordonner, to order.
oublier, to forget.
pardonner, to forgive.
parler, to speak.
passer (se), to do without.
permettre, to permit.
persuader, to persuade.
piquer (se), to take pride in.
plaindre, to pity.
plaindre (se), to complain.
prescrire, to prescribe.
presser, to urge.
presser (se), to hasten.
présumer, to presume.
prier, to pray, entreat.
promettre, to promise.
proposer, to propose.
proposer (se), to purpose.
protester, to protest.
punir, to punish.
rassasier (se), to be sated.
rebuter, to discourage.
rebuter (se), to be weary.
recommander, to recommend.
refuser, to refuse.
regretter, to regret.
réjouir (se), to rejoice.
remercier, to thank.
repentir (se), to repent.
reprendre, to censure.
réprimander, to reprimand.
reprocher, to reproach.
reprocher (se), to reproach one's self.
résoudre, to resolve. When active, followed by *de*; passive, by *à*.
ressouvenir (se), to remember.
rire, to laugh.
risquer, to venture.
seoir, to be becoming.
rougir, to blush.
scandaliser (se), to take offence.
sommer, to summon.
souffrir, to suffer.
souhaiter, to wish. *De* may be suppressed.
soupçonner, to suspect.
souvenir (se), to remember.
suffire (unip.), to suffice.
suggérer, to suggest.
supplier, to beseech.
tâcher, to endeavor.

tarder, (unip.), to long.
tenter, to attempt.
trembler, to tremble.
se trouver bien, to derive benefit.
se trouver mal, to fare ill.
vanter (se), to boast.

EXAMPLES.

Il cesse de pleuvoir, it ceases raining.
Je vous conseille de partir, I advise you to set out.
Je crains de vous déranger, I fear to disturb you.
Il est défendu de fumer ici, smoking is forbidden here.
Dites-lui de venir, tell him to come.
Vous méritez d'être puni, you deserve to be punished.
Il risque de tout perdre, he risks losing everything.
La forteresse fut sommée de se rendre, the fortress was summoned to surrender.

13. After the following prepositions and conjunctions:—*près*, *hors*, *avant*, *au lieu*, *loin*, *afin*, *à moins*, *de crainte*, or *de peur*, *à force* (by) *faute* (for want of), *plutôt que* (rather than). Ex.:—

Avant de partir, before departing.
Au lieu de pleurer, instead of crying.
Loin de se corriger, far from amending himself.
A force de prier, by much entreaty.
Dieu nous afflige afin de nous corriger, God sends us afflictions (in order) to amend us.
Je sors, de crainte (or *de peur*) *de vous déranger*, I go for fear of disturbing you.

THEME 54.

1. I advise you to stay here and (to) begin your studies. 2. I beg you to come at six o'clock. 3. The first step[1] towards good (*vers le bien*) is to avoid evil. 4. It is (*c'est*) the duty of a Christian[2] to please God, to hurt nobody, and to do good, even to his enemies. 5. He is not able to go so far. 6. You are very amiable in having come to pay[3] us a visit. 7. It is dangerous to trust[4] everybody. 8. The law of nature forbids us to do injustice (*tort*) to others. 9. A simple and temperate diet[5] lays the foundation[6] of firm health, [which is] capable of enduring[7] the greatest hardships.[8] 10. I cannot help[9] recognizing in the laws of nature a wonderful

art; and I hesitate not to say, in the language of Scripture,[10] that every star hasteneth[11] to go whither the Lord sendeth it.

1. *Le pas.* 2. *Chrétien.* 3. *Faire.* 4. *Se fier à.* 5. *Nourriture.* 6. *Prépare.* 7. *Supporter.* 8. *Les fatigues.* 9. *M'empêcher.* 10. *L'Ecriture Sainte.* 11. *Se dépêcher.*

THEME 55.

1. I was astonished, after such news, to see the man so quiet. 2. Before one writes (*Inf.*), one must know what one wishes to say. 3. Instead of working, he went to walk that day. 4. I longed[1] to see my native country[2] again; accordingly[3] I determined to embark[4] for Europe. 5. By much entreaty, I induced[5] my friend to accompany me. 6. For fear of offending him, I preferred to remain[6] silent. 7. The enemy retired,[7] in order[8] to make believe that he had given over[9] the siege. 8. When one advised Philip to expel[10] from his dominions[11] a man who had spoken ill of him; "I will take care[12] [not] to do it," replied Philip; "he would go everywhere and speak ill of me."

1. *Il me tardait.* 2. *Pays natal.* 3. *C'est pourquoi.* 4. *S'embarquer pour.* 5. *Engager à.* 6. *Me taire.* 7. Reflective verb. 8. *Afin de.* 9. *Renoncer à.* 10. *Chasser.* 11. *Etat.* 12. *Se garder bien.*

THE INFINITIVE WITH *à*.

We place the preposition *à* before the Infinitive of a verb:—

14. When the English Infinitive is passive, or can be changed to the passive without altering the sense. Ex.:—

La moisson à espérer, the harvest to be hoped for.
Cette maison est à vendre, this house is to be sold.
Je n'ai pas de temps à perdre, I have no time to lose.

15. After a substantive, when the following verb is or may be expressed by *in* with the Pres. Part. Ex.:—

J'aurai beaucoup de plaisir à vous voir.
I shall have great pleasure in seeing you.

16. After any adjectives which take a verb in the Infinitive to complete the sense, provided the verb preceding the adjective is not used impersonally. Especially after:—

Accessible, accessible.
aisé, easy.
attentif, attentive.
bon, good.
disposé, disposed, inclined.
difficile, difficult, hard.
docile, obedient.
habile, skilful.
facile, easy.
lent, slow.
prêt, ready.
prompt, quick.
propre, fit, proper.
sensible, sensible.
sourd, deaf.
utile, useful.
inutile, useless.
(See also L. VIII., Gov. of Adj.)

EXAMPLES.

Cette leçon est facile à apprendre, this lesson is easy to learn.

Ce fruit n'est pas bon à manger, this fruit is not good to eat.

Ce thème est-il difficile à traduire? is this exercise hard to translate?

Nous sommes disposés à croire que, etc., we are disposed (inclined) to believe that, etc.

Soyez prompts à faire le bien, be quick to do good.

NOTE. Compare the following sentences, in which the verb preceding the adjective is used impersonally (see L. XX., § 10). Ex.: —

Il n'est pas facile de prononcer ce mot, it is not easy to pronounce that word.

Il est difficile de vaincre ses passions, it is difficult to conquer one's passions.

Il semble difficile d'apprendre cette langue, it seems difficult to learn that language.

The other way would be: —

Ce mot n'est pas facile à prononcer.

Cette langue paraît difficile à apprendre, etc.

THEME 56.

1. This wood is to be sold. 2. These rooms are to let. 3. We have not a moment to lose. 4. There is much pleasure in taking a a walk. 5. Is this house to sell or to let? 6. It is to let. 7. I perceived in him a kind[1] of repugnancy to learn Greek.[2] 8. You know his courage in facing[3] dangers. 9. This girl spends all her time in playing. 10. There is more glory in dying like Nelson than in living in unmerited[4] honor. 11. Is German easy to learn? 12. It is not so easy as French. 13. That is easy to say, but not so easy to do. 14. That forest[5] is dangerous to pass. 15. I am ready to follow you, but I fear that you are not fit to guide[6] us.

16. Be attentive to seize the opportunity.[7] 17. The just man is slow to punish but quick to reward. 18. Are you disposed to do what I tell you? 19. I shall be quick to perform what you command me.

1. *Une sorte de répugnance.* 2. *Le Grec.* 3. *Affronter.* 4. *Au sein des honneurs qu'on n'a pas mérités.* 5. *Forêt,* f. 6. *Guider, conduire.* 7. *L'occasion.*

---

17. The following verbs also govern the Infinitive with *à*: —

Abaisser(s'), to stoop.
aboutir, to end in.
accorder(s'), to agree, to coincide.
accoutumer, to accustom.
acharner(s'), to strive furiously.
admettre, to admit, to permit.
aguerrir(s'), to become inured.
aider, to help.
aimer, to like (v. L. XX., § 6).
amuser(s'), to amuse one's self with.
animer, to animate, to incite.
appliquer(s'), to apply one's self.
apprendre, to learn, to teach.
apprêter(s'), to prepare.
aspirer, to aspire.
assigner, to assign, to summon.
assujettir(s'), to subject one's self to.
attacher(s'), to strive.
attendre(s'), to rely upon, expect.
attendre, to put off, delay.
augmenter(s'), to increase.
autoriser, to authorize.
aviler(s'), to debase one's self.
avoir, to have.
balancer, to hesitate.
borner(se), to confine one's self to.
chercher, to seek.
complaire(se), to delight in.
concourir, to concur.
condamner, to condemn : also the ref.
condescendre, to condescend.
consentir, to consent.
consister, to consist.
conspirer, to conspire.
consumer, to consume.
contribuer, to contribute.
convier, to invite. Sometimes followed by *de*.
coûter, to cost. When used impersonally it is followed by *de*.
décider, to decide.
déterminer, to determine.
déterminer(se), to resolve.
disposer, to dispose.
disposer(se), to prepare one's self.
divertir(se), to amuse one's self.
donner, to give.
employer, to employ.
encourager, to encourage.
engager, to induce.
enhardir, to embolden.
enseigner, to teach.
entendre(s'), to be skilful, to be a judge.
entreprendre, to undertake.
essayer(s'), to attempt.
étonner(s'), to wonder.
être, to be.
étudier(s'), to make it one's study.
évertuer(se), to strive (may be followed by *pour*).
exceller, to excel.

exciter, to excite.
exercer(s'), to practice.
exhorter, to exhort.
exposer(s') to expose one's self.
haïr, to hate.
habituer(s'), to become used to.
hasarder(se), to venture.
hésiter, to hesitate.
induire, to induce.
instruire, to instruct.
intéresser, to interest.
inviter, to invite.
mettre, to set, to put.
mettre(se), to begin.
montrer, to show, to teach.
obstiner(s'), to persist in.
offrir(s'), to offer one's services.
opiniâtrer(s') to insist upon.
parvenir, to succeed in.
passer, to spend (time, etc.).
pencher, to incline.
penser, to think, to intend.
persévérer, to persevere.
persister, to persist.
plaire(se), to delight in.
plier(se), to bend, bow, comply.
porter, to induce.
pousser, to urge, compel.
prendre plaiser, to take pleasure.
préparer(se), to prepare.
prétendre, to lay claim, to sue. When signifying *to mean, to intend*, it governs the infinitive without a preposition.
provoquer, to provoke.
réduire, to constrain.
réduire(se), to be reduced.
renoncer, to renounce.
répugner, to be repugnant.
résigner(se), to be resigned.
résoudre(se), to resolve.
rester, to remain. Also used imp.
réussir, to succeed.
risquer, to risk.
servir, to serve.
songer, to dream, think, purpose.
suffire, to suffice. May be followed by *pour*. When used impersonally, is followed by *de*.
tarder, to defer, to delay.
tendre, to tend, to intend, to aim.
tenir, to be anxious, desirous.
travailler, to labor.
viser, to aim.
vouer, to devote.

Examples: —

J'aime à danser, I like to dance.
Mon fils apprend à chanter, my son learns to sing.
Je vous autorise à vendre mon jardin.
I authorize you to sell my garden.
Notre bonheur consiste à vivre suivant la nature.
Our happiness consists in living according to nature.
On m'a invité à faire une promenade.
I have been invited to take a walk.

18. The Infinitive preceded by *à* is idiomatically used after the verb *être* to translate the English *progressive* forms, such as: *I am*

singing, I was writing, etc. The French *Je suis à chanter, J'étais à écrire*, are, however, not so much used as the English participial inflections, which are generally rendered by the simple verb *Je chante, j'écrivais, etc.*

19. The Infinitive with *à* also occurs in abbreviated expressions which in reality are simply contracted subordinate sentences. Examples: —

A l'entendre, on dirait qu'il est innocent.
To hear him, one would say he is innocent.

A vous voir, on croirait . . .
To see you, one would think . . .

Il était le premier à se jeter sur l'ennemi.
He was the first to throw, i. e. who threw himself on the enemy.

Je ne suis pas homme à me laisser offenser
I am not the man to allow myself to be offended.

Je me plaçai de manière à pouvoir tout observer.
I placed myself in such a posture as to observe everything.

20. Verbs with *à* or *de*. The following verbs require either *à* or *de*, according to the sense in which they are employed: —

1. *Commencer*, to begin, is generally followed by *à*. Ex.: —

On a commencé à jouer, they have begun to play.

But if it exprèsses simply a fact without any idea of continuation, *de* is used after it: —

Puisque j'ai commencé de rompre le silence.
Since I have begun to break the silence.

2. *Continuer à* denotes an uninterrupted continuation of the action. Example: —

Si vous continuez à travailler si fort, vous ruinerez votre santé.
If you continue to work so much you will ruin your health.

Continuer de denotes an action repeated, but after successive interruptions. Ex.: —

Mon ami continuait de m'écrire.
My friend continued to write to me.

3. *Défier* requires *à* when it means *to challenge, to provoke* (to a competition), and *de* when it means *to set at defiance*, or, defy to do something.

4. *S'efforcer*, synonymous with *faire des efforts*, to exert one's self, to take pains, takes *à*. Ex.:—

Il s'efforçait à faire son devoir.
He took pains (exerted himself) to do his duty.

S'efforcer de means to endeavor. Ex.:—

Je m'efforcerai d'obtenir cette place.
I shall endeavor to get that place.

5. *Être*, to be, when joined to *ce*, is followed by *à* if it denotes *turn*, and by *de*, if it denotes *duty* or *right*, as:—

C'est à vous à parler, it is your turn to speak.
C'est au maître d'ordonner, c'est à moi d'obéir.
It is for the master to command, it is for me to obey.

6. *Laisser*, to leave, meaning *to transmit*, is followed by *à;* meaning *to cease* or *abstain*, by *de;* and when used in the sense of *to permit* (*to let*), it governs the next verb without a preposition.

7. *Manquer à* denotes the omission or neglect of a duty:—

Pourquoi avez-vous manqué à faire votre exercice?
Why have you neglected to do your exercise?

Manquer de signifies to fail, to be on the point of:—

J'ai manqué de perdre la vie, I had nearly lost my life.

8. *S'occuper* takes *à* in the sense of to employ one's time, to work at. Examples:—

Il s'occupe à lire, he occupies himself with reading.
L'auteur de "Paul et Virginie" s'occupait à recueillir les matériaux de cet ouvrage.
The author of "Paul and Virginia" occupied himself in collecting the materials of this work.

S'occuper de signifies *mettre ses soins*, to pay attention to, to think much of. Ex.:—

Il s'occupe de détruire les abus.
He is thinking how to abolish abuses.

9. *Venir* governs the Infinitive with *à*, when it signifies to happen. Example:—

S'il venait à apprendre que vous êtes ici.
If he happened to know that you are here.

Venir is followed by *de*, when it is used to express a thing just happened (see P. I., L. XLVII.). Ex.:—

Mes sœurs viennent de sortir.
My sisters have just gone out.

10. *Tarder à* signifies to delay. Ex.: —

Ne tardez pas à lui envoyer de l'argent.
Do not delay sending him some money.

Tarder, as an impersonal verb: *il me tarde,* I long, governs the Infinitive with *de.* Ex.: —

Il me tarde de le revoir, I long to see him again.

21. The following eleven verbs may take either *à* or *de*: —

Consentir, to consent.
contraindre, to compel.
demander, to demand.
forcer, to force.
s'empresser, to be eager.
s'engager, to engage, agree.
s'entêter, to be obstinate in.
essayer, to try.
obliger, to oblige.
oublier, to forget.
tâcher, to try.

Examples: —

Il ne demande qu'à manger et à boire.
He demands nothing but to eat and drink.

Elle demanda au ciel de lui pardonner sa faute.
She prayed to heaven to forgive her fault.

Le banquier s'engagea à (or *de*) *payer la somme de mille francs.*
The banker agreed to pay the sum of a thousand francs.

THEME 57.

1. When the captain began to speak, all the soldiers listened[1] attentively. 2. In the spring the trees begin to cover themselves with leaves. 3. They continued to live in peace. 4. We have continued to write to him, but he has not yet answered us. 5. The unfortunate never fail to complain. 6. I have failed to do what I had promised you. 7. I will endeavor to satisfy him. 8. It is long before he comes (he delays to come). 9. I long to have finished my work. 10. At last I longed (*il me tarda*) to see again my native country. 11. That woman is occupied only with ironing.[2] 12. Do not fail to be here at a quarter to six. 13. Come [and] see us this evening. 14. Is your brother at home? 15. No,

he has just gone out. 16. We have just received your letter. 17. He agreed to inform you of the result.[3]

1. *Écouter*. 2. *Repasser*. 3. *Résultat*.

INFINITIVE WITH THE PREPOSITIONS *POUR, PAR, APRES, SANS*.

22. *Pour*. Whenever the English *to* before an Infinitive expresses a *design* or *purpose*, and can be changed into, in order to, *pour* must be used. Ex.: —

Il attend de l'argent pour payer ses dettes.
He is expecting money to pay his debts.

J'ai fait mon possible pour les réconcilier.
I have done all in my power to reconcile them.

Je l'ai fait moi-même pour ne pas vous déranger.
I did it myself not to disturb you.

23. The proposition *pour* is also used after the adjective following *assez*, *trop*, *suffisant*, or after the verb *suffire*. Ex.: —

M. R. est assez riche pour acheter cette campagne.
Mr. R. is rich enough to buy that estate.

Caroline est trop jeune pour faire cet ouvrage.
Caroline is too young to do this work.

24. The French usage differs from the English in employing the Infinitive instead of a separate clause, when the dependent clause has the same subject as the principal clause : —

Je crois être blessé, I think I am wounded.
J'espère mériter votre confiance, I hope I deserve your confidence.
Je voudrais être riche, I wish I were rich.

THEME 58.

1. I travel to see the world. 2. The army was too fatigued to renew[1] the attack. 3. I will do everything to oblige you. 4. God has not given us hearts to hate one another. 5. He is going into the country to shoot.[2] 6. Some people are hated without deserving[3]

it. 7. It is necessary to know the human heart to judge well of others.[4] 8. After having terminated some affairs at home, I shall begin by paying[5] some visits. 9. Nobody can be happy without practising[6] virtue. 10. If the emperor Titus passed one day without doing good[7] to (*à*) anybody, he used[8] to say: "I have lost that day."

1. *Renouveler l'attaque.* 2. *Chasser.* 3. *Mériter.* 4. *Des autres.* 5. *Faire.* 6. *Pratiquer.* 7. *Du bien.* 8. *Il avait coutume.*

READING LESSON.

ALEXANDRE SELKIRK.

(Suite.)

"Une longue habitude me fit manger la viande sans sel et sans pain. Dans la saison j'avais quantité de bons navets[1] qui avaient été semés par l'équipage[2] de quelque vaisseau et qui couvraient plusieurs arpents[3] de terre. Je ne manquais pas non plus d'excellents choux[4] que je cueillais sur une espèce de palmier et que j'assaisonnais avec le fruit du piment, qui est le même que le poivre de la Jamaïque, et dont l'odeur est délicieuse.

"Mes souliers et mes habits furent bientôt usés à force de courir à travers les bois et les broussailles.[5] Cependant mes pieds s'endurcirent[6] si bien à la fatigue, que je courais partout sans peine.

"Revenu[7] enfin de ma mélancolie, je me divertissais quelquefois à graver mon nom sur l'écorce[8] des arbres avec la date de mon exil, ou bien à chanter et à dresser[9] à la danse des chats et des chevreaux. Lorsque je n'eus plus d'habits, je me fis un juste-au-corps[10] et un bonnet (*cap*) de peaux de chèvres que je cousis ensemble avec de petites courroies;[11] un clou[12] me servait d'aiguille. Je me fis aussi des chemises d'un morceau de toile que j'avais. Quand mon couteau fut usé jusqu'au dos, j'en forgeai d'autres avec quelques cercles de fer que j'avais trouvés sur le rivage, et je les aiguisai[13] sur des pierres.

"C'est ainsi que la nécessité m'apprit à pourvoir à tous mes besoins."

"Pendant mon séjour[14] dans cette île déserte, j'ai vu plusieurs fois des vaisseaux qui passaient, mais il n'y en eut que deux qui vinrent y mouiller.[15] Incertain de quelle nation ils étaient, je m'en approchai pour les examiner. Mais quelques Espagnols qui avaient déjà mis pied à terre, ne m'eurent pas plutôt aperçu qu'ils tirèrent[16] sur moi et me poursuivirent jusque dans les bois, où je grimpai sur un arbre. Je ne fus pas découvert, quoiqu'ils rodassent[17] dans les environs et qu'ils tuassent quantité de chèvres sous mes yeux. Enfin j'aperçus vos navires que je pris aussitôt pour anglais. J'allumai un feu sur un rocher près du rivage pour vous donner le signal de ma détresse.[18] Vous me comprîtes et, grâces à votre humanité, je puis espérer de revoir ma patrie."

1. Turnips. 2. The crew. 3. Acre. 4. Cabbage. 5. Brushwood. 6. To harden. 7. Recovered. 8. Bark. 9. To train. 10. Jacket. 11. Strap. 12. A nail. 13. To sharpen. 14. Stay. 15. To anchor. 16. To fire or shoot at. 17. To run about, ramble. 18. Distress.

QUESTIONNAIRE.

Comment mangeait-il la viande ?
N'avait-il pas autre chose à manger ?
Manquait-il de choux ?
Où les cueillait-il ?
Avec quoi assaisonnait-il ses choux ?
Avait-il toujours des souliers et des habits ?
Comment se divertissait-il quelquefois ?
Lorsque ses habits furent usés, que fit Selkirk ?
De quoi se servit-il pour coudre les peaux de chèvres ?
De quoi se fit-il des chemises ?
Quand son couteau fut usé, que fit-il ?
N'a-t-il jamais vu de vaisseaux qui passaient ?
De quelle nation étaient-ils ?
Que firent-ils lorsqu'ils l'eurent aperçu ?
Fut-il découvert ?
Qu'aperçut-il enfin ?
Pourquoi alluma-t-il un feu sur le rivage ?
Ce signal fut-il remarqué ?

XXI. VINGT ET UNIÈME LEÇON.

THE PRESENT PARTICIPLE.

1. The Present Participle is invariable in French. Ex.: —

Une femme mourant de soif.
A woman dying of thirst.
Une preuve convainquant tout le monde.
A proof convincing everybody.
Une mère consolant sa fille.
A mother consoling her daughter.
Une pluie fécondant la terre.
A rain fructifying the earth.

2. When the Present Participle loses its verbal nature and becomes a participial adjective, it follows the noun, and agrees with it as an adjective. Ex.: —

Une femme mourante.
A dying woman.
Une preuve convainquante.
A convincing proof.
Des paroles consolantes.
Consoling words.

3. The Present Participle is often used in English as a substantive, which is not the case in French. It can sometimes be rendered by a noun, in most cases by the Infinitive (see Lesson XX., § 1). Examples: —

La lecture est un passe-temps agréable.
Reading is an agreeable pastime.
Sa passion dominante est la chasse.
His ruling passion is hunting.
I like dancing, *j'aime à danser.*

4. When an English Present Participle has reference to a substantive which is not in the Nominative Case, it is rendered in French

by the Present or Imperfect of the Indicative, with the relative pronoun *qui* before it. Ex.: —

Il portait une bouteille qui contenait du poison.
He carried a bottle containing poison.

5. An English Present Participle preceded by any preposition but *by* and *on* (§ 7), such as, *of*, *from*, *before*, *after*, *for*, *without*, is rendered in French by the Infinitive with *de*, *à*, *pour* or *sans* (as we have seen before). Ex.: —

L'art d'écrire est très-ancien.
The art of writing is very old.
Je connais sa manière de penser et d'agir.
I know his manner of thinking and acting.
Ne l'empêchez pas de faire du bien.
Do not prevent him from doing good.
Je l'ai rencontré avant de partir.
I met him before leaving.
On ne peut pas trahir la vérité sans se rendre coupable.
One cannot speak against the truth without being guilty.

6. Sometimes the English Present Participle is used substantively with a possessive pronoun before it; then it must be rendered in French by the conjunction *que* and the Indicative or Subjunctive, according as the case requires. Ex.: —

Je doute qu'il soit un honnête homme.
I doubt his being an honest man.
Nous avons appris qu'il s'est fait soldat.
We heard of his becoming a soldier.

THEME 59.

1. Miss Mary is an obliging young lady. 2. I listened[1] [to] her encouraging words. 3. He has given us consoling news. 4. These books are very interesting. 5. That mother, in her supplicating[2] attitude, would have appeared touching, even without the surprising eloquence of her discourse. 6. The young soldier, preceding all the others, seized[3] the standard.[4] 7. That mountain, commanding an extensive[5] view, was very well calculated[6] for our observations. 8. Caroline, weeping bitterly,[7] threw herself into her mother's arms.

9. I have seen your brother (§ 4) playing in the garden. 10. Alexander asked the physicians standing[8] by (*autour de*) him if he should die of (*de*) his illness. 11. The soldiers of Alexander, forgetting their wives and children, looked upon[9] the Persian gold as[10] their plunder.[11] 12. It ceased raining. 13. He risked losing his life. 14. I am afraid of losing her confidence. 15. The desire of appearing clever often prevents one from becoming so. 16. He left[12] without paying his debts. 17. I heard of his being (§ 6) married. 18. We noticed[13] his looking at it (*le*). 19. He wrote to me without[14] his father's knowing it.

1. *Écouter qch.* 2. To supplicate, *supplier.* 3. *S'emparer de qch.* 4. *Le drapeau.* 5. *Étendue*, f. 6. *Propre à.* 7. To weep bitterly, *fondre en larmes.* 8. *Se tenir.* 9. To look upon, *regarder qch.* 10. *Comme.* 11. *Butin*, m. 12. *Partir.* 13. *Remarquer.* 14. *Sans que* with the Subj.

THE GERUND,—PRESENT PARTICIPLE WITH *EN*.

7. The Gerund is the Present Participle with the preposition *en* prefixed. It generally denotes 1, either a means by which the object of the leading clause is attained, or 2, a simultaneous action, that is, an action during the transaction of which another is acted by the same subject. It is always invariable, and corresponds to the English Present Participle preceded by the prepositions *by*, *in*, and *on* or *while ; or* is sometimes rendered by the simple Participle without preposition. Ex.:—

1. Denoting a means:—

On se forme l'esprit en lisant de bons livres.
We form our minds by reading good books.
Nous avons obtenu la paix en faisant de grands sacrifices.
We have obtained peace by making great sacrifices.
Il se sauva en sautant par la fenêtre.
He saved himself by jumping through the window.

2. Denoting a simultaneous action:—

La déesse sourit en voyant Télémaque.
The goddess smiled on seeing Telemachus.
Il me dit cela en tremblant.
He trembled as he told me this.

Je l'ai rencontré en allant au château.
I met him in going (as I was going) to the castle.
Je lis le journal en déjeûnant.
I read the paper while breakfasting.

NOTE. The English *by* with a Participle is rendered in two cases only by *par* and the Infinitive, viz., with *commencer*, to commence, begin, and *finir*, to terminate with, to do something at last. Ex.: —

Je veux commencer par réciter ma leçon.
I will begin by saying my lesson.
Il finit par me demander pardon.
At last he begged my pardon (he ended by asking).

8. To enforce the simultaneousness of the two actions, *tout* is often placed before the Gerund. Ex.: —

Tout en pleurant il ne put s'empêcher de rire.
Whilst crying he could not forbear laughing.

THEME 60.

1. We learn the news by reading the newspapers. 2. By observing these rules, you may avoid mistakes. 3. By studying much, you will become learned. 4. More glory is[1] acquired by defending one's fellow-citizens[2] than by accusing them. 5. In going[3] this way we shall meet him. 6. I met my friend as I was going to the post-office. 7. By paying all his debts, he reëstablished[4] his credit. 8. He told me, trembling, that he had lost all his money. 9. You may easily get[5] praise, by complying[6] with the (*aux*) wishes of the people[7] with whom you converse, and by preferring others to yourself.

1. *On acquiert.* 2. *Concitoyen*, m. 3. *Prendre.* 4. *Rétablir.* 5. *Obtenir des louanges.* 6. To comply with, *se conformer à qch.* 7. *Des personnes.*

READING LESSON.

GESLER CONDUIT TELL À KUSNACH.

Tell, dans la barque, était moins ému des cris des soldats, du bruit des vagues écumantes, du sifflement des vents déchaînés, qu'il ne le fut en découvrant la caverne de Grutli. Il attendait le trépas,[1] et ne songeait qu'à l'avantage que son pays pourrait tirer de la mort du gouverneur. Il jouissait en silence de la peur, des gémissements,[2] du tourment qu'éprouvait Gesler, lorsqu'un des rameurs, tout-à-coup s'adressant à cet homme cruel: "Nous sommes perdus," dit-il, "il n'est plus en notre puissance de maintenir au milieu des flots la barque emportée[3] par le vent du nord qui, dans un instant, va la briser en pièces contre les rochers du rivage. Un seul homme, le plus renommé, le plus habile de nos trois cantons dans l'art de braver les tempêtes du lac, peut nous sauver de la mort. Cet homme est ici: le voilà! le voilà chargé de tes chaînes! Choisis, Gesler, choisis promptement entre le trépas ou sa liberté."

Gesler frémit[4] à cette parole. Sa haine violente pour Tell combat dans son âme pusillanime l'amour même qu'il a pour la vie; il hésite encore, il ne répond point, mais les prières, les murmures des soldats et des rameurs qui lui demandent, qui le pressent de sauver leurs jours et les siens, en délivrant[5] son prisonnier; la crainte d'être mal obéi, s'il se refuse aux vœux de tous, et la tempête qui augmente, déterminent enfin Gesler. "Qu'on brise[6] ses chaînes," dit-il, "je lui pardonne tous ses crimes, je lui rends[7] la vie et la liberté, si son adresse nous amène au port."

Les soldats, les rameurs, s'empressent[8] de rendre libre Guillaume. Ses fers sont tombés, il se lève, et, sans prononcer un seul mot, il s'empare du gouvernail.[9] Faisant mouvoir sous sa main la barque, comme l'enfant fait plier la baguette[10] qu'il tourne à son gré, il oppose la proue[11] aux deux vents, dont les forces ainsi divisées la tiennent en équilibre. Profitant ensuite d'un moment de calme, il tourne de la proue à la poupe,[12] maintient la barque dans la direction qui seule peut la sauver, fait prendre les rames à deux seuls rameurs, dont il dirige les efforts, et s'avance, malgré les vents, malgré les flots et la tempête, vers le détroit[13] qu'il veut repasser. Les ténèbres[14] empêchent Gesler de s'apercevoir qu'il retourne aux mêmes lieux d'où il est parti. Tell continue sa marche; la nuit presque entière s'écoule;[15] il est rentré dans le lac d'Uri, il aperçoit la lueur mourante du signal donné sur le mont d'Altdorf. C'est cette lueur[16] qui lui sert d'étoile ; il connaît le lac depuis longtemps, il en évite les écueils,[17] il s'approche pourtant du rivage qui borde le canton de Schwitz ; il pense à Werner Stauffacher ; il calcule que Werner doit être en marche, et que les chemins encombrés de neige, le forceront de côtoyer[18] le lac. Dans ce faible espoir, il navigue, en feignant d'ignorer les lieux où la tempête pousse la barque, en augmentant les terreurs de Gesler et de ses soldats.

(*To be continued.*)

1. Death. 2. Sighs. 3. Carried away. 4. To shudder, tremble. 5. To liberate. 6. To break (see p. 372, § 15). 7. I give. 8. See p. 388, § 9. 9. The helm, rudder. 10. The rod. 11. The prow. 12. The stern. 13. The strait. 14. The darkness. 15. To pass away. 16. Light. 17. Cliff. 18. To follow *or* march along the coast.

QUESTIONNAIRE.

Tell était-il ému de quelque chose ?

Qu'attendait-il ?

A quoi songeait-il ?

De quoi jouissait-il en silence ?

Qu'est-ce qui détermina enfin Gesler à delivrer le prisonnier ?

Que dit alors un des rameurs à Gesler ?

Qui était le batelier le plus habile dans les trois cantons ?

Le rameur nomma-t-il cet homme ?

Entre quoi Gesler avait-il à choisir ?

Quel parti (*decision*) prit-il ?

Que firent les soldats et les rameurs ?

Quand les fers furent ôtés, que fit Tell ?

Quelle manœuvre fit-il après ?

Racontez ce que fit Tell ensuite.

Gesler s'aperçut-il que Tell retournait vers les mêmes lieux d'où ils étaient partis ?

Vers quel lac Tell dirige-t-il la barque ?

De quel rivage s'approche-t-il ?

A qui pense-t-il ?

Que calcule-t-il à son égard ?

Que feint-il ?

XXII. VINGT-DEUXIÈME LEÇON.

THE PAST PARTICIPLE.

Every possible difficulty in regard to the agreement of Past Participle may be solved by the application of one of the three following rules :—

1. The Past Participle, when used adjectively, is placed after the noun and agrees with it as an adjective. Ex.:—

Une fleur flétrie, a withered flower.
Une lettre bien écrite, a well written letter.
Des maisons bien meublées, well furnished houses.

2. The Past Participle accompanied by the auxiliary *être* agrees with the *subject*, except in reflective verbs. Ex.:—

Cette lettre est bien écrite, this letter is well written.
Mes deux tantes sont mortes, both my aunts are dead.
La ville fut prise, the town was taken.
La nuit sera bientôt passée, the night will soon be over.

3. The Past Participle accompanied by the auxiliary *avoir* (and by *être* in reflective verbs) agrees with the *direct object*, but only when that direct object precedes. Ex.:—

La lettre que j'ai reçue.
The letter I have received.

Les lettres que j'ai reçues.
The letters I have received.

Les dames que nous avons rencontrées.
The ladies we have met.

Les affaires que vous avez entreprises.
The affairs you have undertaken.

Où sont les livres?—je les ai perdus.
Where are the books? I have lost them.

Où est ta plume?—je l'ai perdue.
Where is thy pen? I have lost it.

Où sont les fruits que vous m'avez envoyés?
Where are the fruits you sent me?

But there is no agreement in the participle when there is no direct object, or when the direct object comes after the participle. Example: —

J'ai reçu une lettre — deux lettres.
I have received one letter — two letters.

J'ai rencontré une dame — deux dames.
I met one lady — two ladies.

J'ai perdu les livres.
I have lost the books.

J'ai perdu la plume.
I have lost the pen.

Nous avons mangé.
We have eaten.

Ils ont répondu à notre lettre.
They have answered our letter.

Mes frères avaient dormi.
My brothers had slept.

4. In reflective verbs, as *être* takes the place of *avoir*, the participle agrees with the second pronoun, if that is a direct object. Examples: —

Ils se sont presentés.
They presented themselves.

Elle s'est blessée.
She wounded herself.

But when the second pronoun is an indirect object, the participle remains unchanged, unless the direct object precedes, as in verbs conjugated with *avoir*. Ex.: —

Ils se sont presenté des fleurs.
They presented flowers to each other.

Ils se sont ecrit deux lettres.
They wrote a letter to each other.

But the participle must agree if the direct object (*fleurs, lettres*) precedes. Ex.: —

Les fleurs qu'ils se sont presentées.
Les lettres qu'ils se sont écrites.

APPLICATION OF THE ABOVE RULES.

As the application of the above rules may present some difficulty, special rules will be given, though all that follows is really embraced in §§ 2 and 3.

5. The Past Participle of a neuter or intransitive verb conjugated with *avoir* never agrees, when conjugated with *être* it always agrees with the subject. Ex.: —

Les deux heures que j'ai dormi.
The two hours during which I slept; *que* is equivalent to *pendant lesquelles.*

Ils sont tombés, they fell. *Elles sont tombées.*

Hence also the Past Part. *été* is always invariable: *Elle a été*, *Elles ont été*.

6. The Past Participle of an impersonal verb is always invariable, as:

Les pluies qu'il y a eu cet hiver.
The rains we have had this winter.

7. A Past Participle does not agree with *en* (of it, of them, some), because *en* is not considered as a direct object. Ex.: —

Avez-vous des fleurs? — Oui, il nous en a donné.

But the presence of *en* does not prevent the participle from agreeing with the real direct object if that precedes. Ex.:

La bonne opinion que j'en avais conçue.
The good opinion I had conceived of it.

8. A Past Participle between two *que's* is invariable. Ex.: *Les livres que vous avez cru que je vous donnerais*, the books you thought I would give you. The first *que* is not the object of *cru*, but of *donnerais*.

9. The Past Participle followed by an infinitive agrees when the object that precedes is governed by the participle, if the object depends on the infinitive the participle is invariable. Ex.: *La dame que j'ai vue peindre*, the lady I saw painting. *La dame que j'ai vu peindre* means, The lady whom I saw *painted*, that is, whose

portrait I saw taken. *La dame que j'ai entendue chanter*, the lady I heard singing; but, *La chanson que j'ai entendu chanter*, the song I heard sung, — because *que* is governed not by *entendu* but by *chanter*. For the same reason *Je les ai laissés partir*, I allowed them to go; but, *ils se sont laissé surprendre par l'ennemi;* they allowed themselves to be surprised by the enemy. In this last sentence *se* is the object of *surprendre*, as it is equivalent to, They allowed the enemy to surprise THEM.

10. The past Participle of the verb *faire* followed by an infinitive never agrees, because *faire* thus connected with an infinitive is considered for all purposes of government as forming but one verb with it. Thus in *Je le fais passer*, *le* is the object of *faire passer;* in *Je lui fais passer le pont*, *le pont* is the direct object, and *lui* and not *le* must be used, as *faire passer* cannot have *two* direct objects. Hence *fait* is invariable in the phrase: *Une femme s'est présentée à la porte, je l'ai fait passer*, a woman presented herself at the door, I let her pass.

11. After the Past Participles *dû*, *pu*, and *voulu* an infinitive may be understood, in which case they remain invariable, as: *Je lui ai rendu tous les services que j'ai dû . . . que j'ai pu* (that is *lui rendre*), I rendered him all the services I should . . . I could (render him). But, *Les sommes qu'il m'a dues*, the sums he owed me — *dues* agrees with its object *que* which precedes.

12. The Past Participles *attendu*, *excepté*, *passé*, *supposé*, and *vu* are sometimes employed as prepositions. They then precede the noun they govern, and are invariable.

Other instances might be adduced, but a strict application of §§ 1, 2, 3, and 4, will be found to cover all cases of doubt.

THEME 61.

1. She is loved. 2. We are satisfied. 3. My sisters are satisfied. 4. My aunt has arrived. 5. My cousins (*fem.*) have arrived. 6. This house is sold. 7. The two houses are sold. 8. These letters are written very well. 9. My mother has gone out,

and my sisters have also gone out. 10. Mary's grandmother appears afflicted. 11. The trees have been felled.[1] 12. Virtuous people are esteemed, and the impious[2] (are) despised. 13. The rule[3] which I have learned is very easy. 14. The woman I have seen is very handsome. 15. Where is the letter which you have received? 16. Here it is (*la voici*); it is written in (*en*) French. 17. The horses which we have sold were very old. 18. How many horses have you sold? 19. We have sold them all. 20. Which house have you taken?[4] 21. How many books has he bought? 22. Where is my pen? 23. I have not seen it. 24. Where are my sisters? 25. I have not seen them. 26. Here are the apples (which) you have given me; I have not eaten them. 27. The young ladies have been much amused[5] in your company. 28. Gentlemen, you are mistaken.[6] 29. She has repented of her neglectfulness.[7] 30. I saw (*have seen*) them play before my house. 31. The singers[8] whom I heard singing yesterday were Tyrolese.[9]

1. To fell, *couper*. 2. *Impie*. 3. *Règle*, f. 4. *Louer*. 5. *S'amuser*. 6. *Se tromper*. 7. *Négligence*. 8. *Chanteur*, m. 9. *Tyroliens*.

THEME 62.

1. That girl has run too fast; she is out of breath.[1] 2. My aunt has travelled in Italy. 3. His mother (has) lived[2] in this house for (*pendant*) two years. 4. These young men (*gens*) have studied French and German. 5. We (have) met some ladies in the street. 6. Miss Eliza has brought a bunch[3] of flowers. 7. For whom has she brought them? 8. She (has) brought them for you. 9. Have you read these two books? 10. No, sir, I have not yet read them. 11. I have read another book which your brother has lent me. 12. The carpenter[4] has built a new house, and he has sold it this morning to Mr. B. 13. The rain which has fallen this morning has spoiled the roads. 14. We have bought twenty acres[5] of land.[6] 15. The excessive heat which we had[7] last summer has occasioned diseases.[8] 16. There came a person that I did not know. 17. Why are these plants so wet?[9] 18. I (have) ordered[10] them to be

watered.[10] 19. The measures[11] I was obliged[12] to take have not had the expected effect.[13] 20. The landlord[14] caused[15] them to be paid.

1. *Hors d'haleine.* 2. *Demeurer.* 3. *Bouquet.* 4. *Le charpentier.* 5. *Arpent*, m. 6. *Terre.* 7. Put the Comp. Pres. of the impersonal form *il fait.* 8. *Maladie.* 9. *Mouillées.* 10. *Faire arroser.* 11. *Mesure*, f. 12. Part. of *devoir.* 13. *Effet*, m. 14. *L'aubergiste.* 15. *Faire.*

THEME 63.

1. Where is your gold watch? 2. I have sent it to the watchmaker.[1] 3. I thought you had allowed[2] it to be stolen. 4. The two horses which I (have) advised you to buy are worth (*valent*) a thousand francs. 5. Happy the princes who have always used[3] their power[4] for the good[5] of their people. 6. You must (*il faut que vous*) finish the letter which you have begun to write. 7. The apples which I have forbidden you to eat are not ripe. 8. How many men[6] commit the same faults which they had resolved to avoid.[7] 9. We have showed[8] him all the honor (*pl.*) it was our duty [to show him]. 10. My friend rendered me every service[9] he could. 11. Have you bought some cigars?[10] 12. Yes, I have bought [some]. 13. Are not these trees very high? 14. I have seen higher ones. 15. The ship which we saw launched[11] has now the name of Arion. 16. The play[12] I saw performed[13] last night has been very much applauded. 17. Imitate the virtues which you have heard praised (*Inf.*). 18. We used[14] all the means we could.

1. *Horloger.* 2. *Laisser.* 3. *Employer.* 4. *Pouvoir*, m. 5. *Le bien.* 6. *Que d'hommes.* 7. *Eviter.* 8. *Fait.* 9. *Tous les services qu'.* 10. *Cigarre*, m. 11. *Lancer.* 12. *La pièce.* 13. *Jouer.* 14. *Employer.*

XXIII. VINGT-TROISIÈME LEÇON.

THE PARTICIPLE ABSOLUTE.

1. The Participle Absolute is used, as in English, instead of accessory and subordinate clauses beginning with a conjunction which have the same subject as the leading clause. Ex.: —

Régulus s'éloigna de Rome, tenant les yeux fixés à la terre, et laissant sa femme et ses enfants.

L'ennemi, voyant (as he saw) *notre petit nombre, recommença le combat.*

Néoptolème, poursuivant son discours, me dit, etc.

Le charpentier, laissant son ouvrage à moitié fait, alla dîner.

L'empereur Conrade, ne voulant plus tenter la fortune, abandonna subitement la Terre-Sainte, etc.

Ne sachant que faire, il prit ce parti.

2. When the accessory sentence expresses an event which has taken place before another expressed in the principal sentence, the compound form of the Participle Absolute (*ayant vu, ayant fait, etc.*) is used. Ex.: —

Le comte de Toulouse, ayant sommé (having summoned) *la ville de se rendre, la déclara sa possession.*

Le roi ayant tout sacrifié pour le bonheur de son peuple, fut enfin la victime de ses bonnes intentions.

Lysandre ayant fait un riche butin (booty) *dans la prise d'Athènes, envoya à Lacédémone tout l'or et l'argent qu'il avait pris.*

THEME 64.

1. As the two combatants would not yield,[1] they were pierced with wounds.[2] 2. As Mentor heard the voice of the goddess who was calling her nymphs into the wood, he waked[3] Telemachus. 3. Crantor, seeing that I was already very near him, redoubled his zeal, and attempted[4] to barricade my way. 4. That mountain, commanding an extensive[5] view, was well calculated[6] for our observations. 5. I cannot accompany you into the country, having some business that

requires my presence here. 6. How many people do we see, who, knowing the value of time, waste[7] it improperly.[8] 7. Wishing to make something of my son, I have put him into your hands. 8. Newton, having taken the average[9] of years during which the kings of the various[10] countries have reigned, reduced each reign to about twenty-two years. 9. Napoleon, seeing that the battle of Waterloo was lost, drew his sword and wished desperately[11] to fling himself into the tumult of the battle. 10. Franklin, [after] having looked everywhere for employment,[12] reëntered at the printer[13] Keimer's.

1. *Céder.* 2. *De coups.* 3. *Eveiller.* 4. *Chercher à barrer.* 5. *Etendu.* 6. *Propre à.* 7. *Perdre.* 8. *Mal à propos.* 9. *Le terme moyen.* 10. *Différent.* 11. *En désespéré.* 12. *De l'occupation.* 13. *Chez l'imprimeur K.*

3. The Participle Absolute can also be used in the place of subordinate sentences beginning with a conjunction, if they have a different subject. Ex.: —

Le roi étant mort, son fils lui succéda.
The king being dead his son succeeded.
La ville ayant été prise, les soldats la pillèrent.
The town being taken, the soldiers pillaged it.
Le repas étant fini, nous nous mîmes en route.
When diner was over, we set off.

Étant is sometimes omitted. Ex.: —

Le repas fini (for *étant fini*), *nous nous mîmes en route.*
When dinner was over, we set off.
L'opération achevée, le roi remonta à cheval.
The operation being performed, the king mounted again on horseback.
Cette disposition faite, nous entrâmes dans la salle de réception.
When this arrangement was made, we entered the parlor.

THEME 65.

1. My mother being ill, I cannot go out to-day. 2. Franklin, seeing that all his efforts were useless, went back to his country, in order to brave the storm[1] with his countrymen. 3. Wishing to see him, I went to his house. 4. Mary and her brother Henry, perceiving a pretty butterfly,[2] endeavored to catch[3] it. 5. The gates being closed, we could not enter. 6. Philip sent deputies to the Scythians,[4] demanding (*pour demander*) a part of the expenses[5] of

the seige; the Scythians, alleging[6] the barrenness[7] of their land, replied that, having no riches sufficient to satisfy so great a king, they thought [it] more[8] unfit to pay but[9] a part, than to refuse the whole.[10] 7. The wound still bleeding,[11] she fainted.[12] 8. Everybody will respect the magistrates who, forgetting their own interest, observing the law, favoring[13] virtue and restraining[14] vice, seek the welfare[15] of their country.

1. *L'orage*, m. 2. *Papillon*, m. 3. *Attraper*. 4. *Scythe*, m. 5. *Les frais*. 6. *Alléguer*. 7. *La stérilité*. 8. *Moins convenable*. 9. *De ne payer qu'une partie*. 10. *Le tout*. 11. *Saigner*. 12. *S'évanouir*. 13. *Favoriser*. 14. *Réprimer*. 15. *Le bien*.

READING LESSON.

GESLER CONDUIT TELL À KUSNACH.

(Fin.)

Enfin l'orient[1] se colore, et la tempête semble s'appaiser aux premiers rayons de l'aurore. Le jour naissant découvre à Tell les roches voisines d'Altdorf, avant que le tyran ait eu le temps de les reconnaître; Guillaume y dirige sa barque et la fait marcher plus rapidement. Gesler, dont la férocité revient à mesure que le danger s'éloigne, observe avec des yeux sombres. Il veut, mais il n'ose pas encore le faire charger de liens.[2] Ses soldats et ses matelots[3] reconnaissent bientôt où ils sont, en instruisent le gouverneur, qui s'avançant vers Tell avec colère, lui demande d'une voix terrible, pourquoi la barque, qu'il a guidée, a repris le chemin d'Altdorf.

Guillaume sans lui répondre, pousse la barque droit[4] à un rocher peu éloigné de la rive,[5] saisit d'une main prompte l'arc et la flèche[6] qu'un archer tenait à la main, et, rapide comme l'éclair, s'élance[7] de la barque sur le rocher. Là, sans s'arrêter, il saute sur un autre roc, gravit[8] aussitôt la roche escarpée,[9] et se montre sur le sommet, semblable à l'aigle des Alpes quand il se repose auprès des nuages, et qu'il promène ses yeux perçants sur les troupeaux des vallons.

Le gouverneur étonné pousse un cri de fureur, de rage. Il commande aussitôt qu'on débarque, et que ses soldats, dispersés, environnent de toutes parts le roc où il voit le héros. On obéit; les archers descendent et préparent déjà leurs arcs; Gesler, qui marche au milieu d'eux, veut que leurs flèches réunies s'abreuvent toutes du sang de Guillaume. Guillaume aussi a ses desseins. Il ne s'arrête, il ne se montre que pour attirer l'ennemi. Il laisse approcher cette troupe armée jusqu'à la juste distance où son trait[9] peut donner la mort. Il regarde, fixe Gesler, pose sa flèche sur sa corde, et, l'adressant au cœur du gouverneur, il la fait voler[10] dans les airs. La flèche vole, siffle,[11] frappe au milieu du cœur de Gesler. Le tyran tombe, bégaie sa fureur, et son âme s'exhale au milieu des imprécations. Tell a déjà disparu; plus léger que le faon,[12] s'est précipité du sommet du roc, il court, il vole sur la glace; il gagne, traverse des sentiers[13] déserts, et prend le chemin d'Altdorf.

Florian.

1. The east. 2. Fetters, chains. 3. Sailor. 4. Straight. 5. Bank. 6. Arrow. 7. Jumps. 8. To climb up. 9. Steep. 10. To fly. 11. To hiss. 12. The fawn. 13. Path.

QUESTIONNAIRE.

Que découvre le jour naissant à Tell?
Que fait Gesler?
Quelle était l'intention de Gesler?
De quoi les soldats et les matelots instruisent-ils le gouverneur?
Quand Gesler aperçut les roches d'Altdorf, que demanda-t-il à Tell?
Guillaume lui fit-il une réponse?
Où pousse-t-il la barque?
Que saisit-il d'une main prompte?
Où s'élance-t-il de la barque?
A qui ressemble-t-il quand il se montre sur le sommet?
Qu'est-ce que le gouverneur commande alors?
Fut-il obéi?
Gesler que veut-il?
Jusqu'où Tell laisse-t-il approcher la troupe?
Qui veut-il frapper?
Sa flèche l'a-t-elle atteint?
Que fait Tell alors?
Quel chemin Tell prend-il?

XXIV. VINGT-QUATRIÈME LEÇON.

GOVERNMENT OF VERBS.

1. Many verbs which in English require a preposition, such as *at, of, from, to, with, for, etc.*, take in French a direct object. Such are :—

approuver, to approve of.
attendre, to wait for.
chercher, to look (seek) for.
connaître, to be acquainted with, to know.
considérer, to look upon.
désirer, to wish for.
devenir, to become.
écouter, to listen to.
envoyer chercher, to send for.
espérer, to hope for.
expier, to atone for.
fournir, to supply with.
prier Dieu, to pray to God.
regarder, to look at.
rencontrer, to meet with.
résoudre, to resolve upon.

Examples :—

Attendez-vous votre frère, are you waiting for your brother?
Qu'êtes-vous devenu, what has become of you?
Il faut envoyer chercher le médecin, we must send for the doctor.

2. The following verbs which in English usually require a direct object take in French the preposition *à* :—

Apprendre } *qch. à qn.*, to teach one
enseigner } something.
conseiller qch. à qn., to advise.
convenir à qn., to suite any one.
déplaire à qn., to displease one.
désobéir à qn., to disobey one.
dire à qn., to tell some one.
faire tort à qn., to wrong one.
se fier à qn., to trust one.
nuire à qn., to hurt, injure one.
obéir à qn., to obey one.
ordonner à qn., to order.
pardonner à, to pardon, forgive one.
parvenir à qch., to attain.
permettre à qn., to allow one.
plaire à qn., to please one.
remédier à qch., to remedy.
renoncer à qch., to renounce, abdicate something.
résigner à qch., to resign something.
résister à qn., to resist one.
ressembler à qn., to resemble one.
subvenir à, to relieve.
succéder à, to succeed.
se soustraire à, to keep out of the way.
survivre à, to outlive, survive.
toucher à qch., to touch something.

Examples:—

Pouvez-vous enseigner le latin à mon fils?
Can you teach my son Latin?

Il faut obéir à vos parents.
You must obey your parents.

On ne peut pas plaire à tout le monde.
You cannot please everybody.

Ne vous fiez pas à lui.
Do not trust him.

THEME 66.

1. Who teaches your brother French? 2. Mr. R., who is a very good teacher. 3. This ribbon does not please my sister. 4. You have wronged your neighbor; you have hurt his credit;[1] at least he says so (*le*). 5. A good christian forgives his enemies. 6. Miss Mary resembles her mother [very] much. 7. Will you allow your pupils to to take a walk this afternoon? 8. Yes, I will allow them to go with you. 9. Children must obey their parents. 10. The officer disobeyed the orders of the king. 11. The son succeeded his father. 12. The riches of the count would have relieved the wants[2] of the poor. 13. He who wishes to please everybody, runs the risk[3] of pleasing (*de ne plaire*) nobody. 14. Louis the Fourteenth survived his son, the dauphin, and his grandson.[4] 15. Do not touch anything.

1. *Crédit*, m. 2. *Besoin*, m. 3. *Courir risque.* 4. *Petit-fils.*

---

3. Verbs which require in English the prepositions *of* and *from* are generally followed in French by *de*. Besides these, the following also require *de*:—

Accabler de, to overwhelm.
s'acquitter de qch, to discharge.
s'affliger de, to be afflicted at.
s'apercevoir de,* to remark, to perceive.
approcher de, *s'approcher de*, } to approach.
s'armer de, to arm one's self with.
avoir besoin de, to want, to require.
avoir pitié de, to pity.

* *Apercevoir*, when not a pronominal verb, governs the direct object and applies to visible things, as: *J'aperçus une flamme.*

avoir or *prendre soin de*, to take care of.
brûler de, to burn with.
charger de, } to load with.
combler de, }
se contenter de, to be satisfied *or* contented with.
couvrir de, to cover with.
se défier de, } to distrust.
se méfier de, }
dépendre de, to be dependent on.
envelopper de, to wrap up in.
faire de, to do with (to make use of).
faire présent de, to present with.
féliciter qn. de qch., to congratulate on.
fourmiller de, to swarm with.
honorer de, to honor with.
jouir de qch., to enjoy.
médire de qn., to traduce, to slander.
se mêler de qch., to meddle with.
se moquer de qn., to laugh at.
mourir de, to die of.
munir de, to furnish, provide with.
se passer de qch., to do without.
périr de, to perish *or* die of.
profiter de qch., to profit by.
pourvoir de, to provide with.
punir de qch., to punish for.
récompenser de qch., to reward for.
regarder de, to regard with.
se réjouir de, to rejoice at.
remercier de qch., to thank for something.
remplir de, to fill with.
se repentir de, to repent.
rire de, to laugh at.
se souvenir de, to remember, to recollect.
sourire de, to smile at.
triompher de, to triumph over.
se tromper de, to mistake.

Examples: —

Approchez-vous du feu, come near the fire.
Je me suis défié de ses promesses.
I distrusted his promises.
On m'accabla de reproches.
They overwhelmed me with reproaches.
Elle sourit de notre embarras.
She smiled at our embarrassment.

THEME 67.

1. He was overwhelmed with reproaches.[1] 2. You must discharge that obligation. 3. Death pities nobody, neither rich nor poor. 4. Come near the window. 5. Nature wants few things. 6. She is contented with little. 7. Have you not perceived this mistake? 8. No, sir, I have not perceived it (*en*). 9. The ground[2] was covered with snow. 10. The general honored me with

his friendship. 11. Your brother presented me with this silver pen-holder.[3] 12. The impious[4] mock at virtue and religion. 13. Do not meddle with my affairs. 14. Distrust that man; he will laugh at your benefits[5] when he no longer requires them. 15. Never traduce (slander) anybody. 16. Mr. A. is a very strong man; he enjoys good health. 17. If he repents his faults, I will pardon him. 18. I cannot do without his help.[6] 19. I hope (that) you will profit by this experience. 20. Remember your promise. 21. I remember that story very well. 22. Everybody rejoices at that victory.[7]

1. ***Reproche***, m. 2. ***La terre.*** 3. ***Porte-plume***, m. 4. ***Impie.*** 5. ***Bienfait***, m. 6. ***Secours***, m. 7. ***Victoire***, f.

4. Verbs with different *governments*. The following verbs have different governments according to their different significations: —

1. *Abuser qn.*, to deceive.
   abuser de qch., to abuse, to misuse.
2. *Assister qn.*, to assist, to help.
   assister à qch., to be present at.
3. *Changer qch.*, to change, to alter, to exchange.
   changer de qch., to change, to change one thing for another.
   changer en, to turn into.
4. *Convenir de qch.*, to agree (construed with *être*).
   convenir à qn., to suit.
5. *Croire qn.*, to believe some one.
   croire qch., to believe something.
   croire à qch., to believe in something.
   croire en, to believe in.
6. *Demander qn.*, to ask *or* inquire for some one.
   demander qch., to ask for somothing.
   demander à qn., to ask a person.
   demander qch. à qn., to ask something of some one *or* to ask some one for something.
7. *Echapper* and *s'échapper de*, to escape from, i. e. out of.
   échapper à, to escape from, i. e. to avoid, to be preserved from.
8. *Se fâcher de qch.*, to be sorry for.
   " " *contre qn.*, to be angry at.
9. *Insulter qn.* or *qch.* (dir. obj.), to offend by insults.
   insulter à qn. or *à qch.*, to deride, to scorn, to insult.
10. *Jouer à qch.*, to play at a game.

jouer de l'argent, to play for money.
jouer d'un instrument, to play (on) an instrument.
se jouer de qn., to laugh at, to deceive.

11. *Manquer* (neuter verb without a government), to be wanting *or* missing.
manquer qn. or *qch.*, to miss, to fail in.
manquer de qch., to be wantiug in, to be short of.
manquer à qn. or *à qch.* (also *contre qch.*), to fail in, to omit.

12. *Répondre à qch.*, to answer.
répondre de qch., to answer for.

13. *Satisfaire qn.*, to satisfy, to content.
satisfaire à qch., to fulfil duties to . . . , to satisfy.

14. *Servir qn.*, to serve one, to be at one's service.
servir de qch., to serve as something, for some one.

15. *Souscrire qch.*, to subscribe, to sign.
souscrire à qch., to approve of, to subscribe to.

16. *User qch.*, to use up, to wear out.
user de qch., to make use of, to use.

Examples: —

On a changé les conditions, they have altered the conditions.
J'ai changé de logement, I have taken other lodgings.
Que demandez-vous, what do you ask for?
Demandez à votre mère, ask your mother.
J'ai demandé mon argent à mon oncle, I have asked my money of my uncle.
Répondez à ma question, answer my question.
Pouvez-vous répondre de sa probité, can you answer for his honesty?

5. Special remarks on some verbs.

1. *Acheter qch. à qn.*, to buy something of some one.

2. *Aider qn.*, to succor, to support, to give means of doing.
aider à qn., to help, to aid physically in doing something.

3. *Applaudir*, to applaud something, governs the dir. obj.
applaudir, to applaud a person, governs the ind. obj.

4. *Approcher qch.* (active verb), to approach, to advance, to bring *or* push near.
approcher qn., to approach — to have free access.
approcher de qn. or *de qch.*, to approach some one *or* something, to go *or* draw nearer (see § 3).

5. *Emprunter*, to borrow, governs the indirect object of the person when

represented by a personal pronoun (such as *lui, leur, nous, etc.*). But it requires *à* or *de* when the person is expressed by a noun (as: *à* or *de mon frère*, of my brother.

6. *En croire qch.*, to trust, to depend upon.
7. *Hériter qch. de qn.*, to inherit something from some one. If, however, no person is mentioned, the thing follows the preposition *de*.
8. *Persuader qn. de qch.*, to convince a person of the truth of a thing. *persuader qch. à qn.*, to persuade one to do something.
9. *Redoubler qch.* (dir. obj.), means to redouble, i. e. to reiterate. *redoubler de qch.*, to redouble, i. e. to augment in force.
10. *Penser à* means to have one's mind upon. *penser de*, to have an opinion of.

Examples: —

Approchez la table, approach the table (bring it nearer).

Tout le monde peut approcher notre prince.
Everybody has free access to our prince.

Ne vous approchez pas tant du bord.
Do not go so near the edge.

Pensez à moi, think of me.
Que pensez-vous de cela, what do you think of that?

6. On the verb *faire*. The verb *faire* when followed by an Infinitive with a dir. obj., requires the person in the ind. obj., the two verbs being considered as one verbal expression the sense of which is is always active. The reason of it is that an active verb cannot have two direct complements (see L. XXII, 10). Ex.: —

Je lui ai fait écrire cinquante mots.
I have made him write fifty words.

Sa mère lui a fait raconter cette histoire.
His mother caused him to relate that story.

But if there be no direct object after the Infinitive that follows *faire*, the person stands in the direct object. Ex.: —

Je les ai fait partir, I have made them depart.

Nous les avons fait renoncer à leur prétentions.
We have made them abandon their pretentions.

7. The verbs *écouter*, *entendre*, *laisser* and *voir*, also, are sometimes used in this manner, as: —

Je lui ai vu maltraiter son chien.
I saw him ill-treat his dog.

But this is not generally adopted, and it is better to say: —

Je l'ai vu maltraiter son chien.
J'ai vu le petit garçon (dir. obj.) *maltraiter son chien.*

8. When the Infinitive is followed by a subordinate sentence with *que*, the indirect object is preferred, as: —

Je lui ai entendu dire qu'il partirait.
I heard him say that he was going to leave.
J'ai entendu dire à son père qu'il lui pardonnerait.
I heard his father say that he would forgive him.

THEME 68.

1. The jailer[1] has deceived the prisoner with respect to (*sur*) the lot[2] which awaited him. 2. Have you not abused our patience? 3. We have abused it (*en*). 4. The hour from 10 to 11 does not suit my sister. 5. We have agreed on the price.[3] 6. Let us always assist the poor. 7. I could not be present at the funeral.[4] 8. I have changed my opinion. 9. Could you change me this napoleon? 10. Industry is the true philosopher's[5] stone that changes all metals into gold. 11. Whom have you asked for? 12. I inquired for my eldest[6] brother. 13. Have you asked your friend for money? 14. I have not asked him for any. 15. Do not believe that man, he is a liar.[7] 16. I do not believe in his promises. 17. We believe in God. 18. The little bird has escaped from his cage. 19. Can[8] you play at chess?[9] 20. No, Sir, but I will play at cards with you, if you like.[10] 21. I play (on) the violin and my sister plays on the piano. 22. We often play together. 23. I was too late, I missed the train.[11] 24. A soldier must (*doit*) not fail in courage. 25. The pupil redoubled his application, when he heard that a prize[3] would be given. 26. The man is too poor, he cannot satisfy his creditors.[12] 27. Do you make use of spectacles?[13] 28. Yes, I always wear spectacles; I am short-sighted.[14] 29. Make him read a chapter[15] or two. 30. I made him relate[16]

the story a second time. 31. Charles the XII made all that multitude cross[17] the river, without retaining[18] a single soldier prisoner.

1. *Le geolier*. 2. *Le sort*. 3. *Prix*, m. 4. *Funérailles*, f. pl. 5. *Philosophe*, m. 6. *Aîné*. 7. *Menteur*. 8. *Savoir*. 9. *Aux échecs*. 10. *Vouloir*. 11. *Le convoi*. 12. *Créancier*. 13. *Lunettes*, f. pl. 14. *J'ai la vue basse*. 15. *Chapitre*, m. 16. *Raconter*. 17. *Repasser*. 18. *Sans en retenir*.

XXV. VINGT-CINQUIÈME LEÇON.

IDIOMATICAL EXPRESSIONS.

Idioms are modes of speaking peculiar to one language, which cannot be literally translated into another.

Avoir, to have.

Avoir vingt ans, to be twenty years old.
Avoir mal aux yeux, to have sore eyes.
Avoir mal à la tête, to have a (*or* the) headache.
J'ai froid aux mains, my hands are cold.
Vous avez beau parler, it is in vain for you to talk.
J'ai de la peine à le croire, I can hardly believe it.
Avoir froid, to be cold, —*chaud*, to be warm.
Avoir honte, to be ashamed.
Avoir raison, —*tort*, to be right, —in the wrong.
Avoir bonne mine, to look well.
N'avoir que faire de, to have no occasion for.
Avoir grand soif, —*faim*, to be very thirsty, —hungry.
Avoir quelque chose, to have something the matter with one.
Avoir peur, to be afraid.
Avoir sommeil, to be sleepy.
Avoir soin, to take care.
Avoir besoin, to have need, want.
Avoir sujet, to have reason.
Avoir regret, to regret.
Avoir envie, to desire.

Avoir coutume, to be accustomed.
Avoir lieu, to take place.
Avoir beau, to be in vain.
L'avoir belle, to have a favorable opportunity to do it.

Etre, to be.

Etre en état de, to afford.
Etre à son aise, to be in good circumstances.
Etre mal avec quelqu'un, to be out of favor with some one.
Etre de moitié, to go halves.
Etre à la portée, to be within reach.
Etre sur le point de, to be very near to, to be going to.
Il en est de . . ., it is with, it is the case.
Etre riche de, to be worth, to possess. When a person is the subject, *valoir* is never used in this sense.
Il est riche de douze mille piastres, he is worth twelve thousand dollars.
Etre en retard, to be late.
Etre à même de, to be able to.
Etre en peine de, to be uneasy about.
Etre en vie, to be alive.
Etre en chemin pour, to be on the way to.
Etre au fait, au courant de, to be familiar with.
Etre à la veille de, on the eve of.
Etre de trop, to be in the way.
Etre bien avec, to be on good terms with.
Etre brouillé avec, on bad terms with.
Etre aux prises avec, to be in open rupture, quarrel or battle with.
Etre d'avis, to be of opinion.
Y être, to be at home.
Etre d'accord, to be in tune.
Ce piano n'est pas d'accord, this piano is not in tune.
Nous sommes d'accord, we agree.
Vous n'y êtes pas, that is not it.

Faire, to do, to make.

Faire savoir qn., to let one know, to send word.
Faire chaud, faire froid, to be warm, — cold (of the weather).
Se faire des amis, to get friends.
Faire faire, to get made.
Faire semblant de, to pretend.

Faire attention, to pay attention.
Faire cas de, to value, to esteem.
Faire un tour de promenade, to take a walk.
Faire voile or *mettre à la voile*, to set sail.
Faire de son mieux, to do one's best.
Ne faire que, to do nothing but.
C'en est fait de moi, I am undone, it is over with me.
Vous feriez mieux de rester, you had better stay.
Faites-moi grace de tous ces détails, spare me particulars.
Faire raccommoder, to have mended
Faire la cuisine, to cook.
Faire tort à, to injure.
Faire bouillir, to boil.

THEME 69.

1. How old was your father when he died? 2. He was seventy. 3. And your mother? 4. She was almost[1] eighty. 5. I do not remember to have ever been so[2] thirsty as I was yesterday. 6. Warm yourself, if you are cold; my feet are not cold, because I have walked much, but my hands are so cold, that I cannot write. 7. There are some walks[3] in our park which are three hundred feet long. 8. You are in the wrong, and he is in the right. 9. It is in vain for you to ask money from a miser, he will never give you any. 10. Is it cold this morning? 11. Yes sir, it is very cold; however, I do not think it is quite so cold as it was yesterday. 12. The weather is very inconstant; it was hot yesterday, it is cold to-day; it rained this morning; it is fine weather now, but perhaps it will rain again before (it be[4]) night.

1. *Près de.* 2. *Si.* 3. *Allée*, f. 4. *Faire* (Subj.).

Donner, to give.

Donner dans le piége, to be caught in the snare.
Donner sur le jardin, to look out on the garden.
Donner carte blanche, to give full powers.
Donner sur l'ennemi, to fall upon the enemy.
Ne savoir où donner de la tête, to know not what way to turn.
Ce vin donne à la tête, that wine flies up to the head.

Donner un coup de main, to help.
Donner à pleines mains, to give largely.
Se donner des airs, to take a great deal on one's self.
Se donner la peine, to take the trouble.

Jouer, to play, etc.

Jouer d'un instrument, to play (upon) an instrument.
Jouer à quelque jeu, to play at some game.
Jouer une pièce de théâtre, to act a play.
Jouer un tour à qn., to serve (play) one a trick.
Se porter, to be (in reference to health).
Il se porte bien, he is well.
Aimer mieux, to have rather, to choose rather.
Aller à bride abattue, to go at full speed.
Dormir la grasse matinée, to sleep very late.
Prendre en mauvaise part, to take amiss.
S'y bien prendre, to go the right way to work.
S'y prendre mal, to go the wrong way to work.
Se passer de, to do without.
Trouver mauvais que, to take ill if.
Trouver son maître, to meet with one's match.
Trouver à redire, to find fault with.
Savoir bon gré, to be thankful for.
Tenir parole, to keep our word.
Ne tenir qu'à, to be in a person's power.
Il ne tient pas à moi que, it is not my fault.
S'en tenir à, to stand to.
Faire tenir, to forward.
Venir à bout de, to bring about, to accomplish.
En vouloir à, to have a spite against, to be vexed with.
Je voudrais pouvoir, I wish I could.
Il y va de votre vie, your life is at stake.
Venir de, to have just done something.
En venir aux mains, to come to blows.

THEME 70.

1. How do you do this morning? 2. I am very well, I thank you. 3. And how does your sister do? 4. She is not well; she has been ill for these two months, and I fear she will never be well again. 5. And your brothers, how are they? 6. The youngest is

very well, but I do not know how the eldest does, because we have not heard[1] of him for[2] these two months; he was very well when he wrote to us last.[3] 7. It is with the diseases of the heart as with those of the body, some are real,[4] and some imaginary. 8. It is with men of learning as with ears[5] of corn; they raise their[6] heads while they are empty, and when they are full, they begin to droop.[7] 9. It is with your son as with other children. 10. I do not think it will be with my son as it was with yours.

1. *Avoir de ses nouvelles.* 2. For these—*depuis.* 3. *La dernière fois.* 4. *Réel.* 5. *Epis de blé.* 6. Def. Art. 7. *Pencher.*

THEME 71.

1. I have great pain[1] in my side. 2. He has sore eyes. 3. He has a sore foot. 4. My lips are sore. 5. She had the toothache yesterday, now she has a headache; to-morrow, perhaps, she will have the ear[2]-ache. 6. When I was young, I often had the headache. 7. Why do you not eat, if you are hungry? 8. I am not very hungry, I can wait [till] dinner time,[3] but I am very thirsty, and I will thank[4] you for[5] a glass of wine. 9. It is very cold to-day. 10. It was cold yesterday. 11. It will be hot soon. 12. I am thirsty. 13. He is hungry. 14. My sister is not well, she has not been[6] well for three weeks, she has a headache to-day. 15. At what o'clock did you rise this morning? 16. I rose at four o'clock. 17. It is in vain for you to say so, I do not believe you.

1. *Bien mal.* 2. *Oreille.* 3 *Le dîner.* 4. *Prier.* 5. *De me donner.* 6. *Se porter*, use the Present tense.

ENGLISH VOCABULARY

OF THE WORDS THAT OCCUR IN THE THEMES.

A.

Able (to be), *pouvoir*, irr. see p. 190.
About, *environ*, see also p. 301.
Absolve, v. a., *absoudre*, irr. see p. 175.
Abstain, *s'abstenir*, irr. see p. 187.
Abundance, *abondance*, f.
Abuse, *dire des injures*, *maltraiter*.
Accept, *agréer*, *accepter*.
Accompany, *accompagner*.
Account, *compte*, m.
Acquaintance, *connaissance*, f.
Acquire, *acquérir*, irr. see p. 187.
Act, *agir*.
Action, *action*, f.
Admirable, *admirable*.
Admiral, *amiral*, m.
Admit, *admettre*, irr. see p. 180.
Advantage, *avantage*, m.
Affair, *affaire*, f.
Afraid (to be), *avoir peur*.
After, *après*.
Afternoon, *après-midi*, m. f.
Again, *encore*.
Against, *contre*.
Age, *âge*, m, [old age, *vieillesse*, f.]
Agree, *convenir*, irr. see p. 187.
Agreeable, *agréable*.
Agriculture, *agriculture*, f.
Alike, *pareil*.
All, *tout*; all that, *tout ce qui*, see p. 127.
Alley, *allée*.
Allow, *permettre*, irr. see p. 180.
Almost, *presque*.
Already, *déjà*.
Also, *aussi*.
Always, *toujours*.
Ambitious, *ambitieux*.
Amiable, *aimable*.
Among, *parmi*.
Amuse, *amuser*, *entretenir*.
Ancestors, *ancêtres*, *aieux*.
And, *et*.
Anger, *colère*.
Angry, *fâché*.
Angry (to be), *se fâcher*.
Animal, *animal*.
Anoint, *oindre*, irr. see p. 175.
Answer, v., *répondre*.
Answer, n., *réponse*, f.
Any (with neg.), *aucun*, *pas de*.
Anybody (after neg.), *personne*.
Any more (after neg.), *plus*.
Appear, *paraître*, irr. see p. 178.
Appetite, *appétit*, m.
Apple, *pomme*, f.
Apply to, *s'adresser*.
Approach, *approcher*.
April, *avril*, m.
Arm, *bras*, m.
Army, *armée*, f.
Arrive, *arriver*.
Art, *art*, m.
Artist, *artiste*.
As, *comme*; (so) as — as, *aussi — que*.
Ashamed, *honteux*.
Ashes, *cendre*, f.
Ask, *demander*.
Assiduity, *assiduité*.
Assist, *assister*, *secourir*, irr. see p. 184.
Assistance, *secours*, m.
Astonishing, *étonnant*.
At, *à*, *en*; see p. 302: at home, *à la maison*; at your house, *chez vous*; at first, *d'abord*; at once, *tout d'un coup*; at all, *du tout*.
Attack, *attaquer*.
Attain, *atteindre*, irr. see p. 175; *parvenir*, irr. see p. 187.
Attention, *attention*, f.
Attentive, *attentif*.
Attract, *attirer*.
August, *août*, m.
Aunt, *tante*, f.
Author, *auteur*.
Avarice, *avarice*, f.
Avaricious, *avaricieux*.
Avoid, *éviter*.
Avow, *avouer*.

B.

Bad, *mauvais*.
Ball, *balle*, f., *bal*, m.

Bark, *aboyer.*
Barley, *orge*, f.
Battle, *bataille*, f.
Beard, *barbe*, f.
Beat, *battre*, see p. 107, *frapper.*
Beautiful, *beau.*
Because, *parce que.*
Become, *devenir*, irr. see p. 187.
Bed (to go to), *se coucher.*
Bee, *abeille*, f.
Beer, *bière*, f.
Before, *avant*, *devant*, see p. 298.
Beg, *prier*, *mendier*, — for a thing, *demander*, *solliciter.*
Begin, *commencer*, *se mettre à*, see p. 180.
Behind, *derrière.*
Believe, *croire*, irr, see p. 177.
Belong, *appartenir*, irr. see p. 187.
Better, *meilleur*, *supérieur.*
Better, adv., *mieux*, to be better, *valoir mieux.*
Between, *entre.*
Beyond, *au-dessus*, *au delà*; *delà*, *outre.*
Big, *grand*, *gros.*
Bite, *mordre.*
Bird, *oiseau*, m.
Bitter, *amer.*
Black, *noir.*
Blame, *blâmer.*
Blood, *sang*, m.
Blush, *rougir.*
Boarding-house, *pension*, f.
Body, *corps*, m. Everybody, *chacun*, *tout le monde.* Nobody, *personne.*
Boil, *bouillir*, irr. see p. 186.
Bonnet, *chapeau*, m.
Book, *livre*, m.
Boot, *botte*, f.
Born (to be), *naître*, irr. see p. 181.
Boy, *garçon*, m.
Box, *boîte*, *cassette*, f.
Bottle, *bouteille*, f.
Brave, *brave*, *courageux.*
Bray, *braire*, def., see p. 197.
Bread, *pain.*
Break, *rompre*, see p. 107, *casser*, *briser.*
Breakfast, *déjeuner.*
Bring, *apporter.*
Brother, *frère*, — in law, *beau-frère.*
Build, *bâtir*, *construire*, irr. see p. 172.
Burn, *brûler.*
Business, *affaires*, *occupation*, f.
But, *mais.*
Butter, *beurre*, m.
Buy, *acheter.*
By, *par*, see p. 302.

C.

Cabbage, *chou*, m.
Calf, *veau*, m.
Call, *appeler*, — to mind, *rappeler.*
Camel, *chameau*, m.
Can, see p. 190–1.
Candle, *chandelle*, f.
Cane, *canne*, f.
Cap, *casquette*, f.
Carnival, *carnaval*, m.
Care, *soin*, m.
Carriage, *voiture*, f.
Carry, *porter.*
Cast, *jeter.*
Castle, *château.*
Cat, *chat*, m.
Cattle, *bétail*, m., pl. *bestiaux.*
Cease, *cesser.*
Celebrated, *célèbre.*
Chair, *chaise*, f.
Chamber, *chambre*, f.
Chase, *chasse*, f.
Chastise, *châtier.*
Cheese, *fromage*, m.
Cherry, *cerise*, f.
Child, *enfant*, m. f.
Choose, *choisir.*
Church, *église*, f.
City, *ville*, f.
Class, *classe*, f.
Clean, *net.*
Clean, v., *nettoyer.*
Cloak, *manteau*, m.
Cloth, *drap*, m.
Clothe, *vêtir*, irr. see p. 183.
Cloud, *nuage*, m.
Coach, *carrosse*, m.
Coast, *côte*, f.
Coat, *habit*, m.
Coffee, *café*, m.
Cold, *froid.*
Color, *couleur*, f.
Come, *venir*, irr. see p. 187, *arriver*, — down, *descendre*, — in, *entrer*, — in again, *rentrer.*
Comfort, v., *consoler.*
Comfort, n., *agrément*, m.
Command, *ordre*, m.
Command, v., *commander*, *ordonner.*
Commence, *commencer.*
Commerce, *commerce*, m.
Complain, *se plaindre*, irr. see p. 175.
Compel, *contraindre*, irr. see p. 175.
Comrade, *camarade*, m.
Conceal, *cacher*, *taire*, irr. see p. 178.
Conceive, *concevoir*, irr. see p. 189.
Conduct, n., *conduite.*
Conduct, v., *conduire*, irr. see p. 172.
Confess, *avouer.*
Confidence, *confiance*, f.
Conflagration, *incendie*, m.
Conquer, *vaincre*, irr. see p. 174; *conquérir*, irr. see p. 188.
Conqueror, *vainqueur*, m.
Consent, *consentir*, irr. see p. 184.
Consequence, *suite*, f.
Consider, *considérer.*
Constrain, *contraindre*, irr. see p. 175.
Construct, *construire*, irr. see p. 172.
Contain, *renfermer*, *contenir*, irr. see p. 187.
Contented, *content.*
Continue, *continuer.*
Convince, *convaincre*, irr. see p. 174.
Cook, *cuire*, irr. see p. 172.

Cool, *frais*, fem. *fraiche.*
Copy-book, *cahier*, m.
Corn, *blé*, m., — market, *halle aux blés.*
Correct, *corriger.*
Cost, *coûter.*
Country, *pays*, m., *campagne*, f.
Courage, *courage*, m.
Course, *cours*, m.
Cousin, *cousin*, m., *cousine*, f.
Cover, *couvrir*, irr. see p. 185.
Cow, *vache*, f.
Creator, *créateur*, m.
Creditor, *créancier*, m.
Crime, *crime*, m.
Cry, *crier*, *pleurer.*
Cup, *coupe*, *tasse*, f.
Currant, *groseille*, f.
Custom, *coutume*, f.
Cut, *couper*, *tailler.*

D.

Damp, *humide.*
Danger, *danger*, m.
Dark, *sombre.*
Daughter, *fille*, f.
Dawn, v., *poindre*, irr. see p. 175.
Day, *jour*, m. *journée*, f. day-light, *jour.*
Deaf, *sourd.*
Dear, *cher.*
Death, *mort*, f.
Debt, *dette*, *f.*
Deceive, *tromper*, *décevoir*, irr. see p. 189.
December, *décembre*, m.
Decision, *décision*, f.
Deer, *chevreuil*, *cerf*, m.
Defect, *défaut*, m.
Defend, *défendre.*
Delight, *se plaire à*, irr. see p. 178.
Demolish, *démolir.*
Deny, *nier*, *disconvenir*, irr. see p. 187.
Depart, *partir*, irr. p. 183.
Departure, *départ*, m.
Depend, *dépendre.* — upon or on, *compter sur.*
Depict, *dépeindre*, irr. see p. 175.
Describe, *décrire*, irr. see p. 176.
Deserve, *mériter.*
Desire, *désir*, m.
Despise, *mépriser.*
Destroy, *détruire*, irr. see p. 172.
Die, *mourir*, irr. see p. 186.
Difficult, *difficile.*
Difficulty, *difficulté*, f.
Diligent, *appliqué.*
Dine, v., *dîner.*
Dinner, n., *dîner*, m.
Direct (a letter), *adresser.*
Directly, *tout de suite*, *à l'instant.*
Direction, *adresse*, f.
Disappear, *disparaître*, irr. see p. 178.
Discontented, *mécontent.*
Discover, *découvrir*, irr. see p. 185. *inventer.*
Disease, *maladie*, f.
Displease, *déplaire*, irr. see p. 178.
Dissatisfy, *mécontenter.*
Dissolve, *dissoudre*, irr. see p. 175.
Distinguish, *distinguer.*
Distress, *affliger.*
Divide, *diviser*, *partager.*
Do, *faire*, irr. see p. 180.
Dog, *chien*, m.
Door, *porte*, f. door-way, *portail.*
Doubt, *douter.*
Doubtful, *douteux.*
Draw, *tirer*, *attirer*, — after, *entraîner* — (pictures), *dessiner* — upon one's self, *s'attirer.*
Dream, *songer*, *rêver.*
Dress, *habiller*, *parer*, *vêtir.*
Drink, *boire*, irr. see p. 177.
Drop, *goutte*, f.
Drunk and drunken, *ivre.*
Dry, *sec.*
Duck, *canard*, m.
Dumb, *muet.*
During, *pendant.*
Dust, *poussière*, f.
Duty, *devoir*. m.
Dwell, *demeurer*, *habiter.*
Dye, *teindre*, irr. see p. 175.

E.

Ear, *oreille*, f.
Early, *de bonne heure.*
Earth, *terre*, f.
Easily, *facilement.*
Easy, *aisé*, *facile.*
Eat, *manger.*
Edition, *édition*, *impression*, f.
Educate, *élever.*
Education, *éducation*, f.
Effort, *effort*, m.
Egg, *œuf*, m.
Elect, *élire*, irr. see p. 177.
Elephant, *éléphant*, m.
Ell (measure), *aune*, *f.*
Elm (tree), *orme*, m.
Eloquently, *éloquemment.*
Embarrass, *embarrasser*, *déranger.*
Embellish, *embellir.*
Employ, *employer.*
End, n., *bout*, m. (object) *fin*, f. *but*, m.
End, v., *finir*, *cesser.*
Enemy, *ennemi*, m.
Engine (steam), *machine à vapeur.*
Enough, *assez.*
Enrich, *enrichir.*
Enter, *entrer.*
Entertain, *entretenir*, *amuser.*
Entertaining, *amusant.*
Envy, *envie*, f.
Equal, *égal*, *pareil.*
Equality, *égalité*, f.
Error, *faute*, *erreur*, f.
Escape, *échapper*, *se sauver*, see p. 105., *fuir*, irr. see p. 183.
Esteem, *estimer.*
Evening, *soir*, m. *soirée*, f.

Event, *événement*, m.
Ever, *jamais*.
Everybody, *chacun, tout le monde*, — thing, *tout*, — where, *partout*.
Evil, *mal*, m.
Example, *exemple*, m.
Execute, *exécuter, s'aquitter de*.
Exercise, *exercice, thème*, m.
Exhaust, *épuiser*.
Exist, *exister*.
Expect, *attendre, s'attendre à*.
Extinct, *éteint*. To become — *s'éteindre*.
Extinguish, *éteindre*, irr. see p. 175.
Extract, *extraire*, irr. see p. 174.
Extreme, *extrême*.
Eye, *œil*; pl. *yeux*, m.

F.

Fable, *fable*, m.
Face, *face*, f. *visage*, m. *figure*, f.
Fail, *faillir*, def. see p. 197, *manquer*.
Faint, *défaillir*, def. see p. 197.
Faithful, *fidèle*.
Fall, *tomber, choir, dechoir*, def. see p. 189.
Fall, *chute*, f.
False, *faux*.
Falsehood, *mensonge*, m.
Family, *famille*, f.
Fan, *évantail*, m.
Far, *loin*, from far, *de loin*.
Fat, *gras*.
Fate, *sort*.
Father, *père*, —— in-law, *beau-père*, godfather, *parrain*.
Fault, *faute*, f. *défaut*, m.
Fear, *peur, crainte*, f.
Fear, *craindre*, irr. see p. 175.
Fearful, *craintif*.
Feather, *plume*, f.
February, *février*, m.
Feed, *nourrir*, (graze) *paître*, irr. see p. 178.
Feel, *sentir*, irr. see p. 184.
Feign, *feindre*, irr. see p. 175.
Fellow-traveller, *compagnon de voyage*.
Ferocious, *féroce*.
Fertilize, *fertiliser*.
Few, *peu*, a ——, *quelques*.
Field, *champ*.
Fight, *combattre*.
Fill, *emplir, remplir, rassasier, combler*.
Find, *trouver*.
Fine, *beau*.
Finish, *finir, terminer, achever*.
Fire, *feu*, m.
Flag, *pavillion, drapeau*, m.
Flatter, *flatter*.
Flatterer, *flatteur*, m.
Flee, *fuir, s'enfuir*, irr. see p. 183.
Flesh, *chair*, f.
Florin, *florin*, m.
Flour, *farine*, f.
Flourish, *fleurir*, see p. 102.
Flower, *fleur*, f.
Fly, *mouche*, f.
Fly, *fuir, s'enfuir*, irr. see p. 183, *voler*.
Fog, *brouillard*, m.
Follow, *suivre*, irr. see p. 174.
Folly, *sottise, folie*, f.
Fool, *sot, imbécile, fou*.
Foolishness, *sottise, bêtise*.
Foot, *pied*, m.
For, prep. *pour*.
For, conj. *car*, as ——, *quant à*.
Forbid, *défendre*, God ——! *à Dieu ne plaise!*
Forehead, *front*, m.
Foreign, *étranger*.
Foresee, *prévoir*, irr. see p. 192, *pressentir*, irr. see p. 184.
Forest, *forêt*, f.
Forget, *oublier*.
Forgive, *pardonner*.
Fork, *fourchette*.
Formerly, *autrefois*.
Forsake, *abandonner*.
Fortnight, *quinze jours*.
Fortune, *fortune*, f.
Forward, and forwards, *en avant, sur le devant*.
Found, *fonder*.
Freeze, *geler*.
Frequently, *souvent*.
Fresh, *frais*, fem. *fraiche*.
Friday, *vendredi*.
Friend, *ami*, m. *amie*, f.
Friendly, *amical*.
Friendship, *amitié*.
Fruit, *fruit*, m.
Full, *plein*.
Fulfil, *remplir, satisfaire*.
Furniture, *meubles*, pl. m.

G.

Gain, *gagner*, —— (a victory) *remporter*, — (affection, hatred) *attirer*.
Game, *jeu*, (chase) *gibier*.
Gape, *bâiller*.
Garden, *jardin*, m.
Gardener, *jardinier*, m.
Gate, *porte*, f.
Gather, *cueillir, recueillir*, irr. see p. 184.
General, *général*, m.
Generous, *généreux*.
Genius, *génie*, m.
Gentleman, *gentilhomme*.
Gentleness, *douceur*, f.
Get up, *se lever*.
Gift, *don*, m.
Girl, *fille*, f.
Give, *donner*.
Glad, *aise, content*.
Gladly, *volontiers, avec plaisir*.
Glass, *verre*, m.
Glitter, *reluire*, irr. see p. 171.
Glory, *gloire*, f.
Glove, *gant*, m.
Go, *aller*, irr. see p. 194, — away (set out), *s'en aller, partir*, irr. see p. 183,

—far from, *s'éloigner de*, —for, *aller chercher*, —on, *continuer*, —out, *sortir*, irr. see p. 184, —out, *éteindre*, irr. see p. 175.
God, *Dieu*, m.
Gold, *or*, m.
Good, n., *le bien*.
Good, ad., *bon*, *sage*. To be —— for nothing, *ne valoir rien*.
Good-will, *bienveillance*, f.
Goodness, *bonté*, f.
Govern, *gouverner*.
Gown, *robe*, f.
Grammar, *grammaire*, f.
Grandfather, *grand-père*, *aïeul*.
Grandmother, *grand'mère*.
Grant, *accorder*.
Grass, *herbe*, *verdure*, f.
Graze, *paître*, irr. see p. 178.
Great, *grand*.
Green, *vert*.
Grief, *douleur*, f, *peine*, f.
Grind, *moudre*, irr. see p. 174.
Ground, *terre*. On the —— *à*, *par terre*.
Grow, *croître*, irr. see p. 178, —lean, *maigrir*, —old, *vieillir*, —pale, *pâlir*, —red, *rougir*, —tall, *grandir*, —thin, *maigrir*, —worse, *empirer*.
Guilty, *coupable*.

H.

Hail, n., *grêle*, f.
Hail, v., *grêler*.
Half, n., *moitié*, f.
Half, ad., *demi*.
Hand, *main*, f.
Handkerchief, *mouchoir*, m.
Handsome, *beau*.
Happen, *arriver*, *survenir*, irr. see p. 187.
Happily, *heureusement*.
Happiness, *bonheur*, m.
Happy. *heureux*.
Hard, *dur*, *difficile*.
Hardly at all, *ne—guère*, —ever, *presque jamais*.
Hare, *lièvre*, m.
Harvest, *moisson*, *récolte*.
Haste, and Hasten, *hâter*, *se dépêcher*, *s'empresser*.
Hat, *chapeau*, m. To put on one's —, *mettre son chapeau*, *se couvrir*. To take off one's hat, *ôter son chapeau*, *se découvrir*.
Hate, *haïr*, see p. 102.
Hatred *haine*, f.
Hay, *foin*, m.
Head, *tête*, f.
Heal. *guérir*.
Health, *santé*, f.
Hear, *entendre*, *ouïr*, def. see p. 198.
Heart, *cœur*, m.
Heat, *chaleur*, f.
Heaven, *ciel*, pl. *cieux*, m.
Heavy, *lourd*, *pesant*.
Helm, *gouvernail*, m.
Henceforward, *désormais*, *dorénavant*.
Here, *ici*, *y*.
Heretofore, *autrefois*.
Hide, *cacher*.
High, *haut*, *élevé*.
Hill, *colline*, f. *coteau*, m., *montagne*, f.
Hinder, *empêcher*.
History, *histoire*, f.
Hit, *frapper*, *atteindre*, irr. see p. 175.
Hive, *ruche*, f.
Hoist, *hisser*.
Hold, *tenir*, irr. see p. 187.
Hole, *trou*, m.
Holiday, *congé*, m.
Home, *au logis*, *à la maison*, *chez soi*, see p. 37.
Honest, *honnête*.
Honor, *honneur*, m.
Hope, n., *espérance*, f., *espoir*, m.
Hope, v., *espérer*.
Horse, *cheval*, m.
Hot, *chaud*.
Hour, *heure*, f.
House, *maison*, f.
How, *comment*, *combien*, *que*, —long (since when)? *depuis quand?* —many (much) *combien*.
However, *quelque*.
Human, *humain*.
Hunger, *faim*, f. To be hungry, *avoir faim*.
Hunter, *chasseur*, m.
Hunting, *chasse*, f.
Hurt, *nuire*, irr. see p. 172, *blesser*, *gâter*.
Husband, *mari*, *époux*.

I.

Ice, *glace*, f.
Idea, *idée*, f.
Idle, *paresseux*.
If, *si*.
Ill, adj., *malade*.
Ill, adv., *mal*.
Illness, *maladie*, f.
Image, *image*, f.
Imagine, *imaginer*.
Immortal, *immortel*.
Importune, *importuner*.
Impossible, *impossible*.
In, *en*, *dans*, see p. 297, and p. 304.
Inch, *pouce*, m.
Increase, *accroître*, *croître*, irr. see p. 178, *augmenter*.
Incredible, *incroyable*.
Inconstant, *inconstant*.
Incur, *s'attirer*, *encourir*, irr. see p. 184.
Indeed, *vraiment*.
Infamous, *infâme*.
Infringe, *enfreindre*, irr. see p. 175.
Inhabit, *habiter*, *demeurer*.
Inhabitant, *habitant*, m.
Injure. *nuire*, irr. see p. 172.
Ink, *encre*, f.
Inkstand, *encrier*, m.

Inquire, *s'enquérir*, irr. see p. 188.
Inquisitive, *curieux*.
Inscribe, *inscrire*, irr. see p. 176.
Instruct, *instruire*, irr. see p. 172.
Interrupt, *interrompre*.
Into, *dans*, see p. 297.
Introduce, *présenter*, *introduire*, irr. see p. 172.
Invent, *inventer*.
Invite, *inviter*.
Iron, *fer*, m.
Island, *île*, f.
Ivory, *ivoire*, m.

J

January, *janvier*, m.
Jealous, *jaloux*.
Jealousy, *jalousie*, f.
Jewel, *bijou*, m.
Join, *joindre*, irr. see p. 175.
Joy, *joie*, f.
July, *juillet*, m.
June, *juin*, m.
Just, *juste*.
Justice, *justice*, f.

K.

Keep, *tenir*, irr. see p. 187, (observe) *observer*.
Kill, *tuer*.
Kindness, *bonté*.
King, *roi*, m.
Kingdom, *royaume*, m.
Kitchen, *cuisine*, f.
Knee, *genou*, m.
Knife, *couteau*, m.
Know, *connaître*, irr. see p. 178, *savoir*, irr. see p. 191.
Knowledge, *science*, f., *savoir*, m., *connaissance*, f.

L.

Labor, n., *travail*, m., pl. *aux*.
Labor, v., *travailler*.
Laborious, *laborieux*.
Laconic, *laconique*.
Lady, *dame*, f.
Lamb, *agneau*, m.
Language, *langue*, f., *langage*, m.
Land, *terre*, f.
Large, *gros*, *grand*.
Last, v., *durer*, *continuer*.
Last, adj., *dernier*, *passé*.
Lasting, *durable*.
Late, adj., *feu*, see p. 247.
Late, adv., *tard*, *en retard*.
Laugh, *rire*, irr. see pp. 194 and 107.
Law, *loi*, f.
Lawyer, *avocat*, m.
Lazy, *paresseux*.
Lead, n., *plomb*, m.
Lead, v., *mener*, — into, *induire en*, irr. see p. 172.
Leaf, *feuille*, f.
League, *lieue*, f.
Learn, *apprendre*, irr. see p. 181.
Learned, *savant*.
Least, *le moindre*. At the —, *du moins*, (at all events), *au moins*, in the —, *du tout*.
Leave (of absence), *congé*, m.
Leave, v., *quitter*, *laisser*, *cesser*. Take — of, *prendre congé de*.
Left, *gauche*, f.
Leg, *jambe*, f.
Lend, *prêter*.
Less, *moins*.
Let, *laisser*, — us go, *allons*, — him know, *faites-lui savoir*, (to hire) *louer*.
Letter, *lettre*, f.
Liar, *menteur*, m.
Liberty, *liberté*, f.
Lie, *gésir*, def. see p. 198.
Lie, *mentir*, irr. see p. 184.
Life, *vie*, f.
Lift up, *lever*, *élever*.
Like, *pareil*, adv., *comme*.
Likely, *probable*, *vraisemblable*.
Lily, *lis*, m.
Limit, *limiter*, *borner*, *restreindre*, see p. 175.
Line, *ligne*, f.
Linen, *toile*, f. Unbleached —, *toile écrue*.
Lion, *lion*, m.
Listen, *écouter*.
Little, adj., *petit*, adv., *peu*, *ne — guère*.
Live, *vivre*, irr. see p 181, (dwell), *demeurer*, *habiter*.
Loadstone, *aimant*, m.
Lock, *serrure*, f.
Locksmith, *serrurier*, m.
Long, adj., *long*, fem. *longue*, adv., *longtemps*, *depuis longtemps*.
Look at, *regarder*, — for, *chercher*.
Looking-glass, *miroir*.
Lose, *perdre*.
Loss, *perte*, f.
Love, n., *amour*, m.
Love, v., *aimer*, — dearly, *chérir*.
Low, *bas*.
Luxury, *luxe*, m.

M.

Mad, *fou*, *insensé*.
Madam, *Madame*.
Magnificent, *magnifique*.
Maintain, *maintenir*, irr. see p. 187, *nourrir*.
Make, *faire*, irr. see p. 180, — up a quarrel, *ajuster une querelle*, — haste, *se dépêcher*.
Man, *homme*, m.
Manners, *mœurs*, f.

Many, *plusieurs, beaucoup, bien des.* So —, *tant, tant de, autant.* As — as, *autant que.* Too —, *trop.*
Map, *carte*, f.
March, *mars*, m.
Marriage, *mariage*, m.
Marry, *marier, épouser, se marier.*
Master, n., *maître*, m.
Master, v., *dompter, s'emparer de.*
Matter, *matière*, f., *affaire*, f., *chose*, f.
May, *mai*, m.
Meadow, *pré*, m., *prairie*, f.
Meal, *repas*, m., *farine*, f.
Mean, *bas.*
Means, *moyen*, m.
Meat, *viande*, f.
Meddle, *se mêler (de).*
Medicine, *médecine.*
Meet, *rencontrer.*
Melt, *fondre.*
Member, *membre*, m.
Memory, *mémoire.*
Mend, *raccommoder*, — a pen, *tailler.*
Merchant, *négociant.*
Messenger, *messager.*
Metal, *métal*, m.
Middle, *milieu*, m.
Mild, *doux.*
Milk, *lait*, m.
Miller, *meunier*, m.
Mind, *esprit*, m.
Minute, *minute*, f.
Miss, *Mademoiselle.*
Misfortune, *malheur*, m.
Mislead, *égarer, induire en erreur.*
Mist, *brouillard*, m.
Mistake, v., *se tromper, méconnaître*, irr. see p. 179, *méprendre*, irr. see p. 181.
Mistake, n., *erreur*, f., *faute*, f.
Mistrust, *se méfier de, se défier de.*
Mock, *se moquer de, rire de*, irr. see p. 194.
Modern, *moderne.*
Modest, *modeste.*
Modesty, *modestie*, f.
Moment, *moment, instant*, m.
Monday, *lundi*, m.
Money, *argent*, m.
Month, *mois*, m.
Moon, *lune*, f.
More, *plus.*
Morning, *matin, matinée.*
Mortal, *mortel.*
Mother, *mère*, f., — in law, *belle-mère.* Grandmother, *grand'mère.*
Motive, *motif*, m.
Mourning, *deuil*, m.
Mouse, *souris*, f.
Mouth, *bouche*, f.
Move, *mouvoir, émouvoir*, irr. see p. 190.
Much, *beaucoup, bien de.* Too —, *trop.* How —, *combien.* As —, *tant, autant.* As — as, *autant que.*
Mud, *boue*, f.
Murder, *assassiner.*
Music, *musique*, f.
Muslin, *mousseline*, f.
Mutton, *mouton*, m.

N.

Nail, *ongle*, m., (of metal) *clou*, m.
Naked, *nu.*
Name, *nom*, m.
Napkin, *serviette*, f.
Nature, *nature*, f.
Naughty, *méchant.*
Near, *proche, près, auprès.* He is pretty near it, *il ne s'en faut guère.*
Nearly, *presque, à peu près.*
Neat, *propre.*
Neatly, *proprement, joliment.*
Necessary, *nécessaire*, to be, — *falloir*, irr. see p. 190.
Neglect, n., *négligence*, f.
Neglect, v., *négliger.*
Neighbor, *voisin*, m., *voisine*, f.
Neither — nor, *ni.— ni.*
Never, *ne — jamais.*
New, *neuf, nouveau, frais.*
News, *nouvelle*, f.
Next, *prochain, suivant.*
Nice, *joli, gentil.*
Niece, *nièce*, f.
Night, *nuit.*
No, *non, point.*
No, *nul, aucun.*
Nobility, *noblesse*, f.
Noise, *bruit.*
Noon, *midi*, m.
Nose, *nez*, m.
Not, *non, non pas, ne — pas*, — at all, *point du tout.*
Nothing, *ne — rien.*
Notwithstanding, *nonobstant.*
Nourish, *nourrir.*
November, *novembre*, m.
Now, *maintenant, à présent.*
Number, *nombre, numéro*, m.

O.

Oak, *chêne*, m.
Oats, *avoine*, f.
Obedient, *obéissant.*
Obey, *obéir.*
Oblige, *obliger, faire un plaisir, rendre un bon office.*
Obliging, *obligeant.*
Observe, *observer.*
Obtain, *obtenir*, irr. see p. 187, *remporter, acquérir.*
Occupy, *occuper.*
October, *octobre*, m.
Odious, *odieux.*
Of, *de.*
Offend, *offenser.*
Offer, n., *offre*, f.
Offer, v., *offrir*, irr. see p. 184, *proposer.*
Often, *souvent.*
Oil, *huile.*

Old, *vieux*, (*vieil*), *agé*, — age, *vieillesse*, f. How — are you, *quel âge avez-vous?*
Omit, *omettre*, irr. see p. 180.
On, *sur*.
Once, *une fois*, — on a time, *autrefois*. At —, *de suite*. All at —, *tout à coup*, *tout d'un coup*.
Only, adj., *seul*, *unique*.
Only, adv., *ne — que*.
Open, *ouvrir*, irr. see p. 185.
Open, adj., *ouvert*, *sincère*, *franc*.
Openness, *sincérité*, f.
Opportunity, *occasion*, f.
Oppose, *s'opposer*.
Opposite, *vis-à-vis*, *opposé*.
Or, *ou*.
Orange, *orange*, f.
Order, n., *ordre*, m.
Order, v., *prescrire*, irr. see p. 176.
Other, *autre*.
Otherwise, *autrement*.
Ought. See Owe.
Over, *sur*, *au-dessus*. To be all — mud, *être tout couvert de boue*. It's all over, *c'est fait*, or *c'en est fait de. . .*
Overtake, *atteindre*, irr. see p. 175.
Owe, *devoir*, irr. see p. 189.
Owl, *hibou*, m.
Own, *propre*.
Owner, *propriétaire*.
Ox, *bœuf*, m.

P.

Pagan, *païen*, m.
Pain, *peine*, f. On — of death, *sous peine de mort*.
Painful, *pénible*.
Paint, *peindre*, irr. see p. 175.
Painter, *peintre*, m.
Painting, *tableau*, m.
Palace, *palais*, m.
Pale, *pâle*.
Paper, *papier*, m.
Pardon, *pardonner*.
Parent, *père*, *mère*. Parents, *père et mère*.
Part, *partie*, f. To take — in, *se mêler de*.
Party, *partie*, m.
Pass, *passer*.
Passage, *passage*, m.
Patient, *malade*, m.
Pay, *payer*.
Peace, *paix*, f.
Peach, *pêche*, f.
Pear, *poire*, f.
Peasant, *paysan*, m.
Pebble, *caillou*, m.
Peculiar, *particulier*.
Pen, *plume*, f., — holder, *porte-plume*.
Pencil, *crayon*, m., — case, *porte-crayon*.
Penknife, *canif*, m.
People, *peuple*, *gens*.
Perceive, *apercevoir*, irr. see p. 189.
Perform, *faire*, *s'acquitter de*.
Perish, *périr*.
Permit, *permettre*, irr. see p. 180.
Persecute, *persécuter*.
Persecutor, *persécuteur*, m.
Person, *personne*, f.
Persuade, *persuader*.
Picture, *tableau*, m.
Piece, *morceau*, m., *pièce*, f.
Pierce, *percer*.
Pig, *cochon*, m.
Pin, *épingle*.
Pitiless, *impitoyable*.
Pity, n., *pitié*, f. It is a —, *c'est dommage*.
Pity, v., *plaindre*, irr. see p. 175.
Place, n., *lieu*, m., *place*, f.
Place, v., *placer*, *mettre*, irr. see p. 180.
Plain, *plaine*, *campagne*, f.
Plan, *plan*, *projet*, m.
Plank, *planche*, f.
Plant, *plante*, f.
Plate, *assiette*, f.
Play, n., *jeu*., m., *comédie*, — thing, *joujou*, m.
Play, v., *jouer*.
Player, *jouer*, m.
Please, *plaire à*, irr. see p. 178. If you please, *s'il vous plaît*.
Pleasure, *plaisir*, m. To take pleasure in, *se plaire à . . .*
Plum, *prune*, f.
Plunder, *butin*, m.
Pocket, *poche*, f., — handkerchief, *mouchoir*, m., — book, *porte-feuille*.
Poet, *poëte*.
Poison, v., *empoisonner*.
Polite, *poli*.
Politeness, *politesse*, f.
Pond, *étang*, m.
Poor, *pauvre*.
Pope, *pape*, m.
Poplar, *peuplier*, m.
Populous, *peuplé*.
Portion, *part*, f., *portion*, f.
Post-office, *poste*, f.
Potato, *pomme de terre*, f.
Pound, *livre*, f.
Powerful, *puissant*.
Praise, *louer*.
Pray, *prier*.
Precious, *précieux*.
Prefer, *préférer*.
Prescribe, *prescrire*, irr. see p. 176, *ordonner*.
Presence, *présence*, f.
Present, *présent*.
Preserve, *préserver*, (pickle) *confire*, irr. see p. 172.
Pretence, *prétexte*, m.
Pretend, *feindre*, irr. see p. 175.
Pretty, adj., *joli*, *gentil*.
Pretty, adv., *assez*. He is pretty near it, *il ne s'en faut guère*.
Prey, *proie*, f.
Pride, *orgueil*, m.

Principle, *principe*, m.
Print, *imprimer*.
Printing, *imprimerie*, f.
Prison, *prison*, f.
Prodigious, *prodigieux*.
Produce, *produire*, irr. see p. 172.
Project, *projet*, m.
Promise, n., *promesse*, f.
Promise, v., *promettre*, irr. see p. 180.
Proper, *convenable*.
Property, *propriété*, f., *bien*, m.
Proposal, *proposition*, f.
Propose, *proposer*.
Prove, *prouver*.
Punctually, *ponctuellement*.
Punctuality, *exactitude*, f.
Punish, *punir*.
Punishment, *punition*, f.
Pupil, *élève*, m. and f.
Purchase, *acheter*.
Purchaser, *acheteur*, m.
Purpose, *but*, m., *dessein*, m. On —, *exprès*, *à dessein*.
Purse, *bourse*, f.
Pursue, *poursuivre*, irr. see p. 174.
Put, *mettre*, irr. see p. 180.

Q.

Quarrel, *querelle*, f.
Queen, *reine*, f.
Question, n., *question*, f.
Question, v., *interroger*.
Quiet, *tranquille*.
Quite, *tout*, *tout à fait*.

R.

Railroad, *chemin de fer*, m.
Rain, n., *pluie*. f.
Rain, v., *pleuvoir*, irr. see p. 190.
Rainy, *pluvieux*.
Raise, *élever*, *lever*.
Rare, *rare*.
Rashness, *témérité*, f.
Ray, *rayon*, m.
Reach, *atteindre*, irr. see p. 175, *parvenir*, irr. see p. 187.
Read, *lire*, irr. see p. 177. To — again, *relire*.
Ready, *prêt*.
Reaper, *moissoneur*.
Reason, *raison*, f.
Rebuild, *rebâtir*.
Recall, *rappeler*. To — to mind, *se rappeler*.
Receive, *recevoir*, irr. see p. 189, *accueillir*, irr. see p. 184.
Recognize, *reconnaître*, irr. see p. 178.
Recollect, *se rappeler*.
Recompense, *récompense*.
Recover, *se porter mieux*, *guérir*.
Red, *rouge*.
Reduce, *réduire*, irr. see p. 172.
Reed, *roseau*, m.
Reel, *chanceler*.
Reflect, *réflechir*.
Refuse, *refuser*.
Regular, *régulier*.
Reign, *règne*, m.
Rejoice, *se réjouir*.
Relate, *rapporter*, *raconter*.
Relieve, *secourir*, irr. see p. 184.
Rely, *compter*, *s'appuyer*.
Remain, *rester*, *demeurer*.
Remedy, *remède*, m.
Remember, *se souvenir*, irr. see p. 187, *se rappeler*, — me to him, *rappelez-moi à son souvenir*.
Rend, *déchirer*.
Render, *rendre*.
Renounce, *renoncer à*.
Repair, *réparer*.
Repeat, *répéter*, *redire*, irr. see p. 172.
Repent, *se repentir*, irr. see p. 184.
Report, n., *bruit*, m.
Report, v., *rapporter*, *raconter*.
Repose, v., *se reposer*.
Represent, *représenter*.
Reproach, v., *reprocher*, *blâmer*.
Reproduce, *reproduire*, irr. see p. 172.
Require, *demander*.
Resemble, *ressembler*.
Reside, *demeurer*.
Resolution, *fermeté*, f.
Resolve, *résoudre*, irr. see p. 175.
Rest, n., *repos*.
Rest, v., *reposèr*, *s'appuyer*.
Restless, *inquiet*.
Restrain, *restreindre*, irr. see p. 175.
Return, *retourner*, *revenir*.
Reveal, *révéler*.
Revenge, *vengeance*, f.
Reward, n., *récompense*, f.
Reward, v., *récompenser*.
Ribbon, *ruban*, m.
Rice, *riz*, m.
Rich, *riche*.
Riches, *richesse*, f., *biens*, m., pl.
Ridiculous, *ridicule*.
Right, *titre*, m., *raison*, f. You are in the —, *vous avez raison*.
Ring, *sonner*.
Ripen, *mûrir*.
Rise, *se lever*.
Risk, *hazarder*.
River, *fleuve*, m., *rivière*, f.
Road, *chemin*, m., *route*, f.
Rob, *voler*.
Robber, *voleur*, m.
Roof, *toit*, m.
Room, *chambre*, f.
Rose, *rose*, f.
Rotten, *pourri*.
Round, adv., *autour*.
Ruler, *règle*, f.
Run, *courir*, irr. see p. 184, — away, *s'enfuir*, irr. see p. 183, — to, *accourir*, — over, *parcourir*, — aground, *échouer*.

S.

Sacred, ***sacré.***
Sad, ***fâcheux, triste.***
Sadness, ***tristesse,* f.**
Sage, n., ***sage,* m.**
Salt, ***sel,* m.**
Same, ***même.***
Satin, ***satin,* m.**
Satisfy, ***satisfaire,* irr. see p. 180.**
Saturday, ***samedi,* m.**
Savage, ***sauvage.***
Saucer, ***soucoupe,* f.**
Save, ***sauver.***
Say, ***dire,* irr. see p. 172.**
Scarce, scarcely, ***à peine.***
Scholar, ***écolier,* m., *élève,* m.**
School, ***école,* f.**
Scold, ***gronder.***
Scratch out, ***rayer.***
Seal, ***cacheter.***
Season, ***saison,* f.**
Seduce, ***séduire,* irr. see p. 172.**
See, ***voir,* irr. see p. 192.**
Seek, ***chercher.***
Seem, ***paraître,* irr. see p. 178, *sembler.***
Seize, ***saisir.***
Seldom, ***rarement.***
Self, ***même.***
Sell, ***vendre.***
Send, ***envoyer,* irr. see p. 194, — away, *renvoyer, conégdier,* — for, *envoger, chercher.***
Sense, ***sens,* m.**
Sentiment, ***sentiment.***
September, ***septembre.***
Servant, ***domestique.***
Serve, ***servir,* irr. see p. 183.**
Set off, out, ***partir,* irr. see p. 183.**
Sew, ***coudre,* irr. see p. 174.**
Shade, ***shadow, ombre,* f.**
Shame, ***honte,* f.**
Share, ***partager.***
Shed, ***verser, répandre.***
Sheep, ***mouton,* m.**
Sheet, ***feuille,* f. (of a bed), *drap,* m.**
Shine, ***briller, luire,* irr. see p. 171.**
Shirt, ***chemise,* f.**
Shoe, ***soulier,* m.**
Shoemaker, ***cordonner.***
Shop, ***boutique.***
Short, ***court.***
Show, ***montrer.***
Shower, ***ondée,* f.**
Shrub, ***arbuste,* m.**
Shun, ***éviter, fuir,* irr. see p. 183.**
Shut, ***fermer,* — in, *enfermer.***
Sick, ***malade.***
Side, ***côté,* m.**
Sight, ***vue,* f.**
Silence, ***silence,* m.**
Silk, ***soie,* f.**
Silly, ***niais.***
Silver, ***argent,* m.**
Simple, ***simple.***
Since, ***depuis.***
Sincere, ***sincère.***
Sincerity, ***sincérité,* f.**
Sing, ***chanter.***
Singular, ***singulier.***
Sir, ***monsieur.***
Sister, ***sœur,* — in law, *belle-sœur.***
Sit (down), ***s'asseoir,* irr. see p. 192.**
Skate, ***patiner.***
Skin, ***peau,* f.**
Slander, v., ***médire (de).***
Sleep, v., ***dormir,* irr. see p. 183.**
Slide, ***glisser.***
Small, ***petit.***
Smoke, ***fumée,* f.**
Snow, n., ***neiger,* f., — flakes, *des flocons de neige.***
Snow, v., ***neiger.***
So, ***ainsi,* — many, *tant de.***
Soap, ***savon,* m.**
Sober, ***sobre.***
Soft, ***doux.***
Soil, v., ***souiller, salir.***
Soldier, ***soldat,* m.**
Some, ***du, de la, des, quelque.***
Something, ***quelque chose.***
Son, ***fils,* m.**
Soon, ***bientôt.***
Sorrow, ***douleur,* f., *chargin,* m.**
Sorry, ***fâché (de).***
Soul, ***âme,* f.**
Source, ***source,* f.**
South, ***sud, midi,* m.**
Speak, ***parler,* — ill of, *médire (de).***
Spell, ***épeler.***
Spite, ***malice,* f. In — of, *en dépit de, malgré.***
Spoil, ***corrompre.***
Spoon, ***cuiller, cuillère,* f.**
Sport, ***jeu,* m.**
Spread, ***étendre, répandre.***
Spring, ***printemps,* m., *ressort,* m.**
Stagger, ***chanceler.***
Stain, n., ***tache,* f.**
Stain, v., ***tacher.***
Stairs, ***escalier,* m.**
Stake, ***pieu,* m. Our life is at —, *il y va de notre vie.***
Star, ***étoile.***
State, ***état,* m., *condition,* f.**
Stay, ***rester, demeurer.***
Step, ***pas,* m.**
Stick, ***bâton,* m.**
Still, ***encore, tougours.***
Sting, ***piquer.***
Stocking, ***bas,* m.**
Stone, ***pierre,* f.**
Stop, ***arretêr.***
Storm, ***tempête,* f.**
Strange, ***étrange.***
Stranger, ***étranger.***
Strawberry, ***fraise,* f.**
Street, ***rue,* f.**
Strength, ***force,* f.**
Strike, ***frapper,* (of a clock) *sonner.***
String, ***cordon,* m.**
Strong, ***fort.***
Study, n. ***étude,* f.**

Stuff, *étoffe*, f.
Subdue, *subjuger*, *dompter*.
Submit, *soumettre*, irr. see p. 180.
Subtract, *soustraire*, irr. see p. 174.
Succeed, *réussir*.
Success, *succès*, m.
Successful, *heureux*. To be —, *réussir*.
Such, *tel*.
Suffer, *souffrir*, irr. see p. 185, *endurer*, *subir*.
Suffice, *suffire*, irr. see p. 171.
Sufficiently, *assez*.
Sugar, *sucre*, m.
Suit, *convenir*, irr. see p. 187.
Summer, *été*, m.
Sun, *soleil*.
Superfluous, *superflu*.
Support, v., *appuyer*, *soutenir*, irr. see p. 187.
Suppose, *supposer*.
Sure, *sûr*.
Surprise, *étonner*, *surprendre*, irr. see p. 181.
Surprising, *surprenant*, *étonnant*, *merveilleux*.
Surrender, *se rendre*, *livrer*.
Surround, *environner*, *entourer*.
Sword, *épée*, f.
Swim, *nager*.
Symbol, *symbole*, f.

T.

Table, *table*, f.
Taint, *corrompre*.
Take, *prendre*, irr. see p. 180, — part in, *se mêler de*; — charge of, *se charger de*; — away, *ôter*, *enlever*.
Talent, *talent*, m.
Talk, *causer*.
Task, *tâche*, f.
Taste, n., *goût*, m.
Taste, v., *goûter*.
Tea, *thé*, m.
Teacher, *maître*.
Tear, *larme*, f. To burst into —, *fondre en larmes*.
Tear, v., *déchirer*.
Tell, *dire*, irr. see p. 172.
Than, *que*, *de*.
Thank, *remercier*. I — thank you, *je vous remercie*, or simply, *merci*.
That, *ce*, *cela*.
Thaw, *dégeler*.
Then, adv., *alors*, *puis*.
Then, conj., *donc*.
There, *là*, *y*. There is, there are, *il y a*.
Thick, *épais*. An inch thick, *épais d'un pouce*.
Thief, *voleur*, m.
Thimble, *dé* (*à coudre*), m.
Thing, *chose*, f.
Think, *penser*.
Thorn, *épine*, f.
Thought, *pensée*.
Threat, *menace*, f.
Through, *à travers*, *au travers de*, *par*.
Thumb, *pouce*, m.
Thunder, n., *tonnerre*, m.
Thunder, v., *tonner*.
Thursday, *jeudi*, m.
Thus, *ainsi*.
Tiger, *tigre*, m.
Till, *jusqu'à*.
Time, *temps*, m., *fois*, f., see p. 160.
Timid, *timide*.
Tired, *las*, *fatigué*.
To, *à*. To-day, *aujourd'hui*. To-morrow, *demain*. The day after to-morrow, *après-demain*.
Too, *trop*, — much, many, *trop*.
Tooth, *dent*, f.
Toward and Towards, *vers*, *sur*, *envers*.
Towel, *essuie-mains*, m.
Tower, *tour*, f.
Town, *ville*, f.
Tradesman, *marchand*.
Tragedy, *tragédie*, f.
Transgress, *enfreindre*, irr. see p. 175.
Translate, *traduire*, irr. see p. 170, *transférer*.
Translation, *traduction*, *version*, f
Travel, *voyager*.
Traveller, *voyageur*, m.
Treasure, *trésor*, m.
Treat, *traiter*, — ill, *maltraiter*.
Treatment, *traitement*.
Treaty, *traité*, m.
Tree, *arbre*, m.
Tremble, *trembler*, *tressaillir*, irr. see p. 185.
Trouble, n., *peine*, f.
Trouble, v., *troubler*, *inquiéter*.
True, *vrai*, *véritable*.
Trust, *avoir confiance*, *se fier*, *croire*, *ajouter foi*, *s'en rapporter à*.
Truth, *vérité*, f.
Try, *essayer*.
Tuesday, *mardi*, m.
Tutor, *précepteur*, *tuteur*, m.
Tyrant, *tyran*, m.

U.

Ugly, *laid*, *vilain*.
Umbrella, *parapluie*, m.
Unbleached, *écru*.
Uncle, *oncle*, m.
Understand, *compendre*, irr. see p. 181, *entendre*.
Undertake, *entreprendre*, irr. see p. 181.
Undo, *défaire*, irr. see p. 180, *perdre*. *ruiner*.
Unfortunate, *malheureux*.
Ungrateful, *ingrat*.
Unhappy, *malheureux*.
Unheard of, *inouï*.
Unknown, *inconnu*.
Unless, *à moins que*, *de*.
Unsettled, *irrésolu*, *incertain*, *inconstant*.
Unstitch, *découdre*.

Upon, *sur*.
Uprightness, *probité*, f.
Use, n., *usage*, m. To make — of anything, *se servir de*.
Use, *employer*.
Useful, *utile*.
Usually, *ordinairement*.

V.

Vainly (in vain), *en vain*.
Valley, *vallée*, f.
Valor, *valeur*, f., *bravoure*, f., *courage*, m.
Variety, *variété*.
Velvet, *velours*, m.
Verb, *verbe*, m.
Verse, *vers*, m.
Very, *très*, *fort*, *bien*.
Vessel, *vaisseau*, m.
Vice, *vice*, m.
Victory, *victoire*, f.
Village, *village*, m.
Vinegar, *vinaigre*, m.
Violate, *enfreindre*, irr. see p. 176.
Violet, *violette*, f.
Virtue, *vertu*, f.
Virtuous, *vertueux*.
Visit, *visite*, f.
Voice, *voix*, f.
Volume, *volume*, *tome*, m.
Vow, n., *vœu*, m.
Vow, v., *vouer*.
Voyage, n., *voyage*, m.
Voyage, v., *voyager*.

W.

Wait, *attendre*.
Walk, *marcher*, *se promener*.
Wall, *mur*, m.
Walnut, *noix*, f.
Want, n., *manque*, f., *faute*, f.
Want, v., *vouloir*, *avoir envie*, *manquer*.
War, *guerre*, f.
Warm, *chaud*.
Watch, *montre*, f.
Water, *eau*, f.
Weak, *faible*.
Weariness, *ennui*, m.
Wearisome, *ennuyeux*.
Weary, adj., *las*, *fatigué*.
Weary, v., *ennuyer*.
Weather, *temps*, m.
Wednesday, *mercredi*, m.
Week, *semaine*, f.
Weep, *pleurer*.
Well, *bien*. To be well (in health), *se porter bien*.
What, *que*, *quoi*, *quel*.
Wheat, *froment*, *blé*, m.
When, *quand*, *lorsque*.
Where, *où*.
Whip, *fouet*, m.
White, *blanc*.
Who, *qui*, *lequel etc*.
Whole, *tout*.
Whose, *de qui*, *dont*, see p. 126.
Why, *pourquoi*.
Wicked, *méchant*.
Wife, *femme*.
Willing, *prêt*. To be —, *vouloir*, irr. see p. 191.
Willingly, *volontiers*.
Win, *gagner*.
Wind, *vent*, m.
Wind up a watch, *remonter une montre*.
Window, *fenêtre*, *croisée*, f.
Wine, *vin*, m.
Winter, *hiver*, m.
Wipe, *essuyer*.
Wisdom, *sagesse*.
Wise, *sage*, *savant*.
Wish, *souhaiter*, *désirer*, *vouloir*, irr. see p. 191. I should —, *je voudrais*.
With, *avec*.
Without, *sans*.
Witness, *témoin*, m.
Wonderful, *admirable*, *merveilleux*.
Wood, *bois*, m.
Wool, *laine*, f.
Word, *mot*, m., *parole*, f. To keep one's —, *tenir sa parole*.
Work, n., *travail*, *ouvrage*, m.
Work, v., *travailler*.
World, *monde*, m.
Worse, adj., *pire*.
Worse, adv., *pis*.
Worth, *digne*. To be —, *valoir*, irr. see p. 191.
Wound, n., *plaie*, *blessure*.
Wound, v., *blesser*.
Wretched, *malheureux*, *misérable*.
Write, *écrire*, irr. see p. 175.
Writing, n., *écriture*, f.
Wrong, *tort*, m. To be in the —, *avoir tort*.

Y.

Year, *an*, m., *année*, f.
Yes, *oui*.
Yesterday, *hier*.
Yet, *encore*.
Yield, *céder*.
Young, *jeune*.
Youth, *jeunesse*, f.

CPSIA information can be obtained
at www.ICGtesting.com
Printed in the USA
LVHW101929170422
716440LV00004BA/319

9 783752 592603